STEWART HOUSE BRIDES

A CLEAN HISTORICAL WESTERN ROMANCE COLLECTION

CHARITY PHILLIPS

CONTENTS

MAIL ORDER BRIDE
CARRIE

STEWART HOUSE BRIDES

MAIL ORDER BRIDE CARRIE

Wallace, Kansas - 1890

Young and beautiful Carrie Nelson is on her way westward to marry a young rancher in California when she is handed an advertisement flyer for a "waiter-girl" position in Wallace, Kansas. No longer content to move to California and just be a housewife in an unknown land, she decides to change plans and to apply for the position. When she starts working for the Stewart House restaurant, she quickly meets some wonderful new friends including the shy Annie and the wise Rita.

When charming coach driver Leeroy Jackson befriends her, Carrie grapples with thoughts of marriage again. She is unsure at first, but with the support of her waitress friends, all that's left is for her to say "yes."

Is it worth it for her to break her contract at the Stewart House and give up on her newfound independence? Is it possible that Mr. Jackson could love her all the more *for* her independent spirit?

1

Carrie Nelson clutched the newspaper advertisement in her hands as she stepped off the train in Kansas. She'd come all the way from Dublin, Ohio which was a tiny town in the middle of practically nowhere in order to marry a gentleman who owned a large, prosperous ranch in California. Her train stopped in Kansas and Carrie was to continue on as soon as her connecting train arrived, but she was beginning to have cold feet. On the train, a gentleman in a handsome suit had handed her a newsprint flyer, advertising a job opportunity right there in Wallace. She gazed out at the small, dusty town that was in view from the station and gave a sigh. Then she looked back down at the flyer in her gloved hands.

Stewart's House seeks young ladies to work as waiter girls in

Wallace, Kansas! All ladies must be between 18 and 30 years of age, charming, smart, pretty, and possessing good virtue. Come and be interviewed. We'd be delighted to have you!

Carrie flapped the small bit of paper in the air in front of her a bit, scanning the surroundings again as she fanned herself. She had no good reason to stay in this place. She'd made a promise to Mr. Jacobs. The rancher had seemed like such a sweetheart on paper, too... But California was so very far away. This town had one thing going for it that she doubted very much that California could boast: Wallace reminded her of home.

"Excuse me, sir?" Carrie asked a passing conductor on the platform. She kept her large, cloth suitcase at her feet, hesitant to pick it up until she knew which way she was going. "Can you tell me where an eatery called Stewart's House is?"

The conductor looked at her a bit blankly and Carrie started to wonder if the establishment had even been opened yet. It would be difficult indeed for her to try and make roots in a town where her reason for staying didn't even exist yet. After a few moments of curiously glancing around, the conductor pulled aside another railway worker, in a similar blue and gray uniform, and they conferred with each other while Carrie looked on, feeling more and more like this perhaps wasn't the best idea.

Suddenly, the other train operator turned to her with a broad, friendly smile. "The Stewart place is yonder that way," he said, pointing to the left and diagonally. Carrie looked in the direction he indicated and felt butterflies emerge in her stomach.

Is it reasonable to walk there? she thought in her head, but she didn't dare to even ask it. Of course, a lady didn't walk unchaperoned to places in a town that were new to her!

"Thank you, sir," she said politely instead, giving him a cordial nod. "And, um, where might I locate a coach?"

The train worker continued to smile warmly at her, unperturbed by her nervous questions. He'd worked around enough city slickers to know how to handle the oddest questions. "I'll take you to where the coach driver's sit," he told her.

He led her along, carrying her suitcase so she didn't have to bear the burden of it as she walked. Carrie still held fast to the newspaper flyer, as if it was a golden ticket that would help her find what she needed.

"Here y'are, ma'am," the railway worker said to her once they'd reached the front of the train station. He gestured an arm towards the group of carriages that were parked along the curb there.

Carrie gave a small curtsy in thanks to the gentleman, who then proceeded to wave over one of the coach drivers.

He was a good-natured looking man with very slightly graying brown hair and a beard. He took one look at her as he approached and let out a whooping laugh. "You're wanting to go to Stewart's place?"

She reddened. How had he guessed? "Indeed, sir," she said. "Do you often meet girls who are looking for that place?"

The man nodded. "Sure do. Here at the station, anyway. I'll take you there." At once, he picked up her hefty suitcase and loaded it into the back of his sleek, black coach. As he worked, Carrie noticed that there actually weren't that many carriages waiting there. Perhaps five were waiting for riders. This was just another indication to her that the town of Wallace wasn't much bigger than her beloved Ohio town. The transition to living here wouldn't be difficult. Provided this Mr. Stewart wanted her to stay and work for him, of course.

Once he was finished loading the coach, the driver kindly assisted her into the back seat. It was rickety as he drove, and she wondered how often people in Wallace utilized the coaches to get around. As they rode into the main area of the town, Carrie could see that there weren't that many homes. There were a fair amount of businesses, however. She spied a blacksmith's, a general store, a bank, a saloon, and a butcher as she rode past all of them. The carriage parked at last in front of a squat little building beside the butcher's shop.

There was a large sign made up of wooden letters, individually carved. *Stewart's House.* Carrie noticed that *it*, as well as the startling majority of the buildings in this town, was a light brownish color. The color of the dirt outside of it, nearly. She'd never really appreciated the green in Ohio when she lived there, but she really did now.

"Thank you, sir," she said to the coach driver as he helped her down from the back seat. She offered him a smile, feeling fatigued from her travels and yet determined to see this job interview through.

The driver gathered her suitcase from the back. "No problem at all, Miss." He carried her luggage up to the front of the building before placing it at her feet.

Carrie reached into her small purse and produced a few coins for his troubles and his great assistance. He refused to take them from her, shaking his head.

"I wouldn't think of it, Miss," he replied. "You keep your money and I hope it's useful for you. Good luck with the new position." He nodded up towards the sign above them. Then, with a slight shrug, he left her there to sort out her affairs.

Carrie wondered if she would see him again. He seemed to be no stranger to this eatery's business. Taking a deep breath, she knocked on the front door and waited. After only but a moment, the door opened and she was greeted by a young lady in a long, black dress and a white apron, tied at the waist.

This woman didn't appear to be much younger than Carrie's twenty-six years, but she wore a large, white bow in her hair which made her look a good deal younger than she otherwise would have. When she smiled at Carrie, her cheeks dimpled which only added to the near childlike look.

She was otherwise a beautiful young woman, despite the slightly strict, uniformed outfit.

"Welcome to Stewart's House," she said to Carrie gaily. "You must be here to apply?"

Carrie nodded. "Yes," she said back. "Thank goodness I've found the right place."

The other woman reached down and picked up the suitcase as if it were nothing. "Please come inside," she said, ushering Carrie into the place. "You're in luck because it's after lunch now. We're not as busy at this time of day."

She hustled with the suitcase into the eatery, followed by a bewildered Carrie. The space had a shiny wooden floor and several round wood tables upon it. The tables were all covered in red-checkered cloths. There was a bar along the left-hand side of the large space, which had stools sitting up against it for diners to sit upon as well. Carrie guessed that this eatery could easily house a good one hundred people or so. She was impressed.

A couple was sitting at one of the tables, lost in conversation, and there was an older gentleman sitting at the bar. A few young ladies, dressed the same as Carrie's hostess, milled about the floor of the place, attending to the customers or cleaning.

"If you'll wait here a few moments," Carrie's hostess said to her brightly, scooting the suitcase under one of the tables and offering a chair there to her, "Mr. Stewart will be right in to meet you."

Carrie felt a lump form in her throat. She nodded and obediently sat. She didn't know what she'd expected, but she didn't think she'd be interviewed so quickly, nor did she think the owner himself would be interviewing her!

The lovely hostess resumed her work in the eatery, greeting potential customers at the front door and helping to clean and organize things. Carrie idly watched her, wondering how difficult it would be to work in a place like this. As the woman had said, this wasn't a busy time of day, so it wasn't exactly the best representation of the position, she surmised.

What if I don't suit his qualifications, though, somehow? she thought. She'd taken to fidgeting with the flyer she'd been given on the train once more. She knew, too, as she sat there that she was going to have to write to Mr. Jacobs in California and apologize profusely for not continuing on like she was supposed to. She knew that she should've been more decisive about things *before* going on her journey west, but maybe the journey itself had inspired such new thoughts and desires within her?

The advertisement that'd been placed into her hands certainly hadn't helped in the matter. She'd been hoping for an out or some kind of an excuse. This seemed to be just what she'd wished for.

C arrie didn't have long to wait there at the table with only her thoughts keeping her company. A door opened on the left wall of the great room, near the bar, and as promised a gentleman walked out towards her. He smiled a friendly, reassuring sort of smile. He was wearing a fine black suit with deep red accents including a red tie and a red pocket handkerchief. A long, gold chain hung from the front pocket of his suit jacket and he reached in and produced a pocket watch right as she was beginning to wonder what the chain was for.

He was checking the time for their interview.

Then, his attention restored, he came to Carrie's table and bowed low, offering a hand to her. "Thank you for waiting," he said in a clear, confident, and warm voice. "I am Mr.

George Stewart, the proprietor of this eating house. Welcome. And what is your name?"

Carrie looked upon him, somewhat surprised to find that the owner of the eatery was nowhere near as old as she'd imagined. He appeared to be in his mid-thirties. He was clean-cut and clear-eyed, obviously as enthusiastic about starting his own business as she was about finding work for herself there.

"It's an honor to meet with you, sir," she said to him, placing her hand into his and shaking with him. *I feel as though I am a professional already!* she thought, a fire lighting up within her. "My name is Carrie Nelson. I'm from Dublin, Ohio. You probably haven't heard of it. Nearly, no one has."

Mr. Stewart laughed softly. "May I sit, Miss Nelson?" He gestured to the empty chair directly across the table from her.

Carrie nodded. "Certainly, sir. It would be awfully rude of me to keep you standing."

Mr. Stewart sat. He never took his eyes off of her. She blushed a bit, knowing that he was judging her appearance. The job advertisement made it clear that he would care about how she looked, at least a little. Carrie had curly blonde hair that she wore up in a loose bun on the back of her head. Normally, it was a bit more kempt than it was at the moment. Right now, there were some loose tendrils hanging by her ears, framing her face. As she thought about them, she hoped that they made her look pretty and not road-weary. Her eyes were big and China blue, and there was a dusting of freckles across the bridge of her nose and her upper cheeks which made it almost look like someone had sprinkled her with cinnamon.

"How old are you, Miss Nelson of Dublin, Ohio?" Mr. Stewart asked.

She noticed with some surprise that he wasn't writing any of this down. *I hope this means he has a terrific memory, not that I've already been disqualified.* "I'm twenty-six years old," she answered.

Mr. Stewart nodded and smiled another handsome smile at her. "And you aren't married?"

Carrie nodded. "No, sir. I was coming west to meet a husband when I was handed an advertisement for your eatery on the train. It seemed like too good an opportunity to pass up." She offered him a smile.

Mr. Stewart wasn't a man who was going to be so easily convinced. She could see that. "Do you have any suitors back home? Anyone who might come along and steal you away from work?"

Carrie batted her long lashes at him. Even her lashes were a honeysuckle color. Her smooth skin was like porcelain and her lashes hardly showed against it, except in times when she was blushing bashfully. This was one of those times.

"No, sir," she answered. "No suitors."

This seemed to please Mr. Stewart. He leaned back in

chair and crossed his arms in front of his chest. "Have you ever worked before?"

She nodded readily. "Yes, sir. I've worked on my family's small farm. I know how to cook and clean, and how to tend to animals and children."

Mr. Stewart scratched at his chin. "You will stay in the neighboring house we have set up to be the waiter-girls' dormitory. You will be supervised by the lead waiter-girl, Rita. You will be paid eighteen dollars and fifty cents a month, plus room and board. You will be required to wear a uniform like the ones you see Rita and the girls wearing." He gestured with a sweeping motion around the dining room. There was another girl in black dress and white apron nearby, tending to the needs of the couple at the table on the opposite side of the room. The other girl, she assumed, was the one called Rita. "Does this suit you?" Mr. Stewart asked, bringing Carrie back to the situation at hand.

Blinking, she thought it over quickly. "It sounds like more than I ever could've asked for," she said.

"You will be contracted for one year, in which you must devote yourself to working in this eating house. You mustn't marry in that time, and you mustn't wear makeup or any such thing that might sully the fine reputation of this establishment. The aim is to provide orderly, friendly help to patrons when they stop in. They are hungry, tired, and they are looking for a kind, pleasant face. Do you understand?"

Carrie nodded again. "Oh, yes sir. I never wear makeup

anyway." The job sounded like it would be somewhat strict, but it was the sort of strictness that she believed would be good for her. "Really, sir, I could use some order in my life." She smiled shyly again.

He smiled back at her. "Splendid." He stood up from his chair at that and offered his hand to her again, which she took. They shook once more, and then Mr. Stewart turned and headed back to the door by the bar. She realized that that must surely be where his office was located.

Not long after the boss of the establishment departed Carrie's table, the girl called Rita reappeared. She smiled another of her dimpled, welcoming smiles. "Come along with me now," she said. "I will show you to your room in the dormitory. We'll need to take some measurements, too. For your uniform."

"Golly," Carrie said, standing from her chair and grinning excitedly as she followed Rita out of the place. "This all seems too good to be true!"

Of course, there were still a few things that she would need to attend to. She'd have to send a letter along to Mr. Jacobs, and she'd also need to inform her family what had transpired. But she could wait to do such things once she was alone.

Rita led Carrie to a small home across the dirt road from the eating house. She hadn't noticed it before, when she'd ridden along in the coach, but it wasn't really much worth noticing either. It was a squat, dull brown house much like all of the other buildings in this town. There were some red shutters on the windows, and a red door. They were the only things that were noteworthy about its outer appearance. Carrie knew that she had to bid farewell to the idea of living on a California ranch by staying here, but the thought of living with a bunch of like-minded young girls made her feel too happy to worry about it. She hoped that soon she'd be able to boast that she was living amongst friends!

3

After setting her suitcase onto the floor in front of her tall oak wardrobe, Carrie stood still and allowed Rita to measure her with some white and red measuring tape. She felt a bit shy to be prodded and looked at so critically, but she knew that it was all for the uniform that she would have to wear to work in the eatery. "Thank you very much for your help," she said, turning around so Rita could size up her calves for the regulation black tights.

"You're quite welcome," Rita replied, rolling up the measuring tape now that she was finished. "It's no trouble. I enjoy welcoming in new waiter-girls to the House. We're one big family here, as you'll soon see. I'll just get your measurements written down and let the seamstress know to make your uniform. I anticipate that you'll be out on the floor by mid-next week."

She nodded at that as if confirming it to herself. Carrie couldn't get over how lovely Miss Rita was. She had black hair and brown eyes, and her skin was a tannish hue, as if she had been gently baked in sunlight her whole life. The dimples on her cheeks served to bring cuteness to her look and soften things a bit so her striking beauty wasn't so overwhelming.

Carrie wished to be just like Rita. But she knew that she wouldn't have much chance of that. Especially if she was forbidden to wear makeup. "Is the training easy?" she asked. "I mean... I don't mean *easy*, as I should like to have a bit of a challenge, but is it the sort of thing that should come quickly to me?"

Rita gave her a reassuring smile. "I think so," she replied. "I'll make sure to pick someone suitable for helping you. I know all the girls well, because I'm the chaperone here in the dormitory."

"You must keep very busy," Carrie said, impressed.

Rita's eyes crinkled a bit at the corners as she smiled at her. "I like keeping busy," she said.

With that, she left the small room that had been given to Carrie. There were two beds as well as the shared wardrobe, two small wooden desks, and a standing mirror in a black frame. She didn't know who her roommate was to be, but she had a feeling that she'd know as soon as the shift was over in the eating house.

Carrie sat down upon her new bed. The mattress was pretty stiff and the blankets were made of scratchy wool, which was going to take some getting used to, but she was satisfied with what she had.

She decided that, in the free time that remained to her before starting this new job, she should write the letters to the people she'd thought about writing to... Even if she didn't entirely *want* to. It would be best to not dawdle. She'd never forgive herself if she waited and then found out that she had absolutely no free time in which to write again for a year!

Carrie sat down at the desk that had been apparently assigned for her, and brought out some paper and a pen. This wasn't a letter that she wanted to write, and she hoped that he could understand that.

MY DARLING MR. JACOBS,

IT PAINS me to have to write this letter to you. This is not the sort of thing that I could have ever anticipated happening, but here we are... I am afraid that I shan't be joining you in California as we had planned. After much careful consideration, I've realized that I couldn't achieve what I wanted all of the way out west, and chiefly with you. I know that this will surely hurt you and for that

I am exceedingly sorry. But I must be true to my own heart. I cannot go along and lie to you, for that is much the same as not being faithful to you.

I have accepted a position at an eating house along the Kansas railway line and I fully intend to repay your kindness in installments as soon as I begin to earn my wages. Please know that I've never meant to hurt you and I pray that you will find peace and happiness. I shall always hold you in high regard.

Sincerest wishes,
Carrie

SHE FOLDED up her letter and carefully placed it into an envelope, sealing it safely shut with some wax from her candle. She sighed then, feeling that there wasn't any way she could avoid hurting him and letting him down without letting herself down.

Without waiting and giving herself more time to mope, Carrie prepared another piece of paper in order to write to her sister. At least this one would be less sad.

MY DEAREST BEVERLY,

YOU WILL NOT BELIEVE *the journey that I have had! I know that it will come as quite a shock to you, but I've decided to forgo the rest of the trip to California and instead I have taken up residence in a dormitory in Wallace, Kansas. I have accepted a position as a waiter-girl at an up-and-coming eating house. I met with the owner and he's very kind and handsome, and a bit strict but that's to be expected when the man is trying to start a new business. There appears to only be a handful of waitstaff and I am to be among them as soon as I've received my uniform and completed my training!*

I miss you madly, my sweet little sister. I hope that things are going well for you. Kansas is not so very different from Ohio. It's quite a bit dustier and less green... I suppose in that way, it is quite different. But there are a lot of little farm houses here. They do make me homesick. I will write again to let you know how my new job is. I wish you were here so that you could experience all of this exciting new stuff with me.

Give my love to Mother, Father and the little ones.

All my love & kisses,
Carrie

SHE SAT BACK, smiling and missing her home and her family. She didn't for an instant regret venturing forth into the world a bit and having her own experiences, but it was something she'd be getting used to for a while. The biggest adjustment was not having her sister with her. Beverly was her best friend. Carrie didn't think that any of the other girls here could compete with that, but only time would tell.

Feeling sleepy, she placed the letter into an envelope and sealed it. Then she lay down on her new, scratchy bed and did her best to nap a bit. She would do better if she was rested. Hopefully her excitement for her new life would allow her to sleep at least a little!

4

The sound of giggling and chattering roused Carrie from her sleep. The door to her room was ajar and she could see that there was a group of girls standing around in the common room beyond. She was still getting a feel for how this dormitory worked and she was delighted to see that there were spaces for spending time together and that she wouldn't be expected to only get to know her roommate. She didn't even know who her roommate was yet!

Throwing off her blankets, Carrie smoothed out her dress and straightened her hair before stepping into the common area with a friendly smile on her face.

"Oh, Carrie, you're up," Rita said with a smile of her own, coming over to her at once. None of the girls were wearing their black and white uniforms now and Carrie realized that it was nighttime. She'd had quite a nap.

"I didn't realize that I'd slept almost a whole day," she said jovially, nodding and making eye contact with each of the girls. Aside from the statuesque and beautiful Rita, there were some rosy cheeked girls who were more like Carrie as well as a few mousier girls. There were blondes, brunettes, redheads... Mr. Stewart seemed to make sure to hire every type of attractive girl he could find.

"We were just discussing you," Rita said, gesturing for Carrie to sit down on a wooden bench beside her. The room was mostly devoid of furniture, but there were benches lining the walls. It reminded Carrie of a parlor at a dance hall, wherein the ladies could change into their costumes. Perhaps that was what this was for? She knew that she'd learn soon enough.

"Good things, I hope," Carrie said as she sat beside Rita.

There was a titter of laughter from the girls sitting and standing around. There were about fifteen of them all together, including Rita and Carrie.

"Yes," Rita said with a laugh. "Good things. I believe that Miss Annie O'Brien should be your roommate and trainer."

One of the rosy-cheeked young ladies let out a squeak at being called upon and she stepped forward a bit so she could meet with Carrie. "Hello," she said shyly. She had light brown hair, a heart-shaped face, and the largest brown doe-eyes that Carrie had ever seen. "I've been working here at

Stewart House for about a month. I'd be happy to show you the ropes."

Carrie smiled pleasantly. "It's a pleasure to meet you, Annie. It's such a pleasure to meet and be here with all of you! I hope that we shall be like sisters." That would help her not miss her own sister so much.

Rita took her hand and squeezed. "That's what we like to hear."

Before long, all of the ladies went back into their rooms in order to change into their nightgowns. Annie went with Carrie. "This was already my room," she pointed out with a wink to Carrie. "Rita knew what she was doing. That's typical of her."

"What's it like to work with her?" Carrie asked. "She seems so kind and calm, but I know that Mr. Stewart is fairly strict." She removed her skirt and bodice before slipping into her white nightgown with pink flowers and accents on it. She tied the pink ribbon around her waist into a bow for a bit of extra flourish. She didn't normally bother, but she wanted to keep making a good impression for the Stewart House girls.

"Oh, I think you'll find that she is thorough but judicial," Annie replied as she stepped into her own nightgown – a white and green one, with little clovers in the pattern. "She keeps things orderly here, but she doesn't bark commands or any such nonsense, which I imagine Mr. Stewart to be more like."

Carrie noted Annie's subtle Irish accent as she spoke. A

last name like O'Brien meant that it wasn't a mystery where she was from. She smiled and nodded at her. "I get the feeling that he is sterner, but he also doesn't seem bad…"

"To be honest, I haven't really had to work when he was around," Annie confided. "Until today, that is. I was serving the guests after lunchtime, when you came in for your interview."

Carrie gasped in recognition. "Yes! I thought you were familiar."

Annie smiled and blushed a bit. "I'm pleased that he didn't seem bothered by my work. I get so nervous when authority figures are around."

Carrie laid a gentle hand on Annie's shoulder. "You needn't be nervous with anyone around here. I can already tell that much. It's a supportive environment."

Annie looked at her with those large brown eyes of hers. "I think you're right. At any rate, I've got to be braver now that I've got you in my charge." She winked.

Together, the girls helped each other take their hair down. Annie's brown tresses were much longer than her up-do had made it seem. They both combed through their loose hair until it was wavy and shining.

As soon as they were done grooming themselves for something Carrie didn't even fully know, there was a rap upon the door. She opened it and saw that all the girls had regrouped in the wide common room. "Come on out here so we can get to know you better," Rita invited. "Lights out isn't until an hour from now. We've got plenty of time for some gossip."

Carrie and Annie laughed and joined them in the common room, sitting upon a bench beside each other. "We were just talking about what it's like to work for Mr. Stewart," Annie told them all. "And how he's nice but can be strict."

"A little strictness is to be expected when one's trying to get a business off the ground," Rita said, sticking up for their boss. "After all, when he arrived here in Kansas, it wasn't much different from how it was for all of us. He had a dream and a vision, and he's worked hard to make them come to life." Carrie could tell that Rita absolutely revered Mr. Stewart, so she longed to make them both happy in her work.

"What brought you here to Wallace, Miss Carrie?" Annie curiously asked her.

The girls were all obviously eager to hear.

Carrie reddened and batted her lashes bashfully. "Oh, the same reason most of you came westward, I think... I was to marry a gentleman in California, but I decided against it once I saw the flyer for this position."

"Ooohh," the girls all cooed in unison, leaning towards her to hear more.

She felt a bit scandalous discussing it all, particularly because not even poor Mr. Jacobs knew the whole of it yet, but it did feel nice to share her tale of woe with people who wouldn't judge her for it, because they hadn't been there and didn't know the man in question. They might have hypothetical views about it, but that wasn't quite the same thing as knowing the story and judging her actions as 'wrong.' This was why she was rather glad she wasn't with her family when she told Beverly the news.

"I never met the man," she told them. "I wrote in response to his advertisement in the newspaper. I was to be his mail order bride."

A few giggles emerged then and Carrie blushed.

"More than a few of us have been there," Rita said. "I was to marry someone out west, too. But as you say, things didn't work out for me either."

It felt gratifying for Carrie to know that the same thing had happened to Rita. A beautiful young lady like Miss Rita would likely have hundreds of suitors, had she wanted them... "I think that things have worked out well for you, actually," Carrie pointed out. "You're a success here. You've found your own success."

Rita smiled at her appreciatively and nodded her head. "That is true."

When Rita's black hair was down, it was nowhere near as long as Carrie's or Annie's, or most of the other girls. It went a little past her shoulder, but only just. And it was curly all on its own, without the aid of braids atop her head. Carrie's curls were loose and leisurely whereas Rita's meant business.

"Well," Rita said with a slight yawn. "I think we've gabbed on long enough. To bed with all of you. I expect you all to rise and shine early in the morning, to take care of the morning train."

Carrie was struck then by the realization that their shifts were to go along with the trains' schedule. It made sense to her, but it didn't make her any less nervous. "No wonder this place is so close to the station," she said as she went back into her bedroom with Annie. "Would you believe that I took a coach here? The driver must've thought I was a silly thing."

Annie smiled a little as she got into her bed. "Unless you rode with Mr. Jackson," she said. "He'll give a ride no matter how short, because he loves meeting new people. He comes into the Stewart House quite often, too."

Carrie got into her bed, wondering if her coach driver had been this Mr. Jackson. "Come to think of it," she said, "I wouldn't be a bit surprised if that's who my driver was. I didn't think to ask his name."

"If it was him," Annie replied, yawning softly. "You'll see him here soon, surely."

The girls carefully blew out the candles on their bedside tables after that and before long, even though Carrie had napped for hours earlier, they were both fast asleep.

5

With Annie's help and Rita's supervision, Carrie got into her new black and white uniform for her first day on the job. The black dress went all the way to her ankles, and the hem of the white apron nearly joined it there. Annie skillfully tied the large, white bow onto Carrie's head. "It really doesn't take long to complete the look," Annie said with a smile.

Carrie had also been given long black stockings and black shoes with slight heels. She moved her feet around in the shoes, grimacing a little. "I don't imagine that these become more comfortable..."

"Not really," Rita said with a small laugh. "But you get used to them."

It was early in the morning, so early that Carrie couldn't even hazard a guess at what time it was. A man from the station was shouting with the aid of a megaphone to all of the train passengers who could be seen blearily exiting the train cars. Carrie watched them from a front window in the restaurant.

It was the breakfast rush for the morning train.

"Places, everyone. Places!" Mr. Stewart said, walking around and making sure that all of the girls were standing where they were meant to, ready to greet and serve the new influx of customers.

Carrie moved from one foot to the other, standing nervously next to Annie. "I hope my training goes smoothly," she muttered.

"You and me both," Annie replied. She kept watching Mr. Stewart as he roamed the large dining room and Carrie recalled that Annie feared their boss. She took Annie's hand and squeezed.

"I won't let you down," she said.

The double doors in the front of the eating house opened then and a large, rambunctious crowd flocked into the place. Though they had appeared sleepy and out of it when they disembarked from the train, their hunger had clearly taken over. Carrie took a deep breath and went along with Annie, from table to table, doing her best to shadow the more experienced waitress and learn how to competently perform the tasks required.

"This here is Carrie," Annie always introduced at each table. "She's new to Stewart House, so treat her kindly." She would give a wink and the customers would smile and laugh delightedly.

Carrie blushed and laughed along with them. "I've never spilled a drink, I assure you," she told one gentleman as she refilled his glass of nice, cold water.

She had empathy for all of their guests because it wasn't so long ago at all that she'd been aboard a long train ride. The relief that came with stretching one's legs and meeting new people at a whistle-stop like this place must've been quite wonderful. Carrie was surprised she'd never heard of such a thing before, but she was proud to work there now.

She noticed right away that the steaks that Mr. Stewart boasted being 'famous' were truthfully highly sought after. "Is it because they're really good or is it just because they're advertised as 'famous' that they're so popular?" Carrie asked Annie in the back room, as they collected up plates full of the food. They certainly smelled delicious, but smells could be deceiving.

Annie laughed and shushed her. "If Mr. Stewart says they are then they are."

Rita was nearby and she nodded approvingly, looking at Carrie and giving a slight wink. "We don't question what the boss says. We've never had a reason to."

As Carrie placed the steaks onto the white table clothed tables in the dining room, she could certainly see the fervor with which people ate them. "Thank you, ma'am," a male customer said. "Sure smells good!"

Carrie smiled at him. That was good enough for her, she decided. *After all, it's not like I'm being made to eat them.* The meat and produce were brought to Stewart House on the train, in a special ice box car. When Annie explained this to her, Carrie laughed a little. "What can't the trains do out here? We never had so much use of them back home."

"Oh, they've been instrumental out here," Annie said. "Imagine if they could move entire restaurants around the west."

"That's probably the next step," Carrie said.

Once the breakfast and lunch rushes were over, it was time for Carrie's break. She was of course going to work during dinner as well; it was the final shift of the day. After all of the hustle and bustle in the eatery, it was strange for her that she should have some time to relax. She didn't know quite what to do with herself.

"A lot of the other girls take the time to go for walks," Annie told her, stepping out of her uniform and into a different dress along with her. "The town's not very large, so it doesn't take a long time to explore it. I'll go along with you, if you like, so you don't get lost." She smirked a bit.

Carrie chuckled. "Okay, you shall be my tour guide."

The prospect of having Annie with her was good, in her opinion, not only because she didn't want to get lost – even if it did sound silly – but also because it always was better to have a companion when walking around a new place. She didn't know what the other people in town might be like, after all. As they set out on their walk, she saw that aside from the restaurant and the train station, there was a butcher shop, a bank, and a sheriff's office.

They hadn't been joking when they said that Wallace was a small town. It was *tiny*.

"My, my, there's not even a saloon in town," Carrie remarked. "I thought everywhere in the west had saloons."

"Thankfully, we haven't gotten to that point yet," Annie said. "I do believe that the people of Wallace are trying to be more proper than all that. The gentlemen who live here all seem to have reputable jobs."

"Where are all of the gentlemen with their reputable jobs?" Carrie asked her with a laugh, looking around the dusty street. "The only gentlemen I've seen here besides our diners are Mr. Stewart and Mr. Jackson... if it was indeed him."

Annie looked thoughtful at that. "Well, they don't live right in town. They all have farms on the town's outskirts."

Sometimes Carrie got the feeling that Annie had only heard about things but hadn't actually experienced any of them herself. *I shall have to ask Rita later,* she told herself. *She likely knows more about this place.*

The contract at Stewart House was for a year, but that

didn't necessarily match the one that Rita had signed onto. As the head waitress, she may have even gone so far as to sign on for five years! She certainly seemed devoted to the position, and to Mr. Stewart as well.

As they made their way back to the eating house, they came upon the gentleman in his stagecoach – the presumed Mr. Jackson – and Carrie stopped in her tracks even though she was on the sidewalk and he was in the road. He smiled a charming smile at her and tipped his leather hat.

"Good afternoon, ma'am! It's good to see you again," he shouted warmly from his driving seat.

"Oh!" she said, demurring and batting her lashes at him, like she believed she ought to. He was already driving the horses and carriage away when she thought of what else to say. "You too!" she called to him, but he didn't respond and likely didn't hear.

When she looked back at her companion, she could see that Annie was smiling a knowing smile at her.

"He didn't hear me," Carrie said softly, trying not to sound too disappointed. "Was that Mr. Jackson?"

Annie nodded, still smiling. "Sure was. You seem to have made quite an impression on him."

Carrie blushed, shaking her head to clear it a little. It wouldn't do for her to become distracted by warm thoughts or feelings about Mr. Jackson. For one thing, she didn't know him beyond a few friendly encounters. And for another thing, she'd signed a contract with Mr. Stewart. She needed to keep her mind focused on her work.

"Come on now, Annie," she said. "Let's get back to work. They'll be needing us for dinner soon."

6

It wasn't until later, when Carrie was relaxing in her bed clothes, that she remembered that she hadn't actually sent her letters yet. It was all well and good to *write* to Mr. Jacobs and her sister Beverly, but it mattered more that they *receive* the letters. "Is there a post around here?" she asked Annie in their darkened room.

Annie was already in her bed with her blankets tucked nicely around herself, but she hadn't fallen asleep yet. "I don't think there's one in this town," she replied. "But probably there's one in Topeka. The train could take it there for you, I suspect..."

Carrie laughed bitterly. "Just have to find the time to get over to the train station then."

She had a rather difficult time falling asleep that night. There was so much that excited her about this small town and her new job. She knew that eventually the luster would wear off, so she wanted to savor the joyful feelings as long as possible. Who knew what tomorrow would bring for her?

Hopefully, too, someone would be willing to run her letters to the train for her. She wasn't going to have time, with the way her shifts worked out. No train would be coming when she needed it.

When the bell was struck, alerting the girls to wake up, Carrie felt as though she'd only slept for twenty minutes. She rubbed her face and stretched, yawning as she did so. "Really, is it necessary for Rita to go around doing that?"

"If she didn't, I imagine there'd be several stragglers," Annie wisely pointed out. "Mr. Stewart doesn't abide lateness."

The two girls got out of their respective beds and quickly dressed in their uniforms. Carrie's crazy bed head made her quite glad that she had to pin up her hair anyway. She brushed it through a few times and tamed it up as well as she could. The large, white bow did the trick and obscured any unruly frizz on the top of her head.

The breakfast crowd was nearly as large as it had been the morning before. Carrie got the idea that it was always going to be this way, because there surely didn't seem to be any decrease in interest in the West. "It's an honor to be a friendly face that they meet along the way," she said to some of her fellow waiter-girls when they had a moment in the kitchen together. "We're proving to them that the West isn't all wild."

Rita smiled approvingly at her and nodded. "That's the initial premise of this restaurant," she replied. "We're bringing some womanly comfort to a place that, until recently, was all cowboys and Indians."

As the breakfast and lunch crowds died down and the trains began reboarding to continue on their way, Carrie took a moment to remove her shoes and rest her feet.

"He's out there again," one of the girls, Sophie, alerted her as she was passing through with a tray of hot cakes.

"Who?" Carrie asked, not waiting to hear the answer before peeking out the door to look at the dining room. There was hardly anyone there. Her eyes scanned the whole place, trying to figure out who the person might be, about which she deserved a preemptive warning.

"Look at the bar," Sophie whispered, rolling her eyes as she opened the door with her hip, leaving the sanctuary of the kitchens and making her way onto the floor to deliver the sweet-smelling hot cakes.

Carrie didn't need to look at the bar. She knew right away who Sophie spoke of. He was always at the bar, and always cranky. The hot cakes were surely not for him.

"Ugh," she moaned under her breath. She placed the

black shoe back onto her sore, black stockinged foot and headed out there to greet him despite her displeasure. She affixed a smile on her face before she was right there at his side.

"Oh, there you are," the old man grumbled to her in greeting, fixing his beady brown eyes on her. He had a wrinkled face and a long, gray beard. The hair that he still had on his head was nearly white and sat there in wisps as if trying desperately to hold on. Carrie had noticed that he always came to the Stewart House at this time, and stayed for the light liquor that was sold at dinnertime. "My coffee's gone cold," he complained to her.

"I'm sorry, Mr. Taylor," Carrie said to him sweetly, not letting the smile leave her face. "I'll go and make some fresh for you, all right?"

She took his half-empty mug and turned to leave, but he tapped her on the arm so she turned slightly back to him and raised her eyebrows in query. "Bacon and eggs," he said gruffly. "Please."

Carrie nodded. "Sure thing." Even though they stopped serving breakfast in the afternoon, exceptions were always made for Wallace's oldest resident.

She went back into the kitchen before letting out a big sigh. "Bacon and eggs for Mr. Taylor," she called to no one in particular, exasperation slightly edging into her voice even though he hadn't been so terribly rude about it this time.

"I don't know if we have any more eggs," one of the girls said, looking through the boxes of prepackaged food that had been delivered that morning. "They sell out practically every day."

Great, Carrie thought, biting her lip. *I have to tell him that we're out of eggs.* "Well, a plate stacked high with bacon, at least," she replied.

She set to work making a freshly hot pot of coffee and carefully filled a white mug for Mr. Taylor. Once that was on a tray with a matching white plate filled with bacon, Carrie brought the order out to her customer.

The old man sniffed when she set the plate and coffee down in front of him. "You forgot the eggs," he said, setting his shrewd gaze on her again.

"Unfortunately, we're fresh out of eggs, sir," she said. "The breakfast rush just cleared them out."

"I ain't ever heard a stupider thing in all my life," Mr. Taylor cried, indignant. "How can you be out of eggs? How many chickens do you have back there?" He indicated a finger towards the kitchen.

Carrie's face reddened a bit. "We don't keep chickens back there, sir. The eggs are delivered to us every morning via the train..."

"Well, there's chickens in this town, aren't there? I could walk right outside of this infernal place and walk right into a farm with chickens, couldn't I?"

She lowered her gaze to the floor, to her still-uncomfortable shoes. That was how she completely felt right now, too – uncomfortable. "I suppose you could, sir."

Mr. Taylor slammed the palm of one hand onto the bar in front of himself. "Why do I even come here?!" he demanded.

Carrie could feel all eyes on her and the scene that she'd unwittingly gotten herself into. She couldn't even think of what to offer up to him. She didn't know why someone who lived in Wallace might want to stop into the eatery every day, but sure as the sun rose every morning, there Mr. Taylor was at the same spot along the bar every day. As she stood there, looking at him perplexedly, her blue eyes now the size of saucers, she caught sight of someone coming towards them. She only saw them out of the corner of her eye, too frozen to turn and look.

"Why don't you leave this poor girl alone?" she heard the familiar voice ask.

Lifting her eyes up from the floor, she looked and saw Mr. Jackson. *As I live and breathe!* she thought, exhaling a deep breath as she thought it. She couldn't help but smile faintly that not only was he there in the restaurant but he had leapt to her defense.

The old man narrowed his already tiny eyes at the other man. "Hmph! I don't see how this concerns you."

"It just so happens that it's only Miss Nelson's second day here," Mr. Jackson informed the old man. "And she's a friend of mine, so treat her nicely, sir, or I'll give you eggs all right."

Several loud guffaws erupted nearby and Carrie realized

that they still had the full attention of everyone else in attendance. Rita rushed over as soon as Mr. Jackson made that mostly playful threat. "That'll do quite enough, Mr. Jackson, thank you," she said hurriedly.

Carrie worried a moment that Rita was going to kick him out of the restaurant, but then she saw the faint smile on the other woman's face.

"Come along now, Mr. Taylor," Rita said instead, gently taking the old man by the arm. "I think you ought to go where you can get those eggs you spoke of. You're right, there's plenty of farms that might be able to sell you what you're after. But I'll remind you that this is a friendly, civil establishment. I can't have you yelling at my girls."

"Aw, it's not that big of a deal," Mr. Taylor said as she walked him out. "I do enjoy this place. I'm sorry for losing my head. You know I can get cranky without my coffee."

Rita nodded and looked to Carrie, who rushed to pick up the mug of coffee from the counter. She brought it over and handed it to Mr. Taylor. "Our gift to you, then," Rita told him. "See you bring that mug back tomorrow if you expect more."

At the doorway, she and the old man exchanged a smile. He took a sip of the coffee and then looked at Carrie. "I owe you an apology, Miss. I'm sorry. You're not a chicken; you can't control these things."

Carrie laughed and nodded, smiling politely at him. "You're right, sir. I'll try and set aside some eggs especially for you tomorrow."

This brightened the old man quite a bit. He walked off with his coffee and more bounce in his step at that, and Rita turned back to Carrie, sighing.

"I tell you, if that man wasn't a fixture in this town, I'd never allow him back in here. That behavior is bad for business."

Right as Rita said this, Mr. Stewart came out of his back office, tie slightly askew and mug of coffee in his own hand. "What's going on out here?" he asked accusingly, looking from Rita to Carrie and back again. His eyes also found Mr. Jackson, who was still standing by the bar.

"It's okay," Rita reassured him with a smile that had more than a little relief in it. "Mr. Taylor was having one of his outbursts. I told him to calm down and we'd see him tomorrow with his requested order ready for him."

Mr. Stewart raised an eyebrow at that. "Well, see that you do." He pulled his watch out of his pocket and glanced at the time. "Miss Nelson, it's time for you to break."

She nodded to him. "Yes, sir." Rushing over to the bar, she collected the abandoned plate of bacon and the silverware. It was her intention to eat the bacon on her break, since it was just going to be thrown away otherwise. No paying customer wanted someone else's cold bacon.

"What do you do on your breaks?" Mr. Jackson asked her, sidling up to her at the bar so that no one else would hear their conversation. Attentions were still drawn to her because of the scene that had unfolded, but people were beginning to go back to their own conversations now that it was over.

Carrie looked at him searchingly as she held the tray of discarded food against her hip. "I normally just eat something to keep me going the rest of the day... Maybe go for a walk. I've done both of those things my two days on the job so far."

He chuckled, scratching a little at his beard. She noticed as they stood there, looking at each other for perhaps the first proper time, that his eyes were a haunting shade of gray-blue like a stormy day at sea. They'd always been a bit shaded and out of view for her when he wore his hat outside, but now she could see them clearly.

Good lord, he is handsome, she thought, wishing that he wasn't if only because he'd be easier to get out of her mind if he wasn't.

"Would you like to go for a walk with me?" he asked her.

Carrie blushed. She didn't know what to say. She wanted to walk with him and get to know him better, but she didn't know if that might violate her contract with Stewart House or not. "I'd like to, but I don't know if I should."

"Carrie!" Rita called to her, looking surprised. "Go on your break. We can't have you working all hours without a break. You'll collapse."

"Y- Yes, ma'am," Carrie replied with a bit of an awkward curtsy, rushing off towards the kitchens.

Mr. Jackson took her arm to stop her. "Meet me out front in a few minutes?" he implored her.

She blushed again but said nothing to that. Hastening away, she finally set the tray down on a counter in the kitchen and fanned herself with a hand. "Goodness, let my days here be more normal than this!"

7

As before, Carrie went next door and changed out of her work uniform, putting on a pretty dress so she could walk around at leisure during her break from waitressing. She chose a nice green dress with emerald, velvet accents on the hem and on the sleeves. She normally wouldn't have chosen such a dress for just a half-hour's jaunt around the small town, but she had a feeling that today wouldn't be normal at any point anyway.

When she was back out front of the dormitory, she could see Mr. Jackson standing in front of the restaurant, clearly waiting for her there. She didn't know what to do. *If I turn him down, suppose he makes a scene and makes it even worse for me? Mr. Stewart surely doesn't mind if we're friendly with customers, right?* She wished that Annie was with her.

"Good afternoon, Mr. Jackson," Carrie said as she strolled over to him. She worried about Mr. Stewart seeing them together there, so she took Mr. Jackson's arm at once and rather urgently moved along with him. He didn't seem to mind, or if he did he still went along without resisting. They were in front of the bank up the street when Carrie finally slowed down. "What brought you into Stewart House today?"

He smiled at her. Now that the hat was back on his head, his handsome eyes were masked in shadow again. "Honestly, I came in to see you," he said.

"Me?" Carrie asked him. "But why? I'm just a waitress there, like all of the other girls..."

Mr. Jackson slowly shook his head. "I wanted to see how you were doing in there," he said. "And I must say, you're not like all of the other girls, either."

She batted her lashes at him, not quite sure what he wanted her to say to that. "Actually I... I think I am. And what does a coach driver need in a café like ours? You could go anywhere in Kansas to get a meal, if you wanted. There's no train schedule stopping you."

He kept on smirking at her. "You're sure a hard nut to crack, Miss Nelson."

She smiled at him a little bit then. "You can call me Carrie. Everyone else does. Well, except for Mr. Stewart, but my friends call me Carrie."

"Okay, Carrie," he replied with a laugh that she couldn't

help noticing sounded victorious. "In that case, you may call me Leeroy."

Grateful that he wasn't upset to just be friends with her, she stopped walking and offered him a handshake. He stopped and shook hands with her, continuing to laugh in his pleasant way. It was then that she got an idea. She opened up her small, black purse and produced the two letters that she had written. She'd been keeping them there in case she ever had a chance to run them to a train.

"That reminds me," she said to him then. "Do you think you could do me this huge favor and take these letters with you to the station? I need them on board the next train that can get them to a mail post."

"Certainly can do," he said. Leeroy took the letters that she held out for him, glancing down to look at the name and address on the top one. He looked at her then, surprised. "Who's this Mr. Jacobs in California?"

His voice was not accusatory, yet Carrie still felt like sinking into the ground in mortification. The whole situation with Mr. Jacobs made her feel rotten and she couldn't wait to be done with it. "He's the gentleman I was supposed to marry," she answered. "Only I changed my mind."

Something changed in the way that Leeroy looked at her now. He appeared to be disappointed in her. "I see," he said. "Well, I'd better get this sent off right away, then." He tipped his hat to her awkwardly. "I'll see you around, I'm sure, Carrie."

Before she could stop him, he was off down the street, back towards the restaurant and the station. *Odd. We could have walked back together...*

She recounted what happened to Annie when she was back in the dormitory, changing clothes once more. Annie gave her a serious look, smiling an ironic sort of smile. "Isn't it obvious?" she asked her. "He likes you, and when he found out that you had a beau in California, it must've come as quite a shock."

Carrie had to laugh at that. "But I *don't* have a beau in California! I don't have a beau anywhere."

"Well, obviously Mr. Jackson wishes to fix that. Although it sounds to me like he now doubts himself. He didn't know he had competition."

"But he *doesn't*!"

Annie just laughed.

The two girls walked the short distance back to the restaurant. Carrie liked the quiet before the dinner rush. The only people around were the other laborers in town, and a few folks who lived in the nearby farmhouses that Annie had told her about. The train did indeed bring in a lot of the character to the place, but Carrie fully intended to get to know the people who lived in Wallace and made the town what it was. "I'd like to befriend that grumpy old Mr. Taylor," she said as they waited in their places to greet their dinner guests.

Annie let out another laugh. "After the way he was

towards you today?" she asked. "You really are just looking for trouble, aren't you?" She had an awed tone as she said it, more like she wished that she could be like Carrie than like she really was chiding her.

Carrie laughed along with her as they made their way out into the eatery's dining room. The two girls split up then and she had to focus her attentions on her customers, which wasn't a problem considering what she'd just professed to Annie. She wanted to get to know more people around there, and where better to start than at work?

She quickly found that she couldn't stop thinking about Mr. Jackson – Leeroy – now that he'd left in such a rush with her letters. She didn't want to believe it when Annie said that he liked her, because she wasn't the sort of girl who ever believed such things. Besides, she didn't want to entertain romantic thoughts when she wasn't allowed to pursue anything like that... She blushed a little just thinking about it. What she really needed was to try and work without distractions. Now that Leeroy was taking care of her letters for her, she didn't have to worry about them anymore. She was free to fully embrace her new life!

8

M r. Taylor was in a much better mood when Carrie next saw him in the restaurant. It was a few days later, and evidently, he had taken that time to reflect on his behavior because he was nothing but cordial to the waitresses when he showed up again. "I am sincerely sorry for the way I treated you when last we saw each other," he said to Carrie as she placed a fresh cup of hot coffee in front of him.

She smiled pleasantly back at him. "I accept your apology, sir," she said. "How are your eggs today?"

"Oh, scrumptious," he said with a smile that surprised more than her.

"We are always glad to see you here, Mr. Taylor," Mr. Stewart said, coming over to the table at the sight of the old codger's smile. It was certainly unlike Mr. Taylor to do *that*. Pleasant words were one thing, but a genuine *smile*??

"It's okay," the old man said with a chuckle. "You don't have to lie on my account. I was being a spoiled brute. But I aim to do better now."

Sure enough, when he left the eatery later that afternoon, he left some extra money on the table for Carrie to collect for herself. She was completely incredulous.

"We're going to celebrate with this," she told Annie once she was finished picking her jaw up off the floor. The feel of the coins in her palm made her feel ten feet tall.

Annie stared at her. "Blimey!" she enthused. "He really wasn't kidding about making things up to you."

The two girls went off to the dormitory, arm in arm, and went right up to their room. Carrie took off her uniform and set it aside to be washed. "Oh, I never would've believed that only a week would have me so exhausted, but here we are. I'm so ready for a day off!" She put on her emerald green skirt and a white blouse with little pink flowers on it.

Annie, meanwhile, stepped into a blue skirt with a black blouse. She let her hair down and brushed the knots from its waves. "Working hard just makes the time off even more worthwhile," she said. "I can't believe I ever used to lie about all day with nothing to do. It sounds so boring to me now."

Carrie nodded. "I never used to lie around so much as complain about being bored. That's why my mother put me to work, helping her in the kitchen and with the farm animals. But that just felt like childhood chores. It didn't feel as wonderful as this does."

Annie smiled. "Well, of course. You're earning a living now. I bet your mother never paid you."

"Ha! With what?" Carrie let her blonde locks down from their restraining bow, pins and hair net. She swiftly braided her hair into one long, loose braid and let it hang there on her right shoulder. She smirked at her reflection. "I still look like such a girl, though."

"Well, fortunately for you, I think Mr. Jackson likes that about you," Annie said, smirking right along with her.

"If there's one thing I'm worried about," Carrie said, "it's that I might run into him tomorrow. He acted so strangely; I don't know what I should say if I see him again."

Carrie and Annie left the dormitory for their late afternoon break. "What should we do?" Annie asked, looking around at the small amount of businesses along the dirt road.

"Should we use the tip money right away?" Carrie wondered out loud. "I don't know what we would buy with it, though..."

Annie shook her head. "You should save it for tomorrow. We'll have enough time to do some real exploring then."

Carrie looked from business front to business front, pensively holding an index finger to her mouth as she thought. "I wonder if the butcher is any good," she said softly. "That'd be helpful if the train ever fails to deliver the steaks."

Laughing, Annie looked at her like she was being silly. "Mr. Stewart says that the train will never fail us. He's got it all in a tight contract, like he has for us."

Carrie shrugged. "Things can happen, though. Anyway, it would be good to know if the local meat is tasty also because I think I will go absolutely mad if all I ever eat is Stewart House steaks."

Annie wasn't about to argue with that.

The two friends went to the butcher's shop. As soon as they stepped inside, Carrie was struck in the face with a strong wood fire smell. She knew at once that this butcher certainly had pork products, and her mouth watered a little at the thought of eating some freshly made bacon, even though just the other day she'd consumed perhaps ten pieces of the stuff. There was a counter inside, but no chairs. Clearly the butcher didn't mean for anyone to dine in at his establishment. She didn't have to wonder why the local townsfolk might want to visit Stewart House now.

Right as she and Annie were admiring some pieces of meat that were hanging from hooks on the ceiling, a scruffy gentleman appeared from the backroom to the left. He was wearing a white apron over gray shirt and black pants. The apron was alarmingly stained with red. Carrie didn't pause to wonder why that was.

"Can I help you?" he asked them in a gruff voice.

She didn't imagine that he saw many women in his shop. The only women in town apparently worked at his only business rival. Clearing her throat, she smiled at him as if he wasn't glaring back at her. "Hello, sir. We were just wondering if you might make steak here."

He stared at her. "Are you being serious?"

She nodded. "Yes, sir. You see, I'm getting tired of only ever eating steaks which have been frozen on a train for weeks and weeks."

The butcher smiled ever so slightly. "Oh yeah? You want something fresher, don't you?"

Annie nodded, stepping up so she was directly beside Carrie. Now that they'd got him talking, he wasn't so terribly scary. Not the sort of person they would want to chat with all the time, most likely, but not bad.

"You got money?" he asked then.

Carrie reached into her purse and pulled out a few small coins. "Is this enough?"

The butcher laughed. Even his laugh was somewhat gruff. "Not for a whole steak, it ain't. But I can give you a few cuts, sure." He nodded a little and held out his hand for the money, which Carrie gave to him.

With that, he left the room for a moment.

Carrie and Annie looked at each other, grinning and giggling softly. "I think we've made his day," Carrie whispered. "Did you see the way he smiled?"

Annie nodded. "He probably wasn't expecting Stewart Girls to appreciate his steaks. After all, we're conditioned not to."

Their giggling continued until the butcher returned, carrying two slabs of meat, wrapped in newspaper. "You've got an oven, I assume," he said to them. "You'll want to marinate these beauties if you really want to get to the flavor, but I'm willing to wager that your steaks aren't as thick and juicy as mine are."

"Thank you, sir," Carrie said, taking the meat from him and handing one to Annie, who looked a bit disgusted to hold freshly cut meat in her hands. The paper was disconcertingly damp whereas their steaks...well, their steaks never had to be touched by them. "We shall try them at once and let you know what we thought."

Carrie continued to giggle a bit as they left the butcher's shop together, carrying the meat. "Now we can say that we've tried something new here, instead of always eating at the Stewart House."

"I just hope that we're not being traitors by doing this," Annie fretted. "After all, we've got to borrow the oven now..."

Carrie paused to mull that over. "There's no kitchen in the dormitory?"

Annie shook her head. "Of course not. None of us are cooks!"

"Hmm," Carrie said. "I have an idea, but it might be terrible."

Raising her eyebrows, Annie tilted her head at her, reminding Carrie of a puppy. "What is it?"

Carrie weighed the packaged meat in her hand as she

continued to think it over. "How far away do you think Mr. Jackson lives?" she asked aloud, though she didn't necessarily expect Annie to know or answer for her. "And do you suppose he has an oven?"

She didn't know much about how men lived in the west, but she imagined that they weren't totally helpless when it came to cooking up their suppers. After all, they lived without women around for years, didn't they? There was a reason a lot of the locals didn't need to come to the eating house. They had homes where they could eat already.

The only question was, would Leeroy be willing to let them use his kitchen and have lunch at his home?

9

C arefully carrying the steaks wrapped in newspaper, Carrie and Annie walked back towards the train station. Their dinner shift would be starting fairly soon, and then they would have a day off, but they first needed to ensure that their plan for that day would be possible. They would be able to store their steaks in the restaurant's ice box overnight without causing much conflict, but they didn't presume to think they should make the steaks there the next day. It wasn't very good advertising for Stewart House waitresses to be eating non-Stewart steaks *in* the restaurant. Carrie wanted to sample something different, but that didn't mean that she intended to be a traitor to her job.

The girls passed the restaurant where they worked and

went to the station, keeping a look out for the familiar coach driver. *I wonder if he's not going to want to speak with me,* Carrie thought, biting her lower lip a bit as she looked for Mr. Jackson. *The last time we spoke didn't exactly end well...*

Sure enough, Annie caught sight of him there ahead, sitting in the front seat of his coach and watching in case any passersby were in need of a lift from the station. She gently nudged Carrie with an elbow, and Carrie immediately rushed over to his carriage. She smiled warmly at the man that she considered a friend. "Good afternoon, Mr. Jackson," she said. "How have you been?"

Leeroy looked at her, surprised and seemingly taken aback by the fact that she had apparently sought him out. "Hello, Miss Nelson... What're you doing here? Aren't you busy at your place of work?"

She shook her head, still smiling though a bit let down by his reaction to seeing her. "I'm off until supper time. Guess what, though? Tomorrow I'm completely free for the entire day."

"Oh, well, you deserve a day off," he said, still eyeing her somewhat warily. "Do you have any plans?"

Carrie beamed at him. She'd been hoping that he might ask. Annie smiled at her from where she stood, a few feet away so that the coach driver and Carrie could speak more privately. "As a matter of fact, my friend and coworker Annie and I were thinking about trying out some steak from the butcher tomorrow. Among other, as yet undecided things, of course."

Her blue eyes twinkled a bit as she spoke. She couldn't help but notice some warmth returning to Mr. Jackson's cool gray-blue eyes. "Wilfred might not be the best conversationalist, but his steaks are exquisite. You won't be disappointed," Leeroy promised her.

Wilfred? she thought at first before realizing that this meant he was friendly with the stoic butcher.

"Yes, I have a feeling his steaks are divine," Carrie said with a nod. "But as to that... We were wondering if we might be able to make use of your kitchen tomorrow? We have one at work, of course, but I'm afraid that our boss may not take too kindly to us using the oven to make the competitions steak."

Leeroy raised an eyebrow at her. "You want to use my oven?" he asked her. "But what will your beau in California think of that? He likely doesn't want you going off to another man's home, even if you did change your mind about marriage."

Carrie blanched a bit, her mouth hanging open in horror that he'd ever mention Mr. Jacobs, especially in that manner. "I'll have you know that it was not marriage that I wasn't keen on," she said at once. "It was a marriage to him that made me change my mind. But I don't have to explain that to you. May we use your oven or not?"

Leeroy looked at her warily again. She could feel that he

didn't trust her. She didn't know why his opinion of her had changed so drastically just because she had been writing to her former fiancé. Not every girl would even take the time or the ink to write such a letter to forewarn her beau. And this was the thanks that Carrie got for it.

"Sure," he said after a moment that felt like an eternity. "You can come over and borrow my oven, but only if you share some of that steak with me." He nodded in the direction of the steak in her hands, and then smirked as he looked at her.

Men were so hard to read sometimes.

Carrie smiled an astonished smile at him. "Okay," she said brightly. "Thank you, sir!"

The two ladies climbed into the coach with minimal assistance and Leeroy drove them down the street, past all of the businesses. It didn't take long until they were surrounded by pastures and fields, and little farm houses that did indeed remind Carrie of home. She smiled as she looked out of the window, admiring the structures and the sweet, homey atmosphere that now surrounded them. It pleased her to know that one didn't actually have to go far to find familiar home settings. She imagined that for ladies from the big cities, this still would be a culture shock, but for her it was just comforting and nostalgic.

"I feel like my sister could walk out of any one of those front doors," she said to Annie.

Annie, sensing that Carrie was emotional at the sights, took her hand.

"Your sister was who the other letter was for, wasn't it?" Leeroy asked her from the front seat.

Carrie nodded. Then, realizing that he couldn't look at her and safely steer the carriage, she laughed a little. "Yes," she said so he could hear her. The ladies were sitting inside the comfortable interior of the coach, but there was a little, open window through which they could converse with Leeroy.

"I imagine that your sister's reaction to you not going all the way west to California will be somewhat happier than the gentleman's," Leeroy said. There was smile in his voice, but Carrie still wished that he wouldn't keep bringing up Mr. Jacobs. It didn't make her feel good. She'd hoped that she might be able to let the past remain in the past, but he kept bringing it back to her attention when she was least prepared for it.

Eventually, he stopped the stagecoach outside of one of the farm houses. It was small and the light tan color of most of the buildings in town. It was almost as if the buildings came up out of the soil like that and it was up to the people to make them a different color. Leeroy didn't have as much land as the rest of his neighbors, but Carrie found that she was impressed just the same.

"You actually have a farm house," she said, gasping and smiling as she came out of the carriage.

"Don't act so surprised," Leeroy replied, but he was smiling so she knew he wasn't really offended.

"I'm not really surprised," she said, smiling at him. "I'm mostly impressed, is all. I thought you might just be completely dedicated to driving your coach."

He looked a bit shy then, though he still smiled. "Oh, I have dreams about starting my own home and family, just like everybody else."

Carrie looked at him in continuing amazement. Annie nudged her a bit. "Y'hear that, Carrie? Just like everybody else."

It was also not surprising to find out that Mr. Jackson wanted to settle down and start a family out West. Most of the men there wanted such a thing. "Why else would there be a mail order bride service?" she asked simply. "It's not unusual at all."

Leeroy laughed and nodded a bit at her. "Why thank you, Miss Nelson. I'm glad to know I'm not unusual."

He led the ladies into his small farm house and Carrie admired the interior. The inside was much prettier than the outside, with pinewood floors and wall paneling. His living room area contained a brown leather couch that appeared to have been handmade, given its uneven legs and slight imperfections in the upholstering. It looked like he – or someone – had stretched the leather over the frame of the couch without thinking of measuring. Carrie found it endearing.

"My kitchen's this way," Leeroy said to the friends. "But

you can make yourselves at home. You don't have to rush, if you'd rather relax a little. This is your first time out of center of town, isn't it?"

Carrie nodded. "Yes. But unfortunately, we don't have as much time as I'd like. We have to be back for the supper time train."

"Oh, yes, that's right," he said with a nod. "Well, make yourself at home. My kitchen is yours."

He went to the leather couch and sat down, meaning that the two girls could have the kitchen to themselves. He didn't want to get in their way. Carrie couldn't help noticing that he was watching her with renewed interest. Could it be that he hadn't quite given up on her yet? She thought she'd scared him off when he discovered her past beau, but now there was more than a little evidence to the contrary. Why, she wouldn't be there in his home if he didn't like her!

"Oh, this oven will do nicely. We should get the steak into it quickly, though, so it doesn't turn out rotten," Annie advised, snapping Carrie out of her musing.

She followed Annie into the kitchen and admired the oven. Leeroy had a few cooking pans that they could use, which impressed her as well.

"See? I knew this would work out," she said, pleased, as they set to work putting their steaks in the pan and placing them in the oven. "They'll only need a few minutes in there, most likely." She looked around and realized that she didn't know where the matches were. The oven wasn't going to start without a match to light the coals.

Without hesitating, Carrie poked her head back out of the kitchen and called to Leeroy in the living room. "Do you have any matches?"

He chuckled and joined them in the kitchen. "Of course, I've got matches. How do you reckon I cook or keep warm in the winter?" He reached up above the stove into a cabinet and pulled out a few loose matches. "Would you like me to light up the stove for you?"

Carrie and Annie nodded. "Yes, please," they said practically in unison, smiling at each other.

Leeroy lit a match and carefully tossed it onto the black coals in the lower compartment of the oven, closing it down so that the heat would fill up the oven and not be wasted by any rush of air in the room. "That should do it," he said. "Don't forget that I want some of that steak, now."

Carrie giggled. "Yes, sir."

He went away then, back into the living room, and left them to it. They worked on preparing the steaks, adding a bit of salt and pepper that they found in his pantry. She wasn't convinced that they were making it taste better than the famed Stewart steaks, but she was doing her best. It largely depended on the cut of meat anyway.

Annie and Carrie took the pan back out of the oven after it had grilled in there for a while on both sides. "Mmm, well, it smells like steak," Annie said with a grin. "I think that means it's a success."

"Mr. Jackson!" Carrie called back to him. "The steak is ready!"

She cut off a bit from her own portion so that he could have some. She wished now that they'd asked for three cuts, but that surely would've cost more. That reminded her. *I still have the extra money from Mr. Taylor. What should I spend that on?* Annie had told her to save it, but Carrie was always pretty discerning with what she should do with her finances.

Leeroy returned to the kitchen, grinning as he smelled the freshly-cooked beef. "Mmm, smells great!"

Carrie took the two plates of steaks in her hands and turned to him. "Do you have a place for us to sit and eat these?"

Annie picked up her plate as well, looking at him inquisitively.

He put his hands on his hips. "Ever the waitresses, aren't you?" He laughed then and gestured for them to follow him. He had a small, round wooden table in an alcove just off of the kitchen. There were four chairs there, but he clearly only used one of them as it was turned out and all the rest were pushed up against the table. Quickly, he moved to alter this, pulling out two chairs for the ladies as they came over with their plates. Carrie set a plate down in front of Leeroy's chair and a plate in front of her offered one. Annie set her plate down next to Carrie's.

All three of them sat down to their luncheon. "Oh, this is wonderful," he enthused after biting into his steak and savoring the flavor a bit before swallowing. "My compliments to the chefs."

Annie blushed and smiled. "The real compliment must really go to the butcher," Carrie pointed out. "Mister... What did you say his name was?"

Leeroy chuckled. "Wilfred," he replied.

Carrie held up her plate. "To Wilfred!"

Laughing, the other two raised their plates and they pretended to toast the butcher's talents. They happily dined together for a while in comfortable quiet, until at last Carrie looked over at the grandfather clock that Leeroy had in the hall.

"I wish we could stay longer," she intoned, "But duty calls. The passengers from the evening train will surely be hungry."

Mr. Jackson was sad to hear that, she could tell by the way he frowned and looked downcast. "Very well, then. I'll drive you both back, seeing as how my work will be needed at the station, too."

She stood up, looking at the now-empty plates on the table. "I'll tell you what," she said. "In gratitude for your kindness in letting us borrow your oven, we'll take these dirty dishes and clean them in the restaurant's sinks. We have much larger ones, don't we, Annie?"

Annie nodded her head and smiled supportively. "We sure do."

"So, it's settled," Carrie added finally, looking to Leeroy.

He smiled at them and shrugged a little. "Well, shucks. All right, it's a deal. Thank you kindly."

The girls stacked up the dishes carefully and carried them out with them to Leeroy's coach. Carrie was sad to bid him farewell, but the offer of cleaning his dishes meant that she'd surely see him again soon.

Carrie could sometimes be crafty that way.

10

Annie and Carrie rushed into their black and white uniforms and came traipsing into the restaurant behind everyone else. Their hair was a bit disheveled, bows slightly askew, and they were clearly out of breath. They fell in line with the other waiter-girls, as if they wouldn't be noticed right away.

"What on earth?" Rita said to them, incredulous. "Where did you two go? You look like you've just come from the forest."

"Sorry, ma'am," Carrie said, straightening her white bow on her head. "We were having lunch and forgot the time."

Rita raised an eyebrow and smiled in a knowing sort of way that made Carrie vaguely uncomfortable. She walked up to Annie and tightened the girl's apron around her waist.

"Let's talk about your adventures later. I need you out on the floor right now. Focused and friendly."

The sound of a train's whistle alerted them all to the train that was soon to arrive in the station. Then a gentleman's voice rang out loud and clear with the aid of a megaphone. "Coming into Wallace, Kansas! Disembark for suppertime at the Stewart House here. Disembark for supper."

"Places, everyone!" Mr. Stewart said, poking his head into the kitchens where the nervous waitresses waited to go out. "Let's give them all a wonderful dinner time here."

With that, Carrie and the rest of the waitresses filed into the main floor of the eatery, smiling in greeting to all of the newcomers who were there to dine. Rita showed everyone to tables and welcomed them politely, a smile never leaving her face. Carrie watched her a bit, admiring her still.

"Good evening," Carrie said to her first table of customers. "What may I get for you?"

The menu of Stewart House was something that was advertised on all of the trains along the Santa Fe railway, so most people came in knowing exactly what they wanted. "We want to try some of those Stewart House Steaks," one of the customers said to her, smiling an excited smile. She was a young married woman, judging by the sparkling gold band on her finger.

Carrie smiled back at her, trying her best to appear genuine. The steaks really weren't bad; they were just a bit ordinary. The restaurant did have other things, but Mr.

Stewart knew what he was doing by promoting one his more expensive products. "Certainly, ma'am," Carrie said to the woman. "And for you?"

The gentleman next to the woman nodded his head. "The same for me, please."

Carrie didn't need to bother about writing down their orders. "I'll be right back with your meals, then, as well as some water for you. You've had a long, tiring journey, I'm sure."

She went back into the kitchens to place the order. "Two more Stewart steaks, please," she announced. "Which reminds me," she said, pulling Annie aside a bit as soon as she saw her. "We need to get those dishes from our room so we can clean them for Mr. Jackson."

"Mmmhmm, Mr. Jackson, I should have known," Rita suddenly said. Carrie hadn't realized that she was standing close by, keeping an eye on things in the kitchen.

Carrie felt herself blushing, even though she didn't believe she had done anything deserving of a blush. "We were in need of an oven and we didn't want to take up this one here. Mr. Jackson was kind enough to let us borrow his. We told him that we'd clean his dishes as repayment. That's all."

Rita smirked at her slightly. "Oh, I don't really think that's all. But you may use our sinks here, Miss Nelson. Except later, of course. We're much too busy right now."

Carrie had a feeling that there was more to that, but she nodded. "Thank you, ma'am."

She continued to work in the restaurant, serving the steaks and a few other things like meat pies and stews. The supper train sometimes brought some more variety, which pleased her. All the while, she thought about Leeroy's dishes and the conversation with Rita that she was soon to have. It loomed ahead of her and made her more nervous than she thought it ought to. After all, the other woman had been smirking as she spoke with her about it. It's just that there was something in the knowing look that the lead waitress had given her. It felt like Rita knew something that Carrie didn't...

At the end of the evening, she and Annie went back to their room in the dormitory. They took off their uniforms and changed into some simple dresses for the remainder of the night. Normally, Carrie would've gone for something lovely and flattering, but she knew that she had a chore to still perform. "And besides," she explained to Annie when she suggested keeping it simple for her, too, "tomorrow's our day off. We'll want to save our best looks for that!"

"I really only ever have simple things anyway," Annie said as she stepped into her pink cotton dress. "You'd think that my parents wanted me to become a nun."

Carrie laughed and took her friend's hand. "Come on. Let's get these dishes cleaned up and find out what Rita was on about earlier."

"I think it was fairly obvious," Annie said, picking up the dishes and handing off two of them to Carrie – hers and Leeroy's from earlier – "She thinks, like I've said to you before, that Mr. Jackson fancies you. I'm pretty sure everyone who was there in the restaurant and has eyes knows that."

Carrie could only laugh at that. "Oh, honestly, you all can be so silly. He's just a good friend of mine, that's all. Why shouldn't a kind gentleman stick up for me and help me out sometimes, when I need it?"

They took the dishes into the kitchen of the eating house, where Rita was still positioned, barking instructions to passing waitresses and keeping track of orders. Normally she was the first point of contact in the restaurant, but she wanted to be around Carrie and Annie tonight, it seemed. *Possibly because we arrived so rushed and disheveled,* Carrie mentally scolded herself. *We really could've been more discreet.*

Rita kindly stood aside and let them at the sink, where Carrie and Annie set about scrubbing the dirty plates from the day's steak lunch. Carrie did her best to focus on the task at hand, but as she stared at the bubbles filling up the basin, she thought about what had been said about Mr. Jackson and wondered, yet again, if there was truth to it. She kept resisting, but apparently everyone around her could see it except her.

The two girls, task completed, set the dishes to dry and went back to the dormitory. Rita was to be closing up the restaurant soon, and then Carrie was full prepared to receive a lecture about being late and uniform tidiness. "She's usually not so strict," she opined to Annie as they sat in their room, waiting. "That's what makes it so easy to forget that she's in charge and not just a friend."

"I really don't think she's all that angry with us," Annie said, kicking her legs a bit as she sat on her bed. "I think it's just something that Mr. Stewart wants her to stress. It's simply protocol; nothing personal. I feel like I'm the one who's really responsible anyway. I'm supposed to be your trainer. What a fine role model I make."

"It's not your fault," Carrie said, shaking her head for emphasis. "It was all my idea. You could've said no, but I think you deserved to have a bit of fun. And that steak was magnificent."

"Oh, I do hope she won't be mad at us about eating another place's steak."

"It's not as if we came onto the floor, shouting about how much better the butcher's steaks are."

Carrie was rather glad that she had a co-conspirator in this situation. It made her think about Beverly and the shenanigans they'd find themselves in sometimes, and how they'd always find ways to get out of them in the end. "If this is anything like when I used to be reprimanded back at home," she said, "then it shall be a slap on the wrist, is all. I'm more concerned with what she's going to say about Mr. Jackson. It's not like he's proposed marriage to me! We're only friends, no matter how he may feel."

Waiting and stewing about this was weighing her down. All Carrie wanted was to have a good job out west and make a life for herself. Why did everything have to be so complicated all the time? "I miss my sister. She'd understand."

Annie got off of her bed and went over to Carrie's, sitting beside her and taking her hand, squeezing gently. "I understand. You mustn't feel pressured by any of this. After all, we do have a contract with Stewart House for a year."

Rita joined them in their room at last, giving a knock before entering. "Thank you for waiting up for me," she said, looking from Carrie to Annie and back again. "I'm sure you know what I'm going to say. Mr. Stewart has standards that we all must adhere to at all times, not only at work but when we're off work hours as well. You're lucky that he wasn't there to hear your story about lunching with Mr. Jackson, or see the messy state of your uniforms. Are these them?" She went over and plucked both girls' uniforms from the bases of their beds. "These should be cleaned now that you've got a day off." She put them over her arm and then sat on the end of Carrie's bed, softening a bit as she looked at them.

"I don't mean to scold either of you too harshly, but you must understand that Mr. Stewart has given you a real chance here. The restaurant is only successful because we all work hard to keep it that way. And if you're distracted by gentlemen who come to visit you, I want you to know that your secret's safe with me. You just have to be careful so he doesn't notice. Remember, you've got a contract."

Carrie's face reddened all over again. "I'm not distracted by Mr. Jackson," she argued. "He only stood up for me because I'm his friend."

"Well, I think that you'd best tell Mr. Jackson that," Rita said at last. "Before he comes into the restaurant and proposes right in front of Mr. Stewart."

Carrie laughed at that; it just seemed so absurd. But she nodded her head. "I will let him know that I shan't be marrying anyone. He already kind of knows, but if it will make you feel better."

Rita nodded and stood up from the bed. "It would, thank you. Now I'm going to go see that these uniforms get cleaned in time for your next shift. Sleep well." With that, she left the room, closing their door behind her.

Annie was giving Carrie such a pitying look. "Oh, now don't you start," Carrie said, standing up and going to her wardrobe to retrieve some pajamas. "I'm not sad about it because there's nothing to be sad about."

But as she lay in her bed that night, Carrie kept thinking about the way that Leeroy looked at her and spoke to her. She remembered how upset he had seemed when he found out that she'd had a fiancé, and how it was like a candle had been lit as soon as he realized that she was no longer going to marry Mr. Jacobs. She'd thought him so silly to worry himself about it... And she'd worried then about the contract and what the gentleman's crush could do for her career.

I moved out here so that things could be happier and easier, she thought. *But apparently, it's not as simple as that.*

She awoke the next morning along with all the other waiter-girls, momentarily forgetting that she was supposed to be off, until she realized that her uniform was nowhere in her room.

"We really don't have to be awake yet," Annie said to her from her bed, yawning. "Let the other people worry about that."

Carrie looked at her. "Sleep in," she said soothingly. "I think I'm going to go for a walk though. With Mr. Jackson's dishes."

Annie sat up in bed then and smiled teasingly at her. "Oh?"

Laughing, Carrie gently pushed her back down. "He needs his dishes back. A promise is a promise. And I can take care of that other thing, too."

She put on another simple dress – a blue one this time – but then she thought better of it as she looked at her reflection and changed into her green velvety dress instead. There was no sense dressing down just because Mr. Jackson was a friend and not a beau... She didn't want him to worry or think that something was going on.

Going over to the restaurant, she went straight into the kitchen and she collected the dishes which had dried overnight. Then, she went outside and looked around for any sign of the man with the coach. He was normally parked outside of the station, though she had to admit that she'd never seen him there so early. Even though she'd been to his house, she couldn't recall how to get there or where it was, so she just went into the train station and sat upon a bench, the dishes nestled carefully in her lap.

The railway workers were giving her odd looks and she could sense that it wasn't normal for a girl like her to be sitting there in the station, unless she was planning on leaving the town. "I'm not waiting for a train," she called to them. "I'm waiting for someone!"

"Who are you waiting for?" a familiar man's voice asked from beside her.

Carrie turned a bit and there was Leeroy Jackson. He smiled at her, squinting in the sunlight that came from between the rocky hills beyond the station. He looked just as handsome as the day she'd met him, except something about him was different. He wasn't wearing his hat, so she could see his stormy eyes.

She blushed a bit reflexively and looked down at the dishes in her lap. She picked them up and held them out to him. "Your dishes have been cleaned, sir," she said to him, feeling shy and hating herself because of it. *Why should what the other girls say matter? They don't know what it's like between me and Leeroy. We're only* friends!

"Thank you," Leeroy said then, chuckling as he carefully received the offered dishware. "But why are you sitting here in the station waiting for me?"

"I'm off today," she reminded him.

He placed the dishes between his side and his arm, keeping them safe there in the crook of his arm for now. "I'm honored," he replied. "Did you have any other plans for your day off?"

She found that eye contact was difficult at the moment, so she kept her eyes focused on her lap. "Care to show me around town? I've heard you're a superb tour guide?"

He chuckled again. "I'd be delighted. Right this way, Miss Nelson." Leeroy led her to his coach and helped her inside, much like he had done when first they met.

She didn't know what she expected to gain by doing this, but she thought it was the best way to casually spend time with him without getting in trouble or hurting his feelings.

11

During the carriage ride, Leeroy left the little window between them open so that they could talk to each other. Carrie thought about what she should say. *It wouldn't be good to have a conversation about my contract and marriage while he's driving and we have a wall up between us,* she thought. "Thank you again for letting us borrow your oven," she said instead. "I told my boss Miss De La Cruz what you did for us and she said that you were a real gentleman. It was she who allowed us to use the sinks in the restaurant, too."

"That's quite all right," Leeroy replied. "Friends help each other out, right? You're welcome to use my kitchen whenever you like, especially if you clean up afterwards like you did. It was awfully nice of you to share your steak with me."

It was then that Carrie realized that Leeroy was driving his stagecoach back to his house. She recognized the cute little farm houses along the road. "Are you giving me a tour of the farms? I guess this town really doesn't have that much to offer in terms of things to do..."

"I wanted to talk to you about something," he told her. "You won't get in trouble for coming back to my house, will you?"

Carrie thought about it. "I won't if I don't go inside," she said resolutely.

Leeroy nodded. "All right," he replied.

He took her to his little farm house and stopped the coach in front of it. After helping her out, he released the pair of horses from the coach and led them up to the stable to the right of the house. Carrie followed, watching him and surprised to find that the stable belonged to him. It seemed like the more she discovered about him, the more capable he seemed. She'd never taken him for anything more than a stagecoach driver who drove people around from the station. It turned out that he had more in common with her than she had originally given him credit for. After all, she had come out west to start a new life and become a rancher's bride. What was a ranch if not a farm? He even had his own pair of ponies!

Carrie batted her lashes a little at him as she watched him put the horses into their stalls. He turned around to look at her and smirked. "You didn't think I was only renting them, did you?"

She laughed slightly nervously. "No, I didn't. I guess I'd never really thought about it before... You've got quite a nice life set up here for yourself, don't you?"

"You sound envious," he said back.

She smiled, feeling a fresh blush powder his cheeks. She was feeling lightheaded in the best way she'd ever felt it before. "I'm not envious. I'm happy for you."

He smiled back at her. "Do you want to come inside? You don't have to stay too long, so your boss won't worry or be angry."

Carrie sighed softly. "Well, now that I'm here, I suppose there's no harm in going inside and seeing how your kitchen has fared since the steaks."

They went inside his house and Carrie sat down on the oddly-shaped and upholstered leather couch. It even smelled of cows. "Did you make this couch yourself?" she asked him innocently. She just had to know.

Leeroy nodded proudly. "Indeed, I did. Why? Do you like it?"

Carrie nodded back at him. "I do. It's... different. I could tell that it must've been made by someone out here. Someone who hadn't made much furniture before."

He gave her a mock-offended look, frowning overdramatically. "Here I thought you were paying me a compliment..."

She laughed. "I mean it as a compliment. I thought you did great work!"

He smirked at her then. "It was the first furniture I'd ever made. Well, besides a chair." He gestured his head over to the table and chairs where they'd eaten the steaks the other afternoon. "Wood chairs are simple, though. A couch is difficult."

Carrie patted the seat next to her, inviting him to sit beside her. "It's a comfortable couch, even if it's not much to look at."

Laughing, Leeroy came over and sat down beside her. "I feel kind of like this couch, then," he said. "Comfortable, but not much to look at."

Carrie gaped a bit at him. "Don't be silly. You're quite handsome!"

He looked at her with those tempest gray-blue eyes of his. "The kind of handsome that you would write letters to and move all the way out here to meet?" he asked her, his voice growing soft now.

She gazed at him, surprised and confused. "Y—Yes, I suppose so. Why? Are you thinking of placing an advertisement?" Maybe that was why he had acted so strange when he heard about her mail-order groom. He'd been amazed to learn that she was doing such a thing, and wanted to participate?

Leeroy shook his head. Then he took her hand in his. He was so gentle and delicate about it, lightly brushing his palm and fingertips against the back of her hand before letting his hand rest on top of hers, linking their fingers together. Carrie looked into the depths of his eyes, breathing heavily now that he was holding her hand. She was happy and surprised, shocked and fearful. She was overwhelmed.

"I ask because I was sort of hoping that maybe, if you were planning to stay around Wallace, you'd consider marrying me." Leeroy was giving her such a sweet and loving look.

Carrie was very glad that she was sitting down. Surely her knees would have given out otherwise. "Oh, Leeroy," she said softly. "It's much more complicated than that... Mr. Stewart has a contract with us. We sign it when we first are hired. We're not supposed to marry for a year."

"I will wait for you, if you want," Leeroy said immediately.

She smiled at him, though she felt like crying. She was afraid of hurting him and she felt like she had no choice in the matter. "I can't ask you to do that," she said. "You should be free to live your life. You shouldn't have to wait around for me, in case I end my contract or change my mind. That's not fair to you."

"Miss Nelson, I haven't been able to get you off my mind since the day we met," Leeroy confessed. "I had been thinking about visiting you at the restaurant every day before I finally did. I worried that I'd bother you, til I saw that old man bothering you plenty as it was."

Carrie laughed a little. "You rescued me that day," she admitted.

"I wouldn't ask you to quit being a waitress there," he said. "I've come to enjoy the idea of loving a waiter-girl." He smiled.

She blushed. "Love?" *This is way more serious than I thought. Annie was right.*

Leeroy nodded. "Yes, ma'am," he said. "If it takes speaking personally with this Mr. Stewart fellow, well, then point me in the right direction."

Carrie gulped a bit. "Could I please have some water?" she asked him.

"Of course," he said, standing at once and going into the kitchen to get a glass. He took it out back to his spigot and came back a moment later, handing off the glass to her.

She was surprised how cold the water was. She took a few quick sips and then set the glass down on a table beside the couch. "Thank you," she said. "Well, if you're serious, then I guess I can't stop you from talking to Mr. Stewart. But please don't get me in trouble. In case you haven't noticed, there aren't other restaurants for me to work in around here."

Leeroy grinned at her and nodded a little. "I won't get you in trouble, Miss Nelson. I'll only tell him that I've fallen in love with you and I wish to marry you. Why, you can pretend that you don't love me back, if it makes it easier."

"That'd be horrible," she replied, laughing despite the

fear that she still felt about it all. "I will pretend no such thing."

"Then you do love me?" he asked.

She admired him a moment, batting her lashes and blushing. She nodded. "Yes, I do believe that I do. It's the reason I thought to seek your help the other day. I've been thinking about all the little ways I might be able to run into you ever since we met."

Leeroy practically bounded up to the roof at that. "You have? Oh, Miss Nelson, that's wonderful to hear! Let's go see this Mr. Stewart right away!"

Carrie calmed him down soon after this excited outburst. It was decided instead that she should return to work as usual the following day, and that Leeroy should come in to speak with her employer without her. That way, it would be more in tune with Leeroy's plan to declare his love for her and catch her boss off guard, instead of making him mad at Carrie right away.

He drove her in the coach back to the dormitory next to the Stewart House and promised that he'd see her again the following day. "Be ready, my love. We'll be able to be together soon."

Carrie went back into the dormitory and straight up to her room. Annie wasn't in the room anymore, not that she really had expected her to be. It was only the early afternoon now. She remembered the coins that Mr. Taylor had given to her and supposed that the plan to spend them somewhere fun in town was out of the question now.

Carrie had a wedding to help plan. She had to do it in secret though, for now. Now that she was alone, she allowed herself to smile and think about the exciting possibilities that this wedding would bring. *I get to marry that sweet and handsome young man!* she thought, lying on her bed and snuggling into the blankets. She wasn't sleepy, but the happiness and some of the feelings of being overwhelmed had fatigued her quite a bit. Waiting for her friends to come back into the dormitory was going to be torturous.

As soon as the door to the bedroom opened and Annie stepped inside, Carrie sat up and looked at her. "Annie!" she hissed.

"Goodness!" Annie cried out, jumping in her surprise. "Carrie, why on earth were you hiding out in here?"

"Can you keep a secret?" Carrie asked her.

Annie closed the door behind herself so no one else could listen in. "Yes...," she replied a bit warily.

"I just went to see Mr. Jackson," Carrie told her. "I wanted to give him the plates back, and to speak with him about what Rita told me yesterday. But I kind of ended up doing the opposite of that."

Annie's eyes widened. "You told him that you *like* him?"

Carrie nodded. "I told him that I *loved* him."

"Oh my goodness," Annie said, falling onto her bed as

well and looking over at Carrie as they gossiped. "What did he say to that?"

Carrie smiled, surprising herself with how genuine it was. It felt so strange to suddenly so overcome with excitement about getting married, when she had been so concerned about it not so very long ago.

"He asked me to marry him," Carrie said. "Oh, but you mustn't tell anyone. Not yet anyway. He's planning to come to the restaurant tomorrow and ask Mr. Stewart for my hand."

The two girls squealed together in a few minutes of excited anticipation.

After a bit, Annie gasped. "We're going to need to find you a dress," she said. "You can't get married in one of your dresses, though some of them are quite attractive. And you certainly can't get married in your uniform. You need a lace, white gown."

"Do you know anyone in town who makes gowns?" Carrie asked her, suspecting that the answer was no.

Annie shook her head. "But you're living here amongst friends. Surely one of us girls knows how to make a dress."

Carrie gasped a bit and snapped her fingers. "We could use the money that Mr. Taylor gave me for some of the supplies," she said. "There's not a tailor in town, but there is a general store. General stores have thread."

They giggled and gossiped some more, enjoying the fact that they didn't have to work in the eating house at all that day. Carrie wasn't used to having so much free time now that she was a working girl – something that she didn't aim to change, if she could avoid it. Leeroy's farm could surely keep her busy, if she was allowed to help fix things up and turn it into a proper, working farm instead of just the passion project that it currently was.

"How did he propose to you?" Annie asked her. "Was it awfully romantic?"

Carrie smiled and nodded, gazing dreamily off into a corner of the room as she imagined it all over again. "He held my hand. That was the start of it. And he told me that he hadn't been able to stop thinking of me, just like I haven't been able to stop thinking of him. Oh, Annie. You were right about him having a crush. But I never thought that such a thing could really be true! He really loves me and will do anything to be with me. I felt so bad, telling him about my contract."

She was going to have to give up some of her pay, because she was ending her contract before the full year was over. She didn't think it would matter much, since Leeroy had a job and he'd told her that she could keep on working. "I won't have to be very far from you girls," she added, thinking of that as well. "I will be living in Wallace for the rest of my life."

Annie got up from her bed and the two girls hugged.

It was going to be perfect. Carrie couldn't believe that everything had possibly worked out so well for her. And in such a short time, too!

EPILOGUE

Mr. Stewart was none too pleased to bid farewell to Carrie. After all, she was his most recent hire. But there was just no turning Mr. Leeroy Jackson down, especially when Leeroy professed to love her so much. Carrie ended her contract with the eating house, but that didn't mean that she had to stop visiting with her friends.

Annie, Rita and Carrie worked together to make a wedding gown for the big occasion. The money that Mr. Taylor had given her as tip money worked well in the purchase of some nice, white buttons for the back of her gown, as well as some white thread.

Rita was not at all surprised to find out that Carrie and Leeroy were to be married. "I told you, I knew it all along. No man sticks up for a woman the way he did without loving her." She winked at Carrie as she worked on sewing her dress.

"I still say that he was just doing that as a friend," Carrie said back, more teasing than anything now. "He told me that he cared about me a great deal right after meeting me. We're lucky that he didn't come into the restaurant every day just to see me."

Rita laughed. "If he'd done that, I'm sure Mr. Stewart would have sent him out and banned him from coming back."

Carrie and Leeroy were soon married in the small chapel just outside of town. The wedding was attended by all of her waitress friends, as well as Mr. Stewart himself. She was overcome at the sight of them out there in the pews, watching this most important moment of her life. They really had become a family for her. She never could have imagined feeling such sisterly kinship towards a group of people who had not long before been strangers to her.

When the wedding was over, before she and Leeroy could completely run off into the sunset, Rita and Annie took her aside. "We have a surprise for you," Annie said. "We received a letter at the dormitory some weeks back. We were going to mention it to you, but we thought it would be better as a surprise."

Carrie looked to Rita. What was it?

Rita took her hand and led her out of the chapel.

Standing there, in the grass and the dirt, as pretty as the day Carrie had last seen her, was Beverly Nelson.

Carrie let out a surprised "oh!" and rushed to hug her immediately.

"Beverly, you came all this way to see me get married?" Carrie asked her, hugging her tightly.

Leeroy came out of the church and Carrie introduced her little sister to her new husband.

"I've come to join the Stewart Girls," Beverly said to them. "I wanted to come here and be just like you. And this way, we can be close to each other again."

Carrie was so happy to have her sister there with her. And now that Beverly was going to join Mr. Stewart's House, she didn't have to ever feel bad again about leaving it. Her family in Wallace could keep on growing bigger.

THE END

BEVERLY: THE BUTCHER'S BRIDE

STEWART HOUSE BRIDES

BEVERLY: THE BUTCHER'S BRIDE

Wallace, Kansas – 1890

Beverly Nelson is young and smart, with a vision for how things should be at Stewart House, the Western eatery where she works as a waiter-girl. Her sister Carrie is sweet and obedient, but Beverly speaks her mind, which seems to be a bit of a threat for their supervisor, Rita.

When she is told to stop meddling in the boss' business, Beverly can't help but spend time with the butcher next door. She has an idea for how things should run and lets the butcher, Mr. Wilfred Maddox, know what she's thinking.

Instead of being angry with her, he is captivated and thrilled by her ideas. Can Beverly successfully help change things for the better at Stewart House, or will she end up losing her job? All she knows is that a friend like Wilfred Maddox is a valuable thing for her to have... But perhaps Wilfred will see her as something more.

1

"Rise and shine, everyone. Breakfast call will be in approximately one hour and we need you in your places before then."

Beverly rolled over in her bed, wishing she could continue on with her dream. A bright light coming from her window shade prevented such things, but this worked out splendidly because sleeping in was not an option for her any longer. Ever since Beverly Nelson first set her bag down in the Stewart House restaurant, she'd been on the go. Her sister Carrie hadn't been kidding when she informed her in letters about all of the hard work that went into being a waiter girl.

It comes with plenty of rewards too, of course, Carrie had written. *Chiefest among them, at least for me, is independence.*

She threw off the blankets and got out of her bed, stretching as she watched her roommate – her sister's former roommate – Annie O'Brien put on her waitress uniform. The long black skirt, long-sleeved black shirt, and white apron and bow. Beverly couldn't get over the bows. They looked so childish. She wrinkled her nose a little, just thinking about putting that on again.

Her training had to be rather quick, on account of the fact that her sister Carrie had recently left the position and they needed Beverly to take her place. The manager, Rita de la Cruz, had been kind enough – or bossy enough? – to take charge of Beverly's training. And she was the one who barked their orders when they first rose that morning.

"Must she always sound so harried?" she asked Annie as she undressed and changed into her black and white attire, too. Swiftly, she tied on her large, white bow. It sat there in her curled, red hair and made her look like some kind of doll. She grimaced slightly as she looked at her reflection in the mirror.

Annie giggled a little. "Rita can be a bit agitated, particularly in the mornings. But it's only because she wants this place to run smoothly. She's rather fond of this job. You'll notice that soon, if you haven't already."

"Oh, I have," Beverly laughed back. "Golly." She attempted to style her hair bun into a more attractive look, but then nothing could ever be attractive once a hairnet was placed atop it. She sighed slightly. Being flashily attractive was not a part of the job, so she'd best get used to that.

Annie shook her head a bit, smiling at her. "Come on, we don't want to keep her waiting."

Together, the two girls left their room in the dorm, meeting several of the other girls on their way out of the squat, tan-colored building and strolling over to the other small, tall building next door.

Stewart House, a sign out front proudly proclaimed. The eating house inside was larger than one might assume by simply judging from the outside. It was made of one large room with wooden floors and furnishings, including tables and chairs and a bar on the far wall. There was also a kitchen, a small back room for the girls to congregate on their short breaks, and an office for the owner himself. Mr. Stewart was there, bright and early every day, though Beverly couldn't say exactly what all he did. His business was successful and widely discussed, so she had to agree that he was doing things well. To be sure, the place was never empty while it was open.

Beverly and Annie filed into line along with the other waitresses, waiting for their cue from Rita or Mr. Stewart to enter the eating hall. There was a tiny circular window on the white door which led out there, and Beverly could just make out a few of the heads of their new customers. Passengers on the morning train always arrived hungry, that was for sure.

"Smiles, girls," Rita said to them, smiling exaggeratedly as she held the door open and they filed into the restaurant, each going to a different table. There were twenty or so girls and about fifty tables, along with five stools at the small bar, so the waitresses were sure to be on their toes during the entirety of the breakfast rush.

Beverly sidled up to the table she'd been assigned to, all smiles and merriment. "Good morning and welcome to Stewart House. What may I get for you?"

Her table consisted of a middle-aged man with a mustache, a lady, and a small boy. She assumed that they were a family. Ever since the train lines had opened up all over the west, traveling for some sightseeing was becoming more and more common. No one had to stay stuck on the eastern coast any longer. Beverly wished that such things had been around when she was the age of the boy at her table. The man cleared his throat, looking over the menu ravenously. "Two coffees, one juice, and three plates of your finest bacon and eggs, please."

Beverly nodded. "Right away, sir." She scooted off to the back rooms where she could relay their order and have the cooks in the kitchen get to work with their food. In the meantime, she poured a tall glass of apple juice and placed it onto a silver tray along with two white mugs and a pot full of piping hot coffee. Carefully, she carried the drinks tray back out to her table. She placed the juice in front of the boy and the mugs in front of his parents. Then, she carefully poured coffee into their mugs.

"I'll be right back with your breakfast," she told them cheerily.

"Can you please bring some milk and sugar, too?" the woman asked her.

Beverly nodded. "Yes, certainly."

Before she could go back to the kitchen, she had another table to visit. There was very little time for her to focus on one table at a time. The train wasn't going to be stopped there at the station for too long.

The breakfast rush did just that and within the hour, the restaurant cleared up as the train whistles signaled that all passengers must board again in order to continue on with their journey. Beverly was glad for the bit of a break. There were of course still some customers, but the people from town weren't quite as demanding as the customers who came from the trains. It wouldn't be long before she and her fellow waitresses were running around once again to serve the lunchtime train.

"What did you do for fun in Ohio?" Annie asked Beverly as they sat together at a table in the dormitory, taking a break and having a meal themselves.

Beverly smirked at her. "That's a fair question, if you're at all familiar with Ohio," she joked. "As you probably know, my sister and I worked on a farm there. Our family's farm.

Outside of that, I mostly read books or made things to pass the time."

"Made things?" Annie asked her curiously, biting into her ham and cheese sandwich. Room and board was provided by Mr. Stewart, which meant that the young ladies never had to worry about where they would get their meals from. Beverly however wished that sometimes their meals could be a tad nicer, like the ones served at the restaurant. *I know that Mr. Stewart would have to pay top dollar in order to pull that off, though,* she thought.

"Yes," she replied. "I would make dresses and toys for the little children around our town. I also love to cook. I almost applied to work as a cook instead of as a waiter girl, only Carrie convinced me that the pay and placement was better for a waitress."

Annie nodded. "Oh yes, the cooks don't get to live in a nice dormitory like ours. They have to live in a hotel nearby, amongst all the other people who pass through town. I imagine it's nowhere near as pleasant."

Beverly ate her sandwich, daydreaming about what it might be like to open a restaurant out west like Mr. Stewart had done. "I think it must be so wonderful to have your own business. I can see why Mr. Stewart took a liking to this town, too. It's always so busy; it never seems to get dull. And it's right near the railway, so even if one does get bored, one can just hop on a train and go for a new adventure!"

"Yes, I do believe that was what Mr. Stewart was going for," Annie agreed with a smile. "You so remind me of your sister, you know. I can tell just by looking at you that you have an adventurous spirit. That's certainly the kind of spirit that's needed here in a place like this. Why, you fit right in with all of the people who come out here to explore and vacation."

Yes, Beverly agreed to herself. *Except that it's not quite a vacation for me. It's a relocation.*

When the lunchtime rush came, she and Annie and all of the other girls were back in their places, smiling and acting supremely friendly towards all of their new guests. There was a lot of call for Stewart Steaks, a thing that Beverly had never heard of until she started working there. She went back to place her first order with the cooks and saw them open the ice box, pulling out some frozen steaks that looked more like blocks of brick than anything edible.

"People pay to eat those?" she asked Rita innocently enough.

"Of course," Rita said defensively. "Those are the famous Stewart Steaks, advertised on trains throughout the country. A lot of folks come in here because they want to try one themselves."

Beverly didn't think for one moment that people all over the country knew about those frozen hunks of meat. But she supposed that word got around enough when people traveled out west and then came home to report on things. She couldn't imagine ever wanting such a thing herself, though. The stews seemed much more appetizing.

"I thought there might be a butcher in town, is all," Beverly said with a shrug. "I thought I saw one when I arrived."

Rita raised an eyebrow at her. "There is a butcher all right. He's our main competitor."

"Oh," Beverly said dumbly. She supposed that made sense. Competition was often good for business too. She just wondered how it was possible that so many people wanted to eat steaks that were delivered via ice box car when they could just go down the street a ways and enjoy a fresh steak elsewhere. *Perhaps it's just that the butcher doesn't cook.*

Seeing the way that Rita reacted to the very implication that their steaks might not be as good as could be, Beverly decided not to push the topic any further. She'd remember not to question things like that to her.

"She's very devoted to this place," Annie informed Beverly as they enjoyed their longer break before dinnertime. "Be careful that you don't mouth off too much or the next thing you know, she'll have told Mr. Stewart what you've said. She can be strict like that, when she suspects disloyalty or rule-breaking."

"I didn't mean to seem disloyal," Beverly said defensively. "I just wondered if there mightn't be a better way. But Mr. Stewart *is* the professional in this area, not me."

All the same, Beverly hoped that she might be able to

meet this butcher at some point soon, so she could find out if he really felt like a rival. She wondered if he might have been at Carrie's wedding. It seemed that the whole town was there. *That's what I should do,* she thought excitedly. *I'll ask Carrie about it!*

She knew that she'd be safe discussing such things with Carrie, because they shared a sisterly bond like no one else Beverly had ever known.

2

During her long break before the dinner rush the following day, Beverly made her way up the dirt lane to her sister's home. Carrie was married to a local stagecoach driver, and though Beverly knew that she could hire him to take her to his house, she preferred to walk there so she could explore the town a bit. As she strolled, she passed by the butcher's shop. *Maddox Meats* read a sign above the door. She smiled a little to herself. If she had her way, she would be meeting that man soon enough.

Beverly supposed that she had a business mind, which was why she had spent so much of her life making things. Her sister helped care for the home with her mother, but Beverly was the one who enjoyed crafting clothing and preparing meals. Carrie of course could also cook and mend, but her passion was more in helping people in their work than in the creation of things. Carrie's dresses were practical whereas Beverly's were unique and interesting. At least in her opinion. Now that she was working for Mr. Stewart, she wondered if she might be able to offer some of her skills to Stewart House. He seemed largely opposed to change, because things that worked just *worked*, so why change them? That was the impression she got from talking with Rita anyway.

The small town of Wallace was a sweet little place, once Beverly got used to its dusty, tan coloring. Ohio was a great deal greener, and she never thought she would miss the bright sight of corn stalks along the road, but here she was. She smiled as she walked, finding each new sight interesting and wondering how long it would take for things to no longer be so quaint to her. *It shall be a sad day when I'm no longer excited to live here, but Carrie is still in love with the place,* she thought.

Finally, Beverly arrived at her sister's home. It was a cute, little house – the sort of home one could easily imagine a man like Mr. Jackson owning. She was still smiling as she knocked on the door. It would be good to spend some time with her sister again, even if they just chatted about how their lives were going and she didn't bring up the restaurant at all.

After only a few moments, Carrie opened the door and

beamed out at her sister. "Beverly! What a lovely surprise. Please come in. How are things at Stewart House?"

Ah, I should've known it would come up right away. Carrie cares about how I'm settling in, of course.

Beverly entered Carrie's home and walked into the living room, taking a seat on the odd-looking leather couch without question, which made her sister laugh. "Have I done something odd?" she asked self-consciously.

Still giggling a bit, Carrie shook her head. "No, not at all. It's just that Leeroy made this couch and I've always made fun of it for how it looks. He'd be pleased to know you didn't notice."

Beverly smirked at her. "Oh, I noticed. I just kept my comments to myself."

Carrie laughed more at that. "I've missed you, sister. How have you been doing at Stewart House? Getting along with everyone, I hope?"

"Of course! I'm not the sort of person who would berate people to their faces. I've been doing well. Rita showed me how things were done and you know I'm a fast learner. She's quite a character that one, isn't she?"

Carrie nodded her head. "She certainly is. She's incredibly attached to that place, and the way that Mr. Stewart expects things to be run. Have you been on your best behavior with her?"

Beverly nodded her head, laughing a little. "I made the mistake to question why we don't serve fresh steaks from the butcher's shop instead of cooking up the ones that were frozen on the train."

Carrie grimaced ever so slightly, but Beverly noticed. "Oh dear," she said. "Yes, they are very protective of their steaks."

"But it makes no sense!" Beverly exclaimed. "They're selling frozen steaks to their customers when, right up the road, the customers could just as easily enjoy fresh ones. It seems that, instead of taking away from the butcher's clients, they could... I don't know... Have they ever tried working with him?"

Carrie looked at her contemplatively. "I'm not sure that Mr. Stewart has thought to talk to Mr. Maddox about this issue at all. He opened his restaurant there by the station and it's pretty much the only thing he thinks or cares about. I reckon that, if you asked him, he wouldn't be able to tell you where the town's bank is."

Beverly laughed lightly. She wasn't surprised by this. Even still, it bothered her that a businessman of Mr. Stewart's apparent stature in the town had placed such miniscule interest in his surroundings. "I simply think he would do well to reach out to other businessmen in the community," she said. "But it's not my place to question him about it or make suggestions, of course."

Carrie smiled delightedly at her little sister. Beverly had always been rather virtuous and optimistic about things, and Carrie knew that she also harbored her own thoughts on business. No girl who made clothing and housewares like

Bevie could ever truly be satisfied without profiting off of such things, at least in some way. Now that she was older, Beverly clearly had thoughts of making her own way. This was why Carrie thought she'd do well at the restaurant, but perhaps having to follow questionable orders was a struggle for her.

"Would you like a beverage or a snack?" she asked Beverly pleasantly. "How long can you stay?"

"Yes, please," Beverly replied, smiling. "Look at you. The waitress in you is still alive and well."

Carrie laughed.

"I have to be back for dinnertime, but I've still got about an hour or so," Beverly added before Carrie went into the kitchen to fetch some vittles.

Beverly really wasn't all that hungry, but she knew that she would regret it if she passed up the chance to eat before the dinner rush. Being around all of that food in the restaurant – even the frozen steaks – was bound to make her feel starved if she delayed her meal until after work.

Carrie nodded her head and walked into her kitchen to fetch a few things for her guest, as well as for herself. Some sandwiches and tea seemed like the perfect thing for a meal before Beverly had to go back to work. She likely received plenty of meals there, provided by the restaurant, so some homemade sandwiches would be a welcome change. Carrie placed everything onto a tray and carried it out, setting it on the coffee table in front of Leeroy's unique couch. She sat down next to her sister, cringing a bit only to get a laugh out of Beverly.

"How have you been enjoying married life?" Beverly asked her with a smile as she grabbed a sandwich and began eating. A ham and cheese sandwich would do the trick for her. Carrie had brought out a whole trayful, too, in case she wanted more.

Carrie appeared thoughtful. She took a sip from her cup of tea. "Well, I dare not say that it's all been easy. It's been quite a transition again from working as a waitress to working as a housewife. We've got big plans to turn this small house and bit of land into a real profitable farm, and it largely falls to me because Leeroy is always off driving his stagecoach around. The people who come from all over and often eat at Stewart House are sometimes mighty interested in riding around with Leeroy, once they've had some food in them. And of course, some people also stay in town for the night or longer, and they have need of him, too. I told him that he shouldn't begrudge Mr. Stewart for his restaurant, because his business helps bring more work to Leeroy, too."

It was now Beverly's turn to look thoughtful. She carefully set her sandwich back down on its plate and sipped at her tea. "This is precisely my way of thinking about the whole affair with the steaks. It simply doesn't make sense to me why we wouldn't try to work with our neighbors instead of closing off from everyone else and going it completely alone. Doesn't it seem like being friendlier and more cooperative would be beneficial for Mr. Stewart?"

"I agree with you, Bevie. I do," Carrie told her. "But I think you have to be careful in the way you go about it. Perhaps don't tell Rita what you're thinking. She will always side with Mr. Stewart on things like this. Trust me on that."

The two sisters ate the rest of their meal together and promised to visit each other more often, when time permitted, now that Beverly was fully trained at the restaurant and would have more time to look around and explore the quaint little town of Wallace, Kansas.

"I certainly won't mind being your tour guide if you're ever in the need of one," Carrie told her with a friendly smile. "I know that Annie is a good guide as well, but she doesn't want to be in charge of shepherding the Nelson girls around for the rest of her life, surely."

Beverly smiled and gave her sister a hug. "Thank you for the offer. I'll remember that. And thank you so much for giving me your advice. I know that it might not always seem like it, but I promise that I do take it to heart."

With that, she toddled her way back down the dirt road to the Stewart House restaurant. She couldn't afford to be late and make Rita even more annoyed at her. Besides, any minutes lost would mean less money on her end; this she was well aware of. As soon as she got back to the dormitory, she hastily changed back into her black and white uniform. She was grateful for having changed, because any crumbs or

– heaven forbid! – stains on her uniform would only bring her further agony. The girls were all in charge of making sure that their work clothes remained spotless and neat. Rita went around and collected them for washing every few days.

As she went to tie the white bow into her hair once more, Annie came bursting into the room. "We received word that an overly-crowded train is on its way into the station. The eating house is going to be packed tonight! You must hurry and get ready. Mr. Stewart has asked for everyone to meet in the back room immediately. Where were you?"

Beverly blanched a bit at the very idea of a full restaurant. The dinnertime train usually caused the restaurant to be its busiest as it was. Would they even have enough places to put everyone? "Do we have enough tables? Plates?"

Annie took her by the hand once the bow had been tied and they walked together out of the dormitory and into the restaurant via the back entrance. "I don't know," she said excitedly as they walked. "I've never experienced anything like this. Suppose we have to turn some people away. That would be a disaster."

I don't know about that, Beverly thought, a small smile forming on her face despite her best efforts to hide it. *I could think of a few other places they could go, if we're too packed in here...*

The Stewart House being overbooked only meant good business for the other venues in the area. People like Mr. Maddox the butcher would surely be able to accommodate the overflow. "It would be a shame to have to put them out," she said for the sake of Annie and Mr. Stewart. She didn't want to do anything that was bad for the restaurant where she worked, but she couldn't help but see the benefit to other people as well.

3

L ining up with all of the other waiter-girls, Beverly listened to Rita and Mr. Stewart as they flitted about the room, clearly in a bit of a panic over this new predicament. "We're going to need each and every one of you to be on your toes for the entirety of this shift," Mr. Stewart told them.

"There are going to be some guests here tonight that we simply won't be able to accommodate," Rita said. "We ask that you politely inform them that they shall have to find food and lodging elsewhere this evening. There are carriages at the train station that can take them a bit further out."

Mr. Stewart nodded in curt agreement with that. "Of course, we will make every effort to cater to all of our visitors.

If some of them won't mind a wait, you may invite them to sit in the parlor inside the main floor of the dormitory."

Goodness, Beverly thought. *If nights like this keep happening, I daresay Mr. Stewart might need to open another restaurant...*

Now that she was there and hearing the instructions and news firsthand, she felt nervous about what she was about to endure. She did hope that there wouldn't be an angry scene because of this.

"Places, ladies!" Mr. Stewart ordered.

Rita went out of the room and opened the front door of the restaurant, allowing a slew of customers to come pouring in. Everyone was smiling, at least. Beverly wondered how long that might last.

She and the other waitresses left the sanctuary of the back room and went to their first tables. "Good evening and welcome to Stewart House," she welcomed her guests. "My name is Beverly. What would you all like to drink? I imagine you're all quite thirsty from your travels."

Normally, Beverly wouldn't have had to write any orders down because things were usually pretty run of the mill, but on a night like tonight, with so many people there, she thought she was bound to forget something if she didn't take things down. Indeed, she went back to the kitchen with a full sheet's worth of drinks that had been ordered by that table of seven.

As soon as she brought them their drinks of water, milk

and juice, she immediately took their food orders. "One at a time, please," she had to remind them. "I can't write that fast and I don't want to make any mistakes." After a full two pages of food orders later, Beverly went back to the kitchen to inform the cooks of what to make. Of course, practically all of them wanted to try a Stewart Steak.

She did her best not to roll her eyes.

There was always a new table for her to assist and she didn't have time to worry about whether or not her bow was crooked. At one point, she watched as Rita directed a large family to the dormitory. "Is the lobby of the dormitory even presentable for visitors right now?" she asked Annie in her ear as she passed, carrying a full tray.

"I guess it doesn't matter, if it's just a holding place," Annie replied on her way to the kitchen a few minutes later.

The din of the diners became quite loud as they all ate their food and engaged in conversation. Beverly hoped that they would be polite and vacate their tables as soon as they were done, so the people waiting in the dorm's parlor could be tended to next. *I guess one thing is for sure: business is booming for Mr. Stewart.* She would be pretty hard pressed to try to deny that, or question his strategies, now that she'd witnessed and been a part of this.

"Clearly, you need to expand your operations here!" a customer suddenly shouted as he came inside through the front door, complaining to Rita. The poor lady had been stationed at the front of the restaurant in order to direct people elsewhere, and Beverly didn't envy her. "We were given plenty of advertisements on the train that said that you all would serve us!"

"I'm terribly sorry, sir," Beverly said, sidling over in an effort to help Rita more than anything. The customers at their tables could stand to miss her for a brief moment. "But if you explore this town a little, you will find several other venues which offer food, though in not quite the setting you'd been offered and for that I am very sorry. We can't always account for the size of the trains."

The customer glared at her, narrowing his eyes. He was a tall man, and if Beverly was guessing she would've said that he was a lumberjack. He wore red plaid and denim overalls. It didn't take much imagination to come to that conclusion. "What sort of other venues?" he demanded.

"Off of the top of my head, sir, I know that there's a butcher just up the road. He doesn't really have any space for tables and dine-in places, but he makes wonderful meats. You'd be more than welcome there, I'm sure. And there are places to sit within the dorm next door, as you've no doubt been told by Miss Rita here."

The lumberjack man continued to give her a rueful look, but then shrugged his shoulders and left the restaurant, walking out to head towards the butcher shop. Rita let out a relieved sigh. "Thank you," she said.

Beverly smiled at her and gave a little nod. Then she returned to one of her tables so she could remove some of the empty dishes that had accumulated there. It was a small victory, but it was a victory nonetheless. *Maybe now she'll see the value in Mr. Maddox.*

As she worked, she thought about how she'd only ever seen his shop and heard about the butcher. She still hadn't laid eyes on him herself. *I suppose I ought to pay him a visit one day soon, so I can see for myself what he's like. I want to make sure that he is worthy of all of this newfound business.* She smirked a bit. It wouldn't take much for him to be worthy, especially when he was desperately needed to help out in times like this.

The rest of the dinner rush went by without much incident. It helped that several of the people didn't mind waiting, and others simply went off to find vittles elsewhere in town. Beverly thought that the big, successful restaurant running into a problem like this was exactly the kind of thing that would prove beneficial to every business in town.

When the people had cleared out and the girls were all free to go back to the dormitory, Beverly found Annie. "What're the odds that some of those folks went straight to Mr. Maddox and his steaks?"

Annie laughed. "Oh, Beverly. You are incorrigible."

Beverly shook her head. "Not incorrigible, merely stubborn." She let out a little laugh. "When I first heard and then witnessed all of those people coming in from the train, my only thought was 'how are we going to handle this?' But then I quickly realized that it was an answer to my prayers. Maybe now Mr. Stewart will realize that a little competition might be good for this restaurant and this town."

Annie was smiling at her as they walked up the stairs of the dormitory together, finding their room. "Well, no one can fault you for not caring," she said, opening up their door and leading Beverly inside. "But still, Mr. Stewart is a stubborn man, too. He likely doesn't view the fact that other businesses are profiting as a good thing."

Beverly frowned a little at that, and then shrugged. "It might just take time for him to see how it actually helps him to help the others."

She went over to her bed and began removing her uniform. It was time to hand them off to be cleaned. One of Beverly's favorite parts of the day was when she was able to remove the monochrome garb she had to wear most of every day. Once the dress and bow and socks were removed, she stood in her white bloomers and shift, thinking over what to wear for the rest of the night. *Should I really put pajamas on already? There's still plenty of time left this evening...* She looked over at Annie and saw that she was wearing her pink and white nightgown now, brushing through her long, cinnamon-colored hair. Annie wasted no time.

"How can you even think of sleeping after all of that?" she asked Annie with a laugh. "I was thinking of going out and exploring a little."

The other woman looked at her as if she'd just said she was going a bit off her head. "But we have a curfew," Annie pointed out, setting her comb down. "I know you're anxious about the betterment of this town, and it's indeed admirable, but you must do things within the rules. You don't want to be put out of the House, do you?"

Beverly sighed and shook her head. "No, of course not. I'm just restless. I can't help it." Resigned to bedtime, she took out her mint green pajama gown and stepped into it, carefully buttoning and tying up the top of the nightgown once it was on.

"Just because we have to stay inside doesn't mean you have to go to sleep already," Annie pointed out. "But Rita won't take too kindly to you wandering around the dorm either."

Beverly pulled back the blankets on her bed and climbed in, lying down and looking over at Annie as her head rested on her hands on her pillow. "I know I should be tired, but I feel too excited to fall asleep right now."

"You're probably feeling energized from the night's events," Annie said with a smile. She got up and got into her own bed, mirroring Beverly as she looked the short distance across the room at her. "Just try to close your eyes and take your mind off of things. That's what I normally do."

That's easy for you to do, Beverly thought, *because your mind doesn't seem to be addled about any of this. You just listen and follow instructions. In a way, I envy you.* She closed her eyes and did her best to do what Annie suggested, but telling herself not to think about things was in and of itself, a form of doing that very thing.

She imagined the mysterious Mr. Maddox. Was he like Leeroy, bemused by the Stewart House but ultimately appreciative of it? Her sister had told her that he met her once with chagrin but was more than happy to supply her with some fresh steak for her to try. *He doesn't sound all that competitive to me. A competitive man would've driven Carrie from the shop. He's probably just as curious about our operations as I am about his.*

There was nothing to it. Tomorrow, during her time off, Beverly was going to go over to the butcher's shop and see things for herself. Even if it got her into trouble with Rita or Mr. Stewart, though she didn't think that it would. After all, Carrie had gone over and bought steaks from Mr. Maddox; Rita surely must've known about that. *It's one thing for me to buy a steak on my own time. It's quite another if I tried to start selling them here under their noses.* She laughed softly, uncontrollably. *Imagine that. I'd have to be completely out of my mind to try such a thing.*

Rita might've been worried about that, but Beverly was loyal to her job. That was why she wanted so badly to help the Stewart House become successful. Fresh meat would be a good thing for Mr. Stewart's restaurant. Sometimes, what was good for one ended up being good for all.

4

In the morning, Beverly woke before Annie. She didn't exactly feel well-rested, but she couldn't sleep anymore. Quietly, she got out of her bed and brushed her red, curly hair until it was more under control. She changed out of her nightgown and into her freshly-cleaned black and white uniform. Tying the white bow into her hair, Beverly gazed at her reflection in the mirror. She knew that Mr. Stewart wanted his waiter-girls to be young and attractive, but she didn't feel attractive in the garments that she was forced to wear.

When I'm on my break to meet Mr. Maddox, I'd better change into one of my prettier dresses, she told herself. She was grateful that she'd thought ahead and packed along her dresses.

Carrie had done the same thing, although she had been on her way to meet an intended husband when she left Dublin, Ohio. Beverly had always planned to move out west and become a waiter-girl. *But all of these girls must be planning ahead for something better. No one wants to work in a restaurant forever, right? Well, perhaps Rita was an exception. She'd probably be happy to stay at Stewart House for the rest of her life.*

It was difficult to imagine the lovely young woman as a spinster, however. She just had to meet the right gentleman. That's what Beverly's mother's assessment surely would have been.

The familiar knock on their room's door came about half an hour after Beverly's early rising. She flinched a little. "She sure knows how to resonate, doesn't she?"

"Hmm?" Annie said, rising in her bed herself and rubbing gently at her still-closed eyes. Her long, brown hair was a mess on her head. Beverly was glad for her head-start in the brushing department, at least.

"It's time to rise and shine," she told Annie with a smile. "The breakfast train will be here soon."

"You're already dressed!" Annie said then, brown eyes widening as she woke up. "Did I over-sleep?"

Beverly chuckled and shook her head. "No, I woke up a little early today. You know how I had a hard time sleeping last night."

"I'd forgotten about that," Annie replied. She got out of her bed at once and changed into her uniform as well. She then worked at taming her hair so she could fashion the bow into it. "You could've woken me, you know. I might've appreciated the head-start, too."

"Aww, but you were sleeping so peacefully. I didn't see a point in disturbing you." Beverly thought that Annie deserved to get her beauty rest, since her mind didn't seem to be burdened with as many thoughts and opinions as Beverly's was. "You've got plenty of time to get ready. You know how Miss Overachiever likes to wake us up extra early. It's mainly on account of all those girls who *do* over-sleep."

Annie adjusted the bow on her head, smiling at Beverly's reflection in her mirror. "All the same, you needn't be afraid to wake me up sometimes. Especially if it's only a little early."

The two girls left their room hand-in-hand for roll-call and for entry into the eatery next door. There was no way that the breakfast train would be anywhere near as full as that last dinner train was. Beverly prayed that such a thing had been some kind of an anomaly. Even though she enjoyed being able to supply some of the other vendors with customers, she would've preferred to not be thrown into such a situation...especially without much prior warning.

The breakfast customers arrived all rosy-faced and excited to experience the West as well as to dine at the now oft-talked about restaurant in Wallace. "Our reputation is still favorable, I trust," Beverly said with a smile to a group of men at one of her tables.

One of the men nodded at her, grinning. "Oh, yes, ma'am.

It's so good that I hear there are lots of folks who want to come out here *just* to visit this establishment. You don't hear such things said about just any old' eatery."

Several of the other men nodded their heads in agreement with this. Beverly was quite surprised. "I'll have to inform my boss. It will surely make his day."

Come to think of it, she thought. *I really haven't spoken to him since my interview. I should check in with him so that he remembers me and knows what I've been doing.* She would leave out the butcher, of course. She promised her sister.

As soon as the breakfast bunch was gone back to their morning train, Beverly hastened to the boss's office door. She only had a short break before the lunch diners would arrive, so she knew this was the best time to try and speak with Mr. Stewart. She would see him other times, of course, but she wished to speak with him when things weren't quite so busy.

She found that she was rather nervous once she was standing at his door, but she took a deep breath and finally plucked up the nerve to knock on the dark mahogany door. Beverly could hear the shuffling of papers and the deep clack-clack of footfalls upon the restaurant's wooden floor, approaching. She took another deep breath and suddenly, the door was being pulled open towards her.

Mr. Stewart peered down at her. He still held some paperwork in his left hand, as if he had been so caught up in his work that he couldn't set it down even for a moment. "Yes, Miss Nelson? Can I help you with something?" he asked her.

At least he remembers my name, she thought. "Good afternoon, sir," she said. "I just wanted to inform you about the positive comment I received this morning from a group of customers."

Mr. Stewart appeared wary at first, but he allowed her to continue.

Beverly cleared her throat. "They said that folks back east are so enthralled with your restaurant that they're lining up to come west *just* to enjoy our food and hospitality. Isn't that delightful?" She smiled at her boss, unsure how he was receiving this news because his face remained serious.

Mr. Stewart blinked at her. He shook the papers out in his hand. "That's great news, Miss Nelson. Thank you for letting me know. Hopefully that word of mouth will keep spreading." He turned to go back into his office but then he paused and looked at her again, his expression softening a bit by degrees. "How have you been getting on here, by the way? I'm afraid I haven't been the best at checking in, but of course Rita tells me things. She said you're a very capable waitress and fast learner as well."

Beverly smiled and bowed her head slightly. "Thank you, sir. I do believe I've been getting on well here. I hope that I'll prove to be a positive impact on this place, in my own small way."

"Oh, come now," he said, still smiling at her. "It won't necessarily be a small way." With that, he went back into his office to continue working.

Beverly practically skipped away from the office door, a clear bounce in her step. She went into the kitchen and made a sandwich for herself. She had about half an hour to eat and rest up before the lunch shift.

"Something tells me that you're up to something," Annie said to her as they sat together in the small dining room in the dormitory – most often it was used for leisure, not actual dining. She had a book open on the table in front of her and she arched an eyebrow at Beverly when the other girl sat down at the table, half a sandwich on a plate in front of her.

"Whatever makes you say *that*?" Beverly asked her with faux innocence that made them both burst out into a fit of giggles. "I just spoke with Mr. Stewart and let him know that he had customers complimenting the restaurant. I thought it might be a good idea to let him know, so he might be on good terms with me and realize that I fully support his hard work."

Annie continued to raise her eyebrows at Beverly. "This is clearly leading somewhere, though…"

Beverly blushed a little, smiling at her friend and finishing up the remaining bites of her sandwich. "I won't do anything that's against the rules. And I already promised my sister that I wouldn't bother Rita with any of my thoughts on the matter, but I was planning to go over to the butcher shop and meet with Mr. Maddox."

Annie gasped at her. She closed her book. "Your sister did the same thing, and all it ended up proving was that his steaks are delicious but his attitude is not. He doesn't like Stewart House girls."

"Well, have we given him good reason to? As far as he's concerned, we're unwelcome competition in this small down that didn't have many customers to begin with, and now we're hogging all of them."

Annie shook her head at her. "You Nelson girls certainly are trouble-makers."

Beverly held up her hands. "I won't cause any trouble. But, after all, we're neighbors. There's nothing at all wrong with being cordial to someone else in this town."

"That sure did work out well for Carrie," Annie replied. "She ended up married."

Beverly scoffed a little. "Friendship amongst fellow businesses doesn't lead to marriage unless one wants it to. I've never met the man. From the sound of it, he's a brute."

"That's why I'd advise you not to go."

Sighing, Beverly shrugged her shoulders. "I'll bring you back a treat that might change your mind."

The lunch shift loomed over them and before long, Annie and Beverly were back in their places in the small back room of Stewart House, awaiting the arrival of the latest customers. Beverly liked the lunch shift best because the folks arrived hungry, yet they didn't seem to have as much of a rushed attitude. For some reason, dinnertime was always the worst for her. She imagined that it had more to do with the long train ride and less to do with her, though.

One thing she was glad of was that fewer customers asked for steaks during the lunchtime service. A few people still did, since they were the big advertising draw for the place, but Beverly was pleased to find that many more were ordering sandwiches and even grits. *This is more like it,* she thought. *More like what I'm used to.* That wasn't to say that whatever she was used to was strictly *normal* or even *how it was done*, but she had an easier time dealing with things that made sense to her. This infatuation with frozen steaks didn't make any sense to her.

"This is one of my favorites here," she honestly told a customer who'd ordered a ham and cheese melted sandwich.

The customer – a young woman close to Beverly's age – smiled at her. "Thank you," she said. "That's good to know."

Sandwiches weren't the most exciting thing that Stewart House offered; Beverly knew that. But she tremendously enjoyed their satisfying simplicity. She hoped to continue making and eating sandwiches like that once she left. Watching the cooks in the kitchen, even for a few moments, was enough to learn the general recipes for a lot of their dishes.

A good wife knows how to make good sandwiches for her husband, she caught herself thinking. Even if she wasn't really after that sort of thing, it was true. Most gentlemen hoped to find a wife that could cook and Beverly believed that she could provide that for a man, at the very least. This restaurant position really was a good match for her; she just wished that she could do more.

Finally, the lunch rush ended and Beverly was free to go on her longer break. It was meant to be a break for some leisure activities and perhaps a bit of rest – that was Mr. Stewart's intent when he set up this schedule structure for his waiter-girls – but Beverly had other plans.

5

The first thing that Beverly did on her break was go back to the dormitory and change clothes. She wanted to 'dress to impress' so she put on one of her nicest dresses, a light blue number with little darker blue flowers on it and a matching dark blue sash around her waist. It was a dress that she'd had since she was eighteen, and it still fit her the way it always had. It had impressed gentlemen at parties when she was a younger girl, so why wouldn't it impress the butcher?

As she left the dorm, she ran into Annie on the steps. Annie took one look at her and sighed a little. "It doesn't take a genius to know what you're doing," she said. "You'd better hope that Rita doesn't see you out in that. She'll likely put two and two together."

"Aww, Annie, you worry too much," Beverly replied, gently tapping her friend on the end of her nose as she walked on past her. *There's no harm at all in greeting Mr. Maddox and being friendly. Golly, was Carrie under such scrutiny for going out on the town with Leeroy?*

The difference was that Leeroy apparently had a sparkling reputation whereas the butcher was regarded as an unfriendly brute... Beverly chose to believe that this was only because people hadn't taken the time to really talk to him. *I don't want to seem disloyal to Mr. Stewart, and I of course appreciate very much that I have a job and a place to live,* she thought. *But I can't help feeling that this is the right thing to do.*

Beverly walked along the dirt road, trying her best to avoid getting dirt all over her lovely blue dress. This town had clearly been built with cowboy boots and horses in mind, not ladies in dresses, but she ended up only slightly dirtying the hem when at last she stepped through the open doorway and into Mr. Maddox's butcher shop.

A little bell sat on the counter and Beverly didn't hesitate on her approach. She picked up the copper bell and gently shook it, hoping that this was meant to get Mr. Maddox's attention and not meant for something else. She could feel butterflies in her stomach as she waited there, and she had no earthly idea where they'd come from. *There's no reason to be nervous,* she told herself. *He's just a man...*

At that moment, the tall, scruffy butcher walked into view. He was wearing a white apron over an all-black outfit, which caused Beverly to smile a bit in spite of herself. *His work outfit matches mine.* There were some pink stains on his apron and she didn't have to try to imagine what they might've come from. She tried her best to not think of them at all.

"Hello?" he asked her, fixing his icy, blue gaze upon her. She thought that he was quite handsome, for all of his dark, brooding appearance. His light eyes certainly worked in his favor. "May I help you with something?"

"Yes," Beverly said. "Hello. My name is Miss Beverly Nelson." She extended her hand to him. "I am a waiter-girl over at Stewart House."

He took her hand and gently shook it, stopping and letting it go as soon as the name of the restaurant was mentioned. He looked at her shrewdly. "I see," he said. "Nelson. Do you have a sister in town?"

Her surname was not that uncommon, really, but for once it really was shared with someone around town. Beverly's smile grew ever wider. "I do. My sister Carrie Nelson. Well, Carrie *Jackson* now."

"That's right," he said, still eyeing her rather suspiciously, like she might try to rob his shop or something ridiculous like that. He plainly didn't trust anyone who came from Mr. Stewart's restaurant. "I forgot that she's married to ol' Leeroy now." He whistled a low whistle and shook his head a bit. "She came in here once and asked to try some of my steaks. I still see her around sometimes. I believe she doesn't work there anymore, though."

Beverly nodded. "That's right, sir. She got married so her contract ended. Mr. Stewart only keeps us girls on as long as we're unwed."

"Such a strange system," Mr. Maddox scoffed. "Why should anyone care if you're married, so long as you can hold a tray or whatever it is that you ladies do there?"

"You know, sir, I agree with you," Beverly said sincerely. "I think he aims to promote decency in town, is all. He also hopes to bring new ladies to the attention to the men around here, I do believe. Bring a woman's touch to Wallace..." Now that she said the words out loud, it began make sense to her, although she didn't know that having them work as waitresses with a one-year commitment contract was the best way for them to marry the local gentlemen. She supposed that it all came down to purity. She sniffed a little and batted her lashes at Mr. Maddox. "I don't quite go in for all of that, though."

Mr. Maddox continued to stare at her, shifting his weight a bit. "Why did you come here?" he asked, then he cleared his throat. "Beg your pardon, ma'am, I only mean that... What can I help you with?"

She realized then that she hadn't asked for a sampling of his meats or anything like that. She'd only barged in and introduced herself – fairly awkwardly – and left him to wonder what her purpose was. Beverly blushed slightly and nodded. "Of course. I'm sorry. It's just that I've heard a lot about you, from my sister and my friend at the restaurant. May I please try some steak?"

He gruffly told her how much it would cost and she swiftly handed over the money. With that, Mr. Maddox left her standing there and went into the back room. She looked around the small area of the shop. There weren't any places to sit. She didn't really think there was a reason to want to sit in the place, though. There were large hunks of meat hanging from the ceiling pretty much everywhere about the room. The air smelled like a wood fire and bacon, which succeeded in making her stomach growl.

Even if this steak is as good as Carrie claims, she thought. *I'm having a difficult time imagining Mr. Stewart working with this man.* She frowned a bit. She didn't know why she had ever thought that it might be simple.

When he reappeared behind the counter, Mr. Maddox was holding a small, white parcel. He handed it over to Beverly. She was shocked to find that it was damp on the bottom, but she refrained from thinking about it. "I recommend that you cook that today," he said. "For best flavor."

He studied her face for a moment. "Why did you really come here?" he asked her. "Taking pity on the poor butcher? Is that it?"

"Oh, no! No, that's not it at all," Beverly said with such rapid earnest that she likely sounded like she was being sarcastic or lying. She calmed down a little with another deep breath. "It's just that, I noticed that we sell steaks at our restaurant that come frozen from a special refrigerator car on the train. They're sent out on a regular basis. And it bothered me to hear that we're serving our customers steak that has been frozen and reheated, essentially."

Mr. Maddox looked at her, scratching his scruffy, dark beard. He'd clearly heard about the frozen steaks before. "Your sister has mentioned this to me previously. She felt similarly, but of course nothing really came of it."

This made Beverly a little sad, not that she expected her sister – dear though she was – to take a stand for the butcher or anything like that. "Carrie is a sweet spirit, but she was likely not thinking of anything other than her own meals. I, on the other hand, have an idea that you might be interested in. At least, it's the beginning of an idea, anyway."

Mr. Maddox continued to blink at her. "What'd you say your name was again?" he asked her thoughtfully, a small smile forming on his lips now that he'd heard this from her. Her attitude appeared to change things in his mind.

"Beverly," she said, smiling at him and offering her hand again. "Beverly Nelson. I am interested in finding some kind of beneficial relationship between you and Mr. Stewart."

He took her hand and shook it, looking into her eyes. She could see that he was still quite a bit confused but there was something else in his expression now. He was impressed with her, and interested in what she had to say. Beverly's chest swelled a bit when she realized this.

He's taking me seriously now, she thought with pride. *Which is more than I can say for the other girls. Then again, they do know Mr. Stewart. I think he might be the tougher nut to crack... But I wouldn't have to do that alone.*

"I like the sound of that," he said. "And you can call me Wilfred, if you like. Mr. Maddox just makes me think of my old man, and let's just say there's a reason I left his home, oh, ten years ago."

Beverly giggled a little. "Yes, sir. It's wonderful to finally make your acquaintance, Wilfred. I've heard a lot of things about you, but I had to find out if they were true for myself."

"Were they?" he asked her, smiling.

She shook her head. "Not so much," she said with a laugh. "Which just goes to show you that it's better to find things out for yourself."

Wilfred chuckled and nodded at her. "It does indeed."

Realizing that she was keeping him from his work and she had her own work to get back to, Beverly nodded a little and held up the white paper bag. "Well, I will go and cook this up and see if my idea is a sound one," she told him. "I trust that we'll be seeing each other again soon."

"I hope so," Wilfred Maddox replied, giving her a look which indicated to her that he meant more than just in regards to discussing her thoughts and plans for the businesses.

Beverly blushed and left the butcher's shop. She carried the bag of steak back to the dormitory in order to give it a try.

She had enough time for dinner before the dinner train arrived. *What did that look mean?* she thought as she walked. She didn't have to use much imagination to figure out what he had been thinking as he looked at her. Clearly being impressed with her went hand in hand with thinking that she was pretty.

He can like me all he wants, she thought. *That will help me, in the long run. He'll trust me more if he likes me.* That was, after all, why she wanted to speak with Mr. Stewart in a cordial manner at work, too. Beverly hoped to be known as a clever and resourceful girl by both gentlemen. She just hoped that Mr. Maddox – *Wilfred* – thinking of her amorously wouldn't get in the way of her plans for the future.

6

As soon as Beverly returned to the dormitory, she set about cooking up the steak that Mr. Maddox had so graciously given her – for a price, of course. She had to use the stove in the restaurant, but she did well to sneak in and cook it while Rita and Mr. Stewart were busy elsewhere. "Thank you ever so much for helping me," she said to the cook. There was a small kitchen on the main floor of the dormitory, but it didn't have an adequate stove and the last thing Beverly wanted to do was to ruin the nice steak she'd been given. That wouldn't lead to a fair assessment of it.

Once it was cooked, she put it on a plate and took it back to the dorm, sitting down at the small table within. She cut into the steak and took a bite, immediately moaning a little as the flavors fell upon her tongue. *This is outstanding!* She looked around her, wondering where Annie was so she might tell her about it. She knew that Annie had gone along with Carrie before, so she'd had the steaks too. *I feel as though Mr. Maddox – Wilfred – is Wallace's best-kept secret. But if I have my way, he won't be a secret much longer...*

She finished up the last delicious morsel of steak and then brought the dish she'd borrowed to the sink in the dormitory's small kitchen, washing it up so it could be used in the restaurant. No one would need to miss it. She brought it back to the Stewart House and surreptitiously placed it back in the kitchen.

"Miss Nelson?" Mr. Stewart's voice suddenly asked from behind where she stood.

Beverly froze. So much for going completely undetected. She turned around to look at her boss and gave him a smile. "Yes, sir?"

He was eyeing her blue floral dress. Instead of finding it attractive, like Mr. Maddox clearly had, he seemed rather appalled to see it at all. "What on earth are you doing in here in that frock?" he demanded. "Dinner train arrives in ten minutes!"

Beverly took a deep breath and held her ground. She'd broken no rules. "I was returning a dish to the kitchen, but I am certainly going to go change now," she said evenly, not letting the smile fade from her face for a moment.

"Well, hop to it!" Mr. Stewart said.

Nodding, she rushed off. As soon as she was outside, running to the dorm, she laughed softly. "You'd think the place was in danger of burning down because I dared wear a colorful dress while on its hallowed grounds," she said aloud to herself.

She climbed the stairs of the dormitory and swiftly changed into her black and white garbs as soon as she was safely within the confines of her room. Annie wasn't there because she was already dressed and ready to go, surely. *I guess I shouldn't have taken my time to clean that dish,* Beverly thought. When she clambered into the back room in the restaurant, falling in line with the other girls gathered there, Rita gave her a sharp look. Beverly shrugged at her a little, knowing that a lecture was going to greet her later that night.

The dinnertime shift was nowhere near as difficult as the other night. There were still more people than at any other time of day, but there wasn't an overflow of guests to the restaurant and things more or less retained their order. Beverly was relieved for the more relaxed experience. *I wonder if word got around about our seating issues?* she thought.

Once again, Annie wasn't really around Beverly all that much. The few times she saw her, Annie was assisting another table. She was laughing and smiling like always, but Beverly missed having the other young woman as her confidant. *Have I said or done something that upset her?*

She sidled up to her as the evening was winding down.

"Hello there," she said with a smile. "How have you been? I feel like we haven't properly chatted since this morning."

"I've been fine, thanks for asking," Annie said, the slight Irish lilt in her voice sounding more clipped than usual.

She was obviously peeved at Beverly for some reason.

Beverly pouted a bit. "Aww, you're not still upset with me for going to see Mr. Maddox, are you?"

"I'd rather not discuss him anymore, if you don't mind," Annie replied. "It's only that I worry about you. I don't want you to lose your job and damage Mr. Stewart's reputation."

Beverly furrowed her brows at Annie. "I'm sure Mr. Stewart's reputation will remain pristine no matter what I do or who I talk to. Good gravy, you make it seem as though I've been meeting up with the Devil himself. *You've* met Mr. Maddox before; you surely know he's not an evil person. He just wants to perform well in his business, same as Mr. Stewart."

Annie looked at her, eyes slightly downcast as she sighed. "I never said that he's a bad person. I just think that you don't listen to advice or follow instructions, and I don't want you to do something you regret. As far as Rita sees it, you're meddling in things and have been doing so ever since you first questioned Mr. Stewart's method for serving steak. I worry about you because you're my friend and you're my friend Carrie's little sister. I know that she wants you to do well, and you're working here largely under my watch. Suppose something unfortunate happens to you. She won't think of me very well in that case, will she? She will think it's partially my fault."

"Oh, Annie..."

"No, it's true. She'll think I put the idea into your head. Which is kind of true," Annie said, wringing her hands as she fretted. "I never should've mentioned that blasted butcher!"

Suddenly, Beverly felt hot as all eyes in the room were now on her and Annie. Their little conversation had attracted all the other girls' attention. Including, as it turned out, Rita's. She'd come into the room while Annie and Beverly were chatting during a brief break from the throngs of diners.

Rita crossed her arms in front of her chest and fixed her eyes on Beverly. That glare was as if she was underlining in ink the fact that she was going to give her a lecture once the night was over. This truly felt like the longest day of Beverly's life.

"I have a headache," she murmured to Annie, who had gone white as soon as she noticed their supervisor there.

"Go back out on the floor and see to the remaining diners," Rita directed the girls in the room. "And if you don't have a table, then grab a broom and get a head start on cleaning up." Her gaze never left Beverly's until she had left the room.

Clutching the broom handle as she swept up from the night's events in the restaurant, Beverly felt tears forming in her eyes. She bit her lip and willed herself not to cry. *What are you even going to start crying for? You've done nothing wrong. Everyone seems to be overreacting, but there's no need to start worrying too.* That look that Rita had given her had chilled her to the bone, though. She hadn't felt so nervous to speak with someone since the time she was twelve years old and angered her mother for playing with the lambs instead of shearing them.

"I really don't think I've done anything wrong," she said out loud when no one was around to hear her. She placed the broom and dust pan into their respective spots in the back room and made sure to extinguish all of the candles in the restaurant before leaving.

Mr. Stewart was there, no doubt. He could handle the rest.

When she arrived in the dormitory and went up the stairs, Rita was waiting for her in the meeting area in the hall between the girls' rooms. Beverly was expecting to find her there. "May I sit?" she asked.

"Of course," Rita replied with a short nod.

Beverly sat on one of the chairs that rested against the wall in the long, rectangular space. The hardwood floor was dusty; more thought and care went into the restaurant and its' guests than went into the girls' living conditions. She told herself not to think about it any further because it would only serve to upset her even more. *I've become so pessimistic,* she thought. *I don't like that.*

Rita stood over her, arms still folded across her chest like she was a teacher and Beverly was her misbehaving student. That wasn't actually far from what the situation was, except that Beverly insisted that she was *not* misbehaving. "I believe you know why I wanted to meet with you," Rita said sternly.

"Yes," Beverly replied haughtily. "But I promise you that I haven't been doing anything nefarious. I went to meet with Mr. Maddox because I always strive to be friendly towards my neighbors and people that I'll likely be dealing with."

"Even after you've been told not to meet with him?" Rita rhetorically asked her. "Even after you've been told that our way of doing things is not up for debate or changing?"

Beverly thought this was quite a closed-minded way of seeing things. "You don't plan on ever implementing changes?" she asked her incredulously. "Have you ever considered that the railway business might not last forever? Or that the west itself may stop being so attractive to people back east? Stranger things have happened and will likely continue to—"

"That's enough," Rita said testily. "May I just state for the record that you're lucky that your sister was quite a good friend to me when she was working here. She was diligent and she spoke rather highly of you, so I'm not keen to be rid of you, even if you do prove to be a nuisance to both myself and Mr. Stewart."

Beverly looked down at the floor again. "Yes, ma'am," she said softly.

"As for Mr. Maddox," Rita went on, "it's not for me to say what you do or don't do when you are out of our restaurant and dormitory during the day. Only that that man has been less than friendly towards Mr. Stewart ever since he started up here, so it doesn't give him much confidence in you when you make time to deliberately go off to see his rival."

"But I don't see *why* they must be rivals," Beverly complained. "They really should be working *together*. That's all I've been trying to say."

Rita sighed and sat down next to her. She could tell just by looking at the older woman that she was exhausted, and she didn't believe that it was merely because of the 'trouble' she had caused. "What I'm trying to tell you," Rita said more calmly now, "is that you must let the men deal with things and figure all of this out. They don't need you pushing them along as if they can't work things out on their own terms. They've both been working out here side by side longer than you've been here. Keep out of it and see what happens. You've got to be patient when dealing with two pig-headed gentlemen."

With that, she smiled at Beverly. It was a slight gesture, but it felt good to Beverly to see Rita smiling again. She thought that the supervising waiter-girl must surely hate her by now.

"Now, please go to sleep. I shall forget all of this nonsense if you forget it, too," Rita told her. "And I shan't tell Mr.

Stewart about the steak as long as you don't try anything like that again."

Beverly nodded obediently. "Okay," she replied, standing up from the chair. "I promise to let it go."

When she was in her bed that night and the candles had all been snuffed out, she thought to herself before falling asleep, *Telling Mr. Maddox about this won't hurt anything.*

7

W hile out on her long break before dinner a few days later, Beverly strolled down the dirt road. She could've been heading towards any number of places, or even her dear sister's farm house. However, she was wearing a pretty yellow dress which would have surely tipped off at least Annie had she seen her on her way out again. She was going to pay a visit to the town's butcher. Rita had forbidden her from fixating on the two business owners working together, but she hadn't forbade her from talking with Mr. Maddox again. *I'll tell him what Rita said,* Beverly thought as she walked. *And that will be the end of it.*

She didn't anticipate that this visit would take very long. She had a sandwich waiting back at the dormitory with her name on it. This matter certainly wasn't something for her to starve over, now that it was basically out of her hands. "I'll just walk in and tell him that it's all up to him now, and then I'll go back to the dorm, eat my sandwich and get back to work as if none of this had really happened."

Setting foot in the small butcher's shop changed her mind.

Beverly didn't have to ring the little bell on the counter this time, because Mr. Maddox – *Wilfred,* she reminded herself to call him – was already standing there behind the counter, as if he had been waiting for her to arrive and greet him. She blinked at him, smiling and blushing uncontrollably.

"Hello again, Beverly," he said, smiling back at her. He appeared quite glad to see her looking so happy to find him there.

"Hello," she replied, batting her lashes at him and carrying on in a way that would've normally made her roll her eyes had it not been coming from her. "Have you been expecting me?"

Wilfred chuckled. "Would that I had the power of premonition. No, I've merely been working at being a better salesman in my store. Believe it or not, I've given a lot of thought to the proposal brought forth the last time you visited, about the Stewart House opening up a business relationship with my little shop here."

She was still blushing, but it was a bit of a nervous blush

now. *Oh dear, I hope I haven't caused him to get ahead of himself... It was only an idea, not a proposal.*

"I wanted to stop by today to let you know a little bit more about that, as a matter of fact," she said carefully. She hoped that she wouldn't disappoint him with her news. "You see, Mr. Stewart and some of his upper staff aren't so keen on the idea of things changing. They told me as much today, when I brought up my little idea about you two gentlemen working together in regards to the steaks, as opposed to competing. I've been told to stay out of it. The head waitress tells me that gentlemen are too... How did she put it? Pig-headed."

Wilfred regarded her with ever widening eyes. She couldn't believe that she had ever thought of them as icy. It was true that they glowed with a sort of ethereal inner light, but they were more like clear blue water than ice. She wondered if perhaps she had caused the ice within him to thaw.

He furrowed his dark eyebrows as he looked at her at the conclusion of her tale. She knew that it was a lot to tell him at once, but he deserved to know the whole of it. "It seems to me that this Rita woman doesn't have a lot of faith in the owner of the establishment if that's the way she thinks of him. I don't know Mr. Stewart well, as you know, but I've got enough respect for the man to know that he is shrewd and smart about things. He's not bullish, elsewise how would he have such fine ladies under his employ?"

Beverly smiled at him, relieved that he had taken her

news so well. "I couldn't have said it better myself," she admitted. "So, I came here to tell you that and to see if maybe you'd like to take over from here. You're under no obligation, I promise you. I just thought all of this might be worth your while, if you were interested."

"Oh, I'm more than interested," he told her, giving her that strange, inquisitive sort of look he'd given her previously. An almost flirty gesture. "I'm captivated."

Beverly didn't think her cheeks would ever stop being hot now. She batted her blonde-red lashes at him as she smiled. Now that she had told him the latest and how he must take over from there, she didn't quite know how she was supposed to end this conversation. She didn't want to bid him farewell just yet. Especially since he was acting flirtatious again. It flattered her and made her even more curious.

"I should probably head back now," she said coyly. "After yesterday's chat, I have a feeling they'll be wanting me to return quickly. They don't actually know I'm here, talking to you... I thought it would be better if they didn't."

"You don't think you'll get in trouble simply for talking to me, do you?"

Beverly shrugged her shoulders a little bit and she felt rather sad. "It's a possibility, I'm afraid," she told him honestly. "They would rather I didn't stir up trouble by conversing with the townsfolk."

The smile on Wilfred's face slowly faded away. "That's a shame... Well, as you say, I shall simply have to take matters into my own hands. Thank you for coming in to visit with me again even against such pressure to avoid me. I appreciate it more than I can articulate." He offered his hand to her and she graciously took it.

They shook hands and Beverly felt tremendously sad. She had hoped to start a friendly, business-minded relationship with this gentleman and now she could feel him being forced from her grasp. "I... I hope to see you around, Wilfred."

She left his shop before he could see her eyes welling up with tears.

Why did I ever have to open my big mouth? If I hadn't told Annie and Rita my ideas, I'd still be able to spend time with Wilfred. It wasn't fair, but she didn't see any way that she could fix it now. The gentlemen would just have to work things out on their own. Or not. Beverly wished that she could force them to do what she wanted, but she knew that it was wrong of her to even think of that as an option. No one should be forced to do what they didn't want to do... She supposed that she could be a bit controlling at times.

Beverly took a detour and went to her sister's house instead of going directly back to the restaurant. She didn't want to get into trouble again, but she also didn't want to give Rita the pleasure of seeing her back so soon from her break. She had other things that she could do to fill her free time, after all.

"Beverly!" Carrie said with an excited smile upon

opening the front door to her farmhouse. "To what do I owe this pleasure?"

"I was in the neighborhood and thought I'd stop by," Beverly chided. Everything was technically 'in the neighborhood' there. The two sisters hugged and Carrie invited Beverly inside.

They sat together on the strange couch of Leeroy's creation. "I'm afraid that I don't have any sandwiches or tea ready for you," Carrie said. "But I could easily whip you up something, if you like."

Beverly dismissed that with a gesture, smiling and also shaking her head a little. "That's not at all necessary. I don't have that much time. There's a sandwich waiting for me back at the dorm. I just wanted to stop by to say hello and see how you're doing."

Carrie gave her sister a serious look. "You went to visit Mr. Maddox again, didn't you?"

"Is it that easy to figure out?" Beverly asked sheepishly. She was annoyed at herself for feeling so defensive about it. The man himself didn't pose a problem, either to her or her job!

Carrie laughed softly. "Oh, Bevie, I could read your expression better than most, surely. I'm guessing it was a pleasant visit at any rate. And not entirely related to the Stewart House..."

"I don't know what you're talking about," Beverly countered. "I don't think my expression should say much of anything. I told him that the powers that be wish that we don't meet up anymore. He said that it was now up to him to proceed with my suggestion, and I left it at that."

"But you're glowing," Carrie told her. "He surely must've paid you a compliment of some kind at the very least."

Beverly thought about it. "I suppose that he seemed most bothered when I told him that I shan't be able to speak with him anymore without getting into trouble with Rita. The news that they wanted to take matters into their own hands instead of allowing me to scheme with him didn't seem to set him off quite as much as when I implied that it meant I wouldn't come to see him anymore at all."

"And you like that he was bothered by that," Carrie said with a smile. "Just admit it, darling sister. I won't betray your little secret."

"What secret is that?" Beverly asked, her face growing hot once more.

Carrie beamed at her. "That you and Mr. Maddox have little crushes on each other."

It wasn't long after this that Beverly – a bit awkwardly – took her leave. She didn't know how she was supposed to respond to that. As much as she thought she should deny it, there was no denying that Wilfred had been flirtatious with her and she had felt pleased about it. She didn't think he had been outwardly flirty so much as sweet and endearing. Things she never could have imagined the bearded, stoic butcher to be. He hadn't exactly been the friendliest towards her when they first met, but could there be something to what Carrie said? *I certainly didn't set out to make him admire me or anything like that... And I was never thinking of gaining a husband while working out here.*

But Beverly had to concede that the idea of Mr. Maddox courting her made her happy. Even if it was only a school-girl type daydream, she couldn't deny that she liked the thought of being with him. She'd set out to try and help his business and she thought she had laid a good foundation out for him, if he took it from there. In the meantime, if he should appreciate and be attracted to her because of her helping him, Beverly certainly wasn't going to stop him from doing so.

Of course, this is all just the fantasies of a pair of silly young ladies, she thought as she walked off back towards the dormitory. *He is probably a bit flirty with any woman he sees in his shop, considering he hasn't seen that many.*

Though Carrie hadn't ever mentioned him reacting that way towards her...

8

The next several days passed slowly for Beverly. Now that she was no longer allowed to go off and conduct friendly, business-related meetings with Wilfred, she found that she didn't have much enthusiasm for actually going anywhere else at all. She started taking after Annie and reading books to pass the time when she wasn't working. She was bored, but she thought being bored was better than continuing to risk her job and her place of residence.

I've done my part, she thought. *Now I must have faith that Wilfred and Mr. Stewart will take it from here. If he has faith in my idea and he truly likes me as Carrie believes, he won't let me down.*

Being patient was one of the hardest things Beverly had

ever forced herself to be, but she decided to be smart and do things the proper way that Rita had requested. She didn't want people to keep being annoyed with her, even if she disagreed with them over it. She did want to play nice and not let anyone down, least of all her sister. Carrie was so proud of her for taking up the job that she'd vacated, so Beverly didn't want to damage that pride.

During the dinnertime shift, she was surprised to see Mr. Maddox appear in the restaurant. He walked right up to Rita and spoke with her. Beverly stared in shock, doing her best not to drop her tray of Stewart Steaks and beverages for two of her tables. *What's he doing here?* she wondered, thinking by the look on his face that he meant business. She hoped that it was a good kind of business and he wasn't going to try to start anything with her boss or her supervisor.

As soon as he finished talking with Rita, he nodded towards her and walked through the eatery to the back office door, knocking so that Mr. Stewart would know he was there.

Beverly gave the steaks and drinks to her two tables of diners and then strode over to Rita at the front entrance of the restaurant. "What's all this about?" she inquired curiously, placing a hand on her hip and letting the empty tray drop to her side.

Carrie would've told her to keep her questions to herself for the time being. Annie would've told her to ask someone else or ask after the fact. But Beverly did what she thought was best.

Rita regarded her with a tight-lipped expression. Finally, she sighed. "He asked to speak with Mr. Stewart because he has some kind of business proposition."

Beverly's eyes lit up at once. "Oh!"

While they talked, Mr. Stewart's office door opened and Wilfred Maddox stepped inside the office. The door shut behind him.

"Don't get too excited," Rita told her. "Remember, this is between the two of them." Still, she gave her a small smile. Beverly chose to read *well done* into that smile.

She did as she was told and got back to her work, checking on tables and delivering plates of food to the guests. The fact that Mr. Maddox stayed sequestered in the office with Mr. Stewart indicated to her that their conversation was going well, which gave her hope. Again, she told herself not to get too excited. *Suppose they're merely visiting with each other. After all, Mr. Stewart doesn't take the time to reach out to others in town. Maybe this is just Mr. Maddox – Wilfred – extending an olive branch?*

They stayed in the office together until the last of the customers were finishing up their desserts. Beverly jumped a bit when Mr. Stewart's office door opened and the two men came out, patting each other on the back, all smiles. She'd always wondered what Mr. Stewart's genuine smile looked like and there it was.

He's rather handsome when he's not being so stern.

The two gentlemen shook hands and then Wilfred left

Mr. Stewart's side. He walked past Beverly and paused to give her a grin and a wink before departing the restaurant.

She watched him leave, mouth agape, and then looked over at her boss. Mr. Stewart smiled at her and gave her a slight nod. "Make sure you sweep up before you leave for the night, Miss Nelson," was all he said before turning and going back into his office.

The man was enigmatic. She did as she was told and made sure the floor was swept and things were tidy before blowing out all of the candles and departing for the dormitory.

"I don't know what he was here for," she later told Annie, undressing from her uniform and putting on her day dress from earlier, not wanting it to go to waste. "But he gave me a wink as he departed and Mr. Stewart was looking at me awfully strangely, too."

Annie set her brush down on her vanity and looked at Beverly with a smile. "Perhaps they were discussing the business that you brought to Mr. Maddox's attention. I wouldn't count that out of the realm of possibility, only don't take credit for it and stay out of it as best as you can now."

This attitude didn't entirely make sense to Beverly. It seemed to her that if her idea was now in motion, she should be allowed to be a part of it. After all, she'd thought of it and spoken up when no one else had. She relayed these thoughts and feelings to her friend. "It isn't fair. It's almost like theft or plagiarism."

Annie laughed softly. "That's what being a woman is like sometimes," she said. "But if you like him, and we all know you do, you'll simply support him in this. Because he will likely make you part of it anyway, in the end."

Beverly's head hurt now. She wasn't sure that she liked only being 'part of it.' But perhaps Annie was right and it was the best she could hope for.

She had strange dreams that night about Wilfred and his butcher shop. Upon waking, she couldn't remember what she'd dreamt exactly but she woke up smiling.

"You look well-rested," Annie said to her with a smile right back at her.

"I am," Beverly replied, wiping her eyes a bit with the backs of her hands. "I had wonderful dreams, but I can't remember any of them now."

"Oh, I hate when that happens," Annie said, her smile becoming sympathetic as she looked at her thoughtfully. "Were they dreams about Mr. Maddox?"

Beverly blushed a little, which she hated because it instantly gave away the answer. Annie giggled.

"As I said," Beverly said tersely. "I can't remember what they were about, but Mr. Maddox may have been in them."

Annie couldn't seem to stop smiling. "I know we're not supposed to talk about or support this, but I think you two sound awfully sweet together. As long as you're behaving and doing as Mr. Stewart requests, I don't see any harm in you having a crush."

Beverly's face reddened. "I do *not* have a crush. Don't be silly. I merely *admire* him. That's all." Annie gave her a look that said she didn't fully believe her. Beverly rolled her eyes. "It is possible for a gentleman to admire a woman without being in love with her."

It was going to be difficult to try to convince her friend of that, though, so she decided to just drop it. She got out of bed, stretched and went to her own vanity desk, where she could brush her hair and prepare herself for the wearing of the restrictive uniform and working in the busy restaurant.

"I wonder why he came to Stewart House last night," Annie said thoughtfully. "It doesn't really seem like a place he'd be interested in dining at. You must have sold him on our menu or something like that."

"I don't think it was the menu he was interested in," Beverly said. "But I don't want to think about it too much and possibly make it not happen with my meddling, as Rita calls it. Whatever they want to have happen will happen." *I just wish I could be a part of it.*

Her red hair brushed, she set down her brush and changed into her work uniform. The bow never managed to sit on the top of her head in a way that she liked, but it wasn't up to her and her taste. If it was, she wouldn't even wear the bow. Or the apron. She could style the black dress into something much more flattering, but those accessories prevented the dress from ever being what anyone would consider pretty.

"Are you okay?" Annie asked, watching her as she gazed sadly at herself in the mirror. "Something tells me that you aren't very happy working here anymore."

"No, I mean, yes," Beverly said, shaking her head. "I am happy working here. I'm fine. I've just had a lot on my mind lately. I really rather suppose that Rita and you were right: I should've stayed out of things. I've only ended up disappointing myself and making myself get into a rut over nothing at all."

Annie fixed her with a sympathetic look. "Well, it's a new day," she said optimistically, rising from her chair and coming over to give Beverly a hug. "You don't ever have to think about any of that again, if you don't want to."

Beverly wished that her mind worked like that. She envied Annie's positive outlook about things. It seemed that nothing that went on in the restaurant ever upset her, not even when customers were rude or she got in trouble for being ever so slightly late. Through it all, Annie smiled and was gracious.

The girls finished getting themselves ready for work and then they went down the stairs together, holding hands all the way until they were in the back room of the Stewart House. At once, Rita came over to them. "Mr. Stewart wishes to speak with you right away this morning, Miss Nelson," she said softly so the others wouldn't overhear and become too curious.

Beverly blinked at her, confused as to why, but she

nodded. "Yes, ma'am," she replied softly. "Thank you for letting me know."

Once the restaurant was open and the customers were invited in to be seated, Beverly scooted off to the office door towards the back of the eating house. She lightly knocked on the door and, to her surprise, it was already open. It moved beneath her fist.

"Come on in, Miss Nelson," Mr. Stewart's voice beckoned to her.

She gulped and took a deep breath. *I can't imagine what all this fuss is about, but they're certainly not keeping me well at ease,* she thought. It was almost funny the way they were acting all official and secretive about something. She hoped that this meeting wasn't so Mr. Stewart could send her packing or anything like that. Rita hadn't made it seem like it was a meeting about something bad, but then one never knew with Rita. She wasn't an easy lady to read in the slightest.

She entered the small office, unsure of how she should feel or act. Nevertheless, she smiled as soon as she saw Mr. Stewart sitting there behind his desk. He stood up as soon as she came into the room, giving her a low, polite bow. "Please have a seat," he told her, gesturing a hand towards one of the small, cushioned chairs in front of his desk.

Beverly sat. She could feel her heart pounding in her chest and she was the most grateful she'd ever been that the uniform dresses were high-necked. She was convinced her pounding heart could be seen through her skin.

"What did you want to see me about, sir?" she asked him in as pleasant a voice as she could muster. Her training had done her well.

He leaned forward towards her, smiling. "Mr. Maddox has quite a proposition for me," he told her. "And it involves you."

9

Beverly stared at her boss across the wide desk that was festooned with papers and pens and coffee mugs that probably hadn't been cleaned in days. "I don't understand," she said. "What have I got to do with whatever Mr. Maddox spoke to you about?"

Mr. Stewart continued to smile at her. Now that he was doing so much smiling, she found it strange and she didn't quite like it. His smile said that he knew a big, important thing about her that she didn't. That of course was precisely the case now. "Mr. Maddox has asked me to join our business, in a way. He offered to supply me with his steaks to sell to our diners in the restaurant, provided I give him two things in return."

She raised an eyebrow. She was impressed that Wilfred

had gone ahead with the business deal, and so quickly. But she didn't know what his terms might be. "What did he ask in return?"

Mr. Stewart cleared his throat a bit and Beverly could see that he was a little nervous about what he had to tell her. Some of his bravado disappeared now that she was there before him, asking all the questions he had to know she would ask. "Well, first of all, he asked that I make sure to promote his butcher shop, because he of course has all kinds of tasty meats there. He doesn't only sell steaks, or beef for that matter."

Beverly nodded. That seemed like a fair deal to her. She wouldn't want Mr. Maddox to give up his business that he'd worked so hard at for so long. After all, he'd been there longer than Mr. Stewart had. "I see," she said. "That makes sense to me. That shouldn't be too difficult to do."

He nodded at her. "That's the easier part," he agreed. "But he requested something else, too, and I told him that I'd need to discuss it with you first. And he'd need to discuss it with you, too, of course."

She stared at him, blinking and furrowing her brows. *Does he wish to have me no longer here?* she wondered. *Or perhaps he wishes for me to work for him in his shop!* She tried not to get too far ahead of herself. "What is it?" she asked innocently.

"He asked me if he could have your hand in marriage," Mr. Stewart said plainly, swiftly averting his eyes and looking down at the stacks of paperwork on his desk instead. Such talk clearly made him the most nervous.

Beverly didn't have time to consider his nerves. "Marry me?!" she asked, quickly standing from her chair in her surprise. "He wants to join your businesses together, but I'm to be one of the terms??"

"When you put it like that, it sounds like I'm selling you to him," Mr. Stewart said, laughing uneasily. "Of course that's not the case. It's up to you. That's why he asked me to tell you his intentions, and I told him to ask you himself and let you think about it."

Beverly blushed but she didn't smile. "It's highly irregular for someone to ask a lady's *boss* if it's okay to marry her!" she exclaimed. It wasn't all that different from a gentleman asking a father for his daughter's hand in marriage... But Beverly hoped that those times could change a little.

"He knows about your contract," Mr. Stewart told her. "He didn't want to steal you away without my knowing how he felt about you. And he thought it would be better for you if he took the first step."

I did tell him to make the first move... Beverly bit her lip. Her stomach was doing backflips and somersaults. "Well... Thank you for letting me know this. I suppose I shall be less shocked when he comes to ask me, then." Now that the initial surprise was over with, she felt quite happy and she let out a laugh. "Goodness! Quite a bit of theatrics over me, don't you think? I assume it's okay with you if I were to...?"

Mr. Stewart laughed and nodded his head. "Yes," he said. "I might be a tough businessman, but I'm not the sort of person who stands in the way of another man's happiness. I will be sad to lose you, obviously, but your sister left us as well not that long ago and we've moved on okay. And you'll surely be helping Mr. Maddox in his business. You're a smart girl, Miss Nelson. He shall be lucky to have you."

Beverly almost felt like crying now. She offered Mr. Stewart her hand and they happily shook. "Thank you, sir."

"Best of luck to you," he said back.

She felt a bit dizzy as she made her way back out onto the floor of the restaurant. She didn't know how she was supposed to focus on her work now that she knew that a proposal was looming. Of course, she would focus and do a good job as always, but it seemed like it was going to be rather impossible to stop thinking about Mr. Maddox and what he wanted to say to her. Beverly never would've expected that he'd bring that up to her boss. The more she thought about it, though, it did go along with the way their interactions had gone. The way his pale blue eyes lit up whenever he looked at her. The way he seemed excited whenever they spoke, like they shared a common goal rather than just him wanting something and her going along with it.

Yes, we could make quite a pair, she thought with a smile. *And it seems as though he's done the most difficult work for me already.*

Wilfred didn't appear in the restaurant again right away, and Beverly began to inwardly fret that he might've changed his mind about her. She wondered if she should go to him instead, but then she remembered the words of her friends and her sister. *Let him handle it,* she reminded herself. *If he wants to do this, he will come to you. Just like he came to speak to Mr. Stewart.*

After a few days went slowly, agonizingly by, Beverly was startled when Rita appeared at her bedroom door one morning. The older woman was beaming at her and seemed a bit misty in her eyes. "Miss Nelson, you won't be needing to put on your uniform today," she informed her. "Mr. Maddox requests your company in the parlor downstairs."

Beverly inhaled deeply. She nodded to Rita and thanked her, closing the door to the bedroom and letting the air escape her in a sigh. "He's here," she told Annie, who was in the midst of putting her black dress on. "He wants me to meet him in the parlor!"

"Oh, that's wonderful news!" Annie cried, pulling her dress on and giving her a hug.

"Which dress should I wear?" Beverly asked. She was in a bit of a panic now. It had all been well and good to put on cute dresses to go flirting with him and things like that, but today was surely going to prove to be the most important day of her life. And she needed to be dressed appropriately for it.

The two friends hastily went over to her wardrobe and rifled through the dresses that hung in there. "I think this one is sweet," Annie said, pulling out Beverly's green dress. She was pretty sure that she'd worn that for Wilfred before, but she didn't believe he would remember. *What man remembers an outfit?*

Smiling, she changed into the dress and admired herself in the vanity mirror. Meanwhile, Annie stood behind her, brushing her hair and even tying some dark green ribbons into it. "You look beautiful," she said sweetly.

"I hope he agrees with you," Beverly said. She turned around and smiled at her friend, hugging her once more. "Thank you for all of your help. And for not telling me to shut up even though I know I would have deserved it."

Annie laughed, shaking her head. "I never thought that."

Collecting herself, Beverly left her room and slowly made her way down the staircase. She'd never been so nervous in all of her life. She'd have a lot of things to pack later, if this went well. She couldn't imagine it going any other way, unless Wilfred had changed his mind and high-tailed it out of there while she was getting dressed...

She got to the bottom of the staircase and went into the small parlor just to the side of the front door to the dormitory. There was a tall shadow on the wall which could only belong to Mr. Maddox. Beverly did her best to clear her throat without making a sound and then she calmly walked into the room.

Wilfred was standing there, looking quite dapper in his black shirt and black pants. He wasn't wearing his apron, which helped him appear more put together and, admittedly, less like a butcher. He gazed upon her and smiled a shy, small smile. She smiled back at him.

"Hello," he said to her. "You look lovely."

Blushing, she bowed her head a little in gratitude. "Thank you. You look handsome. Believe it or not, I don't really miss your stained apron."

He laughed and she laughed with him. She'd never felt so nervous before with him, but she thought that had to mean something. If she didn't care for him or how he felt about her, then she wouldn't have wasted nerves on him. She likely wouldn't have even agreed to meet with him now like this. *I can't believe this is real,* she thought.

"I know what you're thinking," he said, startling her from her thoughts. "And I don't expect you to say yes right away. It would be rather presumptuous of me if I did."

Beverly looked at him, her cheeks clearly going a bit rosy as she stood there in the doorway to the room, waiting for him to propose. "Do you mean you've... reconsidered?" she asked.

Wilfred laughed. "No, no. I meant what I said to George... Mr. Stewart. I only mean... I don't wish to rush you if you're not ready. After all, as you say, this is the first time you're seeing me out of my place of work, really. We could spend some time getting to know each other first. If you'd rather."

She smiled at him and moved towards him a little more. "How about," she began, gaining more confidence as she went, "you ask me now and we get to know each other... and if I change my mind, I'll let you know."

Wilfred laughed a sort of gaspy laugh, as if he'd been holding in a breath ever since she first joined him in the room. Perhaps that's exactly what he'd been doing. He'd been standing awfully still, like he was afraid to move. "Very well," he said to her. Then he awkwardly got down on one knee, wobbling a little bit as he balanced there. She felt his hand trembling as he took her hand in his. He gazed up at her. "Will you marry me, Miss Nelson – Beverly, sorry. Will you marry me, Beverly?"

She let out a short laugh and clapped her other hand over her mouth. Even though she knew this was coming and had ample time to prepare herself for this, it still took her by surprise. *I can't believe this is really, truly happening to me!* "Yes," she said to him, keeping her voice as calm as possible as she took her hand from her mouth and brought it to her chest, feeling her beating heart there now. "Yes, please."

10

It was decided, through mutual agreement amongst all the parties involved, that Beverly should continue to work as a waitress at Stewart House throughout her courtship with Mr. Maddox. That way, she would be staying in the dorm and remaining a proper and respectable lady instead of running off into the sunset with her new fiancé. Meanwhile, Mr. Stewart and Wilfred began implementing their plans for a partnership. Soon, the steaks that Stewart House sold to customers were all made fresh by Mr. Maddox from the butcher shop next door. The customer enthusiasm went up, which Beverly couldn't have seen as being possible until it happened. For a time, customers were even coming in asking for steaks for *breakfast*!

"One thing's for sure," she said to Annie, Rita and the rest of the girls who were around in the backroom of the restaurant. "Stewart House does really well by word of mouth."

When she wasn't working and Wilfred was off from his job at his shop, they spent all of their free time together, going for walks and getting to know one another better.

"Before I moved here to Kansas, I never would've thought that I'd be engaged to someone that I really just met," she confided in him one afternoon as they roamed around the fields just outside of town. She liked being surrounded by the tall, green grass because it reminded her of Ohio. "Carrie told me about her betrothal to that Mr. Jacob man in California and I thought she must've lost her mind."

Wilfred laughed. "But this isn't really the same, is it?" he asked her. "After all, we didn't just meet and we didn't write letters to each other through the mail for months without seeing each other."

"That's true," she said. "But otherwise..."

He chuckled, shaking his head. "I never thought you'd say yes," he confessed.

"Really?" she asked. "Why not? You're handsome, successful, sweet..."

"And a trifle moody," he pointed out. "I know that I can be gruff and awkward, but I don't mean to be. I just thought that you might not want to be with me in that way."

She smiled at him, taking his hand. "You weren't like that

with me for long," she said. "I guess I just chalked it up to you being shy around women."

He gazed at her in that flirtatious way of his. His eyes now had a loving look to them. She loved looking at them. "You really are so smart," he said. "That's one of the first things I loved about you."

She smiled at him, head feeling like it was about to float clean off of her shoulders. "If you keep saying things like that, I guarantee you that I won't change my mind."

Wilfred threw his head back and laughed again. "I love you, Beverly."

She leaned over and kissed him on the cheek, causing him to go a bit pink. It tickled her to see that shade on him for once, instead of her always being the first one to blush. "I love you, Wilfred."

In this way, the two lovebirds went around town together whenever they had the chance. They normally went for walks and talked. Occasionally, Wilfred would surprise her with little gifts such as a bouquet of wildflowers or a gold ring for her to wear on her finger and show off to all of her friends back at the restaurant. Beverly couldn't remember the last time she had been properly courted like this, and even though she was fairly forward-thinking in terms of women being strong and able to think for themselves and run businesses if they had a mind to, she had to admit that it made her swoon whenever he acted all chivalrous towards her.

After several months of this, much like they had been

writing letters to each other but much more enjoyable, in Beverly's opinion, Wilfred took her aside and asked her again. "Will you marry me, Miss Nelson?"

She smiled at him. "Yes, I will, Mr. Maddox. But only if you never call me 'Miss Nelson' again."

He laughed and they kissed. It was a light peck on the lips, but to Beverly it felt like a buzz of electricity all through her.

Beverly went to the dormitory that night after work and packed up her things into her suitcase. It felt strange to her that she should be packing like she was going somewhere far when really, she was only moving into the house next door.

"I'll be over to visit you all the time," she told Annie, who was clearly sad to be seeing her go, even if there was still a whole day of wedding celebrations to go through first.

"I hope not," Annie quipped. "I hope to be out of here soon too." She flashed Beverly a smile.

Beverly nodded at her, proud to see that Annie also had bigger plans for her life. It seemed the only girl who really felt tied to Stewart House was Rita. "Just don't let them hear you say that, or you'll be in hot water like I was."

The following morning, Beverly dressed in her light blue gown with little, dark blue flowers all over it. It wasn't a white dress, but she hadn't had time to make herself a dress like that and she didn't reckon that it mattered what color she wore.

"What this town needs is a dress shop," she declared as

Rita placed a sheer veil on her head and Annie worked the brush through her red curls.

"Oh, Beverly, you're always planning something," Rita said with a laugh. "Plan your day. Start from there."

She and Annie went with her to the chapel in town. They timed the wedding well, between breakfast and lunch, so that the restaurant could be closed and Mr. Stewart could be there. Beverly carried a bouquet of purple and blue flowers and her sister Carrie met her at the chapel to be her matron of honor. Leeroy was there as well, serving as Wilfred's best man.

"Beverly Ann Nelson," the minister asked solemnly. "Do you take Wilfred Maddox to be your lawfully-wedded husband? To have and to hold, to love and to cherish, to honor and obey, forsaking all others until death do you part?"

Beverly smiled tearfully. "I do," she said, gazing at Wilfred.

The minister turned to him next. "Wilfred James Maddox, do you take Beverly Nelson to be your lawfully-wedded wife? To have and to hold, to love and to cherish, to honor and protect, forsaking all others until death do you part?"

Wilfred gazed back at Beverly and gave her a little wink like he had done in the restaurant that evening. The evening when he had asked Mr. Stewart for permission to marry her.

"I do," he replied.

A cheer rang up in the crowd gathered there to witness. Beverly laughed a little as she glanced out at all of the people who were there. She didn't know all of them; most of them knew Wilfred, of course, but she was glad that they were there all the same.

The minister cleared his throat a bit so that he could regain everyone's attention. "Then, by the authority given to me by our lord and savior Jesus Christ as well as the great town of Wallace, Kansas, I now happily pronounce you husband and wife. You may kiss the bride."

For a moment, Beverly and Wilfred stood there, smiling at each other and holding hands, but then he moved forward and so did she. They planted their lips onto each other's at the same time, which prompted the crowd to all cheer again. She could hear the voice of Carrie happily shouting well wishes at them.

The chapel's organ began to play music and Beverly and Wilfred took each other's hands again, rushing back down the aisle once more. She wasn't quite sure what she was going to do with her time now that she was no longer a working girl, but she knew that she would find some way to keep herself busy. She was certainly not going to sit idly by while he worked in the butcher shop *and* the restaurant!

But she told herself not to worry about that right now. Like Rita had told her, she must plan for the rest of this wonderful day and take things one day at a time from then on out. And plans she certainly had.

Wilfred and Beverly were wed and he would never call her 'Miss Nelson' ever again.

EPILOGUE

It wasn't long at all before Beverly began to help Wilfred with his business. She was much too enthusiastic and full of ideas for him to ignore or send back into the other rooms of his home. The butcher shop was the front room of his house, and even though she found the rest of his home to be quaint and nicely furnished – nothing to complain about like Leeroy and his chair – she thought that his business was the place to be whenever it was open.

"I'm perfectly capable of doing anything that you can do," she told him. "I'm not afraid of getting my hands dirty. Have you seen what the floor of a restaurant looks like after a day?"

Wilfred always laughed and couldn't argue with her, so in time she got her way. She became his assistant, mostly helping with the organizing of displays and bringing in new customers by standing outside the shop with a tray of cuts and a smile. She could thank her training at Stewart House for that.

Her favorite part of the job, and the one thing she jumped to ask to do, was going over next door to deliver the fresh steaks to the cooks in the restaurant. It wasn't the only way that she could see all of her old friends, but it was the easiest and the way that made the most sense in her mind.

One day, not long after she was married and had moved in with Wilfred, she found out that Annie was no longer there at the Stewart House. Rather than being sad, after a moment of missing her, Beverly felt very proud of her friend. She knew that it only meant that Annie had moved on with her life. *I bet she found a fellow for herself*, she thought, pleased as punch for her sweet, shy friend.

One major thing that she noticed by working in the butcher shop was that the clientele didn't change the way that it did in the Stewart House. The people who came in to buy from her husband were largely townsfolk and occasionally people who'd heard of the shop from the waiter-girls next door. Wilfred was happy because the work was much steadier now that he was working alongside Mr. Stewart rather than competing against him for people's attention.

Beverly kept herself much too busy to miss working in the restaurant, although sometimes she wondered what her friends were up to there. The staff of Maddox's Meats consisted of only her and Mr. Maddox, naturally. She did rather miss having her friends to work alongside.

One day, to her great surprise and joy, the door opened and who should appear but Annie O'Brien! Beverly greeted her with a hug and a wave of nostalgia rushed over her.

"It's so good to see you," Beverly told her, taking her hand and squeezing it. "You'll have to tell me everything that's happened to you since I left the old dormitory."

As Annie smiled at her and told her all about her adventures, Beverly grinned just to see her there. In that moment, she realized that no matter what happened and how soon or late the girls left the restaurant, they would always be around to visit each other and share in each other's lives.

THE END

ANNIE: A BRIDE FOR THE FARMHAND

STEWART HOUSE BRIDES

ANNIE: A BRIDE FOR THE FARMHAND

Wallace, Kansas – 1890

Annie O'Brien is a shy, but incredibly loyal waitress at the Stewart House restaurant. Devoted to her employer, she lives for the days when the restaurant is its busiest and there's lots of work to be done. The nice thing about hard work, she quickly discovers, is that it helps keep her mind off of her broken heart. For the last year, she's kept a well-guarded secret, even from her closest friends: she was stood up at the train station where she was supposed to meet her mail order beau, James Prescott.

That all changes when one day, out of the blue, a man by the name of Thackery Prescott shows up in her life. It turns out that this man is the same gentleman who had been writing to her, but his train had run into trouble and he was unable to meet her that day.

Can Annie find it in her heart to forgive Thackery for his disappearance? Or will her loyalty to Stewart House cause her to turn down the only love she ever knew?

1

"All of these girls seem to be man-obsessed. I'm grateful that I at least have you here. You'd never run off and get married so quickly, Annie." Rita stood tall and solemn in the bedroom doorway, watching as Annie O'Brien smoothed her cinnamon brown hair with her brush and tied it back with the regulation white ribbon. She looked up at Rita and smiled. It may not have been entirely true, but she fully intended to make her friend and supervisor happy.

Rita left the doorway soon after, to go and wake up some of the other girls, who were likely still sleeping. Annie sighed a bit and looked over at the empty bed in her room. It'd been vacated only the other day. *Admittedly, Beverly hadn't been around as much as Carrie was, but still it was nice to have a friend as a roommate.* Mr. Stewart would likely be bringing in several new waiter-girls soon, but for now Annie was bunking in a room by herself.

The quiet, shy girl didn't really mind having the space and time to herself when she wasn't working, however. It would be a nice little break from the dramatic situations that usually came with having a roommate – drama that was typically, as Rita opined, man-related in nature. She would be able to sleep better after a long day at work in the restaurant if she didn't have to drift off with someone else's worries keeping her awake at night.

It wasn't easy being empathetic.

As soon as Annie was dressed and ready to start the new day, she made her way down the stairs and out the door of the dormitory. She walked over to the restaurant next door and met with all of the other sleepy-eyed girls as they waited in a cluster for the front doors to open and the breakfast crowd to rush in. Annie didn't mind a busy day at work, especially now when it would help keep her from feeling lonely once she'd stopped relishing her alone time and started missing having someone to talk to and laugh with.

"Is this going to be another full train of hungry people?" she asked.

"When is it not, these days?" Mary, one of the other waitresses, answered.

Annie smirked at her. She was happy to hear that. A full train meant lots of work to be done. Above all else, she wanted Rita and Mr. Stewart to notice all of the effort she was putting in for them. *I didn't come all the way to Kansas for no good reason,* she thought. *I wanted to really work and make a good living for myself.*

Of course, she hadn't really come all the way to Kansas just to work in the restaurant; that was merely something she told herself now. The real reason just left her feeling rather heartbroken. She'd never mentioned it to anyone before, but she'd come all the way from Massachusetts to marry a man in the west. He was supposed to meet her there at the station in Wallace and then proceed on the railway with her from there. They had made plans to meet each other halfway. However, when she arrived, she waited and waited and he never appeared.

Broken-hearted, she discovered the Stewart House right up the road and the rest was history. Annie had sworn off romance and was married to her work there from that day forward.

When the double doors of the restaurant were opened by Rita, the waiter-girls poured into the eating house in order to greet all of the guests and direct them to tables. "Good morning!" Annie happily chirped to everyone she came upon. "Good morning. I hope you have enjoyed your travels thus far."

A lot of the other girls didn't like it when there was a large crowd in the restaurant, but Annie lived for the moments when she had a whole bunch of tables to greet and serve. She supposed it was why she was one of the waitresses that had worked there the longest amount of time. Many of the girls moved out west to try and find a handsome rancher husband; Annie had moved out west to find a job and a purpose, as far as she was concerned.

She approached one of the tables, where a lanky, sandy-haired gentleman was sitting, seemingly dwarfing everything in his vicinity – chair, table, the meal itself all seemed much smaller when compared to him. Annie ignored his immense height and simply smiled up at him. "How are you doing this morning, sir? Would you like me to refill that orange juice for you?"

The gentleman had a light brown cowboy hat resting in the seat that was next to him. *He must be another one of those boys heading out yonder to California or Oregon to try to make it big,* Annie thought without judgment or prejudice. She knew that a lot of men and boys had dreams of striking it rich in the west. If it wasn't for that exodus, she likely wouldn't have her job, so how could she judge him?

He looked up from his nearly empty plate of eggs and grits and smiled at her. It was the whitest smile Annie thought she'd ever seen. It was at least the nicest smile she'd seen from a rancher or cowpoke out here. As such, she beamed back at him.

"As a matter of fact, I would," he said to her. "Thank you, Ma'am." Annie detected the hints of a New York accent in his voice, which didn't surprise her in the least. "May I also please get some more of your grits? They're mighty fine."

She nodded. "Of course. Right away." She flashed another smile at him as she collected up his glass and plate. As she walked away back to the kitchen, she could feel his eyes on her. She was getting about as much attention as she was giving him, she supposed. *He likely noticed me paying attention to everything, so he's returning the favor now.* She hoped that her apron and bow were still straight.

"Fresh order of grits!" she called to the cooks as soon as she was in the kitchen. She set the used plate down in the sink basin to be cleaned. There was still some food on it, but at Stewart House the dishes were either pristine or full of fresh helpings of food. There was no in between for very long.

While the cooks were at work refreshing the customer's grits for her, Annie retrieved the bottle of orange juice and poured another generous glass. The restaurant received box loads of fresh oranges daily and then it was left up to the team of cooks to squeeze them into juice. Nearly everything was delivered via train, not just the oranges or the customers. Mr. Stewart had really taken advantage of the railway lines, which Annie was excited by. The Stewart House seemed to be growing ever more popular, and the new technology meant that they were on the cutting edge whereas a lot of the other businesses out west were a shade behind them.

Annie grabbed a silver tray and placed the glass of

orange juice onto it along with the refilled plate of grits and a fresh, new napkin. Smiling, she left the kitchen and made her way back out to the handsome young traveler who was sitting at a center table all alone, apart from his hat. "Here you go, sir," she said to him brightly. "If there's anything else I can get for you, please don't hesitate to let me know."

With that, she left to tend to her other tables so he could eat to his heart's content. She noticed with some curiosity that the breakfast rush consisted of more men than any other day since she had worked there. Hardly any women had come along for breakfast. *I reckon that's because most of these gents are off to start their futures, or to get back to them as the case may be.* Likely, some of these young men had gone home to visit their families. That was another wonderful perk of the railway system.

Annie had been living in Kansas for almost a year now. She came from a suburb of Boston. Growing up in a large family with Irish immigrant parents, she'd had to work from a pretty young age, most often helping with her younger siblings by doing chores around the farm when she was old enough to help out. *I'm grateful that I was able to just get out and work instead of always sitting at home, waiting for a wealthy suitor to come along and offer to marry me.* She rolled her pretty brown eyes at such foolishness. Cinderella was a fairytale. In life, she'd found, hard work earned you useful skills and strength that one didn't get from just running off and getting married straight out of school.

That was a big part of why Mr. Stewart's stipulation that his waiter-girls remain single for at least a year wasn't a problem for her at all. Annie was devoted to her job and anyone who knew her would easily vouch for that. As a reward for her efforts, she seemed to be Rita's shining star, which left her absolutely tickled. She gladly supported her friends as they ran off and got married, but she knew that with every new wedding announcement, she became stronger and more worthy in the eyes of both Rita and Mr. Stewart.

Perhaps at the end of the year, I shall get a raise, she thought happily as she refilled some glasses of water at a table. *It's never been mentioned before, but I think that has more to do with the fact that hardly anyone else has lasted this long.*

As she worked that morning, she continued to feel the eyes of that young farmer on her. He'd taken a keen interest in her and she didn't know why. Several times she passed by him and asked him if he would like a refill or another helping of his breakfast, but he always shook his head with a smile.

"No ma'am," he said at last when she asked. "As a matter of fact, I believe I'm ready for the bill if you're ready to give it to me."

"Oh," she said. "I hope you didn't think I was trying to rush you out of here! Please take your time." Annie looked at the grandfather clock near the front of the restaurant, checking on the time to see when the travelers would have to head out in order to get back on the train.

The young man smiled at her ever more. "I didn't think you were rushing me," he replied. "But I know you're busy, and I suspect I'd best be heading out soon."

Annie went into the back room to tally up the total for his meal, returned and placed the check down gently in front of him. The man squinted a bit at the hastily penciled in numbers and words that she had written there.

"What's the matter?" she asked him, smile fading a little in her concern. "Do the numbers not add up? I'm afraid I'm not the best at arithmetic, even at my age." She giggled a little in order to try and diffuse the tension.

The young man looked up at her and gave a forlorn sort of sigh. "Nah, that's not the case at all. I'm willing to bet that your math is just fine. I can't read very well, is all."

Annie gave a start, and then smiled at him. *Of course!* she thought. *How silly of me. That's fairly common out here.* "I see," she said. "That's no trouble at all."

She picked up the bill and proceeded to read it off to him, careful to review her itemized list as slowly as he seemed to need so that he'd understand and follow her.

"Thank you very much," the gentleman said, reaching into his pocket and pulling out a fairly ratty leather wallet. "Here y'are." He handed over the amount of money that she'd taken down as the total.

Annie graciously took the money from him. "You're more

than welcome, sir. It's been my pleasure to assist you this morning. If you're ever in Wallace again, please be sure to stop in to the Stewart House so I can say hello."

With another bright smile, she turned and made her way to the back room so she could safely hand off the money to Mr. Stewart. Annie beamed, knowing that she was bound to get a decent cut as a tip for the good job that she'd done this morning.

2

The rest of the morning and afternoon were not quite so interesting for Annie. It really wasn't every day that a customer paid so much attention to her, or reacted so happily towards her service. It made her job worth doing, in her opinion, to see such a big smile – and the extra bit of pay that came as a result didn't hurt either.

Annie was excited to take her break after the lunch rush had wound down. She went into the dormitory and changed out of her work uniform so it would remain pristine, putting on a simple blue dress before heading down to the small kitchen area that was afforded to the girls there. Not finding much in the pantries there, she brought out some bread and some strawberry jam. It certainly wasn't the most exciting lunch, but it was better than nothing.

It was in these quiet moments of downtime that she most missed her friends. *I suppose I can go next door and visit with Beverly,* she thought. *She might be on break now, too!* Quickly, she wrapped up her sandwich in some paper napkins and carried it out of the dormitory. She walked a little ways down the dirt road and turned into the open doorway of the butcher shop.

Beverly was standing behind the counter, packaging up some meat for a delivery later on. She lifted her head and saw Annie there, and beamed. "Well, hello!"

Annie smiled a bit shyly back at her friend. "Hello again," she said, stepping fully into the shop. "I'm not sure if you're busy at the moment, but it occurred to me that while I was on my break I might stop in and see how things are going here for you?"

"That's so sweet of you," Beverly said to her. "Please, won't you sit a moment?" She gestured to a table nearby with two chairs, something Annie hadn't seen there in the shop before. *This was surely Beverly's suggestion.* She was well aware that her ambitious friend had big visions for her new husband's place of business.

Annie went over and sat at the small table as directed, smile growing bigger as Beverly came around the counter and joined her in the chair opposite. "So, you must have news," she said to her.

"Not so much," Annie said with a little laugh. "I mostly missed you, is all. I thought you wouldn't mind a visit while I eat my lunch." She placed her carefully-wrapped sandwich onto the tabletop and Beverly looked at it in surprised amusement.

"I've got something that'll fill you up better than that," she said, getting back up at once and going into the back room. Annie proceeded to eat her jam sandwich while Beverly was gone. When she came back to the table and returned to her seat, she was holding a few delicious looking slices of perfectly seared steak wrapped loosely in paper as well.

"I wouldn't normally share this with someone who'd just popped into the shop, but you're basically family at this point," she said with a smile. She placed the juicy meat in the middle of the table so that Annie could partake in some.

Annie balled up the paper that had once contained her sandwich and gratefully dug into the generous meal that Beverly had offered. "Mmm, this is lovely. Thank you. Have you been enjoying your new life here? It certainly seems like it."

Beverly giggled a little and nodded her head. "Of course!" she declared. "This has always been what I wanted out of life... I obviously didn't know before that I wanted to be a butcher's wife and all of that, but I adore Wilfred and I've been really enjoying the handling of the business while he works on making his meats."

Annie listened to her friend, smiling and nodding along

with her. It wasn't exactly what she wanted out of life, but she was glad that Beverly had found the happiness that she'd clearly been aching for when they worked together at the restaurant. "I know you were always restless and not quite content before, so it's really marvelous to see you so happy now."

I suppose I really ought to pay Carrie a visit one of these days soon, too, Annie thought. She was afraid that she wasn't the best when it came to keeping in touch with people. Her shyness didn't help with that, surely.

The two ladies carried on their friendly, easy-going banter for a bit longer but then Annie knew she had to return to work in time for the dinnertime arrivals. She stood up from her chair and Beverly gave her a big hug.

"Please don't be a stranger," she beseeched. "After all, we're neighbors! And kind of coworkers still." She winked and Annie laughed.

"Okay, I'll be sure to stop in to visit you more often," Annie replied. "Whenever life's not too crazy."

Beverly chuckled. "Well, maybe don't stop in when life's too boring either. Then we won't have anything to talk about."

Annie left the butcher shop, carefully disposing of her paper trash in a bin by the door as she went. Visiting her friend did help her to feel less alone. *Of course I'm not alone,* she thought. *I'm never alone with all of my good friends here.* It felt strange to her, but something seemed to be missing from her life now that Beverly and Carrie had both gone away from the Stewart House. It was almost as if a light had dimmed and left her desperate to adjust and see clearly again.

When Annie arrived back at the restaurant later that afternoon leading into evening, she found quite a kerfuffle waiting for her. The dinner train that was going to be stopping in the station momentarily was said to be another full one; full of eager patrons who were bound to come bustling through the doors of the establishment, hungry and impatient. *Bring it on,* Annie thought with a satisfied smile. These kinds of evenings were what she lived for. This was just the thing she needed to take her mind off of the strange, out of sorts feeling she'd been trying to keep at bay all day.

She found herself rubbing her hands together with anticipation as Rita told her and the rest of the girls to head out and greet the tables of customers. Annie went right up to the first table in her area of the eatery. "Welcome to Stewart House! My name's Annie. What may I get for you?"

The customers were all smiles back at her, for the most part, and didn't seem to notice her slightly overzealous demeanor. *It's strange,* she thought as she took an order down in her notepad. *I'm never shy when I'm out here assisting customers. I wonder if it has more to do with them than it does with me. Helping people makes me feel cheerful.*

There was one such customer, however, who wasn't smiling when she returned to his table. "Miss," he told her, getting her attention as she made her rounds. "Do you have a moment?"

She stopped walking on her way and came over to his table. "Yes, of course." Annie beamed. "What may I help you with?"

The gentleman gestured at his bowl of beef stew. "This is completely cold," he complained. "What, did you leave it back there and let it turn into ice before bringing it to me?"

Annie felt her smile fade from her face somewhat, but she did her best to keep it there just the same. "My apologies, sir," she said at once, bending down and carefully scooping up the bowl from in front of him. "I'll be sure to run this right back and fetch a fresh, hot bowl of stew for you right away."

The gentleman grunted a bit. "See that you do."

He was a middle-aged man with dark hair and a beard. The usual sort of man who came in via the railroad. Annie got the impression that he'd made this trek before, probably off to mine in Oregon or some such thing. She didn't recognize him from any other evening, however. Perhaps word of mouth had finally convinced him to check out the Stewart House, or perhaps he just so happened to be passing through on one of the trains that stopped in Wallace.

"Is this your first time dining with us, sir?" Annie asked politely as she returned with a fresh bowl of stew, placing the bowl down carefully in front of him. She preferred using the silver trays, but exceptions had to be made in a pinch such as this.

The man nodded his head. "Sure is," he said. "I figured it was about time that I saw what all the fuss was about."

Annie's smile grew bigger at the sound of that. "Did you hear about us on the railway during your journey?"

"Oh, all the time," the man said, spooning himself some stew and placing it into his mouth. His face said it all; he was pleased by the temperature now. "A fellow can't go anywhere anymore without hearing about y'all's restaurant," he added.

"That's good to hear," Annie said. "I guess the word of mouth along with all of the newspaper ads that Mr. Stewart runs are really paying off."

"It certainly appears that way" he replied, giving her a small bit of smile of his own. The fresh stew had been their truce. "I admit that I have my reservations about this enterprise, but when I see the way y'all have drummed up the interest and, well, look around and see all these people, it makes me realize that your Mr. Stewart was really on to something. Besides, anything that gets more young folks interested in moving out here and helping us miners and cowpokes is fine by me."

Annie nodded at him. "Thank you, sir. I'm mighty glad to hear that."

She had been so panicked about his reaction to the stew,

but his mood changed substantially once the error had been corrected. *All the poor man wanted was some nice, hot food after a hard day's work.*

Annie continued to assist other tables, refilling their drinks and bringing out plates of desserts. As she worked, her thoughts drifted from the gentleman she just served to the other, younger man who had visited previously. She smiled when she thought of how she was able to help the young farmer who couldn't read and had needed her extra help with the bill. *I don't know why Beverly could have ever thought that her work wasn't worthwhile here. There are so many nice people in need of assistance.*

She supposed that was what made her different from the other girls: she saw only the good in the things that Mr. Stewart was doing. She never felt restless in her job. How could she? After leaving her home in Massachusetts to come all the way to Kansas, the last thing she wanted to do was to have to pick up and leave again.

Perhaps Mr. Stewart will give me a raise once my contract is up? she thought. *I've been working here nearly a year now, and I believe I've been doing exemplary. Rita will surely vouch for me.* Annie saw no reason why she shouldn't be rewarded for remaining faithful to the job and her boss instead of breaking her contract and running off with the first handsome man she saw.

Annie tried very hard to not judge her friends, but

looking around the restaurant made her sense that, though she missed them when she had down time, the restaurant really didn't need them. There wasn't a gaping hole where Carrie or Beverly should be. They'd be replaced easily enough. *But I dare to dream that it would be different if ever I should leave!*

3

The breakfast rush provided Annie with another busy, packed house the following day. A new girl had been added to her bedroom in the dorm, but today wasn't going to be a good one for Annie to provide training for her. Rita did her best to fill in for that role, and she was much better at it anyway, as far as Annie was concerned. It took a chattier girl with more discipline to really give the new girls the best training. And Annie truly wanted all of the girls to receive the most detailed training possible, so there'd be no mistakes that could cost them customers or money.

"Think of it this way," she told the new girl, Melissa, when she was back in the dorm room on her short break. "You're being trained by the best of us and you haven't been thrown into the very busy environment yet. You've witnessed it, surely, but you haven't actually had to serve your own tables yet. Your timing is quite impeccable."

Melissa smiled at her. She was sitting on the bed opposite Annie's. She was a young girl – Annie guessed that she was about twenty – with long, dark brown hair and large, earnest blue eyes. She was going to have a tough time trying to fill the buckled shoes of the last girls who'd slept in that bed. But of course, Annie would remain impartial and reserve her judgment in that regard. She wasn't required to befriend every girl who came to the Stewart House, as long as she was friendly and cordial.

"How long have you been working here?" Melissa asked her in a dreamy sort of voice. She was obviously swept up by all of this thus far. Every girl that arrived there seemed to start out that way.

Annie smiled at her. "Oh, nearly a year by now," she said thoughtfully. "I've seen a lot of girls come and go from that very bed you're sitting on."

Melissa tilted her head a bit, fixing her with a curious gaze. "What brought you here? I was on the train to meet a man who turned out to be a fraud, so I took heed of the advertisements and here I am. Did something similar happen to you?"

Lightly closing her eyes, Annie tried to think about her answer in a way that was truthful but wouldn't upset her or betray her innermost feelings right then and there to a girl who was practically a stranger. *I've never told anyone the story,* she thought. *And I'm not about to now.*

"It was similar to your tale," she said, opening her eyes. "I came out here on the train for love and a new life, but it didn't work out for me. But I've become rather enamored with the Stewart House, so I suppose it's all worked out for the best."

Melissa was giving her a sad look of empathy now. Annie wished that she wouldn't, but at least the other girl hadn't pressed her for more painful details. The way Annie saw it, the Stewart House had saved her life and though the contract was meant to last a year, she had every intention of letting it extend as long as Mr. Stewart wanted her around.

"We'd best head back over to the eating house now," Annie told the other girl, rising up out of her chair and tidying up her bow in the mirror before leaving the room. She went down the stairs, not pausing to wait for Melissa but soon sensed her walking behind anyway. She smiled a little. It was nice to have a little duckling following her around and learning from her again, even though it was far too busy in the eatery for her to really slow down and learn things at present. Right before they were inside the Stewart House, she turned to face Melissa and beamed at her a little. "Heed Miss De La Cruz's instructions and watch me as I work and you'll get the hang of it soon enough."

As soon as they arrived on the floor of the restaurant, Melissa went to Rita to receive further direction and then could sense Annie watching whenever she was nearby. *Leading by example is the easiest way to teach these girls what's what,* she thought, pleased.

The lunch rush wasn't that busy, so she had more of a chance to show Melissa around and introduce her to a few new tasks that Rita had missed. "You can memorize the orders if you prefer," she told Melissa in between checking on tables. "But I like to keep a notepad on hand just so I don't make any mistakes. I've found that some of the older customers greatly appreciate it."

Melissa nodded. "That sounds good to me. I'm afraid my memory isn't always the best. Especially when so many things have such similar-sounding names!"

The two girls laughed pleasantly with each other. While enjoying this bit of spare time with the new waiter-girl, Annie looked out at the floor and noticed a familiar gentleman sitting alone at a table, his cowboy hat taking up the seat beside him.

Annie immediately smiled, grateful to see the friendly face of a former customer. She strolled over to him right away, even though he wasn't sitting at one of the tables that she was assigned to. "Hello there," she said brightly.

The young man looked up from his bowl of grits. He smiled back at Annie, a look of warm recognition in his sparkling gray eyes. "Why hello," he said. "I was hoping I might find you here again."

Annie blushed a little. "Why wouldn't you find me here? Did you think I'd lose my job?"

He laughed, shaking his head. "Oh no, no! I just know it gets busy here sometimes. You might've been off somewhere else, too."

She bit her lip a little bit as she smiled at him. "It sounds like you were trying to see me."

The gentleman looked down, embarrassed, though he was still smiling. "What would you say if I told you that I was?"

Annie was immensely flattered by this. *What a sweetheart,* she thought. *But surely this has more to do with my helpful service for him last time than anything else...*

"Well, that's awfully kind of you, sir," she said. "Your table's not part of my rotation this lunchtime, but I will gladly fetch you anything you'd like since I'm over here already."

"Can you fetch me your name?" the man asked her, looking up from his bowl and right into her eyes.

Annie batted her eyelashes, surprised to be asked such a thing and in such a way. Customers were always told her name upon coming into the restaurant and sitting down at one of her tables, but this time he wasn't her customer and he'd likely forgotten her name from before. *Surely that's all this is.*

There seemed to be some urgency there in his eyes however, some hunger for information. He appeared rather lost to Annie, much like he had when he'd needed her help with reading his bill. Her heart went out to him.

"It's Annie," she said brightly, continuing to smile her welcoming, warm smile at him. There was really nothing to telling a customer her name, since it went along with the job.

But the man then shook his head a little bit. He smiled at her, but the look remained in his eyes. "What's your full name?"

Annie's smile turned into a confused expression herself. *Was he sent here by someone?* she wondered. The question didn't give her much confidence or much reason to answer his new question.

"What's yours?" she asked. She was beginning to wonder if she was supposed to know him. That didn't seem all that likely though. *After all, he didn't say anything like this before. He didn't ask my name last time.* She feared that someone had asked him to come back and find her again. She hoped not, because she much preferred the sweetness of finding each other again versus him searching for her all along.

The gentleman nodded his head a little. There was still a timidity about him. He didn't seem to enjoy discussing things in this way; he still sounded and looked embarrassed with the way he averted his gaze from hers as soon as she asked him the same question. For a moment, neither of them spoke and the sounds of the restaurant were the only sounds Annie heard, mingling with the sound of her own thoughts. Then the young man looked her in the eyes again. "My name is Thackery Prescott," he said.

Now that she knew his name, she felt that there was no reason that she shouldn't tell him hers, except that she was still a bit suspicious about his motives. *It comes with the territory, I guess,* she thought. Men had not exactly given her cause to trust them much, except for Mr. Stewart but he didn't really count amongst the other men she'd interacted with.

"Pleased to make your acquaintance," she said as a formality. She smiled at him a little and could feel the curious gazes of Rita and Melissa on her back as she stood there, speaking to him as an old friend instead of working. "My name is Miss Annie O'Brien."

The sound of *Miss* seemed to bring the sparkle back to his eyes. He smiled as well and bowed his head politely. "It's lovely to meet you, Miss O'Brien... You've confirmed my suspicions, but I don't want to keep you since you're at work. Is there a time or a place we might be able to meet later on?"

Annie's heart was racing in her chest. She had no idea what his suspicions might be, and it scared her when she tried to guess at them. *Should I do this? I suppose I wouldn't have to go alone...*

"You can meet me after lunch gets out," she told Mr. Prescott. "Which is only about an hour from now. Meet me outside the dormitory next door?" The squat building next to the restaurant was not difficult to find, and it contained parlors on the bottom level which were frequently used for gatherings and whenever the restaurant had an overflow. There would be nothing wrong with meeting Mr. Prescott there and finding out what he was there to speak to her about.

Annie knew that she must tread carefully, so having him meet her at a well-known place was a good, safe idea. The last thing she wanted was to do something which might cause scandal for Mr. Stewart. He liked his girls to remain proper at all times, especially when meeting gentlemen outside of work hours. Now the only question was *who* she could invite along with them, to keep things safe and proper?

4

As soon as the slightly awkward conversation drew to a close, Annie made her way back over to her friends along the back corner of the room. Rita was watching over everything like a hawk and she fixed Annie with a curious head-tilting kind of look as soon as Annie arrived back there with them. "What was that all about?" she asked. "The gentleman was finding things to his liking, I hope?"

Annie nodded. "Oh yes," she replied. "I think he wants to speak with me in private later on."

"Oooh," Melissa couldn't help but squeal a bit.

Annie rolled her eyes, but smiled anyway. It wouldn't do her any good to be rude when what she really needed was her friends to help her with this new situation that she found herself in. "It's nothing like that," she explained. "At least, I find that hard to believe considering I never met him before the other day here at the restaurant."

Rita's eyebrows raised a little. "Oh?" She put her hands on her hips. "Well, in that case, may I suggest that you bring a friend along with you when you meet? It sounds to me like he's taken quite an interest in you. I never thought I'd see the day Miss Annie O'Brien found a suitor. No offense."

Annie blushed profusely. "None taken," she said in a meek voice. *Everyone who works here knows that I'm not interested in a husband. But still, their eyes light up at the first sign of that sort of thing. It's beyond frustrating!* "As a matter of fact, I was thinking of asking Carrie to come along. I trust her to provide good judgment about that sort of thing..."

Melissa looked crestfallen, but Annie reasoned that the new girl was still little more than an acquaintance to her. It didn't seem right or fair to invite someone else along instead of Carrie or Beverly, or even Rita, not that the supervising waiter-girl would go along anyway.

Rita nodded approvingly. "Carrie would probably appreciate the invite," she agreed. "But do make sure she joins you. I can't have you meeting alone with a customer. It wouldn't look right for Mr. Stewart."

Annie nodded her head back at her. "Yes, quite right. If I can't find a companion, I shan't meet with him today."

"I could be your companion," Melissa offered.

"You cannot," Rita said. "I would like you to work alongside me today, and I'll show you what to do in preparation for the dinner rush."

Melissa sighed a bit. "Yes ma'am."

As soon as lunchtime was over and the restaurant was all but vacated, Annie was out of the place. She rushed up the dirt road to Mrs. Carrie Jackson's home. It had been a while since Annie had seen her friend and she prayed that she could spare a moment to help her. She rapped on the door as soon as she stood in front of it, worrying her bottom lip a bit with one of her front teeth until a crack appeared in the skin there.

Annie never thought she'd be doing anything like this. It was usually the other girls who met with men in the 'courting parlors' and left the restaurant. *I really don't think that's what this is,* she thought. *He doesn't know me. He had to ask my name. Perhaps he wants to get to know me, but we shall only be friends because I'm not leaving the Stewart House. Especially not for a* man.

Suddenly, Carrie opened the front door. She smiled as soon as she saw Annie standing there. "Annie! How are you?"

Annie let go of her reverie and smiled back at her friend. She looked like she was doing very well for herself. "Married life seems to be treating you well," she said sweetly. "I'm doing okay myself. I have a favor to ask of you, if it's not too much trouble? And I don't have much time."

Carrie tilted her head a bit in curiosity. "Oh?"

Taking a deep breath, Annie just got right to it. "A

gentleman has asked to meet with me in one of the dormitory parlors this afternoon. He said that he had something he wishes to speak with me about."

"A gentleman?" Carrie asked her, seeming surprised but also delighted. "Have you met him before?"

"Slightly," Annie replied. "It's a long story I shall have to tell you later. Would you be able to accompany me in meeting him, to keep things proper? I'm not sure entirely what he wants from me..."

Carrie was giving her such a sympathetic look, along with a strange, almost pitying sort of smile. "Of course I'll come along with you," she said. "I must admit that it makes me happy to see you pursuing a bit of romance."

Annie blushed a little. "That's not what this is about, I shouldn't think. The man is practically a stranger."

"So was my Leeroy at one point," Carrie said with a wink.

The two ladies rushed along the dirt road together and into the foyer of the dormitory. Thankfully, Mr. Prescott hadn't arrived there yet, but Annie knew that he would be there soon enough. She took the bow from her head and hid it away in her small purse. "Do you think I ought to change dresses?" she asked Carrie. "Will it be bad to be seen outside of work in this?" In her haste, she had gone to Carrie's house in her black and white uniform.

Looking her over, Carrie shook her head. "I think it's perfectly acceptable to be seen in the dorm dressed like that. But you might want to lose the apron."

Annie looked down at herself and realized this was a great idea. If she simply wore the black dress, it wouldn't technically be her uniform anymore. She didn't see the need to run upstairs and change into something prettier when the meeting was likely to be short and nothing to do with how she was dressed, anyhow. "You're so smart," she said, removing her apron and tucking it away in her small handbag as well. "This is why I knew you were the perfect girl to ask to accompany me."

Carrie smiled and bobbed her head a little, pleased.

There was a sudden knock on the front door of the dormitory. Annie jumped slightly in her excited anticipation. "You don't have to sit in the little room with us," she told her friend. "Just... please remain close."

Carrie nodded knowingly and moved off to one of the other nearby parlors on the main floor. She evidently knew just which one had the bookshelves. Carrie had always been fond of books, and marriage had made her much calmer than she'd been when she lived there in that dorm. Annie smiled as she watched her go. She knew her friend wouldn't let her down.

She straightened her back a bit and smoothed her skirts, hoping that she would look her best for the gentleman even though she had no idea what he wanted to discuss. Then Annie pulled the door inward and smiled out at him as he stood there on the porch. Right away, Mr. Prescott removed the cowboy hat from his head and held it in his hands in front of himself, politeness as always. She only got a glance at him wearing it, but it thrilled her anyway to have seen that he did in fact look the part of a cowpoke. It wasn't every day that such a person came into her life. Not since her botched engagement...

Let's not even think about that, she told herself. *Too painful. Let's see what he has to say.*

"Mr. Prescott," Annie said in a pleasant and pleased sort of voice. "Welcome." She stepped aside from the doorway and gestured for him to enter. "This isn't much, but this is the place we waiter-girls call home. Please have a seat in the parlor to your right."

He came inside and walked into the small room off to the side as directed. She closed up the door and followed him in, watching curiously as he placed his hat onto the small coffee table in the parlor. The set-up of the space was clearly meant for gathering, be it a meeting or a friendly chat. Annie knew that Mr. Stewart had created these 'courting parlors' so that the ladies he hired could get to know and eventually marry the gentlemen customers who came to the restaurant. He didn't encourage for this to occur around the clock, of course, but he wanted to make sure that things remained appropriate when it did happen.

Mr. Prescott looked at her and waited to see what the next move should be. "Oh, don't be afraid to have a seat," Annie told him, smiling as she sat on a green dais. She nodded towards the light blue wing chair across from her, with the table in between. At once, he took her lead and sat down in the chair. Or rather, he perched there. She noticed that he remained seated on the edge of the seat, as if he didn't have long to stay or maybe was afraid to... Right away, his left leg began to nervously bounce.

"I suppose I'd best start off by saying that I have every reason to believe in fate now," he said, looking straight into her eyes the way he had earlier. He had an intense gaze, one that made a person want to believe him wholeheartedly, even if no real reason had been given. "When I saw you in the restaurant the other evening, I felt as if I should somehow know you. And then today, when you told me your name, it confirmed it for me – you're the very someone I was meant to meet."

Annie felt slightly queasy. *What is he going on about?* Carrie and Rita had been right. Melissa too. Apparently, Mr. Prescott had engagement on his mind. "Mr. Prescott," she broke in. "I feel as if I must stop you right there before you make me feel too guilty. You see, I'm not looking for marriage or anything like that. I'm a working girl here at the restaurant. I signed a contract and I plan to stick to it."

Mr. Prescott nevertheless seemed undisturbed by this news, or at least his continence was stable. He continued to look into her eyes with urgency and faith that what he had to say would matter to her regardless of what she thought. "I don't expect anything from you. You needn't give up your position here or change the course of your life if you're truly happy here. I wouldn't ask that of you. At least not right off. What kind of man would I be if I did that? All I'm saying to you is... Well, shucks, Miss O'Brien. About a year ago now, we were writing to each other. Don't you recall?"

Annie's heart felt like it stopped for a moment. She stared at him. "But... That can't be true. The man I wrote to was a man called James. *James* Prescott."

He smiled a bit. "Yes, ma'am, that's me. James Thackery Prescott. No one really calls me by my first name, but you see I had the help of a farming friend. He wrote the letters for me. Always using my own thoughts, I promise you."

Annie leaned back in her chair. The room seemed to spin now and she felt rather hot. *Can this possibly be true?!* She stared at him, open-mouthed and unsure of what to say to that. The good thing was that this Mr. Prescott – James Prescott... – wasn't afraid of talking.

"I regret that we didn't exchange pictures, because I would've recognized you right away if we had," he went on as if he'd memorized what he wanted to say to her. He obviously knew she didn't have the rest of the afternoon to spend time with him. And that she might have cause to not want to.

"Why weren't you at the station that day?" she asked him in a quiet voice, not really wanting to know the answer as much as she had wanted to ask him that question for the worst part of a year.

He sighed a little. "It was completely the fault of timing," he said. "I was on a train from California and I was supposed to be there to meet you, but my train ran into some problems just west of Salt Lake City and I was delayed at least a week. Having no way to reach you, both on account of not knowing your new address as well as not being able to write and all, well, I figured this was just God's plan for me. I surrendered to the idea that I wouldn't get to marry a pretty girl and be happy. I arrived here in Wallace eventually, of course, but by that point I decided to just take another job on another farm. And I've been moving around ever since. There was no point in settling if I didn't have someone to settle for."

Annie looked at him searchingly with more than a little skepticism. "You may have simply moved on, but I *did* settle here. I had no choice. But I made the most of it. You broke my heart and abandoned me here, but this place has proven to me that I don't need you. I don't need marriage or love. I make my own fate."

Mr. Prescott was staring sadly at her now. She didn't mean to make him feel bad, but she didn't think he had any right to come to her and complain about not being able to settle. *I don't want him to settle for me. I thought he wanted to start a new life, and he certainly could have done that without me if he'd worked enough at it.* Annie realized that she was thinking more like Beverly than she ever had before, but she *was* upset.

"Thank you for telling me your side of things, Mr. Prescott," she said then. "I really have to go back to work now. Be well in whatever path you choose to take."

With that, she left him there in the parlor and headed back to the restaurant. Carrie meanwhile came forward and escorted the emotionally shaken man out of the dormitory. This plainly hadn't gone the way he had hoped for. Annie supposed that he thought he was just going to be able to pick right up from where they'd left off. *He probably thinks he can still marry me now!* she thought incredulously. *The folly of men.*

5

Annie's mind was fuzzy when she went back to work and began serving the customers during the dinner time rush. Thankfully for her, things were a trifle calmer than they normally were so she didn't feel quite as overwhelmed as she might have otherwise, but the lack of bustling also meant that she was left alone with her thoughts more than she would've liked. *He spoke to me as if I would be willing to just drop everything and leap into his arms as if the past year hadn't happened! As if he hadn't left me standing there, stranded, broken-hearted. He claims it was simply a train delay, but a decent man would've written and explained himself.*

At least he had come to the restaurant again as soon as he thought she might be the one he hoped to find... Though Annie believed that it was too little, too late.

"How did your meeting with the gentleman go?" Melissa asked her innocently, sidling up to Annie as she stood there along the wall of the eating house, watching the crowds as they dined.

Immediately, Annie regretted that she'd ever mentioned such a thing to the younger girl. Not because Melissa had meant her any harm – she certainly wouldn't gossip or anything like that, as far as Annie had noticed – but because it was embarrassing to now have to go around, explaining what had happened to people. *Oh, why can't people mind their own business?*

She let out a laugh as she realized that none of this should upset her, anyhow. Mr. Prescott wasn't worth all that. Now that she'd told him off, she didn't think she'd ever see him around again, so there was no use in worrying about it any longer. And there was no use withholding the rather ridiculous situation from anyone else. What was past was past, and was absolutely harmless to her here and now.

"About a year ago, I was exchanging letters with a suitor out west," Annie explained to Melissa. "He was a farmhand in California. He asked me to marry him, so I travelled all the way to Wallace in order to meet up and continue west with him. He told me that he was open to the idea of settling down in Kansas, as well. He had all kinds of lofty ideas for his future. Ideas that now feel more depressing than pleasant to discuss."

Melissa looked at her sympathetically. "What happened?" she asked.

"I arrived here like I'd promised, but he never turned up. So, I accepted Mr. Stewart's graciously offered waitress job and I've been here ever since."

The realization then dawned on Melissa. Her mouth fell open. "You mean that gentleman was your long-lost beau?!"

A few heads turned towards them and Annie blushed, shushing her friend even as she continued to smile. She felt extremely awkward but she refused to let anyone know it. "Yes," she said. "He sure was. And he told me that I was his reason for coming back here and looking to see if he could ever find me again. He told me that I was his motivation for settling in Kansas and all kinds of nonsense."

Melissa was giving her a dreamy, far off sort of look now. "Aww!" she said sincerely. "It sounds like he really regrets what happened and wants to make things better. Patch things up, you know?"

Annie sighed a little. "I know. But this isn't something that I necessarily want patched up. He really hurt me and I've found a real life here and a job I'm passionate about."

"What's this about a job you're passionate about?" Rita suddenly interjected. "And why aren't you doing *said* job right now?"

Annie blanched a bit. It would figure that the supervisor would overhear at this moment in the conversation, but she also had a point. "Sorry, Rita. We were just chatting. I'll go check on my tables right away."

"Thank you," Rita replied. She wore a curious expression and Annie felt unnerved as she went on her way, knowing that Melissa was likely going to regale the head waiter-girl with the tale of Annie's woe.

There was a reason I didn't share any of this with anyone before, she thought miserably. *I never wanted to be the topic of childish gossip.*

Fortunately, the evening went on with no more upsets or discussions of her and Mr. Prescott. When it was time to close up shop, Annie removed her bow and apron once again and strode next door to the dormitory.

When she arrived inside, one of the other girls came towards her holding a piece of paper. "Annie, this was left here for you," she said inquisitively, handing over the paper which turned out to be a thin envelope. All that was written upon it was "Miss Annie O'Brien" in a hastily-scrawled, childish sort of hand which meant that it could only have been left by one person.

"Thank you, Lottie," she said with a smile, doing her best to pretend that none of this was out of the usual. With that, Annie carried the envelope upstairs and into her room, securely closing the door and leaning her back against it, closing her eyes.

When she opened them again, she realized that Melissa was sitting there on the bed across the room from her. She stared at her, head tilted, appearing as though she wanted to say something.

Annie sighed a bit. "Apparently, I've received a letter," she said, holding the envelope up so Melissa could see it.

"Oh?" she asked. "From who?"

Laughing, Annie shook his head. "Come on now, you know who." She went into the room and sat down beside her vanity. Carefully, she opened the envelope and pulled out the letter. It had been quickly written out on some paper that seemed as though it had been dipped in oil, it was so grease-stained.

Unfolding the letter and grimacing a bit at its stains, Annie read it. She was rather surprised to find it was a well-written letter, and then she realized that as with before he had surely found someone who could help him write it.

Miss Annie,

I'm so sorry. The chat we had today clearly upset you. That was never my intention. I only wanted to let you know what had caused my delay in meeting you. I never meant to hurt you. Please believe me in that.

It is my hope that perhaps we might rekindle what we had before by writing letters again. I have a friend here where I am living, a fellow farmhand, who is willing to help me get my thoughts down on paper. I'm working on a farm in Sharon Springs at the moment, though I am hoping to join you there in Wallace as soon as I can. If that is what you wish.

I'm happy that you've established yourself in town, with the restaurant and all. I wish you only the best. I hope you will write to me.

Sincerest wishes,
Thackery

ANNIE NOTED that he had signed his own name; the lettering was much less neat and spaced out the way a child might when he was learning the letters of his own name. In spite of her continued frustration about the day's events, she found herself smiling.

Melissa noticed that smile. It was impossible not to. "Did the letter make you feel better?" she asked.

Annie wished that it wasn't the case, but it was true. The letter had made her feel better. She looked at her friend and then carefully folded the letter up, placing it back into the envelope so she could easily return to it later. She set the envelope into the top drawer of her vanity. "I'm not sure what he expects of me," she said honestly. "But I do feel somewhat better, yes. It takes a good soul to actually take the time to write a letter after such an event as today's was. I can tell he's sincere. I just fear that he really believes he can pick up right where we left off. As if he hasn't disappointed me and hurt me a great deal."

I also don't know how he expects me to write to him. He hasn't provided a return address, after all. She supposed that she would cross that bridge when she came to it. The post office in town very well might have known where Mr. Prescott lived. Stranger things had happened...

"Surely, he's trying," Melissa said, hugging her legs to her chest as she sat on the bed. "Even if you only become friends through this, that's better than where you were before, right?"

Annie thought that Melissa was sweet for thinking that way. She wanted to give Mr. Prescott the benefit of the doubt and a chance, but she also fully intended to keep her heart safe. And she certainly didn't need the distractions that a person like Thackery would surely bring to her life and her work.

6

Whehen Annie awoke the following morning, she quickly changed into one of her simple dresses that she wore outside of work hours. She threw on a blue skirt and then slipped into a pink bodice, not even caring that it wasn't the best match she had. She wasn't going to have much time before the breakfast train, so she didn't concern herself too much about it. *Hopefully no one of consequence will even see me.*

She sat at her vanity and pulled out a piece of paper and a pen, scrawling hastily.

DEAR MR. PRESCOTT,

I appreciate that you took the time to write a note to me. I admit that our meeting did not put a great deal of confidence in me as to your character, so I was pleased to find that you'd written to me right after to apologize in an attempt to start over.

It probably doesn't surprise you that I wish to take things slowly and that I cannot promise much to you in the way of either forgiveness or companionship. Though I came to Kansas to start a life with you, I've since started a life without you, as you know. I do not wish to change or lose the happy placement which I have found in Wallace. The girl who once wrote to you is different now. I feel as though I am a woman at last, and it is with the clear-eyed pragmatism of a woman that I must tell you that you needn't plan on moving to Wallace. I believe you've also found the right place-ment for yourself in Sharon Springs. I would feel bad if you were to give that up in order to move here because of me, when I cannot give you what you wish.

Best,

Annie O'Brien

SHE GENTLY FOLDED the page and placed it into a clean, new envelope. Not knowing where exactly this letter would be taken to, she simply wrote *Mr. Thackery Prescott* onto it. Then she left the dormitory, taking the letter down the street to the post office. If they didn't know where to send it, she would never know.

"Good morning, sir," she said to the man there at the desk. He looked up at her blearily and nodded a bit.

"Good morning, miss," he replied. "What can I do for you today?"

"I have this letter to send," she told him, placing the envelope onto the wood desk and then sliding it over to him. "The trouble is that I don't know where exactly this gentleman lives, besides the next town over in Sharon Springs."

The gentleman behind the desk took the letter into his hands and peered down at the name on its envelope. "Hmm," he said thoughtfully. "I can send it along to the office in Sharon Springs in the hopes that they can figure out who it belongs to."

Annie didn't think he was using the most reassuring words possible, but she had no other alternative really. "Thank you, sir," she said with a smile and a short curtsy. "I believe it's in good hands with you."

She turned and left the post office, quickly walking back to the dormitory so she could change into her uniform. Rita had washed all of the dresses and aprons last night, so she would need to pick hers up from the bottom floor of the dorm first anyway. *I can get Melissa's as well. She'll appreciate that.* She was in a better mood now that she had her letter on its way to Mr. Prescott. Perhaps she wouldn't have to give it any more thought. Then again, he seemed to be a rather stubborn fellow.

"Where did you go this morning?" Melissa asked her as they dressed.

Annie smiled a little and told her. "I'm not so sure that they'll have any luck finding him, but it was worth a try. Far better to attempt to write to him than to just keep mum. Suppose he came back because he didn't hear from me!"

"That still might happen," her roommate pointed out with a shrug. "What if he can't take no for an answer?"

They tied on their white aprons and large, white bows and then headed down the steps and next door together. Annie was feeling a stronger affinity for the new waitress now that they had gone through the encounter with Mr. Prescott together, more or less. She had no other roommate to chat with about such matters. Talking with Rita wasn't quite the same thing, as she was Annie's superior and could potentially get her into trouble if she said the wrong things. Saying the wrong things was more of a thing that Beverly would do, but Annie found that the other girl's spunk had rubbed off on her, at least a little bit. Rita had clearly noticed this as well, and it wasn't such a pleasing change for her.

As the breakfast train arrived and its passengers spilled into the restaurant, Annie was ready to greet them with a smile and a friendly word like always. It helped her to take her mind off of things with Mr. Prescott, at least for a time. *It's funny,* she thought. *Before he told me who he was, I did think that he was handsome and sweet. It's a shame in a way... But I'm glad that I've moved on with my life.*

Somewhere deep in her mind, she thought, *Keep telling yourself that.*

"Good morning," she said to a table of diners. "Welcome to Stewart House. My name is Annie. May I fetch you some beverages to get you started?"

She went back to the kitchen with their drink orders listed out carefully on her pad of paper. Though she was enjoying herself as she always did, Annie felt that something was missing now. She couldn't think of what until she found herself imagining the handsome farmhand sitting at one of the tables, his hat in the seat next to him.

Now I'm just being ridiculous, she told herself as she placed the drinks onto the table she was serving. *I need to focus on my work! I wish he'd never shown up here. He probably knew what he was doing...*

Once Annie was on her next break, she decided that it was time to visit briefly with Carrie again. They hadn't spoken since the other day when her friend had been gracious enough to come to the dorm and keep an eye on things while she met with Mr. Prescott. Carrie was likely wondering what had become of them.

She knocked on her friend's front door and was surprised when it opened and the tall, friendly-faced coach driver Leeroy was the one standing there instead of Carrie. "Well, how do you do, Miss Annie?" He sounded as if he was greeting an old friend.

Annie smiled and blushed a bit. She could see why

Carrie married him; he was quite a charmer. "Hello, Mr. Jackson. I hope that things are well for you both here."

"Leeroy, Miss O'Brien," he told her with a playful wink. "I think we're friends enough now for you to call me by my given name, don't you?"

She giggled a little. "Yes, sir. I mean. Yes, Leeroy. Is Carrie about? I have something I must speak with her about. She'll be awfully miffed if I don't."

"Oh sure," he said, holding the door open and inviting her to come inside. "She's in the kitchen, planning out today's luncheon."

Annie graciously made her way into the Jacksons' home and followed his directions in order to find Carrie. Sure enough, her friend was standing in the kitchen, assembling a few meal items on the counter.

"Why hello there!" Carrie trilled as soon as she saw that her friend had appeared in the doorway to the kitchen. "How are you?"

Annie went to Carrie at once and gave her a tight hug. "I've been doing well, and yourself?"

"Nothing to complain about," Carrie replied.

"That's good to hear," Annie said. "I just thought it was a good idea to stop by and let you know about what happened between me and Mr. Prescott."

Carrie laughed a little. "I noticed you left him sitting there with a dumbfounded look on his face," she said. "I escorted him out afterwards. I hope that was the correct thing to do. It sure felt like it."

Annie nodded a little. "Oh, it was. I didn't want to see him again... I'm still not sure I want to, but my feelings have become a little less clear. He left a letter for me at the dormitory, apologizing and letting me know more about where he was coming from and what his intentions were."

Carrie raised her eyebrows. "Perhaps we should sit." She led Annie over to the small table in her kitchen and they sat together. Annie explained a bit more of the saga that had gone on with her arrival in the town and Mr. Prescott's failure to show up on the day she arrived.

"I know now that it was an accident and he means to make amends, but I am afraid that he means to move forward as if nothing happened. As if I still want to marry him."

"Well, don't you?" Carrie asked her. "What's changed your mind about him?"

Annie had to think about that. "It's a mixture of things. A complicated mixture. I don't want to have to give up my life here, my job and the way that I've been enjoying things... I'm also still hurt by the fact that I trusted that he would be here and he let me down."

"It was an honest mistake, though," Carrie reasoned. "And who said anything about you having to give up your life here?"

"Mr. Stewart's contract..."

Carrie scoffed a little, waving that dismissively away. "You don't need to keep working for Mr. Stewart's restaurant in order to find happiness and fulfillment here. Trust me, I know. A good husband and a place of your own to work on and cultivate? That's the ultimate source of pride, in my opinion. Because no matter how hard you work in the restaurant, it's always going to be Mr. Stewart's restaurant. You won't ever get all of the credit that you deserve."

"I suppose I have been working there a long time," Annie said thoughtfully. Her head was beginning to hurt with all of these new ideas. "And Mr. Stewart doesn't intend to keep all of his waiter-girls there forever."

Carrie nodded. "Exactly. It's a one-year contract and after that, you're free to pursue whichever path you've chosen. So, I think that you should continue this correspondence with Mr. Prescott and see where it leads you."

Annie took Carrie's hand. "I know that I could count on you to give me some sound advice. Thank you, Carrie. I hope that I hear back from him now."

Carrie smiled and squeezed Annie's hand gently. "From the sound of things, he will," she said confidently. "I'm glad that you've found your knight in shining armor again. It's true that his armor may have lost some of its sheen, but it's still armor all the same. If he truly deserves you, you'll know because he won't disappoint you again."

Annie returned to the restaurant after this brief conversation, glad to have gone to visit Carrie. She could easily vent her woes to Melissa and Rita, but their perspectives were not quite the same as the one that Carrie could offer. After all, Carrie was married and happy with where she'd ended up. Annie hoped to have a future a bit like Carrie's, with a kind and loving man like Mr. Jackson. With a man like the one she'd written to... Even if Thackery had needed help in order to get his sweet words written down. She imagined that he could work on that just as well as she could work on forgiving him.

7

Although she was doing her best to keep her mind off of Mr. Thackery Prescott, Annie was pleased to be handed another letter a few afternoons later, from Rita of all people. "He dropped it off at the restaurant. I asked him if he wanted to stop in for a quick bite, but he said no. He only comes here for you."

Annie blushed a bit as she took the envelope. She didn't necessarily enjoy hearing that, because she knew that her employer wanted customers to come for the meals and the ambiance of his restaurant, not for one of the waitresses. After all, he had made sure to keep them from being particularly eye-catching, but somehow Thackery had seen past the bland uniform and was attracted to her anyway. It helped that he knew who she was already. Mr. Stewart had to understand that.

"Thank you, Rita," she said a bit sheepishly.

Rita held tight to the letter at first so Annie couldn't just take it. She looked right into her eyes. "Don't let this become a regular thing," she intoned harshly.

Annie always got the feeling that Rita would've done well as a schoolmarm. She was nice and well-meaning enough, but there was something stern about her whenever she gave directions to Annie and the rest of the girls. She took her authority very seriously, and she was quite faithful to the business and their boss.

Nodding her head, Annie carefully received the paper from Rita. "Yes, ma'am," she said. "I'll see to that."

She took the letter to the dormitory and sat in one of the courting parlors rather than rushing upstairs to her room just yet. She'd need to send out a new letter today, apparently.

Dear Miss Annie,

I'm very grateful to you for writing back to me. I can tell that you do not wish for your life to change. It is my belief however that your life and mine could change together without you having to make very many sacrifices at all. I don't wish to make you have to quit your position at the restaurant. That is entirely up to Mr. Stewart, of course. If he has initiated a contract with you that requests you don't get married, then I believe severing it wouldn't necessarily be the worst thing. It seems to me that the restaurant is restricting you a great deal more than you think.

It is my wish to see you again, Miss Annie. I long to start a farm of my own in Wallace and have you as my wife. You shall have as much freedom as you'd like with me, I promise you that. There's so much more that you can accomplish out here. You needn't always be a server. I wish to make you happy and treat you like a princess now that we are together again, or nearly anyway.

What do you say?

With great affection,
Thackery

Annie sighed a bit and placed this letter back into its envelope. She didn't know what she was supposed to say to any of this. He clearly wasn't going to stop trying. And Rita was clearly not going to keep her temper about all of these letters. Climbing the staircase, Annie went into her room and sat at her vanity, taking out her pen and some paper in order to scrawl a quick response. She'd need to get back to work for the lunch train soon, but she had enough time to run to the post office as long as she didn't change. Thinking of that, she swiftly removed her apron and bow. *Carrie's so smart,* she thought, recalling her friend advising her to do just that when she wanted to keep her uniform on otherwise. She just hoped she wouldn't get too much dust and dirt on her newly cleaned outfit...

Placing pen to paper, she quickly jotted out a note back for Mr. Prescott.

Dear Mr. Prescott,

I understand that you are decided on how you wish to create a future for yourself here and you don't want to back down from your dreams, but you must take my feelings into account. I know that you say that I will be free to do whatever I like if I should quit my life here and start over again with you, but you fail to tell me how. How shall I fill my days with happiness if I'm to become simply a housewife? I know that my friends who have gone off and gotten married have fared well in that endeavor, but I'm not like them. I believe I'm a great deal more tied to my job here than they were. As such, it's going to take something more than the promise of a married life for me to want to quit the Stewart House.

Please consider my feelings. I was left here, alone, without knowing a soul or what I was supposed to do next. It was a miracle that Mr. Stewart offered me a job and a home. I don't think I should've survived. You must understand my loyalty to this place. I know that it was a mistake on your part and you never meant to leave me here alone, but the fact of the matter is that you did. It doesn't matter how either of us ended up where we are now; all that matters is the here and now.

As such, I wouldn't mind calling you my friend. But you must stop delivering these amorous letters to my place of employment before I get in trouble. My supervisor suspects that you're trying to court me away and no matter how often I say that is not the case, she is annoyed at me and at you, as well.

I would suggest that from now on, if you wish to speak with me, you do so in person at the restaurant. That way, you're providing my boss with patronage.

Sincerely,
Annie

SHE FOLDED up this letter and placed it onto a fresh envelope, scrawling his name onto the back of it once more. As before, she didn't know his address but she figured that, since he was a migrant worker more than a settled farmer, he'd be easily found by the postman in Sharon Springs. Another reason to not be writing these letters to him – it was far easier to just speak with him in person, especially if he insisted on delivering them himself anyway.

What a silly man, she thought with a shake of her head as she went down the street to drop this new letter off with the postmaster there. *I hope he will heed my warning and stop this nonsense before I lose my job.*

On her way, Annie ran into Thackery himself. She let out a surprised laugh of disbelief, shaking her head at him in greeting as he grinned and waved back at her. She was roughly halfway up the street and here he was, walking towards her. Plainly on his way to the restaurant once more. She was glad to have caught him.

"I was on my way to send this to you," she told him, holding up the letter so he could see.

"I think I can guess what it says," Thackery replied. "You're sorry but you can't give up your life here because I failed to meet you at the station and who's to say that I won't fail you again?"

Annie lowered her arm and the letter down to her side. She frowned a little. "More or less," she admitted.

Thackery laughed. "I was on my way to try and meet up with you at the restaurant instead of waiting for another letter from you," he said. "I've been hired by a wealthy farmer in Sharon Springs and I believe, sincerely and truly, that the pay from this job will be more than enough for me to start my own farm."

Annie looked at him doubtfully. "But Mr. Prescott—"

"I know," he said. "I'm not asking for you to upend your life here for me. I'm only asking for you to consider... a promotion of sorts. After all, you can't be a waitress for Mr. Stewart forever. If you marry me, heck, you could open your own restaurant. I wouldn't stop you. Because I know it'd make you happy."

Annie went a bit pale. She moved closer to Thackery. "Please don't even suggest that. I'd never want to compete with the Stewart House. The last man who tried it ended up selling his steaks there anyway. He's got a booming business here and I'm happy for him – for my friends who work there." She bit her lip slightly. "But I do suppose you're right. I can't be a waitress there forever. I'm just frightened. I don't know what else I could do."

Thackery gave her a loving look and Annie felt her cheeks go hot. *I don't know what I've ever done to make him continue to look at me like that,* she thought. She wished he wouldn't because it was making it harder and harder to turn him down. *Perhaps that's why.*

Suddenly, he took her hand and knelt there in the dirt in front of her. He dug a hand into the pocket of his brown, dust-covered pants and pulled out a sparkling ring. There was a gem on it that Annie refused to believe was an actual diamond. "This is what I spent my last hard-earned pay on," he told her, gazing up at her. "Please don't you dare turn me away anymore. I have loved you for a very long time, Annie. Let me show you. Let me prove it to you. Let me marry you and call you my wife."

Annie stared back at him, the breath seeming caught in her throat. She didn't know what to say. He was so sweet and the ring was so beautiful, and suddenly she realized that she was crying. Not just a little, but rivers of tears down her cheeks. "Oh, Thackery, why couldn't you just be here for me when I needed you?"

All at once, Thackery stood back up and put his arms

around her. He kept the ring safe by wearing it on his little finger on his left hand. He stroked her brown hair and cuddled her to him, not saying anything but letting her cry until the tears at last subsided. Looking around a bit, he smiled and pulled back to gaze lovingly at her again. "I know I made a terrible mistake back then," he said to her. "But I swear to you, Annie O'Brien, I won't ever let you down again. I mean it. I've made a plan and by God I'm sticking to it, but I need you with me. I need you in order to follow my dream... our dream, if you still want it."

Annie remembered the way she had felt when they wrote to each other almost a year ago now. She'd been so happy and so in love, and so ready for a change. "I've been so swept up in things here," she said to him then. "I was so afraid of failure that I clung to the only thing I knew I had. I thought I'd lost you forever."

Thackery took the ring off of his little finger. "Then what do you say?" he asked her. "Will you give me another chance? We can do everything you wanted. I love you, Annie. I want only what makes my girl happy."

Slowly, Annie took the ring from him and placed it onto her shaking finger. "I'll give you this chance," she told him. "But you've got to be patient with me. It's a lot to go back to."

Thackery smiled with tears of his own now in his eyes. "I will be," he promised. "I'll always be patient."

"And let me handle this in the way I choose," she said. "I am going to disappoint quite a few people with this news."

He nodded. "I understand. I'll wait for you. After all," he said with a laugh. "I'm still working as a farmhand in Sharon Springs. I'm not ready to start my own farm."

She gazed into his eyes and felt like she was seeing him for the first time again. So handsome and sweet. So hopeful. "You will be soon," she said to him, taking his hand. "I know it."

Bringing her hand to his lips, Thackery kissed it.

A nnie went back to the restaurant after that, still holding the letter in her hand. She'd completely forgotten about it and it wasn't until Melissa tapped her on the shoulder and gestured toward it that she remembered she had it with her. Thackery hadn't read it, but he didn't need to now. She ripped it up and disposed of it in the nearest trash bin.

"It's nothing," she said to Melissa. "I've changed my mind."

That's when Melissa noticed the ring on Annie's finger. "Oh my goodness!" she cried, pointing.

Annie swiftly hid her hand behind her back. "Shh," she said. "I need to find the right time."

"The right time for what?" Rita asked, suddenly

appearing and overhearing the last bit of the conversation. She seemed to have a knack for doing that.

Annie blushed a little, smiling. "Nothing," she said. "It's no big deal. I have something I'm thinking about, that's all. Is today's lunch train going to be a full one? I hope so."

Rita arched an eyebrow at her but she let the topic drop since Annie didn't what to discuss it at present. "Yes, I do believe so," she said instead. "Your favorite kind of train."

The lunch rush went as promised for Annie. There were enough customers in need of her services that she didn't have time to stop and think about what had occurred earlier that midday. However, now that there was a ring upon her finger and a promise had been made, there was no turning back for Annie and she knew it. She was going to give Thackery another chance, and that meant leaving her job. She had complete faith in him that he wouldn't disappoint on her so soon after making this big plan with her. But who could say that would remain the case down the line...?

I must talk to Mr. Stewart tonight, she thought a bit glumly. She didn't want to cause a fuss and she hated goodbyes, but there really wasn't a way for her to slowly break away from the restaurant. *I've broken the agreement, so I must let him know.*

She thought of the Thackery that she'd gotten to know via the letters over months and months. She recalled how connected to him she had felt, how much she loved him. Now that he was back in her life, she felt almost as if she was dreaming. It was much too wonderful to try and ignore any longer. *Fate truly was on our sides somehow!*

After a long and tiring day of working in the restaurant, Annie helped the rest of the girls tidy up and prepare for the following morning, knowing full well that she likely wasn't going to be joining them. *I think he may allow me to stay on for a brief time while I'm getting things organized and moved out... He wouldn't just put me out in the street.* She had to wonder, though. She had broken the contract and as such Mr. Stewart could do pretty much whatever he wanted.

Annie took a deep breath and went to Mr. Stewart's office, gently rapping on the door and then standing aside a bit so she wouldn't be just awkwardly standing right there in the center of the doorway. She wished that she could hide. This was the biggest thing she'd ever done in her life, perhaps even more so than getting the job because she hated confrontation. Mr. Stewart opened the door after a few moments, looking around curiously until his gaze fell upon Annie standing there waiting for him. "Miss O'Brien?" he asked her, surprised to see her there. "What are you doing out of your dormitory? It's closing time, you know."

He looked at his pocket watch, checking to make sure that she wasn't breaking her curfew. Annie was pleased that at least she was following *that* rule.

"Good evening. I'm sorry it's late, but I have some news, sir," she said. "I thought you would want to know right away. I'm engaged to be married. It just happened this afternoon."

She showed him the diamond ring, even though Mr. Stewart hadn't even asked for proof. He appeared shocked at this news, but more in a happy way. She knew that he wished for all of his waiter-girls to get married someday, otherwise what was the point of bringing them out west and keeping them proper for a year? He was giving them work and getting good press and clientele from the girls, but ultimately, he hoped to bring lovely young ladies out west to grow the town and give it a woman's touch. Annie knew that, but still she was nervous about letting him down.

"My, my," Mr. Stewart said, tutting a little bit. He smiled at her then. "You seem awfully anxious about this, but it's a happy occasion! I had no idea that you were interested in all that. Of course, I knew that gentlemen had been courting you. Miss De La Cruz let me know that a gentleman was writing to you. I must confess that I shall be sad to lose you. I hope you'll stay in Wallace." He offered his hand to Annie.

She shook his hand, biting her lip slightly. She felt like she might start crying, but her heart also leapt for joy over the fact that Mr. Stewart wasn't at all mad about what had happened. *I haven't burned this bridge,* she thought. *He still hopes that I shall stick around!*

Of course, now that she thought about it, she recalled that he had been much the same when Carrie and Beverly had married their respective husbands. All the time, she'd been trying to be better than they had been, but Mr. Stewart still seemed quite fond of her friends and the work they'd done at his restaurant. He never really had an ill word to say about any of his waitresses. *I don't know why I was so afraid. I suppose it's more that I must leave him.*

"I shall really miss this place and working for you," Annie told Mr. Stewart. "Thank you so, so much for giving me this job and home when I needed it the most."

"Of course, of course," Mr. Stewart said with another handsome smile. "And while you're getting things ready to move out and be happily wed, please do stay here. I don't want you thinking you must hasten off to an inn or something like that. You're welcome to stay here until that blessed day."

"Thank you, sir," Annie replied. This made sense to her. He was still trying to ensure that things remained chaste between her and her husband-to-be until they were married.

She left the restaurant not long after that, not feeling quite so heavy about it because she now knew that she didn't need to leave right away. When she arrived back in her dormitory room, she found Melissa sitting there on her bed like usual. She was already in her white nightgown, her ringlets down at her shoulders. Annie took the bow off of her head and allowed her own hair down, shaking out her cinnamon curls. She smiled at her friend. It would be much easier to tell her the news. The scariest part was over.

"Now I can tell you," she said, sitting down at her vanity and removing her shoes and apron. "I just got back from speaking with Mr. Stewart. I'm going to be leaving soon. I'm not sure when yet, but soon."

Melissa appeared to be alarmed at first. "What? Why? Are you in trouble?"

Annie shook her head and smiled at her. She held out her left hand so that Melissa could see the sparkling ring that was there on her finger. "Mr. Prescott asked me to marry him this afternoon and I said yes."

Melissa squealed excitedly and bounded from her bed. She came over to get a better look at Annie's ring and then the two friends hugged each other and bounced around in their mirth. Suddenly, there was a knock on their door and the stern face of Rita was staring down at them. Somehow, she always seemed much taller when she had taken on her schoolmarm persona.

"What's going on in here?" Rita demanded, looking between the two girls, from one to the other and back at Annie. "Are you causing trouble, Annie? This isn't like you."

Annie reddened. She hated that for once she was indeed causing trouble... "I'm sorry, Rita. I didn't mean to be so loud. But you see, I'm engaged." She showed her the ring on her finger, flashing it around in the lantern light for maximum 'wow' effect. "I've just come in from telling Mr. Stewart."

Rita looked at her in amazement, but then she smiled. "I knew this was going to happen," she said. "As soon as you started receiving letters, I just knew that you would be next."

Annie was a lovely shade of pink. "I certainly didn't plan

this," she said. "But it just so happens that this gentleman – my fiancé – golly, it feels nice to say that... He was exchanging letters with me back before I moved here from Massachusetts."

Rita's eyes widened. "And he tracked you down here? This is no coincidence."

"No," Melissa agreed with a happy nod of her head. "It's a miracle."

Annie laughed a little. "Well, it's something like that." *I suppose that's what fate is. A miracle. A blessing.* "When he first arrived in the restaurant, I had no idea who he was, of course, but he was drawn to me and met with me again later... I suppose we were just destined to be together somehow, some way."

Rita smiled, touched. She placed a hand on her chest as she stood there in the doorway. "That's the sweetest story I've ever heard. Congratulations, dear! I'm so happy for you!" She hugged Annie and then pulled back to get a good look at her. Annie was wearing the black dress without any of its additional accessories. "Of course, we're all going to miss you here so much. You simply must visit."

"I shall miss you all too," Annie said. "That was one of the reasons I was so resistant at first... But Mr. Stewart says I may work here a little longer as I get reacquainted with Mr. Prescott again. Keeping things respectable, you know." She smiled. "It will also give me some time to prepare to move away."

Annie had no idea what sort of place she would be moving to. Thackery had promised that they'd be able to live in a farmhouse in Wallace, but she thought they'd first have to live in Sharon Springs for a time. He needed to earn enough money to buy his own place, and she didn't think it was fair to keep him waiting forever to marry her... As long as they handled things properly. He was free to court her now. She was more than a little giddy about that.

I've never been the girl who was courted and flirted with, she thought. *Only in letters. And letters don't really count.* Annie was glad, in that way, that they had more time in person to get to know one another.

She went to sleep that night, dreaming happy dreams about what may lay ahead for her when she did finally leave the nest of the Stewart House.

9

Thackery seemed surprised when he found out that Annie was still working at the restaurant when he showed up to spend time with her the next day. He was really tenacious and Annie was no longer surprised by his constant vigilance when it came to pursuing her. *After all, he did say that he wasn't going to leave me alone ever again,* she thought with a smile.

"I'm guessing that the big boss was okay with you being engaged," Thackery said to her, admiring her black and white uniform.

She smiled back at him, nodding her head and blushing a little. "He sure was. He told me that I was welcome to stay while we get things figured out and planned."

"That's terrific," Thackery replied. "It wouldn't be right if he demanded you leave immediately on account of me."

They strolled along the dirt lane together, having a bit of a 'get-to-know-you' chat. Although they'd written letters to each other, that had been a while ago now so they needed some reminding about things. "What's it been like for you?" she asked him. "Being a farmhand and going from town to town...?"

Thackery smiled a wistful sort of smile. "I've really enjoyed it, actually. It's a great way to see the west and all that it has to offer. I moved out here to settle down and even though I haven't yet, I've found that I'm much more content than I was when I lived back east."

Annie looked at him as they walked along the winding path. She smoothed a strand of hair behind her ear. Without her white bow, her unruly locks didn't like staying in place as much. That was one good thing about the silly piece of head-wear. "And you don't think that settling here in Wallace instead of continuing to be a migrant worker will end up making you feel bored or stuck?"

He gave her a sincere look. Whenever Thackery looked into her eyes, she could feel like he was looking into her very heart. "No, I don't think so. Not if I have you with me."

"You're putting an awful lot of faith in me," Annie said. "I'm a little frightened that I'm going to disappoint you now."

Thackery chuckled and shook his head. "As long as

you're my companion in all of this, then I know I shall be completely happy and at peace with whatever comes."

She smiled at him a little. "I did think of something I could do as far as keeping myself occupied, once I'm no longer working at the restaurant. And I think it will be a good help for you, too."

He raised his eyebrows. "Oh really?" he asked her. "What's that?"

"I was thinking that I could become a sort of teacher, for the people in town who might need reading and writing lessons," Annie said. "A tutor, of sorts."

Thackery grinned at her. "That's a terrific idea!" he enthused, nodding his head. "I would like that a lot. I know there are plenty of fellows around these parts who can't read or write so good."

She nodded back at him. "Well," she corrected gently. "Can't read or write so *well*."

"See? You're starting already," he said with another laugh.

They held each other's hands now as they walked, passing all of the businesses in the small town and eventually ending up out near where Carrie lived. Thackery gazed with no small amount of envy at the sprawling farmhouses that were situated there. He still had a long way to go before he could afford a bit of land of his own. Annie thought that she could help him in that effort, too.

Time slipped by, the shadows stretched out ahead of them in the dirt and sand, and it was time for Annie to return to work. She gave Thackery a sweet hug farewell. "This was nice," she said. "We should do this again sometime soon."

"It was nice... Do you ever have a day off?" he asked her. "Not that I'd ever presume to take up your whole day, it's only that I'd like to have more time with you than what I've currently been blessed with."

Annie blushed. "It just so happens that I am available on Saturday, in two days' time."

Thackery grinned at her and kissed her hand. "Saturday, it is. Afternoon again, maybe? Like today? Except hopefully for longer."

She giggled a little. "That sounds delightful," she said. "I shall see you then."

Annie turned and went back to work after that, smiling and feeling the sort of butterflies-in-stomach giddiness that she hadn't felt in probably over a year. After watching her friends all run off and get married, she had to admit that it was nice to finally be the one running off and spending time being courted by a kind and charming young man. *I was never jealous of my friends,* she thought. *But it was largely because I felt as though I didn't deserve this kind of happiness. It seemed to have passed me by. And yet... Here he is. My knight in shining armor has returned.*

When she arrived back at work, Rita gave her a curious sort of look. "You surely had a nice break," she said, raising an eyebrow. "Were you off on an outing with that Mr. Prescott fellow?"

Annie nodded her head. "Who else would I be with?" she asked her innocently. "We're engaged to be married. It wouldn't be proper if I went around with someone else."

Rita laughed a short laugh. "You have me there."

All throughout the dinner rush that evening, Annie imagined what her and Thackery's wedding would be like. She'd never planned a wedding before. Sure, she'd been a part of her friends' weddings recently, but it wasn't the same as being the actual bride. She wondered if she might talk to her intended to see what he might've envisioned for the day, too. He clearly had been thinking about this for a long time.

On Saturday, Annie allowed herself to sleep in a little bit because she didn't have to go to work. She rolled over and dozed off again once Rita had knocked on the door to wake up Melissa. Her roommate didn't bother her or try to wake her up. When Annie rose from her bed, the girls were all gone to the restaurant and she was able to take her time brushing through her long hair and putting on one of her prettier dresses – a white skirt with a blue velvet bodice that her mother had made her just before she moved away to Kansas. *This dress was made for Thackery,* she thought. *This was meant to be my first impression dress.* She smiled a bit sadly at her reflection in her vanity's mirror.

As soon as she was dressed and dolled up in the way that she wanted – her hair pinned up in a fashionable Newport hairstyle with plenty of braids and pins – she left the dormitory room and walked carefully down the staircase. The only other shoes that Annie had besides her work shoes were a pair of white, heeled ankle boots. She was a bit wobbly on them because it had been quite a while since she last wore them, but they went rather nicely with her dress. She knew that this dress would make a great impression on Thackery, even if it wasn't the first one he'd seen her in.

There's something a bit poetic about him first seeing me at the restaurant, actually, she thought with a smile as she walked out the door and along the dirt road to their meeting place. She bit her lip a little, looking around for the gentleman. He wasn't there yet and of course her mind went into a slightly panicked mode. *Where is he? Has he changed his mind? Has he had some kind of accident?*

Her hysteria calmed a moment later when she felt a light tap on her shoulder and she turned to find Mr. Prescott standing there. Much like she had dressed up for their little 'date,' he was dressed in the finest outfit she'd ever seen him in before. He wore black pants, a deep red shirt and a black ascot. He held his usual brown cowboy hat in his hands as he smiled at her and bowed.

"Good afternoon, Miss Annie," he said to her pleasantly. "And isn't it a lovely day?"

She smiled back at him, nodding her head. "Good afternoon, Thackery," she replied. "It certainly is a nice day. I wonder how many more we shall have until it rains or snows again." The winters in Wallace were not terrible, but they weren't always the nicest in which to be outdoors.

He was giving her a thoughtful sort of look now. "I've been thinking about that," he said as they began to walk alongside each other up the road. "If it's not too much trouble, what do you say to getting married here in Wallace before moving with me to Sharon Springs just for a time, til I can save up enough to buy a farmhouse here?"

Annie was taken aback by this idea, but she didn't necessarily dislike it. *I'd have to leave this place... But surely only for a brief time. Until we get things settled. Otherwise, he would have to go back to Sharon Springs without me and I wouldn't want that.* She smiled at him slightly, appearing neither enthusiastic nor against the idea. "If it seems that it is the best option to you, then I won't argue with you. But surely you don't plan to get married frightfully soon. After all, we have to plan for it. I don't even have a dress."

She fidgeted a little with the sparkly ring on her finger. He noticed and, smiling, took her hand in his. "We can take all the time you think you need," he told her. "I wouldn't want you to get married in a dress you didn't want to be wearing."

She plucked up the courage then to ask him if there were any things that he hoped to have for their wedding. "I know it's not normally the gentleman's concern, but I should hate to plan something that you're unsatisfied with."

He laughed softly. "Dearest, as long as I get to marry you I don't really have a preference about anything else."

This was as she had predicted. Annie smiled at him,

letting a small breath of relief escape her. She gently squeezed his hand. "You truly are a blessing to me," she said. "I'm so sorry that I ever doubted you. Thank God that you found me in the Stewart House and saved me from my tower."

He smiled and placed a small peck on her cheek. "To be fair, there are worse towers to be trapped in," he said.

They strolled along the road, hand in hand, as Annie thought about all of the things that she was going to have to think about now. *I never thought that I'd be the one thinking of white lace and flowers,* she mused. *But I suppose that it was bound to happen eventually. I was blinded by my broken heart.*

The first thing she knew was that Carrie had to be her matron of honor and help her with all of these tasks. *Perhaps she can even help me make my dress!* She knew that her friend was a happy farmer's wife now, but Carrie also didn't have too much to do outside of cooking and maintaining the crops. Things like that. Annie believed that she would love to have a wedding to help with. *And Rita and Melissa should be a part of it, too. After all, they were the ones who gently pushed me towards Mr. Prescott in the first place.* She smiled to herself. Yes, planning wouldn't be so difficult with all of her friends helping her.

10

Carrie was more than happy to help Annie with her wedding dress and planning. "This makes me so happy!" she said gleefully, bouncing up and down with Annie. As soon as Annie came over and asked her for her help, Carrie got out all of her fabrics and sewing supplies. It was all strewn about her living room as they discussed everything. "I really like the cut of your dress right now." Carrie looked Annie up and down, mentally making notes about it so she might be able to emulate it.

Meanwhile, Thackery worked out a good time and date for the wedding to take place at the chapel in Wallace. Annie recalled Carrie's lovely wedding there so she knew that it was going to be the perfect setting. Everyone who knew her would be able to be in attendance because they were marrying in the familiar town instead of going off and getting married in Sharon Springs. Annie was still a little nervous about making that journey, but she knew that she wouldn't be alone. Thackery would be accompanying her, and that made all of the difference.

She was going to be so sad to bid farewell to her home and her friends at the Stewart House, but she knew that it was time for her to move on with her life. She was not someone to go against fate. While she made plans with the help of Carrie, Melissa, and Rita, Annie also worked on carefully packing up her belongings so she would be able to move out of the dormitory as soon as the wedding was over and it was time to ride forth to Sharon Springs.

She stopped working as a waitress in the restaurant and turned in her uniform, crying a little as she handed it off to Rita. "I hope you find someone wonderful to take my place."

Rita sniffled a little. "We'll find someone new to fill the position, but no one is going to take your place."

Annie hugged her gently. "I've never been fond of goodbyes," she said. "And I know that I'm not going anywhere just yet, but I just want you to know that this is difficult for me. This is the hardest thing I've ever had to do."

Rita patted her back a little bit. "You don't need to say goodbye, you know. You're going to come back eventually, after all." She smiled, but there was some amount of sadness in that smile. She knew that there was going to be a long period in which Annie was not in Wallace. And there was indeed a chance that she and Thackery would never make it back. Who knew how much money he was going to need to raise in order to start a farm in Wallace?

"We will certainly be looking forward to your return," she said sincerely to Annie.

A few days later, it was the morning of the wedding and Annie was nervously pacing back and forth in her bedroom. Melissa was on hand to help her get dressed into her wedding gown and fix up her hair. Carrie arrived with the new gown in a box and she opened it up to show them her creation. It was a long gown, down to Annie's ankles, with a long-sleeved lace bodice in the same style as her blue velvet one.

"Oh, Carrie, it's absolutely gorgeous!" Annie exclaimed tearfully. She grinned as her friends helped her get into the dress and placed the veil onto her head.

Melissa then placed the white daisies into Annie's hands and the ladies all went out together to get into the special wedding day carriage that had been set up. Leeroy was more than happy to drive them to the chapel.

"This is so bittersweet," she said to her friends as they rode in the carriage together. "It's the first day of the rest of my life, but it means I have to leave you all."

They all held hands as they rode in the carriage and tried not to think too much about the sad farewell that was going to come at the end of the wedding. As soon as they arrived at the chapel, they all went into the small room that was meant for the bridal party. Annie's friends peeked out of the door to see Thackery standing at the front of the room, next to the minister. Now that they were inside the chapel, Leeroy appeared and sat in one of the pews near the front.

The organist began to play the wedding waltz and Carrie, Melissa and Rita slowly made their way up the aisle towards Thackery and the minister. They stood on the left side and awaited Annie.

Annie walked two steps at a time up the aisle, smiling and nodding at friends that she saw in the pews as she walked. Mr. Stewart was there, smiling away. It meant the world to her that he was there.

Finally, she arrived at the front of the aisle and Thackery came towards her, taking her hands and facing her as they stood together in front of the minister.

"Dearly beloved, we are gathered here today to share in the joy and the celebration of these two souls as they are joined together in holy matrimony," the minister said. "James Thackery Prescott and Annie Louise O'Brien, you have come here today to pledge your lives to one another. As it is written in Romans 12:9-10, *Love must be sincere. Hate what is evil; cling to what is good. Be devoted to one another in love. Honor one another above yourselves.*"

Annie and Thackery gazed at each other as they held hands. Even though they were surrounded by all of her friends and people who meant so much to her, she only had eyes for him now.

The minister looked at Thackery. "James Thackery Prescott," he intoned, "do you take Annie Louise O'Brien to be your lawfully-wedded wife? To have and to hold, to love and to cherish, to honor and protect, forsaking all others, in sickness and in health, until death do you part as long as you both shall live?"

Thackery was smiling away at Annie. For a moment, she thought that he might not have heard her. But then suddenly he said, "I do. I surely do!"

The minister now turned his attentions to Annie. "Annie Louise O'Brien, do you take James Thackery Prescott to be your lawfully-wedded husband? To have and to hold, to love and to cherish, to honor and obey, forsaking all others, in sickness and in health, until death do you part as long as you both shall live?"

Annie bit her lip. Then she remembered that doing that was going to mess up her makeup, so she stopped. Gazing into Thackery's eyes, she nodded her head. "Yes," she said. "I do."

A cheer went up from the pews then and the minister smiled at Annie and Thackery. "Then by the power which has been vested in me by our lord and savior Jesus Christ as well as the great little town of Wallace, Kansas, I now pronounce you husband and wife."

There was another cheer. Annie giggled and Thackery laughed. They were both getting antsy for what the future would bring for them soon.

"You may kiss the bride," the minister concluded.

Thackery let go of Annie's hands and gently moved back her veil so he could at last gaze upon her uncovered face. He leaned in and gave her a sweet kiss that left her lips buzzing with excitement.

The organist began playing the exit music and everyone cheered as Annie and Thackery rushed down the aisle, hand in hand. They went out the doors of the chapel and to a new carriage, the one that was going to take them to their new home a town away. Annie's luggage had already been carefully packed up into it by Leeroy and Carrie. Everyone rushed out of the chapel in order to see them off, her friends waving their handkerchiefs and crying happy, bittersweet tears.

Thackery helped Annie into the carriage before getting in himself, and then they were off down the dirt road and onward toward their new life in Sharon Springs.

EPILOGUE

Life in Sharon Springs really wasn't all that bad, as far as Annie was concerned. The people there were nice and she could see that her new husband was quite proud of all that he had accomplished there. Thackery was a well sought-after farmhand, helping out on all kinds of farms both with the horses and with the crops. Annie could see that he had the skills necessary to start up his own farm business; he just needed the funds.

While they were living there, Annie took to living in the small shacks that were given to Thackery while he worked on each farm. It wasn't much of a living arrangement, but it was better than sleeping in an inn away from him. After several long months, Thackery was ready to move on from his work there. He counted up his money and realized that he was only a few more dollars away from having enough to purchase a nice spot of land near Carrie and Leeroy's farm.

"I can help you with that, you know," Annie told him brightly. "After all, I didn't work for nearly a year at the restaurant for nothing." She brought out her purse and showed him all of the money that she had saved up from her time as a waitress.

Thackery was surprised and impressed. "I couldn't possibly ask you to give up your hard-earned pay, though," he said. "This is my dream, not yours."

"Hey," she said to him, giving him a little cuddle as they sat together on their small couch in the living room of the farmhand shack. "When I married you, I took a vow. Your dreams are my dreams now. Your destiny is tied to mine. And besides, I want to share my wages with you. Otherwise what did I earn them for? I don't want my purse to remain full of money that we could be putting to good use."

Thackery realized that Annie wasn't going to take a polite no for an answer, so he decided to allow her to help him. With their combined wages, they had enough money to not only purchase the land but to start building their farmhouse, too.

As soon as they'd moved back into town, Annie decided to pay a visit to all of her friends. She was neighbors with Carrie now, which was a situation she had always hoped for, in the end. She went to Beverly and told her about every-thing that had happened.

"I'm impressed," Beverly said to her with a grin. "You're more business-minded than I thought."

"Perhaps I learned some of that from you," Annie said with a smile of her own.

At last, she returned to the restaurant with her husband in tow. They dined there like normal customers, but of course Rita was ecstatic when she saw them there. "Oh, please don't be strangers!" she bade them. "Come here as often as you like. I know we'd all like to hear about your time in Sharon Springs."

"And what married life is like," Melissa added.

Annie laughed. "It feels so wonderful to be back," she said to them. "I owe my life to this place."

True to her word, she set up a small school in the town. Most of her students were grown men who were in need of reading and writing lessons, though as the small town grew and prospered, she started to see more young children in her class.

Mrs. Annie Prescott would never need know a day without work, and that was just the way she liked it.

THE END

RITA: THE DETERMINED BRIDE

STEWART HOUSE BRIDES

RITA: THE DETERMINED BRIDE

Wallace, Kansas – 1890

Rita De la Cruz has been the supervising waiter-girl at the Stewart House for long enough. She's witnessed all of her friends going off to start new lives with their new beaus, and now, she is ready to follow in their footsteps. She carefully crafts an advertisement for a mail-order husband and is delighted to receive many letters in response. Soon, her days are filled not only with working at the restaurant – which is growing busier by the shift, it seems – but also with writing letters to the sweet men who, like her, are looking for love.

Her friends are all excited for her, but when the owner of the restaurant, Mr. Stewart, discovers that she is meeting with potential suitors, he is infuriated for reasons Rita never expected. Will she be able to leave the restaurant that's become her home and the man who has become her dearest friend?

1

"Rise and shine, ladies!" Rita called, gently knocking upon each door in the hall of the dormitory. "The breakfast train will be arriving in an hour."

She knew that waking up the sleeping waiter-girls wasn't very pleasant for them, but Rita also knew that, if it wasn't for her help, they'd sleep the day away. And how would they earn a living, then?

"Ugh," one of the girls grumbled at her when she opened a bedroom door to check that they were rising from their beds. "I'm up, I'm up."

Rita smiled a dimpled smile. "Just making sure, Elise. After all, time sure has a way of flying by sometimes."

Boy, don't I know that, she thought to herself as she closed the door and continued on her way to perform more of her morning duties. Rita de la Cruz had been working at the Stewart House restaurant for almost two years now. She'd been there from the very start, when Mr. Stewart first opened his restaurant and sent out ads for waitresses. Rita applied when she was twenty-eight years old, living with her wealthy parents in New York City; an heiress who wished to do more with her time than attend parties and donate money at auctions and the like. She entered the restaurant business with much aplomb and enthusiasm. It was a welcome difference from the way Rita had lived before, and the west proved to be a wonderful new experience for her. Of course, all of this was strengthened by the fact that she and Mr. Stewart hit it off so well. The man was a genius in her eyes.

Once she'd gone around rapping on doors, Rita went down the steps of the dormitory and walked out the front door, taking the quick stroll over to the restaurant next door. She was a key-holder of the place, as the lead waitress, so she unlocked it and went into the back room. The trio of cooks were already there as well, preparing and cooking the lots of delicious food for breakfast. Some of the food they made came from the ice box after traveling via train to their location, but a great many items were easily found for them right there in Wallace – the farmers around town had eggs, for example, and the local butcher provided the restaurant with cuts of beef on a regular basis. Rita smiled at them as they set about their work. "Good morning," she said pleasantly. It was nice to be greeted by some ladies who didn't seem quite so bleary-eyed. These women had come from farms where rising with the sun was the norm.

Mr. Stewart of course doesn't expect his waiter-girls to be quite so early to rise, she mused. *But it's clear that these girls have been coddled all of their lives.* Generally, the ladies who were hired to work in the restaurant came from backgrounds like Rita's – they were city girls in search of adventure and employment in a challenging yet rewarding environment. But Rita was noticing that lately, the girls that applied for work were ideal-istic and a bit lazy. She missed her friends Carrie, Beverly, and Annie. They'd been hard workers, but had all stayed a regrettably short amount of time, with Annie being the exception. She was still sad about Annie's departure, even though it had been nearly a month ago now.

At least Melissa is still here, she thought. *I can continue to train her without worrying if she's paying attention or not.* Rita wasn't going to count any of them out of course, but it was draining to deal with girls who didn't seem to care as much as she did.

Rita went into the main room of the eatery, going from table to table and carefully spreading out the white linen table cloths onto each of them. She then went around and placed little potted flowers on in the center of each table so there would be an extra sweet touch there to greet each customer. The flowers had been her idea and she was proud of it. Once she was done seeing to the organization of things before the morning rush, she made her way to Mr. Stewart's office and went inside.

He had a large, oak desk that was festooned with paperwork. The gentleman worked very hard, from generating publicity to purchasing needed items. He was good at a great many things, but staying organized was not one of them. Rita smiled to herself and walked calmly up to his desk, sitting in his large leather chair and carefully arranging his papers into neat stacks, arranged by subject matter and urgency.

Mr. Stewart came into the restaurant not long after and bustled his way into his office like he usually did. He removed his coat and hat and smiled at Rita as he placed them carefully onto the wooden rack to the right of his door. "Good morning, Rita!" he said to her in a chipper voice. "Anything that you recommend I pay attention to first this fine morning?"

He winked at her and she blushed a little as she rose out of his chair so that he could come over and have a seat. He was a handsome, middle-aged man with graying light brown hair and brown eyes with bits of gray in them as well. He was a clean-shaven, dapper sort of fellow and Rita liked that he always appeared dressed in nice suits rather than dressing like so many men in the west. He reminded her of the businessmen from New York City, except there was a friendly openness about him. He was never stuffy, especially towards her. She felt more or less like an equal in his eyes, and this was a big reason why, no matter how she may have felt about the rest of the job, she knew that she must always be loyal to him. She moved to the opposite side of his desk and looked at him with a slight air of authority. She'd been proving herself to him every moment that she'd known him and she wasn't about to stop now. "Mr. Maddox requests an estimate for next month's order," she informed him. "And some new advertisements are needed for the coming season."

"Thank you," Mr. Stewart said to her with a nod, glancing over the papers that she'd neatly arranged in front of him. "How are the new girls?"

"Quality, for the most part," she told him. "A few of them are a bit slow to get used to their new schedule, but I'm sure they will soon. They do seem to learn quickly."

Mr. Stewart nodded his head again. "Splendid." He pulled out his gold pocket watch and tutted a bit. "The train will be here in less than twenty minutes now."

Rita nodded. "Yes, sir. I'll see that everyone's ready and in their places."

She left the office and went back to the small room which joined with the kitchen. Thankfully, the girls had arrived there. Rita smiled at them, inwardly breathing a sigh of relief that the timing had worked out well in the end. She didn't worry about a great many things, but she did get flustered about logistics at times. Especially when the logistics were a bit out of her control because they depended on others.

"Good morning again, everyone," she said to the whole group once everyone had arrived in the room. "In just a few moments, Mr. Stewart and I will open the doors of the restaurant and invite in our guests from the breakfast train."

Rita adopted names like that to describe the morning, afternoon and evening trains that stopped in at the station in Wallace in order for the riders to catch a meal along their journey west. Mr. Stewart had championed the idea of allowing visitors to the west to experience the best, most convenient way to travel and in so doing, he'd garnered much praise and attention from travelers and vacationers.

The new girls, though nervous and hesitant at first, seemed excited to be working this first shift of the day. Rita went out into the restaurant to her hostess area and all of the girls fanned out behind her, going to their various tables and places where they were meant to greet the incoming customers and see to their needs. "Good morning," she beamed as people started coming into the eating house. Rita saw to it that they all found a place at the tables. There were some people who couldn't be seated due to a lack of space, which Rita was becoming used to even though it still alarmed her somewhat.

We seem to never have enough room for everyone anymore, she thought. "Please allow me to accompany you over to our waiting area next door until some of these tables empty out," she said to the overflow of people. Thankfully, there were only ten people who were unable to be seated this morning. The restaurant hadn't had to turn anyone completely away before, but Rita worried a that that day might soon be coming.

She led the customers next door and into the dormitory. In the lobby, there were four little parlor rooms that were intended for small gatherings of people – generally just two people – but they served this purpose quite nicely as well. At least the customers could be seated and relax while they waited.

"I'm terribly sorry about the wait," she said to them. "Please have a seat in here and we will be with you momentarily, as soon as some tables open up for you."

The customers grumbled a little bit, but as soon as she went from parlor to parlor taking their drink orders, they were all smiles and began chatting amongst themselves. Rita quickly went back into the kitchen of the restaurant. She filled glasses of juice or water and carefully placed them onto a silver tray. "Deirdre, can you please assist me a moment?" she asked one of the waiter-girls who was loitering in the breakroom, not doing anything.

Together, she and the other waitress went into the lobby of the dorm and served the drinks to the customers there.

This is something I really must speak with Mr. Stewart about, she thought. *I wonder if it's time for him to expand the eating house a little; make it bigger so we can squeeze more tables in.*

Rita didn't know how likely or feasible that would be for her employer. She knew that the business had become an overnight success, but that didn't mean that Mr. Stewart had the means to expand his restaurant necessarily. He took his budget very seriously. She remembered how he had reacted when former waitress Beverly had come forward with the idea of working together with the local butcher. *He'd hated the idea at first,* Rita recalled. *But eventually he did come around...*

However, as soon as she returned to the restaurant, she noticed that a few tables had cleared out so there really wasn't any reason to go on worrying about it for now. She quickly went back to inform the guests in the dormitory that they would now be seated. She led them back to the restaurant and helped them to the tables that were now available.

A big part of Rita's job was telling people where to go. As the lead waitress, she acted more as a manager there than an actual waitress. Once all of the customers were taken care of, she did rounds around the room, making sure that everyone was happy and the waitresses were all doing a good job. Before long, the train outside at the station gave a toot of its horn, alerting the girls and their customers that breakfast was over.

"Goodbye," Rita said to the passengers as they headed back out the doors and towards their train. "Thank you ever so much for stopping in at Stewart House."

Now that the breakfast rush was over, it was time to do some light tidying up and then, of course, get a bit of rest before the lunch train arrived. Rita looked at the grandfather clock near the front entrance of the eatery. *It won't be long now,* she thought. *I wonder if there are any leftovers in the kitchen that I might be able to grab in the meantime.*

It was a tiring job and Rita felt that she was often living in a flurry of excitement, but she did enjoy it. She couldn't imagine doing anything else with her time, and she certainly couldn't imagine going back to the life she'd led before she saw the advertisement in the newspaper. Then again, now that her friends had all run off and gotten married, Rita often wondered if God had a similar plan in store for her, as well.

2

During her longer break, Rita often met with Carrie and Annie for lunch at one of the other ladies' homes. Ever since they'd gotten married and moved away from the restaurant, Rita found that it was easier to spend time with them as friends and equals. *That's the price I pay for being a supervisor,* she thought. *The girls are intimidated by me until they're away from my authority.* One of the good things, then, about these ladies no longer working for the restaurant was that she could now be close to them and go to them for advice and companionship.

"I know that both of you had your own troubles with the mail order service," Rita said to Carrie and Annie as they sat together at the small dining table in Carrie's house. Her home was cozy, though it had clearly been built for a couple or perhaps a small family of three. "I've just been considering my options lately. I can't stay at the restaurant forever, and even if I could I'm not sure that I would want to. I resisted marriage back in New York because it seemed like such a finality, but now, I must admit, I'm envious of you both." She smiled slightly, letting her dimples show a bit. "I don't want my life or love to completely pass me by."

Her friends gave her a sympathetic look. Annie took her by the hand and gently squeezed a little. "Let's not forget that my mail order story turned out just fine," she said with a shy smile. "It was rocky at the start, but it turned out well in the end."

"That's a good point," Carrie added. "Listen, just because we may have had our difficulties doesn't mean that you will. I think it's a great option, especially since you're already out here. It'll make it easier for the western would-be grooms to know that there's a beautiful single woman right here in their very own town."

Rita laughed, blushing profusely. "Oh, shush. And suppose that the only people who respond to me lived further away? Just imagine if he lived all the way in California. I would hate to be away from all of my friends!"

Annie thought about it. "You could mention that in your advertisement?" she offered. "Say that you're hoping to stick close to home."

Carrie nodded in agreement. "Yes, this could work out nicely! I'm sure there are loads of men around here who are looking to settle down. They just haven't found the opportunity or the chance yet."

"And they also might have difficulty with writing an ad," Annie said. "Which was my husband's case. So perhaps if you do the work for them..."

Carrie giggled. "Make the effort and see what sort of men respond. We'll help you revise it if you'd like."

Rita and her friends continued to lunch together, eating fresh chicken sandwiches and vegetables. Carrie was a wonderful hostess and Rita wasn't surprised at all, given the way she had worked so well at the restaurant. She hoped that the newer waiter-girls would begin to work as hard as her friends had when they were at the Stewart House. *I wonder if I'm becoming bitter and cynical in my older age.* She was going to be thirty soon enough, and though that wasn't really all that old, she was the only person her age that she knew of who wasn't yet married. It was easy to feel cynical.

After a while, it was time for Rita to return to her work at the restaurant. She rose from her chair. "Thank you both so much for meeting with me," she said to them. "Allow me to help you clean the dishes before I head back." They went into Carrie's kitchen and carefully soaked the dishes in soap and water, then Rita dried them each by hand before setting them out to continue drying along the counter. The friends hugged each other and then she departed back to the Stewart House to deal with yet more dirty dishes.

Others have rougher jobs, though, surely, she thought as she walked along the dirt road. She hadn't removed her black dress even though this was her longer break; she simply utilized the trick of removing her bow and apron so that she wasn't walking around in full restaurant uniform in front of onlookers. As soon as she was in the back room of the restaurant, she tied on her white apron and quickly went in search of the nearest mirror so she could tie the big, white bow back into her hair.

That done, she was ready to open up the floor for the dinner shift. "Where is Margaret?" she asked several of the girls, looking around. "Where's Regina and Trudy??" There was no time to wait for the tardy girls to appear, because the dinnertime train unloaded its passengers into the restaurant and it was time to focus on them and their needs. Rita rushed out at once to greet them, smiling at everyone she met.

"Welcome to the Stewart House," she chirped in a friendly voice. "I'm Rita. We're so glad to have you here with us for dinnertime."

Before too long, the young lady named Margaret slipped into the room, anxiously tying her apron strings as she walked in. Her blonde-brown hair was a bit unkempt and her bow was askew but Rita had never been happier to see her. That only left the girl named Trudy... Time ticked away, but she never arrived.

I better mention this to Mr. Stewart, Rita thought, making a mental note to herself. *I should also ask in the break room if anyone knows what's become of her.* She hoped that Trudy wasn't ill or anything like that. She also hoped that the girl hadn't chosen to run away. That had happened a few times in the past, when girls were too afraid of disappointing Mr. Stewart to let him know that they'd had enough or they wanted to be married.

As soon as she could wrest herself away from the restaurant floor, Rita went into the back room and looked around for any of the waitresses who might be aware of the young waiter-girl's whereabouts. A roommate or a friend. Finally, she found Trudy's roommate Felicity. "Do you know where Trudy might be?" she asked her, trying not to sound too angry or desperate.

Felicity bit her lip and shook her head. "She never said anything to me. She went away on her break like she always does and I've not seen her since. Is she in trouble?"

Rita didn't wish to lie. "Possibly," she said. "Unless she's got a good reason for disappearing."

She went back out into the restaurant and finished up the dinner shift with the other girls, serving the tables that would've been Trudy's responsibility. Rita enjoyed being able to act as a waitress instead of simply watching and keeping the girls in line, but she didn't enjoy the fact that she was going to be forced to have a difficult conversation with their employer on Trudy's behalf as well.

As soon as the customers all went back to their train, Rita and the girls tidied up and then she went to Mr. Stewart's office and knocked on the door to give him her usual evening report. "I'm afraid we've had one unaccounted for absence today," she told him right away. "Trudy Nichols didn't show up for the evening shift, though her roommate Felicity told me that she wasn't acting unusual before she went on her break."

Mr. Stewart gazed across his desk at her as she sat there in the chair across from him. For a moment, his mouth just opened and closed a few times. "Did she return from her break?"

Rita shook her head. "Felicity said that the last time she saw her was when she went off on her break."

Mr. Stewart sighed. "I see," he said. "Well, I suppose the contract was too difficult for her to keep. I will review some of our newest applicants and let you know who might be joining us soon."

Rita nodded a little bit. "I'll let you know, of course, if Trudy shows up again. It's possible something has happened to her which has detained her. I'm sure I don't know what, but..."

"I think I have a good idea," he replied, looking right into her eyes. "It happens to the best of us, I'm afraid."

She didn't quite know what was meant by that look he'd given her. *He doesn't know of my feelings on the matter of mail-order brides, does he?* Rita couldn't see how he would know what she was thinking. He hadn't been there at that meeting with her friends, and neither had their husbands. Mr.

Maddox might've brought the news of Rita's intentions to his attention, but Mr. Maddox had been at work in his butcher shop and Beverly hadn't been there at lunch. She was usually busily helping her husband. And even if she had been there, Rita was confident that her secrets would be safe with all three of her friends.

Rita made sure that all of the candles were out in the restaurant and then she made her way back to the dormitory. She climbed the staircase and could hear giggling and chatter going on in several of the rooms. She was relieved that at least the girls who were still around were following the curfew rules that were set into place. She didn't think she could handle chasing anyone back into the dorm tonight.

Walking slowly along the hallway, she noticed that Felicity's door was slightly ajar and Rita's heart went out to the girl. She was one of the newer waitresses, same as Trudy, and now she was going to have to spend the night alone. She didn't imagine that the girls were instant best friends or anything like that – few of the girls became so close right away – but she knew that it could be quite lonely to room in the dorm by oneself.

Rita knew this because she didn't have a roommate herself. It was thought that the supervisor should be afforded certain privileges, including having the privacy of a room to herself. Normally, Rita did enjoy having the serenity of free time spent alone in her room, away from the restaurant's noises and all of the responsibilities. Just the same, she sometimes felt lonely at night, especially now that her good friends had left the dormitory for their own adventures.

She knocked on the door and opened it a bit, offering Felicity a small smile. "I spoke to Mr. Stewart," she informed her gently. "You'll have a new roommate quite soon. In the meantime, my bedroom door will always be open for you if you'd like to chat or anything. I know it can be hard if a friend leaves you here alone."

Rita hoped that she didn't come across as odd by saying this. All the same, Felicity smiled back at her. "Thank you, Miss Rita," she said softly. "I'll remember that."

Nodding a bit, Rita went to her bedroom and readied herself for sleep. *Hopefully tomorrow will be a bit less dramatic.*

3

At work in the restaurant the next day, Rita composed her mail order advertisement in her mind as she worked. The sudden disappearance of Trudy made her wary of leaving so soon. Mr. Stewart would definitely be disappointed to lose her for the same reason that Trudy had likely left for. He had no delusions about his waiter-girls wishing to stay and forgo being married for longer than a year, but he had made that contract stipulation for a reason. He hoped to keep them around for a while. *But he has kept me around,* she thought. *Much longer than the others. Much longer than a year.*

Once she was back in her dorm room for her longer break, Rita took out a piece of paper and she tapped her pen to her lips for a few moments as she thought about the best way to word her advertisement. She knew that Carrie and Annie had offered to help her edit it afterward, but she wished to get it as near perfect as possible right off the bat. Especially because not only would this ad hopefully lead to her finding a future husband, but it also wasn't going to be free. Advertisements cost money, so it was worth carefully considering what to write.

Finally, after much hesitation, she put pen to paper and began to write:

Hard-working, caring waitress in Wallace, Kansas seeking a husband. Twenty-nine years of age. Skilled at the full range of household tasks. Willing to relocate.

Rita didn't know what else she should say. It felt so odd to her, to be trying to offer herself to anyone who was looking in the newspaper, but she supposed that it was just how it worked. Since she still had some time on her break, she carefully folded this paper up neatly and placed it into an envelope, making sure not to close it because she wasn't quite ready to send it off to be printed in the newspaper just yet.

Rita changed out of her uniform dress and into a pleasant cream-colored frock with black fabric along the sleeves and collar. Outside of work, she tended to dress rather modestly because she didn't want to attract too much attention to herself, although that was changing now. She wondered if it might soon be time to dig out her collection of more colorful gowns; the type of things that she once wore to social events in New York. Rita's time as a socialite seemed like it belonged in another life, to another girl altogether. She'd never found that to be sad until now, when she was finally letting herself reminisce a bit about the old days.

Perhaps I should include a picture? she thought as she walked down the road to Annie's home. She didn't want to always find herself knocking on Carrie's door, especially when her other friend had offered to help just as ardently. *It may be that if I was to mention my past life in New York, I'd get even more attention... Oh, but I don't want to gloat!*

Stepping up to Annie's front door, Rita gently knocked upon it, hoping that she wasn't interrupting or bothering her friend. She didn't know what Annie's husband Mr. Prescott might be up to, though she knew that he spent a great deal of time working outdoors on his farm. There'd surely be time for the ladies to relax and chat for a bit.

Annie herself opened the front door and she smiled out at her friend. "Rita! It's such a pleasant surprise to see you. Oh, please come in." She held the door open for her and stepped aside so that Rita could step in.

Gazing around at the little farmhouse, Rita let out a short whistle. "I love what you've done with the place."

"Thank you," Annie said, closing up the door and guiding her over so they could sit together on the low, green couch in the living room. "It wasn't an easy task, either getting him to settle here or getting him to commit to a certain building plan. My husband is many wonderful things, but decisive is not exactly one of them."

They giggled a bit at that as they sat there, smiling at each other. It felt just like old times in a way that Rita couldn't explain. "It's so good to see you so happy and well taken care of. I admit that I was concerned that you'd have to leave Wallace forever, so I'm glad that you convinced him to come back."

Annie giggled a little more at that. "Aww, you're too kind. He knew that I wished to stay close to my friends here, and he didn't want to go against my wishes. But enough about me. What brings you over here? Have you been giving more thought to the mail order service?"

Rita nodded with a smile. She reached into her small handbag. "That's precisely what I was hoping to speak with you about. I've written up a first draft of what I think the advertisement should say. Would you mind reading it over for me and sharing your thoughts with me? By all means, be as critical as you think necessary."

She handed the envelope over to her friend and Annie took it carefully in her hands. Her friend opened it up and brought out the slip of paper. "Oh my, it's not very long," Annie remarked at once. "Of course, brevity is the soul of wit, as the Bard says..." She read it over quickly, a few times. "Still, I think you could do with a few more details about yourself. I know it's an advertisement and you don't want to be too lengthy, but you do want to be eye-catching and to make the gentlemen who read it feel inclined to write to you."

Rita bit her lip thoughtfully. "What do you recommend that I add?"

Annie looked the ad over again, thinking. "Maybe some more about your appearance. Were you considering adding a photograph?"

Rita nodded. "Yes, in fact I was wondering about that as I walked over here. I don't have any recent portraits, of course, but I do have some photographs from when I lived in New York." *I wonder how accurate they would appear alongside the description, though.*

"Ooh, if you've got some fancy portraits from when you lived in the city, I imagine that will be quite attractive for gentlemen out here," Annie replied. "After all, a great many men around here are hoping to meet a girl from back east, which is why Mr. Stewart asked for girls from the region." Annie winked a little.

"That's because the women out west seem to all be married," Rita said with a laugh. "You're probably right. A photograph of me from a party or some such thing will be good to add." She made a mental note of that. "Thank you."

She didn't have enough time to go visit Carrie and ask for her tips, so she entrusted Annie with the advertisement until the following afternoon. "I'll make sure she gets it," Annie promised her, holding the ad tightly as if it was in danger of flying away if she didn't. "And then we can both give you notes tomorrow."

The two friends hugged each other and Rita took her

leave so she could return to the restaurant in time for supper. She hoped that the dinnertime train wouldn't be quite so full or rowdy this time, but she knew that that was a lot to hope for. When she arrived back at the dorm, she quickly dressed in her black and white attire, tying the bow back into her hair and smiling at her reflection, practicing her friendly demeanor for the guests. She was naturally a friendly, sunny sort of person, but even she sometimes became exhausted from keeping up her enthusiasm all of the time.

The evening proved to be pretty standard for Rita – busy but not unbearable. Time went by fairly quickly thanks to the restaurant being busy, and before long Rita was climbing the stairs of the dormitory and heading back to her bedroom. Evenings like this didn't happen so often anymore, so she relished the chance to unwind and to be able to spend more time working on her advertisement. Once she got to her room and shut its door, she knelt beside her bed and pulled out the old, dusty suitcase she had brought with her from New York. It had been blue at one point, but now it was a faded, gray color. She carefully unfastened its buckles and opened it to find her stack of colorful dresses. *At least they're not discolored by time,* she thought with a smile. She gingerly touched some of them, wondering if it might be prudent to save wearing them for such a time as when her groom-to-be should arrive to meet her.

I know that I have a portrait of me wearing this yellow one, she thought, feeling the taffeta beneath her fingertips. It was a bright gown, full of ruffles. The canary shade went well with her black hair and caramel-and-cream skin. *Though obviously the yellow will be up to their imagination.*

Gingerly, Rita dug through the dresses in her suitcase as she recalled placing her photographs into a pocket beneath them. Her theory had been that they would get less folded if she did so, and sure enough she found them lying flat beneath the frocks. She smiled as she pulled them out and then she leafed through them, trying to decide which one would be best. The one where she was wearing the yellow gown was arguably the best, so she carefully replaced the other photographs and brought the chosen portrait over to her vanity. She placed it into an envelope for safekeeping and then placed that into the top drawer of the mirrored desk.

She would need to wait until tomorrow in order to get feedback from her friends and then she could send off her advertisement. *I suppose I should take along that photograph, too, so they can approve it as well.* For some reason, Rita felt somewhat shy about them seeing a photo of her in her younger days. She was embarrassed about her extravagant past, not because she resented her parents or anything like that, but because she couldn't claim to have done much with it. She hadn't used her money in order to help people as much as she would've liked. Her parents wanted her to marry some wealthy son of some wealthy businessman and she wanted more from her life. To be sure, if she'd simply married someone in New York City and continued to live as a

spoiled socialite, things would've been much easier for her...
But Rita knew that she also would've been miserable.

Putting such thoughts to rest for now, she dressed in her
white and lace nightgown, climbing into her bed once her
long, black hair was thoroughly brushed out. She closed her
eyes and smiled a bit.

Imagine if I'd never met Mr. Stewart, she thought. *He's given
my life a much bigger purpose than it ever could've had if I'd
stayed in the city... I shall be sad to leave him, but there's nothing
else for it. I can't be a waitress for him forever. I'd never ask him to
change the rules for me. Besides, life beyond the Stewart House
doesn't seem so bad. It'll be an adjustment, but one that I think I'm
ready for.*

She imagined the kinds of gentlemen who might respond
to her advertisement. For some reason, they all bore a
striking resemblance to her employer: tall with twinkling
gray-brown eyes and a pleasant, knowing smirk.

*He's the only man I've been close with. Clearly, Rita de la
Cruz, you need to get out more...*

4

———

Rita seemed to float through her work the following day. She was present but she wasn't entirely paying attention to things. No one noticed, or if they did they didn't say anything about it to her. Sometimes she was relieved that Mr. Stewart was largely off in his own little world so he couldn't witness her behavior – or the way she observed or failed to observe the other girls at their work. She always became more self-conscious when she knew he was paying attention to her.

Rita finished up her tasks after the lunchtime rush and then went on her break. She walked next door, skipping up the steps of the dormitory and hoping that no one would notice.

"Are you off to somewhere fun today, Miss Rita?" Felicity asked her with a raised eyebrow and a shy smirk.

Rita blushed and stopped her skipping, immediately feeling a tad self-conscious in spite of her other feelings of joy and excitement. *I really don't think she's judging me...* "I'm going to visit with some good friends, yes," she said calmly and smiling a bit herself. "Some former waiter-girls, actually."

Felicity's eyes lit up. "Oh? So, some of the ladies from this place have moved on but stayed here? I've been wondering about that. I suppose this is a pretty friendly town."

Rita nodded. "Oh, it is."

They reached the top of the stairs. She didn't wish to be rude, but she did have somewhere to go, as she'd said. "Have a nice break," she said to Felicity before turning to go into her bedroom.

Felicity smiled back at her brightly. "You too! Tell your friends that the waitresses say hello."

That's awfully sweet, Rita thought. "I will!" Now that she was in her bedroom once more, she quickly removed her uniform, placing it out to be washed by the women on laundry duty. She considered wearing one of the pretty socialite dresses, but decided against it. She wanted to keep them nice for the suitors who might come to meet her, after all. *My friends will understand if I don't want to show off my flashier dresses for them,* she thought. *They can see me in one of them in the photograph.*

She put on a simple but pretty periwinkle dress before safely tucking the envelope containing the photograph into her handbag. "I do hope that the printer will be able to return it to me. It's such a nice photograph. I certainly hope the gentlemen appreciates this potential sacrifice."

Realizing that she was thinking aloud, Rita laughed softly and turned to leave again. She went down the stairs and didn't find any of the girls this time, so she gave a few little skips at the bottom of the staircase. Rita couldn't say why she was in such a good mood; only that she was excited about the possibility that rested in things to come.

She walked to Carrie's house this time since that had been the designated location for their get-togethers. Climbing up onto the front porch, Rita knocked on the door, standing back and smiling as she held her handbag in her hands as if she was gifting it to her friends. When the front door opened, she gave a laugh as not one but three of her friends smiled back at her. Even Beverly had decided to come by!

"My goodness," Rita laughed. "You all are *this* invested in my love life?"

"Oh, you know it," Beverly said with a wink.

It was so good to see the redhead again. It felt as though it had been years when, in actuality, it had only been a few months. Rita stepped forward into the doorway and hugged Beverly. "How have you been? I see you every so often at work, but I know you've been so busy..."

"I've been wonderfully busy," Beverly agreed, still beaming. "But I've been enjoying myself. How about you, Rita? You look well. That's a lovely dress."

"I was just going to suggest," Carrie agreed with a nod, "that you wear this dress when you first meet a gentleman."

"You look like an elegant flower," Annie agreed.

Rita blushed, so happy just to be there with her friends and receiving so many compliments and so much attention from them. In the past, when she worked with them, she never expected to be the center of attention, so it was nice to finally feel like she deserved it a little. She finally felt like one of the girls, instead of the authority figure whose judgment they should fear, at least somewhat.

"Well, let's not all keep standing out here on my porch," Carrie said with a giggle. "Please, Rita, won't you come inside and sit awhile with us?"

The friends all went inside the house, Carrie closing the door once they were all in. They moved into the living room and sat together there – Annie and Beverly on the odd sofa that Carrie's husband had made while Carrie and Rita took up the modest chairs on either side of the sofa, with the deep wood coffee table betwixt them.

"I think this is practically the capacity of this place," Carrie said good-naturedly, laughing a little. "Any more people and folks would have to sit on the floor!"

Rita laughed along with her. "I promise that I won't keep you all here long." She opened the handbag in her lap and carefully pulled out the photograph that she intended to go with the advertisement.

Annie took this as her cue and brought out the piece of paper that Rita had left with her. She unfolded it and right away Rita could see that some notes and revisions had been written directly onto it. *I see that I need to rewrite it before I can send it,* she thought. *It's for the best, I'm sure.* She trusted that her friends knew best. After all, they'd been through such things themselves and she could learn from their experience.

"We don't have too many things that you should change," Annie began. "But we think that your advertisement would work better like this." She handed the paper over to Rita, who traded the photograph with her.

While her friends *ooh*ed and *ahh*ed at Rita's photograph, she studied the edited advertisement. *I should describe myself and my ambitions more. I should state more of what I'm looking for,* she thought as she read her friends' words of advice.

"This is a good critique," she told them, looking up from the paper. They were all still leaning over in order to ogle at her photograph. She smiled a dimply, flattered sort of smile. "I suppose I shall take this back with me and compose a new advertisement tonight."

"I dare say, if you decide to include this photograph" Beverly said, handing it back to Rita, "be prepared for a line out the door of fine gentlemen that wish to meet you."

They all giggled and continued to chatter away about that and about Carrie's, Beverly's, and Annie's husbands as well. Rita's soul felt significantly lifted up and she went back to the dormitory later, feeling quite ready to meet some gentlemen and fill the one remaining hole in her life.

The dinner rush wasn't too dreadful for Rita that night. She didn't think that anything could be bring her down on a day that had been so lovely. It was much easier to smile when things were going right for her. "You've clearly had a good day," Mr. Stewart said to her at the end of the night, just before closing, as she gave him her usual report on things in the eating house.

She blushed somewhat. She was uncomfortable with the idea of Mr. Stewart catching wind of what she was up to, not that she was beholden to him. Even in all this, she wished to stay loyal to her friend and employer who'd trusted her for so long and with so much... *I need to tell him,* she decided then. *He's trusted me too long for me to not confide in him during this important time in my life.* Taking a deep breath, Rita looked him in the eyes. "Sir, there's something I should tell you. It's not exactly work-related, but I feel as though you should know anyway. It'll affect things in time, surely."

Mr. Stewart raised his eyebrows as he looked at her. "Oh?" he asked, setting aside some paperwork so he could be sure to give her his complete, undivided attention. "What is it? Everything's okay with you, I trust? You seem so happy."

Rita could sense his concern now and it made her feel slightly ashamed of herself, though she didn't know why. *Do I have something to be ashamed of? Other than keeping something from him...?* "It's nothing wrong, no bad news," she assured him. He possibly would see her departure as bad news, however. "I just think I ought to let you know that I'm planning to write away for a husband."

Mr. Stewart blinked at her. For a moment, she couldn't tell if he'd heard her or not. He appeared unmoved, vacant. Then at last he cleared his throat. "I see."

"I haven't sent off my advertisement yet," Rita said. "It's not as though I've been making arrangements to leave already or anything like that. Naturally I would let you know, if I was already at that stage, that I was planning to leave." *Good gracious, even saying the words 'planning to leave' make me feel pretty sad.* She told herself that she had to remember that she owed Mr. Stewart a good many things, but she didn't owe him her happiness. She didn't owe him her life and future.

Besides, it's not as though he was planning to marry me. If that should be the case, why, there'd be no need to send away for eligible bachelors! Rita smiled thinly. The very idea was absurd. Mr. Stewart wasn't looking for marriage; he was married to his business. Rita respected him for that, but that meant that he should understand why it was necessary for her to eventually move on with her life.

"I'll keep you updated," she told him finally, nodding her head a bit for emphasis. "I just wanted to make sure you knew so I didn't surprise you or catch you off guard. I don't plan on letting this affect my work, up until my departure."

Ugh, she thought. *Some of these phrases just* hurt.

"Thank you for letting me know," he said after some consideration. He'd leaned back into his chair and was gazing down at the stacks of papers on his desk, seemingly lost in thought. Rita felt terrible; the happiness was gone from her demeanor as well as her mind. All she could think about now was saying goodbye to this man.

This place.

This wonderful, welcoming man. Her friend.

If it makes you feel any better, she thought as she left his office and made her way back home to her bed, *I don't have much confidence that I shall find a better man than you.*

Rita removed her uniform as soon as she was in her room and then pulled her white nightgown over her head. She curled up in her bed without even bothering to put the blankets over herself, and began to cry. She'd been so happy before with the idea and promise of things that lay ahead for her. She was enamored with the possibilities, but now she was more fully realizing the consequences that would also come with moving on. With leaving. And the last thing she saw in her mind's eye, as clear as day, before she fell asleep was the sad, vacant expression of Mr. Stewart as he sat there alone in his office.

Rita couldn't bear to think about seeing that man's frown again, but she knew she would be forced to. She certainly wasn't going to leave without saying goodbye to him. That was a thing that she'd never do, no matter how much the farewell would hurt.

5

Rita rose early the following morning – even earlier than usual for her – and she sat at her desk in her nightgown, writing out her new advertisement. She put her sadness about leaving Mr. Stewart and his restaurant aside and focused on the positives of moving on with her life and finding someone to love her.

WANTED: Handsome, hard-working gentleman in his 30s-40s who is looking for a young bride of good moral character and good standing in Wallace, Kansas. Must be passionate about his work and must be interested in including said future wife in his work. Bride seeking a groom is 29 years old and comes from a wealthy, affluent background in New York City. She came to Kansas to work at Stewart House and now hopes to use her skills in a prosperous, loving household. Interested parties please respond. An in-person meeting shall be arranged for the right candidate. Thank you.

Rita placed this refined advertisement, along with her lovely photograph, into a fresh, new envelope. She packed her uniform carefully into her handbag, choosing to carry her advertisement in her hands instead so it didn't get bent or otherwise ruined on the way to the post office. Quickly, she dressed in a rose-colored dress and went down the stairs and out the front door of the dormitory. Her hair was loosely positioned up on her head, and some dark tendrils of hair were brushing up against her cheeks. *I shall have to tidy up before I go out onto the floor of the restaurant,* she thought as she went. *But I'll have time enough for that later.*

She stood on the porch and attempted to hail a carriage.

As if on cue, who should appear but Mr. Stewart. He was walking along the street past the dormitory on his way to the restaurant. This struck Rita right away as odd because he didn't live on that side of his eating house. He lived to its right, which meant that he was wandering out of his way this morning. *Where is he coming from?* she wondered, and then a new thought chilled her. *Was he out for a prolonged walk because of our conversation? I know he likes to walk when he's stressed...*

She shook this train of thought from her mind then. If she spent all of her time worrying about Mr. George Stewart and his feelings, she'd never get anywhere in life. Which was what she was most afraid of: being stuck, stagnant.

Suddenly, he walked right up to her. Tipping his hat, he smiled at her. "Good morning, Miss De la Cruz. I didn't expect to see you out here and so early. Where are you off to?"

Rita's cheeks flushed a bit and she found it difficult to meet his eyes. "I've got my advertisement to send," she said by way of explanation.

The smile faded ever so slightly from his mouth and some of the light left his eyes. "Would you like me to accompany you?" he asked. She was surprised that his voice remained largely unaffected. And she was surprised, too, that he'd even offered to take her there to send off her reason for leaving his restaurant.

Rita considered for a moment. "Yes," she said, giving him a sincere smile. "That would be very kind of you."

He offered his arm to her and she accepted, linking her arm into his. They walked along the dirt road together. At first, she'd thought that riding in style to the post office would be the best way to get there quickly before work, but now that she was accompanied by the restaurant's owner and boss, she had no reason to worry if she ran a little behind schedule... *I just hope I don't cause us both to be late! He might never forgive me for that either.*

It was rather strange for her to be walking along with her boss on her arm. Rita never thought he'd want to be seen outside of the restaurant with one of his waiter-girls, but now she realized that he cared enough about them to want to keep them safe and happy. It wasn't all propriety, sometimes it was just... affection for them. Her cheeks grew pink again, but this time not due to embarrassment but due to gratification.

When they arrived at the post office, he unlinked their arms so she could go up to the counter and send off her advertisement. Even though he didn't have to, he waited there for her. As Rita turned around to face him again, he waggled his eyebrows at her a bit, smiling that same semi-sad smile. The smile of someone who was trying very hard to maintain their composure. Mr. Stewart offered his arm to her again. "Shall we?"

Smiling back at him, Rita took his arm once more and they walked out of the office and back down the dirt road. There were more people out on the street now, going about their normal activities. "I should change," she said to Mr. Stewart as they neared the dormitory. "I brought along my uniform in my bag, but—"

"Take all the time you need," he replied. "I can manage the girls until you come."

She didn't know what else to say, so she simply gave a short curtsy and then went into the dorm and up the stairs so she could change into her black and white garb, and tidy up her hair a bit too.

He's being very peculiar. But I suppose he wishes to be especially kind to me now that he knows I shan't be here forever. She laughed a little at that. *But then, he really didn't think that, did he?* Rita didn't wish to flatter herself.

As soon as she was presentable in her costume, Rita made her way to the restaurant. Things were in full swing for the breakfast rush, but thankfully everything was under control. The breakfast train was usually nothing to worry about – the customers were sleepy and in need of a hearty meal and more than a little coffee, but they were patient and gracious. There had definitely been times when the morning train was chaotic, of course, but nothing that Rita and the girls couldn't handle.

She spied Mr. Stewart working the floor like a proper waiter and it made her laugh inwardly. He went from table to table, asking how people were doing and fetching orders for them. He noticed that Rita was now standing at the helm like usual and he came over to her, carrying two empty glasses and a bowl.

"It's been a while since I've done this," he said in a rather giddy sort of way. "I must admit that it's quite eye-opening, like a splash of cold water to the face."

"What were their orders?" she asked him, still smiling her amused and slightly touched smile.

Mr. Stewart looked at the glassware and dish in his hands. "Oh yes," he said, handing them over to Rita as if he was in trouble for carrying them. "One glass of milk and one glass of orange juice. And a refill of grits."

"What kind of grits?"

He blanched. "I don't remember. Hold on." He rushed off back to one of the tables. Rita did her best not to laugh out loud. He was the Stewart in 'Stewart House.' It wouldn't do if she was to publicly laugh at him. Their customers didn't know that they were friendly, and it didn't quite matter anyway. Employees weren't supposed to laugh at their employers. Period.

After a few moments of waiting, Mr. Stewart rushed back to her. "Cheese," he said.

She nodded wisely. "I figured as much. Okay, one milk, one orange juice, and one bowl of cheese grits for table number six. Thank you, sir."

Without waiting for him to say anything further – really, she rather hoped that he'd return to his office so the day might progress as usual now that she had arrived – Rita went into the kitchen to place the order with the cooks.

She was relieved to find that Mr. Stewart was back in his office when she returned to the restaurant floor. It wasn't that she didn't enjoy his company or his assistance, but she felt that his role belonged on the management side of things whereas she should be the one in charge of tasks within the restaurant itself. She'd never presume to tell him what to do, but she preferred it when they worked in their own lanes, as it were.

She gave the customers their drinks and grits as they ordered, smiling and thanking them for their patience. The rest of the meal could continue as if she'd never been late or needed Mr. Stewart's help.

As eager as Rita was to leave the Stewart House, she knew that she was going to miss it. Busy shifts such as this one served to remind her of how far she'd come in the world of business and how many skills she had picked up along the way. *No matter what, I'd really rather not have to give up working,* she thought with a sort of sad smile as she stood at her hostess area in front of the restaurant. *I made that intention clear in my advertisement, but will I actually find a man who will understand how important having a job and a sense of purpose is to me?*

6

Not wanting her anxiety to get the better of her, Rita didn't go to the post office to see if she had any mail for weeks after she'd sent her advertisement. She knew that the mailman did sometimes deliver to the dormitory, but the easiest way to get mail was to go to the office. She could open her letters in peace if she wasn't surrounded by the nosy girls in the dorm. She let a month pass, thinking that to be an ideal amount of time to wait. The last thing she wanted was to find that zero men had responded to her advertisement, though that was still a possibility.

Since she knew that it would be a tight squeeze for her to go from there to work, Rita went in her black dress, keeping her apron and bow in her bag for later. She walked briskly up the street, not even bothering with the carriages anymore. *I don't quite know why I had the idea to take one before,* she thought. *It's much easier just to walk.*

As soon as she got into the small mail office, she walked right up to the counter and smiled at the gentleman there. It was the same mailroom receptionist from last time. "Good morning," she said cheerfully. "I'm here to see if there's any mail for me. My name's Miss Rita de la Cruz." She gave him her complete address as well as the address of the restaurant, just in case someone had attempted to send her letter there. After all, she'd mentioned her place of work in the ad.

The clerk smiled back at her and nodded his head a bit. "Let me see what we've got," he said, going into the small room in the back, where stacks of letters and parcels lay. To Rita's surprise and delight, he returned with a large pile of at least ten letters. "Here y'are," he said, chuckling a little. "Somebody's popular."

Rita blushed and couldn't contain her excited grin. There was no way she was going to be able to respond to all of these letters! *I suppose the best thing to do is to read them all and respond to my favorites?* In her brief conversations with Carrie and Annie, she'd learned that that was the way it was generally done. Not everyone who responded to an advertisement got or expected to receive a response.

I just hope I don't hurt anyone's feelings... She looked from the stack of letters, held together by some twine, and then turned her smile on the man once more. "Thank you so much," she said, the giddiness evident in her voice as well as her expression.

Letters in hand, she practically skipped out of the post office. There was no way she was going to be able to read through any of them that morning, though. She had the restaurant to get to. Once she was out of the office and making her way up the street, she gently did her best to stuff the letters into her handbag without folding them too much. She removed her bow and apron so she'd have more room and simply carried them up the street with her, in her fist. *How fortunate that Mr. Stewart wasn't there to see how big of a response I received. If I have to see his sad face again, I hope it shall be as I leave...*

The thought made her feel slightly ill so she pushed it aside. When she got to the restaurant, she went into the back room and placed her purse on the floor where several of the other ladies kept theirs, and then set about putting on her white apron and bow.

"Where have you been?" Melissa chided her with a smile as she watched Rita carefully tying her bow onto her head. "You're glowing this morning."

Rita blushed in spite of herself. She didn't wish to discuss this at work, especially because gossip got around like wildfire amongst the staff in the restaurant. She really didn't want Mr. Stewart to hear about it, if only because she didn't wish to upset him more than she already had... She sighed slightly and looked at the other woman. "I can tell you about it tonight, in the dormitory."

Melissa gave her a conspiratorial smile, as if she was ecstatic to be invited to know something about Rita. Most of the girls knew things about the others' personal lives, but Rita remained fairly stoic about such things. It helped her focus on her job as their supervisor and superior. Much like when she'd known Annie, Beverly and Carrie in the beginning. *It wouldn't do for everyone who works with me to know all of my secrets and innermost yearnings,* she reasoned. *If I become too close to these girls, it'll makes it that much harder to effectively do my duties here. Biases form.*

The breakfast shift went well. The usual amount of groggy but grateful customers came in and were happy to partake in the plethora of the eggs and grits that the Stewart House had to offer. Ever since Beverly and her husband Mr. Maddox had taken over the meat supply duties, Rita noticed that customers were always pleased with the sausage and bacon that they were given. The restaurant had become famous for their steaks back when they were delivered via train and kept in the icebox in the kitchen, but now that the meat was fresher and basically went from butcher to grill to plate, she noticed that the enthusiasm had risen quite a lot. Mr. Stewart continued to revolutionize and then improve upon his operations. Rita was extremely proud. *I do so hope that whoever I end up with is from this town so that I can remain nearby. I don't want to choose a future husband based solely on that desire, but it would be such a plus...*

The restaurant never seemed to be quite so crazy anymore, no matter how many people came in. Rita believed this was largely because they'd become used to larger crowds and they were more prepared for them. It was a sign that they had been in town for longer and they were steadier on their feet. She gazed around at all of the people at their tables and imagined what it might be like if she turned out to be as lucky as Annie. *Imagine if I found my beau in this very restaurant!*

She reminded herself to not get her hopes up. It was good enough that she'd received such a warm reception to her advertisement in the form of that mountain of letters in her purse. She couldn't wait to have a break so she could read at least a few and see what types of gentlemen had responded. The lunchtime shift came and went and before long, Rita was able to go on her break back in her room, with her bag full of letters.

She didn't bother changing out of her uniform, considering that she planned to spend her break inside, reading and possibly replying to her letters. Sitting at the vanity, she pulled the letters out of her purse and placed them on the surface in front of her. She took a deep breath and picked up the first letter at the top of the stack. Carefully, she tore open the envelope and brought out the letter, reading it quickly. It was a short response, not very interesting or detailed. She set it aside and opened the next envelope. This letter had her smiling and even laughing a little bit. This was more like it.

DEAR MISS DE LA CRUZ,

HELLO, and I hope that this letter finds you well. I saw your advertisement in the newspaper and I felt that I must write to you right away. My name is Samuel Grayson. I'm a rancher here in Wallace and as luck would have it I have visited your establishment several times. I really enjoy the work that you ladies do there. How thrilling it must be to work in a place like that. I'm afraid I live in a lowly farmhouse and it's not likely that a girl with a refined background such as yours would be enthusiastic about living on a farm, but I hope to make up for that by assuring you that you would have plenty of things to do here with me. I certainly wouldn't prevent you from working, if that's what you'd like to do. You strike me as very capable, and that's the sort of woman I'm after.

I am thirty-nine years old; about six feet two inches; sandy hair and brown eyes. I can tell by just that one photograph that you're stunning. I hope that you will be interested in meeting me in person. I'd be happy to meet you at the Stewart House if that makes it easy for you.

Please let me know if you'd wish to meet up with me and see how we feel.

Sincerely,
Samuel Grayson

RITA SMILED down at this letter as she held it in her hands. She was pleased to know that he was a rancher in town so she wouldn't need to leave and go far at all! She had limited time, so she decided to quickly write a letter back to this gentleman for now and then see if any others were worthy of a response later on.

DEAR MR. GRAYSON,

How KIND of you to write back to me! I found your letter to be very sweet. You sell yourself short when you say that the life of a rancher is not refined. I believe the work you do is quite important, especially out here where hide and beef are worth so much. I know because our restaurant's most popular item is our steaks. You might know that as well, seeing as how you've visited a few times yourself.

I would greatly like to meet you in person. There is a dormitory next to the restaurant which contains parlors – they're the ideal place for meeting. If you come to the restaurant and say that you're visiting to see me, I'm sure either I or one of my coworkers can lead you over to the right place. I look forward to making your acquaintance in person so we might get to know one another better. Thank you again for your kind and punctual response to my ad.

All the best,
Rita

SHE HOPED that this short note would be enough to keep him interested and that he would turn up at the restaurant one day soon. In the meantime, she surely had plenty of other people to respond to in case it didn't work out. But now was not the time for that. She looked at herself in the mirror and adjusted her bow in her black, wavy hair. She stood up and left her room, the letters still stacked upon her desk, and she went back over to the restaurant in time for the dinner rush.

Rita's tight work schedule didn't allow her a lot of time to do things for herself, however she did have a day off coming up and she planned to fit in as much correspondence that day as she possibly could.

I hope that Mr. Grayson doesn't choose my day off as his day to visit, she suddenly thought. *Though I wouldn't exactly be difficult to track down if I'm in my room in the dorm, or even somewhere else nearby in town. I'm never far.*

At the end of the evening, she met with Mr. Stewart as

usual to give him a report on how the day went and how the girls had behaved. She found that she was much more confident in regards to talking to him than she'd been lately. There was something to be said for receiving nice letters and compliments from gentlemen. It did wonders for the self-esteem, that was for sure.

Rita smiled at Mr. Stewart as she told him about the supplies that needed restocking and the customer remarks for the day. "Melissa is improving each day. I do believe you've got fine material for a supervisor with her," she said. "Of course it will take time, and she also needs to be dedicated to staying here for longer than a year. Felicity is doing very well, too. I worried about her at first, but she's come a long way since her roommate left us. I think it's possible that Trudy was a distraction."

Mr. Stewart appeared thoughtful. He picked up his pen to make a few notes about what Rita said. "So, you're attempting to draft a new supervisor?" he asked her. "Is that right?" His tone wasn't angry or upset, but it was perhaps a bit deflated as if he was somewhat let down that she was still thinking of leaving. They never spoke of it ever since she'd first brought it up, and even now Rita didn't intend to have a discussion about her impending departure, but she knew that it couldn't be completely avoided forever.

"No, sir, not necessarily," she replied with a genuine smile at him. "I'm only saying so because I think it will help you to know how good your girls are. Especially since several of them are fairly new. We're continuing to get the best girls from up and down the eastern shore."

He continued to scribble notes on his bit of paper but Rita chose not to even try to peek. *If I know him as well as I think I do, he's just doodling anyway.* Her smile grew a little.

"Thank you, Miss De la Cruz," he said then with a nod that meant their meeting had come to an end. "I will keep them in mind and keep an eye on them when they're around."

Rita stood up from her chair. Her news made its way to the tip of her tongue, but she refused to tell him. She knew that, though it made her happy to think about, it wouldn't be so for him. She missed the days when she had been able to be confide in him, but now, she was keeping things from him for his own good. *He knows that I've sent off an advertisement. He surely knows what is bound to follow.*

With a small sigh, she left Mr. Stewart's office and walked out of the restaurant, blowing out the last of the lit candles as she went.

7

Rita had forgotten all about her promise that she'd made to Melissa earlier. When she arrived back at her room, she found the girl standing in front of the locked door, an eager jumpiness in her manner. As soon as Melissa saw Rita, she grinned and nodded her head a little. "I hope it's okay that I'm waiting here. You haven't changed your mind, have you? I can easily come some other time..."

Blinking at her and taking a moment to recall what she was talking about, Rita then shook her head at the younger girl. "Oh," she said. "Oh dear! I'm afraid it had slipped my mind, but yes, I'd love for you to stop in now." She offered Melissa a welcoming smile and then unlocked her bedroom door, gesturing for the other girl to come in.

Melissa walked into Rita's room, gazing around with a wonder that Rita found a bit humorous. *It isn't as though I'm a famous person,* she thought with a smirk that she kept friendly. She had a room like all of the others': a bed with a blue and red patterned quilt, a wooden vanity with a mirror, a closet, and plenty of space underneath her bed for her suitcases – full of her colorful dresses and her photographs – and other things that she might not need to access all the time. Rita sat on her bed and gestured to the chair beside her vanity so Melissa could sit there.

"So, what have you been up to?" Melissa asked her as she sat. "I know you're keeping something quite exciting from us."

Rita noticed that Melissa was still wearing her uniform minus the bow. She followed her lead and quickly removed her bow as well, running her fingers gently through her hair so that it could billow and fall against her shoulders and upper back. It always felt heavenly to let her hair down, and she was sure that it was likewise for the rest of the girls. "I suppose I ought to tell someone here, so I don't lose my mind," she said with a laugh. "But you mustn't say a word to Mr. Stewart."

Melissa nodded swiftly. "I won't. I promise."

Rita leaned over and set her white ribbon aside, on her vanity next to the remaining letters that she had to read. Then, she picked up the letters and showed them to the other girl. "I placed an advertisement in the newspaper for a husband," she said calmly. "And these are the response I've received so far."

Melissa's eyes widened. "My goodness!" she cried out in astonishment. "How wonderful! But that means... Are you planning to leave us now, too?" Rita knew that the girl had become friends with Annie fairly recently, only for Annie to run off and get married. She felt sorry to be leaving so soon after that, but the time seemed right to her. *There must be something in the air that's causing the blossoms to float away from this place...*

"Unfortunately, I am planning to leave, yes," Rita replied, wishing that her friend hadn't become quite so glum at this news. "But I'm hoping to stay nearby so I can visit all of you and see how things are doing here. You know that I can't go very long without being here."

Melissa nodded vaguely. She gave Rita a smile and she clearly was still very joyful at the news but she – like Mr. Stewart – was not looking forward to seeing her leave. "You must be awfully excited to start a new life," she said. "I remember how Annie was. And you've been here longer than all of us!"

Please don't make this harder to think about than it already is, Rita thought, but she kept on smiling as if nothing was wrong and she wasn't still facing a bit of inner turmoil. "Yes, I'm hoping to perhaps live on a farm around here, with a husband who doesn't mind visiting the restaurant every so often."

Melissa laughed softly. "Yes, I bet that's what you're hoping for. You might as well try and marry Mr. Stewart, since you're so attached."

Rita's face reddened. It wasn't the first or even the fifth time that the thought had crossed her mind, but it was too silly for her to waste her thoughts or time on. Mr. Stewart wasn't looking to marry, and even if he was, he wasn't about to marry some lowly waiter girl. He deserved the best kind of woman, probably a working girl from New York or Boston. *I wish that I'd had the wherewithal to work back then, but my family was so against it. I wasn't bred to be a worker, and I had to fight for it.*

She knew that Melissa meant well with her suggestion, but it made her rather sad to even ponder that sort of scenario. "Don't be silly," she said at last. "Mr. Stewart isn't the marrying kind and anyway, I wish to leave this place. If we were to get married, this restaurant business would become my life just like it's his."

Rita didn't really think that would be quite so bad, but it was foolish to even waste time daydreaming about something that wasn't remotely possible. "If I truly wanted to stay where I am, I never would've sent off that advertisement."

Melissa shrugged a little. "Fair enough," she said. "Though you needn't get so defensive." She winked at Rita and rose from the chair beside Rita's vanity. "I suppose I'd better go to sleep now. And it looks like you've got a lot of reading to do." She motioned to the letters and smirked.

"Yes, I do," Rita said. "Goodnight, Melissa. Thank you for being someone I could talk to about all of this."

"Goodnight," Melissa replied before leaving, softly closing the door behind her.

Rita got up from her bed and moved to her vanity's chair. She knew that there was no way she could get to all of the letters that night, but she could at least read a few more. As she did so, she started to feel calmer about leaving again. Every time she removed the focus from the restaurant and placed it on the idea of a new kind of adventure, she felt a jolt of excitement. She didn't want to let herself be held back by what was familiar simply because it felt gratifying at the time. That was the way she'd been back when she was a debutante in Manhattan, wealthy and attending parties, trotted out because she made her family look good. Many businessmen back home had wanted to marry the beautiful and flashy Miss Rita De la Cruz, daughter of Spanish immigrants and heiress to a fortune worth thousands. She didn't want to lose sight of that now that she was on her path towards finding a good husband for herself. She didn't think that anything should be *destined* for her. Now that Rita had found her own sort of freedom out there in the dusty plains of Kansas, she wanted to work for what she had and *earn* the good things in her life.

Letter after letter proved to be less than inspiring, and after a while she realized that she really must sleep if she was going to be in good shape to work tomorrow. *The letters can wait for now,* she thought, placing her response to Mr. Grayson into an envelope and licking it shut. *At least I have this one to send off in the morning. I can weed through the rest on my break on my day off.* That would certainly be a good use of her free time.

One of the things that her chatting with her friends hadn't prepared her for was the waiting. She knew that correspondence via the mail was a slow process because she'd mailed enough letters to her parents in her first year there. Still, Rita hadn't anticipated the agony that she had to endure. Even looking at the stack of unanswered letters as she lay there, trying to sleep, made her feel so overwhelmed. Each letter took time and then of course there was the time it took to send each letter, and in addition to that, the time it took to hear back from the person she'd written to. If she heard back at all.

It's enough to drive one a bit mad, she thought as she closed her eyes and really tried to think of something else. After a while, she fell asleep and dreamt of a farmhouse and a life of greeting guests and helping her new husband. When it came time to see who he was, his face was blurred as if he was trapped in a fog. No matter how much Rita squinted or moved around to view him, she could never quite make out the features of his face. All she could tell was that the gentleman had hair that looked a bit dusty, both with actual dust from working on the farm all day and also from a soft dusting of gray.

When she awoke in the morning, Rita was smiling. She sat up in bed and stretched out her arms, yawning softly. *That was a lovely dream, even if it was rather mysterious. I suppose dreams aren't meant to solve one's problems, more like highlight them. And I definitely know that my problems lie in not knowing whom I'm supposed to marry and run off with... Or where I'm supposed to be.*

She dressed quickly, knowing that she had a letter to send off and she didn't want to be late. Late to the post office meant late to work, and also late to meet Mr. Grayson for if he didn't receive her letter then of course he couldn't link up with her at the restaurant and the courting parlors.

Rita carefully placed her letter into her purse along with her apron and bow. She left the dormitory and walked briskly towards the post office. "Hello again," she said to the postmaster there at the counter. "I have a letter that I'd like to send. It's a local letter."

"Sure thing," the gentleman behind the desk said. He graciously took her letter off her hands and carried it into the back room to be placed into the postman's sack. Rita didn't worry herself with trying to figure out the entire process.

"Thank you," Rita said, giving him some coins as payment and also a tip for his kindness. He'd always been so pleasant towards her. *I'd better go now before I begin wondering if the postmaster here is married...* She smiled at him and made her exit.

She had no trouble arriving at work on time, which owed

largely to the fact that she was more rehearsed in this routine now. The rapport that she had with the post office staff surely helped in that regard as well. Rita pulled her apron and bow from her bag and quickly tied them on.

"Good morning and welcome to Stewart House," she said smoothly as she walked out into the restaurant right as the passengers came in through the front doors, smiling and carrying on in their cheerful conversations. "Please take your seats at any of our tables and our waitresses will be happy to serve you."

She did her rounds in the restaurant that morning, feeling fully alive in a way that felt both the same as ever and also entirely new. Her life was changing, and she was happy to find that it was taking its time and allowing her to catch up at her own pace.

8

Over the next two days, during Rita's break times, she carefully read through the rest of the stack of letters on her table and wrote two more responses, exchanging pleasantries and inviting other gentlemen to stop by the restaurant if they were interested in meeting her in person to get to know her a little more. She felt a little strange about it, as if she was selling herself off to the highest bidder – which wasn't entirely dissimilar to the way her parents had made her feel when they were trying to marry her off to whichever business colleague's son or general's nephew that they could introduce her to. Still, she knew that this time was also different because she was in charge of who she ultimately ended up with. *I'm in charge of my own life. I'm making my own destiny now.*

It was complicated, though, this whole finding a beau via letters. She wasn't sure which of them had been the best match for her. She was most looking forward to meeting Mr. Grayson because he'd been the first gentleman to write to her... Or at least his was the first letter she'd read that was meaningful and thoughtful.

If I'm to meet all of them in a short span of time, I'm sure I'm going to become quite overwhelmed. I wish it was possible for me to hire someone to interview these men before I have to meet them. Rita wasn't a shy girl, but she did get anxious when it came to logistics and seeing things through, especially if the result was entirely impossible for her to predict.

Aside from writing and sending letters during her time off, she spent her time as usual, working in the restaurant. She was beginning to feel as though she had two jobs now: managing things at work and corresponding with gentlemen. Rita was exhausted and she was very much looking forward to her day off. *I actually hope I can take the day to just sleep and not think about anything,* she thought.

However, when the day arrived, she learned pretty quickly that she needn't have bothered to take the day off at all because she was needed in the restaurant anyway. She was lying in her bed, sleeping in like she rarely ever got a chance to do when suddenly a knock on her door roused her from her dreaming.

"Yes?" she asked, getting out of her bed to open the door. She blinked drowsily at Felicity. "What is it?"

"So sorry to bother you, Rita," the younger girl said quietly. "There's a gentleman in the restaurant that's asking for you. He said something about our courting parlors, but I wasn't sure if that was what you wanted so I seated him at a table inside the restaurant instead... I didn't know if he wanted something to eat..."

Felicity had such a nervous look about her that Rita almost felt like giggling a bit. "Thank you, Felicity," she said instead, smiling an encouraging sort of smile. "I'll get dressed appropriately and be right over."

She closed the door once the girl was gone, biting her lip in excited anticipation. She felt like dancing but she was also terribly apprehensive now. *Suppose this doesn't go so well? Suppose he didn't want to wait...* Rita took a deep breath and reminded herself that no matter what, it was up to *her* if she wanted to pursue anything with any of the gentlemen. They were calling on her, not the other way around. They must impress her.

Rather than putting on her uniform, since it was her day off, she put on a lovely purple dress, a plum color so dark that it was almost black. For good measure, she put on some matching purple gloves that she had made of lace that went up to her wrists. It wasn't often that Rita got the chance to go out dressed like a proper lady so she intended to enjoy this as much as she could.

She went over to the restaurant next door and sure enough, there was a gentleman sitting rather awkwardly at the front of the room right by the double doors as she came in. This meant that Rita didn't have much time to prepare herself for coming face to face with one of her potential beaus. *Oh, Lord, please let him be one of the gentlemen I wrote to.* She dared not imagine that he was anything else.

"Hello," she greeted him, outstretching one of her hands to him as an introduction. "I'm Miss Rita De la Cruz. I hope you haven't been waiting long."

He stood up awkwardly from his small wooden chair, removing his black cowboy hat at once and holding it in his hands. He was tall and he wore blue denim pants, a yellow and white checkered shirt, and a red-orange bandana around his neck as a sort of western version of an ascot. Rita sized him up as he looked at her, clearly blown away by the mere sight of her in person. She was quite glad that she hadn't worn the yellow gown that she still had in her possession. They might have appeared too bright beside each other.

"Good afternoon, ma'am," the gentleman said to her in a voice that was a trifle squeakier than Rita would've liked but she told herself not to judge him too harshly or so quickly. *After all, he's clearly frazzled.* "Boy, you're prettier than your picture and you're awfully pretty in that." He swallowed and visibly took a deep breath. "I'm Mr. Grayson. Um, Samuel Grayson. I'm so glad to finally meet you in person."

Her cheeks grew hot as she smiled at him. He had a young face with big, green eyes and reddish blond hair. She couldn't quite place his age, though it didn't matter to her

really. She recalled from his letter that he was in his late thir-
ties and that was perfect as far as she was concerned. Finally,
after several moments of shy flirtatious looks, he received her
outstretched hand and gave it a swift kiss on the back of her
little purple glove. Rita had never figured herself for the type
of girl who would swoon because of a rancher, but here she
was. She felt light-headed in the best of ways.

"Would you like to come with me next door?" she asked
him then, noticing that the restaurant around them had
grown quite loud. "This is not an ideal place for us to talk."
She batted her long, black lashes at him and smiled.

Mr. Grayson nodded his head. "Sure," he replied. "I was
just thinking the same thing."

Rita looked out onto the floor of the restaurant, hoping to
catch the eye of one of her friends as they worked around the
tables. Melissa noticed her and nodded her head slightly.
Rita beamed at her and gave a quick wink. It was good to
know that she had her friends looking out for her and paying
attention should anything go awry for her. That brief bit of
communication done, she turned to face Mr. Grayson again
and cheerfully led him out of the restaurant. It felt a bit
strange to her to be leading a gentleman into one of the
courting parlors. Normally for her, the only men who came
into the dormitory were people from overfull trains who
couldn't be seated in the restaurant right away. She couldn't
even recall Mr. Stewart coming into the dorm before; though
she was sure he had at some point. After all, it was he who

had designed it and had it built. He oversaw everything with such scrutiny that she couldn't imagine he'd let inspection of the dormitory slide just because it was going to be inhabited by girls.

She opened the front door to the dorm and led Mr. Grayson into the wide expansive foyer. There were four courting parlors, two on either side of the hardwood hall there. She led him to one on the left-hand side of the room, nearest the front door. Though she didn't want to seem too overly cautious, Rita preferred to be situated close to the door in case she needed to make a swift exit. *It's always good to be on the safe side,* she thought. *Particularly when dealing with strangers.*

Mr. Grayson allowed her to sit down on the plush, deep green Devon chair while he sat in the more straight-backed cushioned chair across from her. The courting parlors did indeed seem like they'd been designed for flirtatious discussions. Or perhaps innocent games of cards. *I do wonder what had been going through Mr. Stewart's head when he added these rooms into his design. Surely, he went into this knowing that each girl was eventually going to leave... I guess I shall never fully understand men and their follies.*

She turned her attention to Mr. Grayson now and smiled at him sweetly. "I hope that you didn't have too difficult of a time finding this place," she said. Pleasant small talk was her strong suit. Venturing beyond that was much more difficult.

Mr. Grayson shook his head at her. "Oh, not at all. As

I've said, I've been here many a time." He smiled back at her and she noticed that he'd never placed his hat back onto his head. It rested on his knee now as he sat there cross-legged. Rita was still rather dazzled to be speaking to a gentleman in jeans. *Mother would be outraged!* she thought merrily. She wasn't interested in the types of men her mother wanted her to marry. Dreams and visions of marrying a man out west had always involved the sort of man that sat before her.

"I'm glad that we left you with a good impression," she said to him. "We try very hard to ensure that everyone feels well taken care of." *But enough about work. You have a life outside of work! ...Allegedly.* "What sorts of things to do you like to do for fun around here? I've been having a more diffi-cult time finding things to do for fun. I'm afraid I haven't been doing such a great job of getting out of my comfort zone and trying new things."

This made Mr. Grayson seem to light up like a firefly. "You'd do well on the back of a horse, I reckon," he proclaimed with another wide, handsome grin. "Maybe one of these days I could bring you to my farm and teach you a thing or two about horseback riding. Would you like that?"

Rita smiled at him. "I would. That sounds very nice."

She was a little bit intimidated by the idea, but it excited her as well. She remembered not to get too ahead of herself. *There are several other men that I mean to meet with at least once. It wouldn't be fair to choose favorites this early on.* But she knew that Mr. Grayson was already in the lead as far as her feelings were concerned.

They sat together and continued to chat for a while longer, and then it was time for them to bid each other adieu. Rita was grateful that she had the rest of the day off to decompress from that experience. *Spending romantic time with men is tiring,* she thought as she sank into her soft mattress, still wearing her purple dress. Who knew if someone else might pop in to meet with her that day? She now knew that she must always be prepared to entertain a visitor, even if only for a brief amount of time. She hoped that there'd never come a time when a man walked in while she was working and insisted to meet with her right then. She knew that Mr. Stewart would never forgive such a thing if that were to happen. Still, though she was worn out from the afternoon's interaction, she'd also enjoyed every moment of it. *I don't think I should mind being Mrs. Grayson,* she thought. *I don't want to get ahead of myself, but I wouldn't mind that at all...*

9

R ita had to go to work the following day but she really wished that she didn't. For the first time in a long while, she'd had a day off that was meaningful for her. She felt accomplished and happy and she wished that she had more time to meet people in the romantic setting of the parlors. Admittedly, she was able to enjoy her time that way because she was safe within the walls of the Stewart House dormitory, surrounded by her friends in case she was ever in danger of anything uncouth. The real world was going to greet her someday soon, and Rita didn't feel completely ready for that yet. *The restaurant is like my cocoon,* she thought as she dressed and went down the stairs and out the front door. *I'm preparing to become a butterfly... or at least a fairly put-together moth.*

The usual morning rush came and went without much that was out of the ordinary. She was drowsy like the customers were, but that also was pretty normal. *I don't imagine that the life of a rancher's wife will allow for sleeping in,* she thought, realizing then with a faint smile that the reason why was so sleepy was that she'd slept in the day before. *It was worth it, though.*

A pair of gentlemen came into the restaurant and Rita walked up to them, beaming brightly and willing herself not to appear at all tired. "Good morning," she trilled. "Welcome to Stewart House." She turned to lead them to a table, assuming that they were to eat together since they'd wandered in together.

"Hold on just a minute," one of the men said. He had black hair and a mustache that was in a style that she could only remember a barber back in New York sporting. Bushy and twirling at the ends. The kind of facial hair that classified as a hobby to some men.

Rita turned back to face them, looking curiously at this man. "Yes?"

"Are you Miss Rita De la Cruz?" he asked, side-eyeing the other gentleman.

She realized now that, though they were there for the same purpose, they were certainly not there together. And neither of them was interested in dining. The bottom of her stomach sank to her knees. "Yes..." she said hesitantly.

"I'm Beauregard Devereux," he replied.

Rita did her best to not laugh. Of course, the gentleman with a name like that had a mustache like that...

"We've written to each other," he went on. "I responded to your ad."

"I, too, was in correspondence with you," the other gentleman finally piped up. He wasn't as eye-catching as his companion. He had dirty brown hair and rather dull gray eyes. He looked like he hadn't slept in a month, which made Rita feel sorry that she'd ever felt tired. "I'm Douglas Bluth."

"Oh yes," Rita said, smiling at the pair of them. She then looked around for Melissa or Felicity, anyone who might be able to help her out of this situation. *I can't handle this at work,* she thought. *I meant for them to meet with me elsewhere...*

Suddenly, her eyes met the gray-brown ones of her employer. Her stomach dropped all the way to the floor. Mr. Stewart! He was never supposed to see her with suitors like this, especially not in the restaurant.

He rushed over at once, clearly sensing some kind of a problem. Her frightened rabbit look that she had given him hadn't helped him feel at ease about things. "What's going on here?" Mr. Stewart demanded of the gentlemen. He looked from Mr. Devereux to Mr. Bluth and back again. Rita couldn't be sure, but she suspected that he found Mr. Devereux's mustache as ridiculous as she did.

The pair of men seemed taken aback by Mr. Stewart's presence, let alone his question. "Why, we're here to meet with Miss De la Cruz," Mr. Bluth spluttered, pointing a thumb in her direction. "I am and he is."

Mr. Stewart crossed his arms in front of his chest in clear agitation. Rita had gone red in the face, and she wasn't feeling very good about herself at the moment. *He was never supposed to see any of this...*

He looked at her next, a glance that was one hundred percent disappointment. Then he looked back at the pair of strangers. "I think you both had better move along," he said sternly. Several restaurant guests had stirred in their seats, craning their necks in order to witness the scene.

"Yes," Rita agreed shakily, clearing her throat in order to be heard better. "I think you'd better go. We will schedule another time. And location."

Mr. Stewart appeared cross. She was relieved that he wasn't forced to remove the men from his establishment himself. They both left, clearly annoyed and arguing with each other as if one of them was to blame more than the other was. Rita's boss turned his head to look at her, mouth partially open but no words forming there. She felt ashamed of herself already so she really hoped he wasn't about to lecture her, especially not in front of everyone.

"Miss De la Cruz," he said in a voice that was restrained and somehow calm. "In my office right now." He said nothing more but went straight to his small back room. She followed close after him, head bowed and afraid to look at anyone else in the establishment. She could feel that all eyes were on her and it was a terrible feeling.

When she arrived in Mr. Stewart's office, she carefully secured the door behind herself. He gestured for her to sit, which surprised her. *He intends for me to stay longer than a moment? I must really be in trouble...* "Miss De la Cruz," he began. His voice was soft and more than a little sad. There was still some amount of restraint to it as well, as if he wanted to say something but would never bring himself to actually say it. "I know that I am forced to accept that you are leaving soon. I know that it is foolish to think that you'd plan to stay here with me. But is it too much to ask that you don't entertain your visitors in my restaurant when you're supposed to be working?"

Rita looked down at her hands in her lap. She was clutching them together so hard that they were beginning to hurt a little. She felt like the most wretched person alive, in that moment. "Words cannot do justice to how profoundly sorry I am," she said to him. "I never meant for such a thing to happen... I should've organized things better."

Then, something that he'd said struck her. *I know that it is foolish to think that you'd plan to stay here with me.* Could there be more to that? More behind his words than just sorrow that he was losing his supervising waitress? Rita wasn't the type of girl to flatter herself, but it sounded as though he was taking it as more than a business loss. He was taking it personally.

She looked at him, right into his lovely eyes. He'd given

her so much and what had she given him? Almost two years of hard work, sure, but she'd also given him a lot of grief, as evidenced by the sad way he spoke and looked at her. "I didn't know that you wished for me to stay so badly," she said. "You should've said so."

"I *did* say so," he argued. "At least, I tried to say so. I was so surprised by the fact that you of all people were planning to leave that I didn't know what I was going to say or do to keep you here. And then, when you were walking to the post office... I was trying to intercept you that morning, you know. I was out for a walk and I saw you there. I'd guessed at where you were going, what you were trying to do."

"But you didn't say anything to me," Rita countered. "You're in charge, *sir*. If you'd told me not to go, I would've listened to you, even if I thought it was unfair..."

She saw a faint flicker of hope flash over his eyes then, like lightning through the dark gray clouds. "Is it too late for me to say something?" he asked her. The restraint had retracted from his voice and was now replaced by a sort of yearning that she never could've expected to hear coming from her employer.

Rita softened a bit in response. She'd been sitting so tensely in her chair but now that melted away as she realized that she was actually far from being in danger of losing her job or something like that. Mr. Stewart was hurt, not angry at her. *He has every reason to be angry at me, but he's not...* "Of course it's not too late," she replied. "It's never too late."

Gazing across his desk at Rita, Mr. Stewart leaned forward so that he could reach out and touch her hands. She likewise reached out towards him and they held each other's' hands in a fairly awkward fashion. Rita didn't care that it was awkward because she was too overwhelmed with surprise and a sort of happy relief that she never expected to be feeling. Mr. Stewart wanted her to stay. "I can't imagine running this place without you," he confessed. "When you told me that someone else could replace you in your position, I thought it was poppycock. No one can fill your shoes. And putting work aside, I just don't want to see another woman coming into my office every day. I want to see *you* every day. I know that I can't tell you what to do with your life. You're smart and determined and I don't want to change that about you. But when you were sending off for a husband, all I could think – all I've been thinking – is, well, why not me? Why couldn't you marry me and save us both the trouble?"

Rita's brown eyes grew large and she smiled a little. "You want me to marry you?"

Still holding her hands even though it wasn't the most comfortable way to sit at his desk, he nodded his head. "Yes, Rita," he said. "You don't need to go looking for someone else. Marry me instead. Unless you truly think that someone you find in the mail would suit you better."

"Oh no, none of them have been better!" she cried out, clutching his long fingers in hers. "The experience has been so utterly exhausting. Some of the gentlemen were pleasant, but just knowing that I would have months and months to try to get to know someone new made me feel so befuddled."

Mr. Stewart chuckled softly. "I thought as much when I saw your poor, sweet face with those men in there. You looked so lost and helpless."

"I'm embarrassed to admit it, but I was," Rita replied.

They smiled at each other for a few moments.

"So, what do you say?" he asked her then. "You never answered. Will you marry me? I want you as my wife and my partner here. You can be in charge as much or as little as you'd like."

He might as well have been serenading her with the sweetest song. It sounded like everything she'd ever wanted. "Yes!" she said in a breathy, still surprised voice. "Oh, yes, please!"

Mr. Stewart stood up from his desk and moved around it so they could embrace. *How funny,* she thought as she hugged him tightly, never wanting to let go. *He proposed like a boss and I wouldn't have wanted it any other way.* She laughed a little.

"What's so funny?" he asked her as they hugged.

She smiled. "Nothing," she said. "I guess just that you're not really going to be my boss anymore but it's going to be better than okay."

He smiled back at her. "Better than okay," he repeated. "I like that."

10

Being engaged to Mr. Stewart now meant that Rita had the task of informing her suitors that she'd chosen someone. She wouldn't have to let all of them know necessarily, but at least the ones with whom she'd made plans to meet. Mr. Stewart allowed her some time off from her duties in the restaurant so that she could send off letters to all of the gentlemen, letting them know her news. *The saddest of all is Mr. Grayson. We might've become friends rather easily.* She reminded herself that there was still a likelihood of being friendly with any of them if they should come into the Stewart House, for that was the goal of the restaurant anyway: to greet people and give them a friendly, entertaining welcome. She amazed herself by being able to write out the several letters in one day, and then she handed them over to her new fiancé who took them at once to the post office. They made a good team even doing that.

"I really must tell my friends," she told him in the evening. She met him in his office like always except this time she had nothing to report from the restaurant. As she had predicted, Melissa had been more than willing to take her place that day. The girl needed more training, but she'd do a good job if ever she was needed to perform in that position. "They've been helping me with this mini-saga of mine. They even helped me write my ad."

Mr. Stewart pulled her into his lap and they sat there behind his desk, smiling cutely at each other. Rita was the oldest girl that had worked for him, but she always felt like a young little thing in his eyes. "I hope that you shall have good things to say about it. And I hope they don't mind that you're marrying their grumpy old boss."

Rita threw her head back and laughed. "None of us have ever thought of you as old or grumpy," she said. "We've always spoken highly of you and that's God's honest truth."

"Even Beverly?"

She looked at him and smiled until her dimples made deep craters in her cheeks. "Well..."

He laughed.

"Tell all of them," he said then. "You can tell the whole town, because I know I will. I get to marry the beautiful Rita De la Cruz, the best waitress I've ever had and surely the best woman I've ever known."

Her eyes twinkled with tears when he said that. "You needn't butter me up now," she said. "I've already said yes."

He kissed her on the cheek. "I'm not buttering you up. It's the truth. I love you, Rita. I didn't set out for this kind of thing, but few men out here really do. Otherwise, why move out west?"

She smiled and rested her head on his shoulder. "I love you, too," she said. She felt so peaceful that she knew this was the happiest she'd ever felt.

The following afternoon, when she had a break from the restaurant duties for a while, Rita went over to Carrie's house, hoping to pay a visit at least with her. She knocked on the front door and was invited in by her friend. "You always have impeccable timing," Carrie informed her. "Annie and Beverly are here for lunch today as well!"

Rita gleefully went in and hugged each of her friends in turn. "How have you all been? You all look well. I'm so glad. I've got a bit of news for you all, so I'm very pleased that you're all here together once again to hear it."

They sat together in the living room as they had before when reviewing Rita's advertisement. "What's the news?" Beverly asked with a smile.

"Have you chosen a husband from one of your letters?" Annie asked.

There was a plate of butter and cucumber sandwiches on the coffee table in front of them and Rita leaned forward a little in order to take one. She took a bite, closing her eyes as she enjoyed the flavors and ruminated on the best way to tell her friends the big news. "I have chosen a husband," she said with a smile and a nod. "But not from the letters…"

Her friends appeared confused, but then Annie smiled. "No!" she exclaimed, a knowing look on her face.

Rita laughed, blushing. "Mr. Stewart – George – asked me to marry him and I've agreed."

She told the three of them the story about the men in the restaurant and how he'd reacted. She told them too about him walking with her to mail her advertisement, and how he'd seemed protective of her while also concerned. "All this time, I thought that he merely hated to lose a good supervisor, so then I offered Melissa as a good replacement and he didn't like that either." She laughed. "He wants to continue to work with me, he says, but as partners not as boss and employee."

Her friends were in awe.

"That's wonderful!" Beverly declared. "Good for you, finding someone who not only supports your working but wishes for you to keep it up." She smiled. "I know that you're like me in that regard. No offense to Annie and Carrie's husbands, but you and I would go crazy being housewives to a farmer."

"Hey," Carrie laughed. "My husband's a farmer *and* a carriage driver, thank you very much."

"You know what I mean," Beverly said, sticking her tongue out at her sister.

"I'm very excited to continue to work beside him," Rita said, blushing as she smiled. "I feel as though I've been given the best kind of promotion. And of course, I hope that all three of you will be my bridesmaids."

The other girls all beamed and nodded their heads in agreement. "First thing we should do is get you a dress," Annie suggested.

"Yes," Carrie agreed. "Have you been thinking about a particular style?"

Rita laughed softly. "I already have a dress I think I should use, but it will need a good deal of altering."

Carrie smiled back at her. "Even better!"

I think it makes the most sense to use my yellow gown, Rita thought. *It's without a doubt my prettiest dress, and George hasn't seen it yet. He never saw the photograph, so it will be a wonderful surprise for him.*

A few days later, Rita went over to visit her friends – at Annie's house this time – and she brought the dress with her, carrying it carefully folded in a box. Her friends all gasped when she opened it to reveal the lovely gown from the photograph she'd shown them. "It's yellow!" Beverly said, impressed. "Such a great, unique choice."

"Oh, this will do quite nicely," Carrie said, gently touching the fabric. "I don't think there has to be too much altering either. Put it on so we can have a look."

They're the ones giving me directions nowadays, Rita thought, tickled rather than peeved about this fact. *We're truly equals and friends now.* She went into one of Annie's rooms to change and, when she returned in the dress, her friends all gasped again. She laughed. "Surely it isn't *that* big of a deal..."

"We always knew you were gorgeous," Carrie said. "But this just... Well, it really emphasizes your beauty."

The trio of ladies took turns examining the dress on Rita, feeling the fabric and making suggestions as to what could be added or changed. In the end, it was determined that it needed some lace around the top of the bust as well as some beaded flowers along the skirt to make it appear more like a wedding dress than a party gown. "I've got some white beads," Carrie offered. "That will be no trouble."

"And I've got some lace," Annie added.

Rita smiled at her friends. She knew that they would come through for her and help her have the best wedding she could possibly have.

Seven weeks went by and then, at last, it was the day of Rita and George's wedding. The ladies walked down the aisle before her, wearing colorful dresses to go along with her colorful wedding gown. As the music played, Rita slowly walked down the aisle. She could hear practically everyone in the room's quick intake of breath when they saw her and she laughed, looking up at George at the front, beside the minister. His gasp was the only one that mattered to her. She fully intended to wow him for the rest of their wonderful lives together.

EPILOGUE

After Rita and George's beautiful wedding, they wasted no time and got right to work with some of the ideas that they both shared. "You want to do something different," he said to her. "I understand that. It just so happens that I've been thinking about opening a hotel next to the restaurant, to make the Stewart House even more of a rest stop for people who are touring the west. They'd be able to stick around and really enjoy things if they had a nice, new place in which to stay. The inns in town are further away and not to my standards."

The new Mrs. Stewart gazed at him lovingly and laughed a little. "You're always about standards," she said. "That's why you're the best in the business."

He opened a notebook on his desk in his office and

showed her the plans he'd made. Not just written ideas but a full diagram of what he intended to create. "You'd have to work here for a while longer, but soon you could be in charge of the Stewart House Hotel. What do you say to that?"

Rita looked from the diagrams to him and then she gave him a kiss. "This is the sweetest wedding gift," she said to him. "But where are you thinking of building this hotel?"

He shrugged, smiling. "We could turn our big house here into an inn. And you can be the innkeeper."

She nodded her head, liking this idea more and more.

Before long, they set this plan into motion. George oversaw the construction and remodeling of his home so that it could accommodate many visiting guests. Meanwhile, Rita was in charge of all of the important details such as the hiring of new staff. There was an area in the hotel that worked well as a small eatery in itself. This was soon used to help take care of the overflow of restaurant customers. Beverly and Wilfred Maddox were more than happy to deliver meat from their butcher shop to the new Stewart House Hotel as well. They never had to turn away customers anymore, which was such a relief to both of them. Their good reputation continued to blossom and Rita was over-joyed to now play an even bigger role in that. The expansion of the business meant that the Stewarts continued to help more and more people, both visitors to town as well as the young, eager girls who came from the east in search of work and to fulfill their dreams of building a better life for themselves.

Each time a wide-eyed new waitress came to them, Rita couldn't help but think about the cyclical nature of things. She and her friends had been like them when they first arrived in Wallace and she now felt like a mother to all of these new girls, in a way. It filled her heart with so much joy to know that she was making such a positive difference in the lives of girls who were, on the whole, just like her.

THE END

MAIL ORDER BRIDE TESSA

STEWART HOUSE BRIDES

MAIL ORDER BRIDE TESSA

Wallace, Kansas – 1891

Getting a job working at the Stewart House Hotel is the answer to Tessa Johnston's prayers. She's from a medical family back in Annapolis, Maryland but she has big dreams of doing something different with her life. Devoted to service work, she finds the hotel is a perfect match for her interests and personality, though the shifts in the diner make her nervous. The overfull trains lead to more people coming in for breakfast and Tessa begins to lose her nerve. Her friend Wendy inspires her to start looking for a prospective husband in the newspaper advertisements.

She begins writing to Samuel Grayson, a handsome rancher

who's been burned by a girl from the Stewart House before but is willing to give it one more try. When Tessa and Samuel meet in person, it's practically love at first sight. Will her service background mesh well with his desire for a house-wife? Tessa is willing to take a chance if he will.

1

Stepping down from the train, Tessa Johnston gazed around the landscape that surrounded her on every side. Kansas was altogether different from any place she'd visited. One of the train conductors plopped her suitcase down at her feet and she pulled out the newspaper clipping that she'd brought along with her, squinting at the words as she held it up. She'd waited long enough for her life to change and she didn't intend to wait any longer. "Excuse me, sir?" she called to the conductor before he could amble off. "Could you tell me in which direction I can find the Stewart House?"

The conductor smiled wryly. He'd been asked this many times before, Tessa could tell. Pointing off into the distance straight ahead from where she stood on the train platform, he nodded his head to her. "If you just continue on straight, you'll come across it. It's situated such that anyone who stops in here at the station can find it right away."

"Yes, of course," Tessa replied with a smile and a determined nod back at him. "That makes complete sense. Thank you, sir."

"Will you be needing any help with your bag?"

She shook her head, still smiling. "No, thank you. I packed lightly." She picked it up off the ground as if to prove it to him. In truth, she hadn't had a whole lot of things to pack in the first place. Tessa wasn't poor, but she considered herself to be practical and didn't see the need for so many dresses or things like that. Her parents always expected her to work, rather than go to parties, so she partially had them to thank for a suitcase that wouldn't strain her back.

Still, carrying the bag out in front of her did make her waddle a little bit as she made her way straight up to the front door of the hotel that sat beside a restaurant. Both were labeled with large, white signs that said in red lettering: "STEWART HOUSE." She set her suitcase down again and looked at the newspaper advertisement. *Well, it says to come to the hotel, not the restaurant,* she thought. *They must have more need there.* She preferred to go where the need was anyway.

Carefully, Tessa climbed the two steps onto the hotel's front porch and then hobbled through the front door. The hotel appeared to be an inn made from an old farm house that had been renovated. There was a desk near the front door, with a bell beside it, hanging on the wall. Setting the suitcase at her feet, Tessa gently pulled the cord on the bell and the *ding* reverberated throughout the house.

There was a rustling nearby and suddenly a woman came down the staircase to Tessa's right. She was a beautiful woman, about ten years older than Tessa, and she was dressed in a black dress with a starched white apron. A white petticoat caused the rustling. She had black, wavy hair that she wore up in braided plaits and eyes that were equally dark and lively. She was dressed for the job of hotel innkeeper, but still Tessa was impressed. The way she wore her uniform made it seem as though it were high fashion.

Is this the Mrs. Stewart that I wrote to? Tessa wondered. She smiled at the woman as she came behind the desk. "Good afternoon and welcome to the Stewart House hotel. How may I help you?" the hostess asked her brightly.

"Hi," Tessa replied. "I recently applied for a position here. I'm Miss Tessa Johnston."

The woman's smile brightened. "Oh! How delightful. It's a pleasure to meet you in person. I'm Mrs. Stewart, but you may call me Rita." She looked at her a bit shrewder now, making sure that she fit the description that every Stewart Girl – even the ones in the hotel – had to possess. Tessa was wearing a simple brown dress with black trim with a thin black petticoat underneath. She had long, dark brown hair that curled a bit, and large hazel eyes, which were right now both earnest and nervous. She wasn't wearing her hair up because the task had been rather difficult when she was on the train. "Come with me and we'll have a little chat in order to get you started and settled," Rita said after a few moments' scrutiny.

She gestured for Tessa to follow her. "What should I do with my suitcase?" Tessa called after her.

Rita turned and fleetingly looked thoughtful. "I will have someone come and take it to the dormitory for you," she said simply. "A room will be arranged for you shortly." She smiled again.

Tessa followed along after her, not really having any other option but to trust that the people at Stewart House would do right by her. Rita led her into the little restaurant area of the hotel and sat at one of the wooden tables, gesturing to the chair across from her. "Your timing is quite good. Customers will most likely be arriving shortly from the restaurant next door. We usually cater to people who wish to extend their stay beyond a quick stop at the restaurant."

"There's a restaurant here at the hotel as well?" Tessa asked, tucking her skirts beneath her.

Rita nodded. "Yes, this eatery is mainly used for breakfast for the people staying in our hotel, but sometimes it serves to accommodate for the overflow of guests that we receive at the restaurant."

"Would I be working in the main restaurant as well?" Tessa asked. *It's not that I don't think I can handle it,* she thought. *I just have more experience with hospitality than serving...*

"Oh, no," Rita said with a chuckle. "No, I need you here. There may be occasions where the restaurant has a need, but my husband typically hires more than enough waiter-girls to handle the tasks there. To be honest, working here will keep you plenty busy, don't you worry about that."

Tessa smiled at her. "Sounds marvelous," she said even as her stomach flopped a bit.

"So, tell me about yourself," Rita said, still smiling. Tessa noticed that she wasn't writing anything down which made her think that she just wanted to hear more of what she'd already read in Tessa's letters. "What inspired you to come all the way out here and work with us?"

Tessa cleared her throat a bit. She reached around her shoulder and brought some of her loosely-curled brown hair forward. "Well, I was ready for a big change. My parents work at a hospital in Annapolis and they wanted me to join them there, but I wasn't interested. I worked for a time as an assistant nurse, but I felt that it just wasn't for me. All of the suffering and death there... I couldn't handle it. Of course, it was a disappointment to my parents. They've raised me to work and earn a living for myself. So, when I saw your advertisement in the newspaper, I thought it was the perfect new opportunity for me." She smiled, hoping that she didn't sound too over-confident but she knew she had a lot to be proud of. She wasn't just some city girl with dreams of the west; she'd been working hard her whole life and wanted to continue to put that work ethic to good use.

Rita nodded a little. "So, you're medically trained?"

"Not fully, but I'm trained enough that if, say, a customer were to choke, I'd know what to do." Tessa ran her fingers through the ends of her hair but resisted overdoing it at the risk of appearing to be a flighty girl.

"Outstanding," Rita replied. "And you're how old?"

"Twenty," Tessa said.

Rita gave her another reassuring smile. "Very impressive," she said. "Well, Tessa, I think you'll do quite nicely here. You will be living in the dormitory along with the other Stewart girls, but you won't have quite the same uniform and of course you'll have different duties, a different schedule and things like that. Pay will be nineteen dollars a month, plus room and board will be completely covered so long as you stay in the dorm. Does this sound reasonable to you?"

Tessa smiled at her. "Yes, very much so," she said. "Thank you."

Rita smiled back, revealing deep dimples in both cheeks. Tessa still couldn't believe that such a lovely woman was in charge of things. She understood why Rita was *Mrs.* Stewart. "Thank you, Miss Johnston. You have no idea how long we've searched for someone like you." Standing up, Rita offered her hand. Tessa stood and shook hands with her new boss.

"Please call me Tessa," she said in a friendly, excited

voice. *That interview was more like a reminder than anything,* she thought.

Rita moved away from the table then, looking around the otherwise vacant dining area. "Feel free to explore the hotel in your spare time today," she said. "And by all means, please head over to the dormitory next door and rest up from your travels. Oh, which reminds me..." She quickly walked out of the diner and back towards the front desk.

Not sure what she should do, Tessa followed. Rita riffled through the drawers in the desk. "Aha," she said under her breath. She handed Tessa a pair of bronze keys. "One key opens your room and the other key opens the front door of this hotel," she instructed. "There's also a ring of keys in this desk which can be accessed with that same key. Make sure you don't walk around with the ring of keys all the time; only use it when you need to assist people to their rooms or for maintenance, things of that nature."

Tessa's head swam with all of this newfound responsibility. She was rather glad that she had some time to orient herself and be trained before diving into her new role at the hotel. "I understand," she said with a quick nod, carefully holding onto the keys as if her life depended on them.

With one more smile, Rita took her leave to get back to work. Sure enough, just as Tessa was beginning to tour around the main floor of the hotel, people arrived to be placed into rooms. She blushed a little, just thinking about how she soon would be working to help them. *It definitely doesn't seem too far removed from the sorts of things I used to do at the hospital,* she thought. *Orienting people into their hospital beds, catering to their needs, managing multiple clients...* She hoped that it wouldn't be too different from what she knew she could do.

It didn't take her long to realize that what she really needed was some rest. *I don't wish to get in anyone's way here when I'm wandering around drowsily from room to room. Perhaps I should nap first and get acquainted with the rest of the place later.*

She knew that there would be plenty of time for her to look around in the days ahead as well. After all, while Tessa trained she would be familiarizing herself with the various rooms and the various tasks that she'd be called upon to perform. She wouldn't be able to be so casual then, but learning as she went was something that she excelled in. It was far easier to train on the job, for her, than to hear a bunch of instructions up front and immediately be expected to know what to do.

Carefully carrying her keys in her fist, Tessa left the hotel and strolled around the restaurant until she happened upon the tan-colored dormitory. It wasn't as tall as she had imagined, but it was wide enough to house the entire staff of the two Stewart properties. She climbed the stairs until she found the door with the room number that matched her key. Room number nine. Her new home.

Tessa unlocked the door and stepped inside. Her suitcase

had been placed on the floor beneath the foot of the bed and she noticed that it contained a dark wooden vanity and an oaken wardrobe. After shutting the door, she pulled off her shoes and climbed onto the bed, falling asleep without bothering to cover herself with the blankets.

2

Awaking from her nap, Tessa briefly forgot where she was. She lifted her head from the feather-soft pillow and looked around wide eyed at her new room. The vanity, the wardrobe, even the sheets on the bed where extremely different from her lodgings at home. The sheets here were white and blue, and topped with a blue quilt. At her home in Annapolis, her mother always used purely white bedding, mainly because it was the easiest for her to make. Blinking in her confusion, it slowly dawned on Tessa that she wasn't in Maryland anymore; she was in Kansas.

Smiling a bit at how silly she'd been, she stood up from the bed and stretched, then bent down to smooth out the wrinkles that had formed on her skirts. It wasn't like her to sleep fully clothed and on top of blankets, but that's just how exhausted she'd been. One minute she was excited to look around her new place of work and the next she'd been completely wiped out. *Hopefully Rita understands... I hope she isn't wondering where I am!*

Tessa felt such affinity for the innkeeper already that she didn't wish to wait around any longer. After carefully locking up her room, she headed out, back to the hotel. There were some guests still milling about, including a few who were sitting in the small diner. She went on a search for the time and found a tall grandfather clock against the wall in a grand salon. Lunchtime had passed and dinner would surely be in a few hours. *I get the feeling that schedules are primarily run by the meals,* she thought.

"Tessa!" Rita's voice suddenly called to her as she wandered around the salon, exploring. She turned and smiled a bit timidly at her new boss. "There you are," Rita said, smiling back and waving her over toward the front desk. "Do you think you're ready to begin training?"

Tessa nodded eagerly. Everything was happening so fast, but she was grateful for that. *I won't be bored if I'm always doing something here,* she thought. She'd spent enough time looking around and she was anxious to learn the where's and how's of things.

"All right," Rita began. "Well, dinnertime is by far the busiest time for us here. The train arrives and the guests file into the restaurant. Some overflow generally arrives here to dine in our eatery. Most of the guests don't elect to stay once the meal is over, but we're here for those who *do* stay awhile. Follow me and I'll show you the rooms, which will be more of what you'll concern yourself with. Restaurant duty here at the hotel is much more lenient and I won't ask you to do it all of the time if you don't wish."

With that, Rita led Tessa up to the second floor to two long hallways that flanked either side of the stairs. The hotel had been decorated with paintings of boats and trains on the walls here and there, calm travel motifs for the weary travelers to enjoy. "There are ten rooms, not including the one occupied by my husband and me, and our study is also housed up here." Rita led her along and gestured to her that the room at the end of one of the halls was the bedroom that was off limits and the room across the hall from it was the study. She went so far as to open the door to each of these rooms.

There's a quilt on their bed that's much like the one on mine, Tessa thought. "Did you make all of the quilts?" she blurted.

Rita nodded, smiling and looking impressed. "Yes, it's a hobby of mine. I haven't had a lot of time for it of late, but it's proved useful now that we've got a hotel. All of the beds needed blankets."

She closed up the private rooms again and then showed Tessa how to knock on each bedroom door and use the ring of keys to go inside in order to tidy things up. It all seemed pretty straight forward. "I can definitely do this," she said. "I haven't been a key holder per se but I've certainly gone into rooms and tidied while I was working in the hospital."

Rita nodded her head. "That's good to hear. Just remember, when you're not on tidying duty, you must keep the ring of keys safely stored away in the front desk. That way, we're not endangering people's private belongings by leaving things open."

Tessa never thought about it, really, but it was a good point. Most of the guests were harmless and there to have a good time and relax, but the train could just as easily bring with it a rascal or two who might try and steal things both from the hotel and from the restaurant. "I understand," she said.

The two ladies went back downstairs to the welcome desk and Rita put the keys away. "One thing that's easier about this job as opposed to working in a bed and breakfast elsewhere is that we don't deliver food to the rooms. If customers wish to dine here, they are welcome to come to either of our eating house options. I do of course try to advertise our breakfast restaurant for our overnight guests."

Tessa wondered if she should have been taking notes, but she didn't think that she'd have any difficulty learning on the job. "How many others do you have working here in the hotel?"

Rita gave it a little thought. She clearly had many girls' names to keep track of. "Clara, Emmie, Wendy, and now you." She smiled. "I encourage you to get to know all of the girls here at Stewart House, because like I said there's a chance for very occasional overlap between here and the restaurant next door. And it always helps to be friendly with your fellow workers."

Tessa made note of the names she'd said. She wasn't sure how she was going to go about meeting the other girls apart from running into them while working – hopefully not literally.

For the rest of the evening, she followed Rita around in order to observe more of the various ins and outs of working in the Stewart House hotel. *It's all pretty self-explanatory,* she thought, relieved. *And if I should ever be confused, there will be others I can turn to for help.* When her training ended for the day, she smiled at Rita and shook hands with her again. "Thank you so much for this opportunity," Tessa said with more confidence in her voice than had been there all day. "I can't wait to get started working here alongside you and the other girls."

Rita smiled back at her. "I'm sure you will do quite well. Let me know if there's ever anything that you need. We take care of our girls here."

Tessa walked back to the dormitory, pleased with her new position and feeling more and more eager to get to work. *I know it gets busy,* she thought as she ascended the staircase back up to her room. *But I doubt very much that a busy restaurant or inn could be anywhere near as stressful or unnerving as a hospital ward.*

She noticed that some of the others girls had their bedroom doors open and she decided that this was as good a time as any to introduce herself. She peeked her head into the first open door and smiled. "Hello," she said to the two girls inside. One of them, a pretty young girl, was sitting on her bed in her pajamas, running a brush through her loose, red-blonde hair. The other girl was sitting at her vanity, tidying herself up for bed as well. She had blonde hair. The girls may as well have been sisters, but Tessa didn't want to assume. "I don't wish to bother you, but I thought I ought to introduce myself. I'm Tessa Johnston. I'm the new girl, working in the hotel."

The girl on the bed lit up at the mention of the hotel. "Oh, wonderful!" she said brightly. "Welcome to Stewart House. I'm Wendy and this is my sister Emmie." She gestured a roll of her shoulder towards the other girl.

I knew it. "It's so great to meet you both," Tessa replied, looking from Wendy to Emmie.

"Come in and sit, if you have a moment," Emmie said, placing her brush down on the vanity and smiling at her as well. "We love to get to know our fellow Stewart Girls."

Tessa stepped into the room and sat on the other vanity's chair, knowing that Wendy wouldn't mind since she was sitting on the bed. "You're so kind," Tessa said. "I've noticed so far that everyone here has been welcoming and warm. I really appreciate it because life amongst the hospital staff in Maryland had been filled with strife.

Wendy's jaw dropped a little. "That sounds so sad."

"You worked in a hospital?" Emmie asked.

Tessa nodded her head. "I worked as a nurse's assistant. My mother's a nurse and my father is a doctor. They met in the hospital, as a matter of fact, caring for the injured soldiers who returned from the war."

The two sisters gasped and looked at her with newfound admiration. "I can see why you might've needed a change," Emmie said. "The restaurant and hotel business is much more cheerful, I'm sure."

Wendy laughed softly. "Oh, definitely," she said. "We never deal with ill people. God forbid we should ever need to. Though I suppose we now have someone who'd be able to help in that case, if that was necessary."

Tessa smiled shyly and blushed. *I don't recall ever receiving so many compliments before I moved here,* she thought. *The people here are too kind.* "I look forward to working with you both. I apologize in advance if I'm a bit slow to learn things, but please know that I'm seriously happy and honored to be working alongside you."

The sisters smiled, touched. Tessa politely said her good-nights and then went back out into the hallway. She was feeling sleepy now and she knew that she must get her rest for the following day, when she was to officially start working in the hotel. She decided to forgo reaching out to the other girls until the next day, when she would be more awake and ready to meet more people. She went into her bedroom and closed her door, choosing not to lock it on the off chance that someone might want to come in and meet her. Many of the others left their doors open, so she didn't want to be seen as unfriendly.

Also, there's always a chance that I might accidentally sleep in for too long, she reasoned with herself as she changed into her fuchsia nightgown. *So, locking the door would hinder anyone who might try to wake me up or inform me of anything important that Rita might've forgotten to tell me.*

Tessa got into her bed, putting the blankets over herself this time. She felt a strange mixture of tired and awake – as if her body wanted to rest but her brain wanted to run laps around the room. She closed her eyes, willing herself not to think about the hotel or the other girls or anything else relating to her new job until the morrow. She knew that it would do no good to think about any of it when she couldn't act on anything until the following day. Nevertheless, she was positive that she'd dream about her new situation and challenges anyway.

At least I'm excited instead of dreading things, Tessa thought as she drifted off to sleep. That in itself was a welcome change for her.

After having quite a few stressful dreams all night, Tessa was relieved when she woke up on the first day of official training for work. She threw her blankets off and stood up, stretching and changing into a simple gray dress, making sure that she still wore her thin, black petticoat because she knew it was needed for the uniform that she'd be required to wear. *Rita's going to give me my outfit today,* she thought excitedly. The black dress and white apron were not the most amazing things to wear, but it was thrilling to be given her regulation uniform and feel as though she was finally one of the Stewart Girls, even if she had a lot of learning to do. *I'm ready,* she thought, brushing her dark brown hair and then pulling it back into a high bun on the back of her head. *I'm ready to be put to the test.*

Tessa left her room and walked over to the hotel. She sat in the foyer by the welcome desk, unsure if this was where she was supposed to meet Rita and be assigned her training partner but thinking that it was the most logical place. *She may be assisting in the restaurant first.* The innkeeper helped her husband with the restaurant as well as the hotel, which meant that she did need all of the help that she could get. Splitting up her duties would be much easier than trying to do a little bit of everything all the time.

Wendy and Emmie appeared soon after Tessa's arrival. They both smiled and waved at her. A third girl also walked in through the front door, tying her apron around her waist. Tessa smiled and nodded to her. *That must be Clara,* she thought. *It's exciting to be working with a bunch of girls my own age or thereabouts!*

"Are you ready?" Wendy asked Tessa in a friendly voice. "It's your big day."

Tessa nodded. "Oh yes, I'm very eager to get started," she chirped with a big grin on her face.

"Rita will be here a little later," Emmie informed her. "She has some business to take care of in the restaurant. But follow us around and we'll show you the ropes."

The three girls ascended the staircase and went from room to room, tidying things up and collecting items for the laundry, turning over the sheets if the room was presently being occupied by a guest. Most of the hotel's current guests were at breakfast, which made the job of cleaning the rooms much easier. At every door, Wendy knocked and said, "Room service." A few of the guests requested that they come back later, which of course they were more than happy to do. "It's what the customer's want, not what our schedule says," Wendy pointed out in a soft voice to Tessa.

Once they were finished going into each room that would admit them and tidying up, Emmie took her leave to go down to the front desk so she could admit newcomers to the hotel. Tessa stayed with Wendy, figuring that shadowing one of the girls for the day would help to give her a more complete picture of what a shift there looked like.

"Do you have a shift at the front desk, too?" she asked Wendy.

"Oh yes," Wendy replied. "We all get a shift there. At least one. My favorite part about it is that there's a little chair so you can sit periodically. Not the whole time, mind you, but when no one's around." Light twinkled in her eyes. *Especially Rita,* Tessa thought, finishing Wendy's statement for her and smiling conspiratorially.

Wendy and Tessa went down the stairs and around the rooms on the main level of the hotel now, making sure that there wasn't any disorganization going on amongst the bookcases and other surfaces. The sitting room was a grand area, filled with gray couches and matching gray chairs. *This looks like a quite nice place to sit and read,* Tessa thought. As they worked, they were soon joined by several guests who'd just come through the front doors from the restaurant next door or perhaps the train station. The chatter in the room reached a rather high volume and Tessa was forced to concede that it might not be the best place to leisurely sit and read at all times...

Wendy sidled over to her, still smiling but also appearing a bit stressed now. The corners of her mouth edged downward. "I need to spend some time in the diner," she told Tessa. "Do you think you'll be okay here for a while? Just continue doing what you're doing, dusting and organizing. Rita will be over shortly, once the rest of the breakfast rush is over. She brings along some waiter-girls usually, too."

Tessa's mind raced, overwhelmed. *Stay here alone? I don't know what I'm doing! What if someone should ask me a question? I suppose Emmie is out there and wouldn't mind if I directed questions and requests to her...* She wished that Rita had given her a bit more information and training. She hadn't known that the innkeeper wouldn't be there to help her on her first day.

"Sure," Tessa heard herself say, doing her best to completely mask her nerves. "I don't think it will be a problem."

Wendy smiled broadly at her and then rushed off to see to the duties in the breakfast diner. Tessa got back to work polishing the bookcase and rearranging the books so they were in an order that made more sense. *Alphabetical by subject, I should think,* she thought. *I doubt very much that people passing through will care about who wrote the books.*

"Excuse me, miss?" a voice suddenly asked from behind her.

In her surprise, Tessa dropped a large, leather-bound volume onto the floor, barely missing her foot in the process.

The man who stood there looked from the book to her face, appearing dubious now. "I'm sorry. Do you work here? I noticed you cleaning..."

"Yes," Tessa said breathlessly, bending down to scoop up the book and place it back on the shelf. "I'm afraid I'm new here and I haven't been given my uniform yet." *He probably doesn't care about that.* "But may I help you with something? I shall certainly do my best."

The gentleman was older, with silvery hair and black eyebrows. His back was a bit stooped and Tessa couldn't help but think that this was a man who was in Wallace for vacation, not so he could become a farmer late in life. He raised his bushy eyebrows at her. "Oh, if you're new here maybe I ought not to trouble you," he said. "Is there someone else I can speak to?"

Thankfully, Rita appeared in the doorway of the sitting room, smiling as soon as she caught sight of Tessa. She rushed over and whisked the old man away, answering his question and promptly coming to his aide.

Tessa breathed a sigh of relief, but she also reddened in the face just a tad. She knew she could've handled the man's requests, if he'd only given her a chance.

Rita came back over to her as soon as she'd finished

assisting the older gentleman. She was all smiles which made Tessa feel somewhat better. *At least she's not frustrated or disappointed in me,* she thought. *I likely looked like such a lost fool, though.*

"Good afternoon, Tessa," Rita said brightly, taking her gently by the elbow. "How has your first day of training been going? How long have you been on your own? Come, we really must get you into a uniform before my husband sees you."

With that, Rita whisked Tessa away from the sitting room and into a small study that was near the front of the hotel, near the small breakfast diner as well. There was a desk in this room, covered in organized stacks of papers and books. There was also a small bed, which confused Tessa. *What does Rita need this bed here for?* She was aware that Rita and Mr. Stewart had their room upstairs, so why must the innkeeper have a bed in her office?

Rita, noticing what had caught Tessa's attention, smiled at her. "Sometimes, when it's calm, I like to try to catch an extra wink of sleep. It's also here if ever one of you girls really needs it, but hopefully that won't be the case. I hope that you all get more rest than I do."

"You seem so cheerful for someone who never gets any rest," Tessa replied, slightly teasingly.

Rita laughed, which was a relief to Tessa. She didn't intend to overstep the boundary betwixt employee and employer. Especially because, though she sensed that they were friendly already, they had still only just met. She strode over to the wardrobe next to the bed – a much smaller one compared to the wardrobes in the dormitory rooms. Even still, Rita had clearly thought of everything.

She pulled out a black dress which had been carefully hanging up in the wardrobe. It matched Rita's, except it was missing the petticoat and the bit of flare that somehow emanated from her. Tessa doubted very much that she was going to be able to emulate her boss in that regard. Rita handed the frock over to Tessa and then, reaching into the wardrobe again, brought out a white apron. "Try all of this on and let me make sure it's a good fit."

With that, Rita left her there in the study, closing the door behind herself so Tessa could have a bit of privacy. She carefully removed the gray dress that she was wearing, laying it flat on the bed for now as she pulled the new, crisp black frock over herself. The black petticoat that she wore went nicely with it, giving the skirt some more volume as Tessa twirled. She wished that she had a mirror with which she could admire herself. *I suppose I can find one in the hall upstairs. Elsewise, I'll wait until I'm back in my room this evening.* Nevertheless, she smiled, feeling like she at last had all of the tools she needed in order to succeed at Stewart House. Tying the apron around her waist, she went to the door and reopened it.

Rita was waiting right outside, acting as a guard in case any of the other girls should come along and try to use the study. As soon as she took one look at Tessa in her new outfit, she beamed excitedly at her and took her hand. "Oh, darling, you look perfect!" she exclaimed in a sing-song sort of voice. "Do you like how it fits?"

Tessa nodded her head, smiling back at her. When Rita was extremely happy, her dimples showed and Tessa adored bearing witness to that, particularly if she was the cause of her smiling. "Yes, it's wonderful," Tessa agreed. "I did have a question, though. Should I go over and return my other dress to my closet?"

"Oh certainly," Rita said, her smile unwavering. "You should take a short break now anyway, since I know you haven't had one yet. Now that I'm over here and can assist you more, we can start more training once you've had some rest, all right?"

Tessa smiled at her and gave a polite little curtsy. "I look forward to training more with you. Wendy has been such a help to me so far, too." She went into the study to retrieve her dress, then she happily marched off to the dorm to put her other dress away and unwind for a few moments.

Blessedly, lunchtime seems less of a hassle than breakfast, she thought as she lay on her bed, arms upon her tummy, fingers intertwined. It felt good to lie down, but her brain was all a-twitter with thoughts about her new job and her new life. It was all so thrilling!

4

Now that Tessa was properly uniformed and Rita was there to offer more in the way of instructions and guidance, everything seemed to fall into place for her. She was given two days of training in all, and then of course she would be permitted to ask questions and seek help from the other girls if she should ever feel confused or stuck with something. "No one here started out perfectly knowing how to do all of this," Rita told her with a comforting sort of smile towards the end of the week, when Tessa was able to move away from shadowing and could take care of a few tasks on her own. "Not even me. So, you're not alone here."

In their downtime from working in the hotel, Tessa and the other girls in the dorm were able to commiserate more.

One of the things that excites me the most about working here is the chance to have real friends in my life after spending all of my early days in the shadows of my parents.

"How long have you been here?" Tessa asked Wendy and Emmie as she sat with them in their room, door open as always. They were so welcoming with everyone and Tessa hoped to be like that with all of the other girls – current and future – as well.

Wendy and Emmie looked at each other and Tessa felt like she could see the gears turning within their minds as they thought back and tried to recall the exact date. "Well we came here together," Emmie replied. "Wendy saw the advertisement and thought it might be an excellent way for us to get away from our parents and explore the world without having to split up."

"We've always been close," Wendy added. "We weren't close with our parents, though."

"I believe it was in the early spring," Emmie said finally, nodding a little as she thought it over. "When this hotel was still pretty new."

It was still new even now, but Tessa understood what she meant. There had to have been a time when the paint was still drying and the guest list wasn't as long. "So, tell me your stories," she said. "I'm assuming that you came from the East Coast like I did."

Wendy nodded. "Yes, upstate New York. The winters there were rough, and our futures seemed bleak. Our father was never around because he did a lot of business in the city, and our mother was of course always busy with the home and finding ways to earn a little extra money any way she could."

Tessa was mystified. She couldn't imagine her parents being apart for more than a few hours. They were best friends and it was very apparent. "I suppose I should be grateful then, for my parents being the way they were. They expected me to be just like them, which was the fault I had with them."

Her friends – she thought of Wendy and Emmie as her friends now – nodded sympathetically. "What matters is that each of us is here now," Emmie said softly. "It doesn't quite matter the reason, it only matters that we came from wherever place and we're here to start over. And we're happy, right?"

Tessa smiled and tears filled her eyes. She nodded. "Yes. I do believe I'm happier than I've ever been now that I'm here."

Wendy and Emmie stood up from their chairs and went to her on the Wendy's bed, hugging her. Tessa laughed. "I've never been hugged by two people at the same time before. It feels amazing."

"That's something else that Rita has been wonderful about," Emmie said. "I can't say the same for Mr. Stewart as he hasn't been working in the hotel as much, though the stories about him have all painted him as a kind and caring soul, too."

Wendy smiled. "So, it is possible to find a man like that out here," she said. "It's not easy, but it is possible."

Tessa looked down at the quilt, blushing even as her smile grew. "Have you been trying to find a husband?" she asked. "I just find working life so much more interesting than romance and all of that. But then, I guess it was bred into me. I wouldn't know the first thing about it."

Emmie and Wendy looked at each other and giggled a little. "Oh, it's a thing worth doing, in my opinion," Emmie said. "And there's a newspaper service that helps. A lot of girls come out west because of it, which you're right about; it's a silly reason to move out here and pin all of your hopes on. But just the same... some of the men in the newspaper advertisements sound awfully sweet."

"I've been writing to at least three of them," Wendy said, turning and opening the drawer of her dresser. She brought out a small stack of letters, setting them down with a *thump* on the bed so that Tessa could take a gander at them.

Isn't it rude to read someone else's mail? She wondered. Still, she peeked at the lovely handwriting that was clearly Wendy's and not that of her Beau. "What does one even discuss with a stranger? I can't think of the first thing I might say to someone I've never met in person before."

"Oh, it's quite easy," Wendy said. "They put a few bits about themselves in the newspaper usually, so you're not starting out completely clueless as to who they are and where their interests lie."

Tessa furrowed her brows a bit, still gazing down at the letters on the bed and wondered if this could ever be the right path for her. "But to get married is to be forced to leave this wonderful place," she mused.

Emmie shook her head at Tessa. "You needn't leave unless you wish to," she said. "In the restaurant, Mr. Stewart requests that his girls remain single but Mrs. Stewart doesn't have such a request. It would be a bit hypocritical, don't you think?"

Tessa thought that over. "But I think we might be hard-pressed to find gentlemen who're okay with us still working."

Wendy giggled a little. "Gentlemen in the east, perhaps, but here there is opportunity for all."

I just don't see it as a utopia like that, Tessa thought, going back to her room as the evening drew to a close and night-time fell upon them. *Surely the gentlemen here are not so far removed from the gentlemen back home in the east. They're just dustier.* She smirked to herself as she got changed into her nightgown and sat at her vanity, brushing the knots out of her long and otherwise smooth hair.

Tomorrow would be a good time to get a newspaper and look into this more. For now, she needed to sleep. Tessa got into her bed and thought no more about it, concerning her mind more with the day ahead, when she would begin to work on her own with limited instruction beyond the daily tasks which were asked of her. She was elated about that, and she didn't think that a prospective husband could ever change that aspect of her. Tessa was made for public service, not for being a housewife.

When Tessa awoke early the next morning, she dressed quickly and left the dormitory, making her way to the post office in order to pick up one of the newspapers that she and the girls had discussed the night before. She didn't have much confidence that anything would come of it, but she was willing to check it out anyway. "Good morning," she said in a friendly voice to the man who worked there.

He was sitting at the front desk and didn't seem at all surprised to be greeted by a young lady in this way. *He's likely used to the Stewart girls coming in here and asking about newspapers...* Tessa instantly felt a wave of embarrassment. She almost turned and left, but then the gentleman spoke in an even tone of his own. "How do you do, miss? Are you here in search of a newspaper?"

She turned to face him, still feeling embarrassed but now she was comforted by the calm, pleasant way in which he regarded her. He was evidently used to such things, but he wasn't judging her. After all, he wanted to give out newspapers. *Otherwise, they're likely to build up, I suppose. He'd rather be rid of them. There's no sense in getting into a tizzy every time someone looks at you, Tess.* "Yes, please, sir. Thank you."

The man chuckled a bit and stood up from his chair, going into the back room to retrieve a paper. Tessa meanwhile looked around at the small post office. It was quite tidy, with chairs for visitors to sit in and tables upon which a person might be able to pen a letter. It was quite a convenient sort of place. Soon, the gentleman who worked there returned and handed over a gray and maroon newspaper with the town's seal and name across the top of it. *It looks just like any ordinary newspaper,* she thought and then she wondered what on earth she had expected. *I guess it wasn't going to say 'Husbands! Husbands! Husbands!' across the front.* She felt herself blushing and she paid the man some coins from her purse, curtsying slightly before making her exit, as awkwardly as she had arrived.

Tessa made her way back to the hotel, making sure to keep the newspaper tucked inside her bag for safekeeping while she was working. She had to fold it up quite a lot in order to get it to fit into her small purse, but she was able to do it. *Just hope no one needs something from my purse today,* she thought. Aside from her money, there blessedly wasn't much else to her purse. Until the newspaper came along, of course. "Good morning," she said to Rita and Clara as she stepped into the hotel lobby, tying her apron around her middle and looking around. There were no other people milling about yet. She didn't wish to get ahead of herself, but she thought that her favorite time of day while she was working was these moments of calm before the storm; before the customers came into the hotel and began listing their demands and needs.

"Tessa," Rita said right away, coming towards her and touching her gently on her elbows. "I'm so glad you're here. Today I'd like you to try something new. But don't worry, I will be there to show you how everything is done and you won't be asked to do it every day unless you find that you really take to it."

Tessa nervously looked from Rita's dark eyes to Clara's shy, nervous expression. "Anywhere I'm needed, I'd be happy to help," she said. "Where are Wendy and Emmie?"

Rita sighed a little bit, reaching up to massage the back of her neck. It was early in the day and already she was stressed. This couldn't be a good sign. "Wendy has requested the day off in order to meet a gentleman in one of the dormitory's courting parlors."

This came as a surprise. Tessa's eyes widened. "Oh? She didn't mention anything about that last night. And what about Emmie?"

"Emmie's upstairs, straightening the rooms," Rita said. "Apparently Wendy's beau surprised her on the street this morning. They've been writing to each other for quite some time."

My goodness, if such a thing happened to me I don't think I would be so happy, Tessa thought. Still, she smiled about Wendy's good fortune and she certainly wished her well.

Perhaps something good would come out of the newspaper advertisements for her, too.

5

"It might be overwhelming for you at first because it's quite different from the calm workflow in the rest of the hotel, but you'll get the hang of it in no time," Rita said as she guided Tessa through the breakfast diner, showing her around the small kitchen and all of the pantries therein. "You won't be alone either. I'll be right here with you. Likely tending to other tables, but near enough if you should need any help."

Tessa's pulse quickened and she gulped a bit, careful to make sure that it wasn't audible. She didn't want her boss to know how anxious she was about this shift in position. "Okay," she said.

I guess today's the day I get to see Wendy's routine while she's working in the diner.

"Fortunately, I don't anticipate it ever being as busy here as the restaurant next door gets. That's because the people here aren't on as strict of a timetable." Rita smiled at Tessa. "Just be sure to greet everyone at your tables and get their orders right. You don't have to rush either. In fact, I'm against rushing because more mistakes are made that way."

This made sense to Tessa. "That's good, because I think I panic when I have to rush."

Rita laughed a little. "There's no need to panic. Now here they come. Look lively." She turned her attention to the guests who'd begun to groggily file in. "Good morning! Please have a seat anywhere you like." She gestured to the tables throughout the small area that comprised the hotel's restaurant.

Tessa followed her example and greeted the guests as they sat. "Good morning! My name is Tessa and I'm happy to be of service to you. What would you like to drink this morning? We've got some nice, hot coffee brewing in the back just for you."

She quickly found that working in the small restaurant wasn't the ordeal that she'd imagined. The guests were quiet and fairly sleepy, and grateful for her help. She also recognized the majority of them from their hotel rooms and when they first came to stay. *I think I could see myself doing this alongside Wendy or Emmie, if I'm needed here,* she thought happily. *There's no reason that I have to strictly work in the hotel.*

This feeling soon changed however, as more and more

people began filing into the diner. Mr. Stewart appeared, leading them in as if he was a tour guide. "This way, please. There should be plenty of room in here for all of you." He looked over and gestured for Rita to come over to him. Tessa watched as the two exchanged some whispered words, and then Rita came towards her.

"Change of plans," she said. "It's about to be quite busy in here. This is overflow from a crowded, hungry breakfast train. You don't have to assist me if you don't wish to, but I'll need you to go and fetch Emmie if you can't."

Tessa looked from Rita to Mr. Stewart and then at the throngs of people who were stuffing themselves into booths or around tables. Would her heart ever be able to stop wildly pounding at the sight of crowds? *I don't know what to do, but I don't want to just give this work to someone else. That strikes me as irresponsible.* She smiled at Rita, nodding her head quickly. "I can handle it," she said in a voice that was surprisingly not quaking. "You'll still be right here with me, right?"

Rita looked at her so fondly that she knew that she'd made the correct choice. "Thank you, Tessa."

Going up to one of the slightly over-populated tables, Tessa smiled at the new customers. "Good morning. My name is Tessa. Busy train today, huh? I'd be happy to get you folks whatever you'd like. May I start off with some drinks?"

She could feel Mr. Stewart's eyes on her as she worked. He was the one in charge of the restaurant and she knew that he was scrutinizing her based on that experience. Things weren't as strict under Rita's control, but Tessa still worried about what Mr. Stewart thought of her. If he didn't like her for whatever reason, he could recommend that his wife fire Tessa and the mere thought of that frightened her. *Focus on your work,* she told herself. *And do as Rita said. Be calm and don't rush, because mistakes happen when you rush...*

Once her notepad was full of their drink orders, Tessa made her way to the back kitchen to pour the drinks into some glasses. After a few moments in which she could clear her mind and try to relax, Mr. Stewart peered into the doorway of the kitchen, watching her at her work. She was taking her time pouring water or juice into each glass, careful not to spill.

"Chop chop, Miss Johnston," he said to her in a voice that was somehow both gentle and urgent. "We've got a lot of tables to serve her today."

Tessa quickly lifted her head so she could look at him there, jumping a little in her surprise and accidentally spilling some milk onto the beech wood counter. "Oh!" she exclaimed. "Okay, I'll be right there!" She rushed to find a rag and sop up the mess.

Mr. Stewart left from the doorway and Tessa cleaned things up, finishing her pouring uninterrupted and then came out with her tray of drinks. She could feel her boss's eyes on her as she walked back to her table and dispensed the beverages. It wasn't a great feeling. *He's probably told her,* she thought, practically shaking in her black-heeled shoes. But Rita was kind. She wouldn't scold Tessa, right? Especially after telling her to remain calm and not rush. Her husband had basically told her the opposite of those directions. Whom should she listen to?

Tessa did her best to just pass out the drinks and go about her business, paying no mind to her boss and Mr. Stewart. *It won't do if I'm frazzled,* she thought. When she was working on bringing out another tray of drinks, her hands were shaking so much that she dropped one of the glasses. Mercifully, it was a glass of water, but a broken glass was still a broken glass.

"I'm terribly sorry!" she said to the customer. Right away, Tessa rushed to get a rag and the broom from the kitchen. Rita walked over as she was sweeping up the broken glass.

"Are you all right?" she asked Tessa. There was surprise and genuine concern in her voice, which made Tessa feel worse instead of better. She didn't want her boss to feel that way about her or her work.

Tessa looked at the floor, very relieved that it had only been water. Juice would've left an awful stain on the rug. "I do believe I'm a bit nervous with all of the customers and with Mr. Stewart being here."

Rita was sympathetic. "Please go and find Emmie?" she asked. Her voice remained gentle and pleasant but Tessa could sense faint disappointment in it as well. Disappointment in her.

Tessa nodded her head and left the diner in search of her friend and coworker. Her eyes filled with tears and she wiped them with the back of her wrist, but no matter what she did more tears just came. She found Emmie in the sitting room, rearranging the books. Emmie immediately stopped what she was doing when she caught sight of Tessa and came over, giving her a loose hug.

She can probably tell I've been crying, Tessa thought sadly. *I feel so ashamed of myself.*

"Are you all right?" Emmie asked her. "What's troubling you?"

Shaking her head, Tessa sighed. "Rita wants you to work in the diner instead. It got quite busy and, in my nervousness, I dropped a glass."

Emmie raised her eyebrows, frowning a little but not pulling back from her or expressing any harshness in her tone. "I'm sorry, dear. We've all been there, though. Rita is good about constantly purchasing new glassware and dishes. I can imagine it being quite difficult to be confronted with large crowds on your first day. Even the toughest among us would be addled." At that, she gently reached over and patted Tessa on her upper arm. "Take a moment to sit down here, hmm? I've almost finished tidying this room. Then you just need to do the usual rounds upstairs, making sure guests' rooms are organized and everyone has whatever they might've requested."

It just dawned on Tessa that Clara had been sitting at the welcome desk all day. *How is that allowed?* She wondered. *I don't wish to stir up trouble, of course. I suppose I better not even ask about it.* Between Clara being able to sit at one post all day and Wendy not coming into work today at all, Tessa was feeling quite miffed about everything. *Perhaps it's good timing for me to start looking into meeting a gentleman from around here...*

She did as was suggested and sat upon the couch in the sitting room while Emmie went off to assist in the restaurant. Rita would be pleased to have a more seasoned worker on hand during the busy shift. Tessa wouldn't hold out hope that the rest of the day would be so forgiving for her. "It's likely to be busy in the hotel later," she said under her breath. "Especially if some of these guests decide to stay in the hotel and extend their time in Wallace."

She sat on the couch for about ten minutes and then finally stood up and continued Emmie's work at the book-shelf. Periodically, Tessa would glance over to see Clara still standing around at the desk at the entrance to the hotel. She seemed quite at home there, but it wasn't right that it was all that she was doing. Particularly because there were no visitors who were coming in and trying to get a room. Clara was effectively watching paint dry all day while everyone else was working like mad.

As soon as she was finished rearranging the books on the shelf, following Emmie's organizational structure, Tessa went back upstairs so she could tidy up the vacated rooms and offer to clean the rooms that were currently occupied. Work seemed to crawl to the stop and Tessa wanted only to sleep as soon as she got back to the dormitory, but then she remembered the newspaper in her purse as she was pulling out her room key.

She smiled slightly to herself and brought it out, holding it in the crook of her arm as she unlocked her bedroom and went inside, closing the door but not locking it. Tessa sat at her vanity, removing her black-heeled shoes, so relieved to no longer have to wear the restrictive things. She sat there in her stockinged feet and opened up the newspaper, spreading it out on the desk in front of her. Flipping the pages, she came upon the page of advertisements. Once again, it didn't cry 'Husbands! Husbands! Husbands!' but nevertheless the advertisements were eye-catching, especially the ones that came accompanied by a photograph.

Tessa blushed as she read through all of these ads, not knowing the first thing about how she would go about choosing one of these gentlemen. *I almost wish I could meet with all of them,* she thought. *They all seem so interesting, and they've all put themselves out there like this. More power to them.*

Finally, her gaze fell upon an advertisement that didn't include a portrait. *Samuel Grayson, a rancher, thirty-eight years of age, seeks a bride to be his companion and help him with the home and livestock. Hoping to find a diligent, enthusiastic young woman to fill his long, lonely days in Wallace, Kansas.*

Tessa's smile grew. This advertisement spoke to her for reasons she couldn't quite articulate. Should she write to him? She didn't see any harm in trying to get his attention.

6

Getting out a pen and some paper, Tessa haltingly began to write to Samuel Grayson, the man who posted the advertisement. She didn't quite know what she was supposed to write, what would interest him enough about her to make him write back, but she knew that she had to try. As much as she appreciated and enjoyed working in the hotel, she was finding that it perhaps wasn't the best fit for her. She didn't believe that was only the self-doubt talking.

DEAR MR. GRAYSON,

You don't know me of course, but I came upon your advertisement in the newspaper and I thought it best that I write to you in an effort to get to know you better. My name is Tessa Johnston and I, too, live in Wallace, Kansas. I currently work at the Stewart House as a hotel concierge and I also have past experience as a nurse's assistant. I'm looking to continue utilizing my abilities wherever else I may go.

I am twenty years old with brown hair and hazel eyes. I believe that I'm pretty; my friends and family have certainly told me so, but it is up to you to decide. I grew up the daughter of a doctor and a nurse in Annapolis, Maryland. I've actually only been in Wallace for about a week now but I have every intention of staying for the rest of my days. Please tell me more about yourself so we might get to know each other better.

I eagerly await your response.

Best wishes,
Tessa

As she carefully folded up her letter and placed it into an envelope, she hoped that he would take the time to respond to her, even if he might not be interested in pursuing anything with her. *I must try my best not to wait around, moping, if I never hear from him.*

Now that she'd responded to one of the newspaper advertisements, it was time for her to go to sleep and get some rest from the brutal day she'd experienced. She prayed that the morrow would be easier on her, and that Wendy would come back to work if only because it made everything less stressful for Tessa.

She awoke the following morning feeling refreshed and ready to take on whatever new challenges that the hotel chose to throw at her. She wasn't keen on attempting to work in the restaurant again, and she was hoping to speak with Rita about what had happened the day prior. *I hope she doesn't think that I'm totally useless,* she thought as she put on her uniform, gazing at her reflection and feeling proud regardless of how stressful things currently were for her. Tessa wasn't one to give up so easily. She fully intended to give it another try. *Particularly if it's a smidge less busy. Or Wendy is there.*

She put her hair up into a neat bun and gathered up the letter in its envelope, placing it into her purse for the time being. There'd be plenty of time during one of Tessa's breaks for her to stop by the post office and mail it off. *Last time I prioritized the mail order situation, I wasn't so focused on work... I should strive to do better today.* She knew that Mr. Grayson could wait. It wasn't like the letter would get to him that much faster if she mailed it in the morning versus later on in the afternoon.

When Tessa arrived at the hotel, Rita was standing

behind the welcome desk, flipping through the pages in the ledger and taking notes in a small notebook. She looked up from her writing and smiled warmly at Tessa. "Good morning, Tessa!" she said, enthusiastic as always. "How are you today?"

Smiling back at her, Tessa placed her purse into the safety of the locked storage cupboard within the desk. She locked it with one of the keys on the ring of keys, and then decided to keep hold of the keys since she was going off to clean the bedrooms anyway. "I'm doing well," she replied. "I wanted to apologize for how overwhelmed I became yesterday. Please let me know if you'd like me to go to the store and purchase some new glasses for you, or anything else I can help you with. I feel so bad."

Rita giggled a little, shaking her head. "Think nothing more of it, please. It's okay."

"I was hoping that I could have another chance at the diner today, if it's not too much trouble for you," Tessa offered. "I believe I can get used to it if I have more practice."

"I realize that yesterday was a difficult first attempt, what with all of the people who came in," Rita said, nodding her head in agreement. "You may certainly try again today. I'm sure Wendy would be happy to have you help her."

Tessa grinned. "Excellent," she said. "I will get started cleaning the rooms." She held the ring of keys up so Rita could see that she was ready to go.

"Several guests checked out last night or first thing this morning, too, so you shouldn't have as much to tidy," Rita said. "Once you've done the rounds up there, come back down and we'll see where best to place you. I don't anticipate today being nearly so tiring."

Tessa did as she was told and went upstairs. Sure enough, most of the rooms were vacant. She removed the blankets and towels from each empty room, placing them into a basket to be carried downstairs and washed. The majority of guests at the hotel were neat enough that the rooms didn't require that much cleaning, which made Tessa happy, too. *I know it can't always be like this, but it's nice when it happens.*

As soon as she was done organizing the rooms and bringing the sheets downstairs to be washed, Tessa found Rita back at the front desk. "What shall I do now?" she asked, swiping a loose strand of dark hair behind her ear.

Rita appeared impressed that Tessa was already done with her first task for the day. It had only been an hour. "Tidy up in the sitting room and here in the foyer," she said. "Then I suppose you can go on a break. Wendy would like your accompaniment during lunchtime, and perhaps dinner, depending on how full the train is."

Tessa was thrilled that she was not only going to be given another chance in the diner, but she was going to possibly be working for longer there. *I just hope I don't make a mess of things again, especially not in front of Mr. Stewart.* She got to work right away in the foyer there by the front desk, straightening up shelves and dusting all of the surfaces. When she moved onto the sitting room, she made a beeline for the bookshelf. Sure enough, Emmie's careful organizational scheme from yesterday was no more. Tessa tutted a little bit as she got to work making it right again. It wouldn't be in the exact order it had been before, but at least it would be in *an* order. Soon, Emmie appeared in the sitting room, sitting on the couch there and clearly there to take a short respite from the morning's duties. She'd been in charge of laundry, a task that Tessa hadn't been required to do yet.

"I don't know why people can't put things back precisely where they found them... or indeed *similar* to where they found them," she said, shaking her head.

Emmie laughed. "Not everyone's as neat as we are," she said. "Alas." Within a few moments, she was standing up from the couch and making her way over to the shelf to witness the damage for herself. "Goodness, you'd think a herd of monkeys had been through here."

Tessa chuckled. "Exactly!"

Despite the disorganized chaos that was going on with the shelves, Emmie still found herself a book to read. She took it and went back to sitting on the couch, crossing her legs at the ankles as she smiled down at the book in her hands. Tessa admired Emmie's laid-back nature. She didn't let the pressures of work get the better of her. She seemed to enjoy herself. Tessa hoped that she could be more like that soon enough.

I also hope that my future husband will allow me to continue working, she thought, biting her lip a bit as she finished straightening the books and excused herself to go back out to Rita at the front.

"I see that Emmie's on a break right now," she said. "Shall I work on something else for a while longer until she's ready to come back?"

Rita looked at her for a moment and her eyes said that she noticed her, but she hadn't quite absorbed her words yet. After a few seconds, she snapped to it and nodded her head. "I think you can go on a break now," she replied. "Em's just on a short break. You may go for a rest and a meal, if you like. Emmie will go on a longer break when you've come back, since you'll be working the diner shifts this evening."

"Are you okay?" Tessa asked Rita. "You look like you could use a rest as well."

Rita laughed an airy, light laugh. "I'm fine," she said. "This is what comes of a slow day. But go and enjoy yourself. We'll be here when you get back." She winked.

Tessa wasn't going to argue with her boss. Rita knew what the right thing to do for herself and for her business. "See you soon," she said after collecting her purse from the desk and she made her way out of the building. She wanted to get some of that rest that Rita spoke of, and perhaps a bite to eat as well, but first things first, she was going to mail off her letter to Mr. Grayson.

Tessa walked along the dirt road towards the post office, wondering if that friendly gentleman would be there again. She'd seen no other workers, though, so the odds were good. As she walked in through the door, she smiled when she saw the kind man sitting right there at his desk like last time. She went right up to him and she almost wished that she had more to do there than just mail one letter. "Good afternoon," she said cheerfully, pulling the envelope out of her purse. "I have this letter to send."

She handed it over to the gentleman and paid him accordingly. "I'm glad to see that you found a use for the newspaper so quickly," he said in a friendly tone, smiling back at her.

"Thank you, I certainly did!" She smiled to him even more and then left the office. Tessa went for a stroll around the town, eyeing the various shops and businesses that were there. The smells that were coming from the butcher shop were quite appealing.

I wonder if it would be a good idea for me to pop into the restaurant and try some of the food that it's famous for... I think it'd be good for me to have experienced some of it for myself, no? Still grinning cheerfully, Tessa strode into the restaurant. She didn't know any of the girls there, but she did recognize a few of them. They were wearing the same uniform she was wearing, except they wore large, white bows in their hair. She was glad she'd removed her apron; she didn't wish for anyone to mistake her for a worker there. Though she worked in the hotel, she didn't know the first thing about how to work in the restaurant. She also didn't think that Mr. Stewart was very fond of her.

7

Tessa was seated in the restaurant and was treated like anyone else would be treated, thanks to the fact that none of the girls seemed to recognize her. She was wearing part of her uniform, but without the apron on, it looked more or less like an average black dress. She tried one of the Stewart House ham and cheese sandwiches and she was pleasantly surprised at how good it tasted. When she went back to work next door, she knew that she would have an easier time singing Mr. Stewart's praises in regards to the food that was offered in both of his establishments.

"How was your break?" Rita asked her in greeting as she came through the front door.

Tessa tied her apron around her waist again, smiling at her. "I think I got a lot accomplished," she said, feeling more positive than she had yesterday for sure.

The diner was nothing like it had been the previous day. The crowds weren't as large and she had more than enough help with Wendy there to guide her and show her the best ways in which to do things. Tessa learned how to pour more efficiently and she didn't have any spills or dropped dishes.

"Impressive," Wendy said to her with a grin.

"It's amazing what some calmness and more practice can do for a person," Tessa replied. "How was your date yesterday?"

Wendy blushed slightly. "Who told you?"

"Pretty much everyone mentioned it."

Laughing, Wendy shrugged. "I think it was a good date. No promises or anything, but I would like to see him again."

I want to talk to her about the gentlemen I found in the paper, but I think we should continue this discussion after work. Rita won't like it if we're standing around, gossiping, when there's work to be done. Tessa simply smiled at her friend and got back to her work waiting on the tables of people and making sure that she made no more mistakes.

Work went by quite quickly for them, which surprised Tessa because it was much slower than it had been the day before. She supposed that it had more to do with the fact that she didn't wish for the day to end like she had the previous afternoon. She had a pleasant time, learning more of the ropes from Wendy and feeling competent instead of feeling like she had such a very far way to go before she could ever consider herself a decent hotel worker.

"I wanted to talk to you some more about the mail order service," Tessa said to Wendy as they, Emmie, and Clara made their way back to the dormitory for the night. "What is it like when one of them – one of the gentlemen from town – meets with you? I heard your prospective beau met you outside on the road yesterday?"

Wendy blushed anew when this was brought up. They walked into the dorm together and up the stairs, going into her and Emmie's room so they could chat privately. It wasn't that Clara couldn't be included in the conversation, but she kind of hung back and stayed out of things as it was.

Tessa sat down in Wendy's vanity chair whilst Wendy closed the bedroom door, removing her apron and shoes before sitting down on her bed. Emmie sat on her own bed, removing her shoes and massaging her clearly aching feet. *That never gets better, apparently,* Tessa thought. "We wrote back and forth for a few weeks," Wendy said to Tessa. "Casual, friendly things. It was easy to meet him because he lives in town. It's not always so lucky. The men in the papers can come from anywhere in the west. I suppose I must've been blessed, though like I said I'm still not sure if he is the right man for me."

Tessa nodded. There was no reason that Wendy or any

girl had to choose the first gentleman she met. There were other people to send letters to, other link-ups to be made, if Wendy so wanted. "I sent a letter to a gentleman today who also lives in Wallace," she said. "I fear that I wrote quite a bit of nonsense, but it's on the way to him anyway." She smirked slightly. "I suppose that I wouldn't really be me if I was well-spoken."

Wendy smiled back at her. "A little bit of nerves are normal. I think that men like it."

Emmie looked between the two of them, shaking her head a little bit. "You girls and your men," she said. "I don't see how any of them could be worth all of this trouble."

"That's because you've never been one for romance," Wendy said teasingly back to her. "But if you looked at the advertisements, you'd probably find someone who interested you, too."

Emmie scoffed. "I don't need a distraction. I like work here. The more focused I can be, the better I do. Maybe someday Rita will let me take her place, or be her assistant or something."

Wendy rolled her eyes. "I don't think that Mrs. Stewart is going to give up running the Stewart House until she has her own children to pass it on to."

Tessa smiled at the pair of sisters. Even when they were disagreeing with each other, she could sense how much they loved one another. She envied them that. And still, she thought that Wendy was onto something. As much as she enjoyed working, it was what she had done her entire life. She felt that it was time for something different... especially if she might be able to get married and continue working in the hotel. "What do you think Rita's reaction would be if we were to get married?" she asked almost but not quite rhetorically. "I hope it wouldn't put her in a bad position."

"Yes, I've thought about that," Wendy agreed. "I don't know how she'd respond, but I believe that she would be more forgiving about it than her husband. Her rules are less strict."

Tessa nodded. "I visited his restaurant for lunch today. The bows he makes the girls wear..."

Emma erupted into a short fit of giggles. "They look pretty silly, don't they? To think that Rita once had to wear such things. You know that she started there as a waitress, right?"

Tilting her head, Tessa smiled as she tried to imagine it. Though it was strange to imagine her taking orders from anyone, she could see how it made sense for her to have fallen in love with Mr. Stewart. They seemed like extensions of the same body much of the time. "But the food is excellent," she said, changing the subject. "That was my main purpose for going in there. I wanted to see for myself the kind of things we were serving to people here. To see what all of the fuss was about."

"She takes this job almost as seriously as you do," Wendy said to Emmie.

Tessa chuckled. "I just like to make every effort to succeed."

The two friends chatted together for a little longer and then Tessa took her leave and went back into her bedroom. She hoped that Mr. Grayson would write back to her and be interested in meeting up like Wendy's beau met with her – except Tessa hoped that there could be a bit more warning in her case. She didn't do well with sudden confrontations. *This could be something we discuss,* she thought. *He just needs to write back to me first...*

Work became easier for her as the days and weeks went by. Tessa soon found that working in the small diner was not unlike when she was working in a slightly crowded sitting room. She could still go through with what she was supposed to do and speak one-on-one with customers. She learned how to be better at taking her time as she went from table to table and then from table to kitchen and back again. It started to become second nature to her, and eventually she wasn't overthinking things as much as she used to. Occasionally, a full train would arrive and some of the customers would come to the hotel for their meal. Tessa stopped seeing this as a big, traumatic event and started seeing it more as an opportunity to help people. The demand was higher at those times, and Tessa did well when she had people to help.

During these weeks, every morning, Tessa stopped by the post office to see if there was anything for her. She got so used to seeing the postmaster sighing and shaking his head at her that she was completely caught off guard when, one fine day, she realized that he was actually smiling and holding up a letter for her.

"Oh!" Tessa cried out, gently taking it from his hands. She sat in the office and carefully ripped the envelope open so she could read the letter right away. Mr. Stewart had interesting, sort of scratchy handwriting. She got the feeling that he had learned to write fairly recently, from the look of it, but this endeared him to her even more.

My dear Miss Johnston,

How thrilled I was to receive your response to my advertisement! You sound like a remarkable young woman. I have placed ads in the newspaper for quite some time now, with little success, so it pleases me very much that you have taken the time to write to me. As I wrote in the ad, I work on a ranch on the outskirts of Wallace. I'm not planning on leaving any time soon. It sounds to me like you are an industrious sort of person and I promise you that I'm not aiming to make you quit your position at Stewart House if it makes you happy. My wish is to have a wife who keeps me company here and knows her way around a home. I would never ask for you to work on the ranch itself, and of course caring for the animals would be more akin to caring for pets than anything else: feeding the horses and the cows and things like that.

We would be able to work it out with your schedule, provided that you continue to be interested and I am keen on having you come here to be with me.

As this letter service is not the most optimal for neighbors such as we are, might I have the honor of meeting you in person? It may surprise you to read, but I've actually been to the Stewart House to meet a girl before, so I'm familiar with the parlors they have there. I believe I'm familiar with your boss as well, for what it's worth. She's a mighty fine woman herself, and she was very kind to me even if our courtship didn't work out in the end.

Anyway, I don't wish to waste paper on the subject of that. Please let me know right away if you're interested in meeting up with me and getting to know me more in person. I feel that it is the most pleasing way of getting to know a person, and it is also quite a bit more comforting, in my opinion. I especially treasure being able to look in someone's eyes as I'm speaking with them, and hearing their voice.

I anxiously await your reply. Thank you ever so much again for writing to me!

Fondest regards,
Samuel

TESSA GRINNED down at the paper in her hands, feeling not unlike Wendy now. She looked over at the clerk in the post office and felt embarrassed to see that he was watching her, a look of amusement on his face. "Thank you!" she called to him, clutching the letter and envelope to her chest and standing up, quickly walking back out of the post office and onto the busy street.

8

Tessa was over the moon that Samuel had not only written back to her but he wished to meet her soon! She was relieved that he'd asked first and hadn't just tried to show up unannounced one morning. *He already seems to understand me a little,* she thought, laughing that off as soon as she'd thought it. Of course, he didn't know that she could be a bit jumpy about spontaneous situations. He was just being a decent, polite gentleman.

At her first opportunity, she sat at her vanity and wrote back to him, hoping that the letter would reach him swiftly. *I really must inform Rita about what I'm doing, and what I hope to do if it all works out. I don't want to leave unless I must.*

Carefully tapping her pen into the ink, Tessa began writing. She wrote furtively, but neatly so that he'd still be able to read her handwriting.

DEAREST SAMUEL,

YOU DO me quite an honor by writing back to me. I'm not as surprised as you may think that you've already met with a girl from the Stewart House. Indeed, I believe a great many of the girls here are in search of a husband like you. I'm only sorry that you weren't chosen before, though I'm grateful that I have the chance to be with you, if that is according to God's plan. Another chance is a wonderful way of putting it. I pray that I may be the answer that you've been hoping to find.

I'm so glad to read that you wouldn't expect me to leave my job here. I think that once I discuss the matter with my boss it shall be perfectly fine for me to continue my position here as a married woman. After all, Mrs. Stewart is married and it's never been a problem for her or her husband. Though it might put a strain on things if I should be working here and unable to assist you on your ranch. This is one of the many things we should discuss when we are together in person soon. I shall be more than happy to meet you in the hotel and have a chat in one of the courting parlors next week. I've heard an awful lot about them and I do believe they are as sweet as everyone has said they are.

With fondness,
Tessa

S<small>HE TOOK</small> this letter to the post office on her next break and then she had only to wait. She didn't anticipate that the gentleman would take that long to come and meet her. Even now, she'd have to be a bit on her toes, but at least it wouldn't be as big of a surprise as it had been for Wendy.

There was one thing that she decided she really must do before she continued to move forward with all of this. She had to talk with Rita about her intentions and ask for permission. *There's no contract about it,* she thought. *But that doesn't mean that she's okay with each of us getting married. And it likewise doesn't mean that she'd allow us to continue working once married.* Tessa bit her lip and told herself not to worry until there was a reason to worry.

She'd written to Samuel that they could meet the following week, but of course that didn't have to be set in stone. The passage of time forced them to be flexible, because the time it took for letters to be delivered by the mail service wasn't controlled by either of them. Then Tessa had a new thought: *The post office in town is likely his post office, too! Why did I never think of that?* She had no way of knowing which man who stopped in during the week was Mr. Grayson, but there was a good chance that he would come to visit with her right after stopping in at the post office and receiving his letter from her! *So, we're not really at the mercy of the mail so much as we've each been waiting for the other to check their own mail.*

Tessa had to laugh at that a little, though she was careful not to laugh too uproariously whilst she was at work. She didn't want any strange looks from any of the guests or her friends. Now that she knew that the clock was indeed ticking, she went to the front desk to see Rita.

"I have to talk with you about something," she said, trying to keep her voice light and friendly to avoid sounding too grave and serious. She didn't wish to scare her boss prematurely, particularly because Rita might not have even thought of it as something about which one needed to be grave.

For her part, Rita simply raised her eyebrows at her. "Of course," she said, gesturing an arm towards the couch in the sitting room. The two of them went into that room and sat down together, facing each other and knees lightly brushing as if they were two friends engaging in some juicy new gossip. "What is it? You're not still feeling out of sorts about things in the diner, are you?"

Tessa shook her head. "No, I think I've really been improving there."

Rita smiled and nodded. "I do too. I am so impressed with you, Tessa. I knew that you had it in you and you only needed more practice. That's really my fault for rushing you."

"What I want to talk to you about doesn't exactly concern the hotel, although I suppose it does by association with you..." Tessa cleared her throat a bit, wishing that she was better at choosing her words. "That is to say, I enjoy working here very much and I hope that what I have to tell you won't affect that in any way."

Rita began to look deeply worried.

"With Wendy's guidance, I looked into the advertisements for brides in the newspaper," Tessa went on. "I've been writing with a gentleman who lives in town and he wishes to meet me soon. I wanted to let you know before we actually did, just in case you had some objection. I should've mentioned it to you before, but I guess I just didn't have much faith in it working so well, so quickly."

Rita's expression changed from worried to exuberant. Her mouth turned into a wide-open grin, the kind of grin that was more pleasantly surprised than just happy. "This is terrific news! Of course, I don't think that you should have to leave your position here, if you don't wish to. You know, I did the same thing before, when I was working at the restaurant. It didn't quite work out the way it was meant to, for me, but I know that many of the other girls have had great fortune with it."

Tessa smiled back at her, so relieved that Rita wasn't disappointed that she'd chosen to go on this new path away from the hotel, even if she didn't have to or plan to leave. "I'm so glad to know that you're okay with it," she said. "I wasn't going to go through with it if you disapproved."

Rita laughed softly, shaking her head. "My dear, your choices shouldn't be up to me," she said. "I know you like this job, and I appreciate that very much, but I don't wish to dictate your life for you."

Tessa felt like she'd just been given a wonderful gift, even though Rita really hadn't done anything... She'd always been in control of what she could do next. *I should've known that she'd be supportive.* She opened her arms and she and Rita hugged, giggling a little as if they were both equals instead of boss and employee. It felt so nice. She told herself not to get used to it, but she enjoyed it just the same.

During the rest of the work day, Tessa felt like she was walking on clouds. She hadn't been keeping things from Rita for very long, but still she felt like a weight had been lifted from her shoulders. She was free to meet Samuel and see what he was like.

A few days later, Emmie found Tessa in the upstairs hallway. She had a big smile on her face. "You have a visitor," she announced.

Tessa looked at her and held tight to the wet rag she was holding so she wouldn't drop it onto the hardwood floor. She smiled, knowing in her heart exactly who this visitor was. "Do you think I can sneak off to change into something a bit nicer?"

Emmie winked at her. "I'll cover for you." She went back downstairs to greet the gentleman at the front of the hotel. Tessa kept her apron on and coolly moved past them, overhearing what her friend said to the tall, sandy-haired gentleman in the doorway. "She'll be down to meet you shortly. She's finishing up some tasks first."

Tessa was able to walk out past them thanks to Emmie diverting his attention. There were plenty of black-and-white clad girls wandering around the premises, so she wouldn't catch his eye until she was ready to.

Giddily, Tessa walked to the dormitory and walked up the stairs at a faster pace than usual, though she was careful not to trip. As soon as she got into her room, she threw off her uniform and changed into one of her other dresses. She wished that she had a more exciting wardrobe, but she thought that her lavender colored frock would be good enough for a first-time meeting. *I don't imagine that he'll really care too much about what I'm wearing, as long as I'm not wearing my uniform.*

Once she was wearing the nicer dress, Tessa also took her long, dark hair out of the bun on top of her head. She brushed her hair until it was smooth and silky once more, curling slightly near the ends. She didn't think that she was a great beauty like her friends were, but she didn't think that she was bad to look at either. *Your eyes are youthful and bright,* she thought, complimenting herself a little, something she wasn't used to doing. *He likes you on paper, so he will probably like you even more in person. Most likely.*

Tessa tried to calm the butterflies that now flew aimlessly around her tummy. She took a deep breath and made her way down the staircase, going back to the hotel and praying that Mr. Grayson would still be waiting there for her. When she stepped inside, she found Emmie there, still standing at attention at the front desk. The two friends smiled at each other and Tessa raised her eyebrows, questioning Emmie without actually asking her out loud.

Emmie nodded her head in the direction of the sitting room. *Oh goodness,* Tessa thought. *He's probably rearranging the books on that shelf, isn't he?* She had to laugh a little. If being a bit messy was the only flaw that she could find with Samuel Grayson, then she knew she would be more than happy. She cleared her throat a bit, straightening her hair as best as she could with the assistance of the mirror on the wall, and then she stepped into the room.

There were several people standing or sitting around, talking together quietly or reading books from the shelves. The tall, sandy-haired man from the doorway before was standing next to the bookshelf, reading through the titles but not actually touching any of the books. Tessa breathed a small sigh of relief and then smiled at him as she approached.

It wouldn't really much matter if he did make a mess...

9

As Tessa strode up to Mr. Grayson, he turned around to face her, evidently sensing that there was someone behind him even though she'd been fairly quiet. He looked at her and smiled politely. Her lavender dress was the first clue to him that she was Miss Johnston and not just some worker at the hotel. "Good afternoon," he said to you. "Are you Miss Tessa?"

Feeling a blush creep up her cheeks, she nodded as she smiled. "Yes. And you're Mr. Grayson, correct?"

He nodded back. For a few moments, they both shyly stood there gazing at the other person, a bit unsure how to move forward now that they were together. *In truth, we haven't written to each other for very long. A lot of things must be said in person rather than on the page, and it's a little daunting this way. But it's also... Well, it's more natural.*

After several moments of silent smiling at each other and admiring each other's features – Mr. Grayson had reddish-blond hair, so it was more coppery than sandy, and his eyes were emerald and twinkling – he gestured over to the couch that was currently unoccupied but perhaps wouldn't be for long. "Care to sit with me and chat a little?"

Tessa did as she was bid and sat next to him on the couch, a cushion apart. She wondered if she ought to suggest that they go into the diner or restaurant where they could have some tea and sandwiches, but he didn't appear to be interested in vittles at the moment. "I'm so glad we're together in person at last," she said with a small, shy smile. "I hope I didn't leave you waiting for too long."

Mr. Grayson, still smiling, chuckled a bit and shook his head. "Like I said in my letters, I'm pretty used to waiting. I don't mind. And sometimes when I wait I'm given glorious gifts for it. You are a vision, Miss Johnston, if I may say so. I was expecting to meet a pretty, lithe young thing but here you are, a beautiful woman. Do you know that I felt your presence as soon as you entered the room?"

Tessa blushed, flattered. He was very sweet, though he hadn't seemed to notice her before when she was in her uniform so she had to believe that he was making things up. *Perhaps he'd simply been expecting to find me when he sensed me. And in that case, it's to be expected that he would've sensed me eventually.* She giggled a little bit, demurely bringing a hand up to her mouth so the giggling wouldn't make her appear too simple or girly. He'd just praised her as being more like a refined woman, so it was no time to start acting childish.

"That's very kind of you," she said after a moment of this. "I didn't want to startle you by tapping your back, so I'm glad that you noticed me first. Were your travels here comfortable for you?"

He chuckled again. "Spoken like a girl who works with train passengers every day," he said with a wink. "I came on one of my horses, and he's a good old boy so I suppose you could say I travelled comfortably. Have you ever ridden a horse, Miss Tessa?"

She laughed pleasantly. "Most likely when I was a little girl," she said. "But there wasn't much need for me to ride them when we had carriages."

Laughing, Samuel shrugged. "You do have a point. If you lived and worked in a city, you probably had more use for carriages. But if you like, perhaps one of these days you can come visit my ranch and I can teach you how to ride a horse. You'd look like a princess atop her steed. I can already imagine it."

Just then, Wendy and Emmie peeked their heads into the room. They saw Tessa sitting there with her beau and they grinned approvingly at her. All the same, she felt embarrassed to be seen there like that as opposed to in one of the courting parlors or the diner. No one else around knew that she was supposed to be working and she felt anxious to be reminded this way. *I know they don't mean to, but they're reminding me of my obligations here.*

She looked at Samuel. "I'm afraid that I really should be getting back to work now," she told him. "But by all means, please meet with me again?"

"Are you free tomorrow morning?" he asked her, rising from the couch after she did.

Golly is he eager. He clearly likes me! Smiling at him, she nodded her head. "That would be fantastic," she said. "Shall we meet next door in a courting parlor or in the diner here? Which do you prefer?"

Mr. Grayson thought about it for a few moments. "I've tried my luck in the courting parlors before. I think I'd rather chat with you in the diner. I hear their breakfast is wonderful." He smiled sweetly at her.

Tessa wondered if he still harbored feelings for Rita. There was a high chance that he would see Rita in the hotel the more he visited with Tessa... But she had to believe that he'd moved on from all of that. He'd said as much in his letter. "Breakfast tomorrow it is," she said. "I'll look forward to it, and I shall make sure that my coworkers remain on their best behavior."

He laughed and gently took her hand, giving it a swift kiss. "Adieu until then," he said. "Thank you for giving me this opportunity."

Tessa watched him leave, smiling at his choice of words.

She'd given him a second chance. She clearly was important to him already. And she thought he was so sweet and handsome. *I should think of it less as taking Rita's beau and think of it more as being the girl who chose to be with him.*

As soon as Samuel was gone, she changed back into her uniform and joined her friends at work. They were full of questions, a lot of which she wouldn't be able to answer until she met with him again and continued to get to know him. "He offered to show me how to ride a horse," she told them. "And he was excited to see me again. That's a good sign, right?"

Her friends laughed and smiled with her. Even Rita joined in a little, but then she told them – in a friendly manner – that they must return to work. "The guests don't know about your personal lives, and I'd prefer to keep it that way. Marriage and beaus are more the topic for the girls next door."

How funny it is that Mr. Stewart makes his waitresses sign a contract, pledging to not marry, when that's precisely the sort of thing that happens after working there a while. She supposed that that last bit could be said for the hotel as well. Rita had employed several young, single girls and she must've known that they'd be in search of husbands eventually. *Except for Emmie,* she thought with an amused smirk.

The following morning, Tessa didn't bother putting on her work clothes, thinking that the day would mostly be spent with Mr. Grayson. She'd given Rita a bit of forewarning and she had her blessing to take the day off for such things, as Wendy had not so long ago. Rifling through her small collection of dresses in the wardrobe, Tessa settled on a baby blue gown with little pink and yellow flowers lining the hem and the collar of the bodice. She'd had the dress for a long time, since she was quite a bit younger, but it still fit her perfectly. She brushed her hair and smiled at her reflection. Her hair looked much better when it was loose and free to brush against her shoulders and back. When she wore it up in a bun and then took it down, it tended to bulge a bit at the back no matter what she did. *It's probably much better for my hair if I don't wear it up every single day,* she thought.

As soon as she felt that she was ready to embark on this second – possibly longer lasting – date with her new beau, Tessa left her room, feeling both like skipping down the stairs and like hiding. She was excited to spend more time with Samuel, but she was nervous just the same. It was one thing to sit and chat for a few casual moments, but it was another thing entirely to devote one's whole day to spending time with someone. *I hope I shall get a few chances to relax on my own,* she thought. *Perhaps while he visits the lavatory or tends to his horses.*

She thought she was silly for needing a few breaks every now and then, but maybe everyone was like that in some way? Everyone needed some time to themselves to reflect and make decisions. And she'd be making quite a few decisions soon enough.

When she arrived at the hotel, she was surprised to find that Samuel Grayson wasn't there yet. Surprised and a little relieved. She took a moment to fix up her hair a bit more, gazing at herself in the mirror. "Aww, Tessa, you're a vision," Rita said behind her. She turned around and hugged her boss.

"I really do hope he thinks so, too," Tessa said in a slightly quavering voice. "I feel like I'm doing a job interview again, only this time it's for life..."

Rita laughed softly. "Darling, don't think of it that way. You make it sound so tedious. Marriage is a lot of work, yes, but it's truly magical if you find the right gentleman. You get to spend the rest of your days with a friend rather than having to go through life's ups and downs on your own."

Tessa did like the sound of that. "I guess I never really gave it much thought until Wendy was writing letters and telling me about it. It does seem much nicer than work... Meaning no offense, of course. You know I'll still gladly work here for you, if you'll have me."

Rita smiled at her and fluffed up some of Tessa's curls. "I'm truly honored to have you remain working for me, if that's what you choose."

Suddenly, a man cleared his throat nearby. The two ladies looked over at the front doorway and there was Samuel Grayson, standing next to the front desk and looking as charming as ever. He looked from Tessa to Rita and back again. "Isn't this a picture?" he said jovially as he strode into the room.

He didn't seem upset to see Rita at all, which was such a relief to both of the ladies, to be sure. Tessa looked from him to Rita.

"How are you, Sam?" Rita asked him in a pleasant tone. "You look well."

"I've been quite well, thank you," he replied, still smiling. "I've been doing much better now that I have little Tessa here to keep me company with soothing words and kind patience. How's married life treating you? You seem like quite a success here."

He waved a hand grandly, signifying the whole of the hotel. Rita laughed softly. "Oh, I think I've been doing all right," she said. "I've certainly been enjoying myself. And I'm so glad that you and Tessa found each other, truly. You have my blessing, not that you need it. You've already had the Lord's."

Samuel bowed slightly, clearly proud to have been spoken to in such a manner by a good woman who was even still – after all they'd been through together – a dear friend to him. "I thank you." He looked at Tessa. "Shall we, then?" he asked her, offering his arm.

Tessa took it, feeling at once like a princess as he had described. He wasn't a prince or anything like that, but he might as well have been, in her eyes. They walked together into the small dining area and took a seat at a table that was secluded, even though there weren't that many other people in there to begin with. "So, tell me more about yourself," he said. "You said you're from a medical family?"

Tessa nodded and told him all about her parents and the often overcrowded hospital in Annapolis. It was a long story, and not really any kind of happy one, but it was her past life and he was interested. "I wished to put my interest in helping others toward a different sort of service," she concluded. "One that dealt less with the ill and dying and more with enjoyment and life."

"I can certainly understand that," Samuel said. "I don't think I would last as long as you did as a nurse."

They smiled at each other.

"Tell me more about yourself," Tessa said then. "Did you always dream of being a rancher out here? Where do you hail from originally?"

Samuel seemed pleased that she wished to ask so many questions about him. She got the feeling that it didn't happen very often. "My mother and father moved out here to Kansas when I was a little boy," he said. "They came from North Carolina originally and they'd had enough of the fighting and war so they wanted to come out here where there was peace and quiet and new promise to be found. I suppose that I *have* always wanted to be a rancher. It's just about the only thing I know how to do. I guess I'd say that I'm a pretty good cook."

You don't hear that from every gentleman, surely! Tessa

beamed at him. "I shall have to try your cooking and judge that for myself," she said, mostly jokingly. "How marvelous that you know how to cook, though. I know my way around a kitchen, of course, but I wouldn't say that I'm the best at making meals."

Samuel looked at her adoringly. "We can figure it out together."

They enjoyed a meal together that morning, feasting on eggs and bacon. Tessa was pleased to be tasting more food that the Stewart House had to offer. How wonderful it would be if she could be experiencing newly married life as she continued to experience working in the hotel and learn all the things she could do there, too. *My life is certainly full of new experiences now!*

They didn't meet again the following day, which Tessa thought might be for the best because Rita and the hotel did still need her to work. She and Samuel saw each other again a few days later, meeting in the courting parlor which Tessa believed made it feel all the more *official*. They were officially courting now. He was intent upon marrying her, or else he wouldn't be calling on her so often. She was extremely flattered and seeing him never failed to make her smile uncontrollably now. She could never hide it, even if she wanted to.

"I hope you won't think that I'm rushing or being too rash," he said as he sat across from her in the small parlor room, gingerly taking her hand. "But I would like to marry you."

Tessa blushed and smiled. She couldn't say that she was surprised exactly, after all it was the main intent of their writing together. "I would like to marry you," she said back. "I think that, though we've only known each other a short while, we've become good friends already."

Samuel nodded excitedly. "Exactly. And I don't wish to waste another moment. I want to bring you home to my ranch and ride horses with you, and spend evenings in the kitchen, cooking with you... I even look forward to dropping you off at the hotel in the mornings, if you can believe that."

She grinned and nodded back at him, eager to make all of that and more a reality very soon. She clung to his hand, happy to be holding it and sitting there with him like a proper couple. "Rita's already given us her blessing, after all."

Samuel laughed delightedly. "That's very true." He brought Tessa's hand up to his lips and gently kissed it. "Leave all of the arrangements at the chapel to me," he said. "We shall be married within a month!"

In his excitement, he leaned across the table and quickly kissed her cheek. Tessa felt like she might swoon, but she held it together. She had so much planning to do! And she of course had all of her friends with which to share the news!

EPILOGUE

Tessa left Samuel to figure out the business with the minister and the timing of everything. Meanwhile, she alerted Rita and her friends that she was going to be getting married. "It shouldn't change anything here though, really. I shan't be living in the dormitory anymore, but otherwise I'll still be here all the time." She smiled and her friends smiled back at her.

"Tess, we're just happy for you!" Wendy exclaimed, hugging her. "We won't begrudge you moving into Mr. Grayson's home and being with him. We wouldn't even be too upset if you stopped working here, because we want what you want."

"We're very glad that you'll keep working here, though,"

Emmie added, smiling. "Things wouldn't be the same around here without you."

"Although there'd be more glasses," Tessa quipped as they all gently laughed along.

She'd only ever broken one glass, but she thought that had been a turning point for her at the hotel. She learned from her own mistakes and she embraced some new ideas about the path she should take in her new life in Kansas.

Rita was kind enough to help make Tessa's wedding gown, using her own white fabric and lace. She, Wendy and Emmie would compose Tessa's bridal party. Tessa was over-joyed to have them be a part of this special day in her life. She owed them a lot and she certainly planned to repay Wendy and Emmie by helping them with their future weddings, if they chose.

On the morning of the wedding, Wendy and Emmie helped Tessa into her wedding gown, brushing her long hair until it was smooth and shiny. Emmie placed the veil onto Tessa's head and they each 'ooo'ed and 'ahh'ed as they regarded her reflection. "You're such a beautiful bride," Wendy said, smiling tearfully for her friend. "I never doubted that you would be, of course."

The four friends took a carriage to the wedding chapel. One of Rita's friends was the driver and he was very friendly and helpful. "I never get tired of helping girls go to get married." When they arrived at the chapel, Tessa and her friends went back into the small bridal room so they could continue preparing for the ceremony. Rita was wearing a lovely pink gown and carrying a bouquet of matching red and pink flowers. Wendy and Emmie wore matching light blue dresses and they looked even more like twins than they usually did. They each carried a multicolored bouquet of wildflowers and wore some similar flowers in their hair. *They look like sweet, summer nymphs,* Tessa thought, smiling as she looked at them.

"I appreciate all three of you more than I can ever say," she said tearfully.

Soon, the music started and it was time for the four of them to make their way up the aisle towards Mr. Grayson and the minister. Rita went first, as the matron of honor. She slowly walked up the aisle, smiling and nodding her head in greeting to all of the wedding guests that she knew. Next, Wendy went up the aisle, followed by Emmie. When it was Tessa's turn, she took a deep breath and walked forward. All eyes were on her as she walked up the aisle to greet her soon-to-be husband, Samuel.

He was the only one she was paying attention to. He looked so handsome in his gray wedding suit. *Gray like Grayson,* she thought as she beamed. Her cheeks hurt from smiling so much but she didn't mind. It was the most wonderful kind of pain she'd ever experienced. It was only because she was so, so happy.

As soon as she'd reached the front of the room, Samuel came to her side and took her hands in his, turning to face her. The minister stepped forward towards them, standing almost completely between them but back enough that they could be in their own little romantic bubble.

"Dearly beloved," he began, "we are gathered here today on this most sacred of occasions to witness the union of these two souls in holy matrimony. Tessa Marie Johnston and Samuel Elijah Grayson, on this day you have chosen to begin life anew as husband and wife. This decision must not be taken lightly. As it is written in Proverbs 3:3-4, *Let love and faithfulness never leave you; bind them around your neck, write them on the tablet of your heart. Then you will win favor and a good name in the sight of God and man.*" He looked from Tessa to Samuel as they thought over what he'd just said. Tessa was biting her lip in her excitement. She couldn't wait to begin her life anew.

The minister rested his eyes on her. "Tessa, do you take Samuel Elijah Grayson to be your lawfully wedded husband? To have and to hold, to love and to cherish, to honor and obey from this day forth, forsaking all others, in sickness and in health, from this day forward, until death do you part?"

There's no question in my mind! "Yes," Tessa replied readily. "I do." She beamed at Samuel. She'd been smiling so long that her cheeks no longer hurt. They'd gotten used to smiling so much, and she felt that they certainly would have to get used to it for she would be smiling for the rest of her life!

The minister turned his attention to Samuel. "Samuel," he said, "Do you take Tessa Marie Johnston to be your lawfully wedded wife? To have and to hold, to love and to cherish, to honor and protect from this day forth, forsaking all others, in sickness and in health, from this day forward, until death do you part?"

Samuel kept his focus squarely on Tessa. He was smiling sweetly back at her. She felt like she could get lost in those emerald green eyes of his and be happy there forever. "I do," he said.

A cheer rang out from the crowd of onlookers. Most of them were strangers to Tessa but she had a feeling that they wouldn't be for long.

"Then, by the powers vested in me by our Lord and Savior Jesus Christ and the wonderful little town of Wallace, Kansas, it is my honor and privilege to pronounce you husband and wife," the minister loudly announced. Another cheer erupted from the pews. He smiled at the newly-married couple. "You may kiss the bride."

Samuel carefully lifted the veil from Tessa's face, leaned forward and planted a soft, loving kiss onto her lips. Tessa kissed him back with all of her heart. She never could have believed, several months ago, that she would be so in love with someone like she loved Samuel. And now she was the happy, new wife of a successful, handsome rancher!

The organ began playing music again and she and Sam left the chapel, quickly making their way to the carriage that awaited them. He brought her to his ranch house and she gazed around at everything that he had made for himself and that now belonged to her, too. He introduced her to his horses and cows with such exuberance that Tessa felt like she couldn't possibly love him more than she did in that very moment. They kissed each other and he helped her onto the back of a gentle, brown mare. He rode a black stallion beside her and together, they went for their first ride of what was to be many joyous rides to come.

THE END

EMMIE'S UNEXPECTED LOVE

STEWART HOUSE BRIDES

EMMIE'S UNEXPECTED LOVE

Wallace, Kansas – 1891

Emmie Sheffield and her sister, Wendy, have spent their whole lives being best friends and confidantes. Things are going well for them at the Stewart House hotel, but Wendy clearly has dreams of getting married and settling down instead of spending the rest of her days as a working woman.

Emmie, on the other hand, has no desire to get married and instead prefers to spend her time reading books, fantasizing about someday opening a library in town. Her desires quickly shift when she receives a letter of response from a smart and charming young lawyer named David Cline. The trouble is, she never sent a letter to him in the first place!

Upon discovering that her friend set the wheels in motion in an attempt to play matchmaker, Emmie decides to write back to the gentleman out of kindness and for fear of hurting his feelings. They soon begin a wonderful correspondence and, before long, Emmie catches herself dreaming of life as a happily married woman. This dream is made easier for her by the fact that her new beau shares the same absolute passion for books as she does and she soon makes plans to meet him in person to test the waters.

Will Mr. Cline turn out to be as incredible in real life as he comes across in his beautiful letters, or has Emmie's head been in the clouds so long that she's lost touch with reality?

1

"Excuse me, Miss?" a tall, slightly portly guest asked Emmie, rousing her from her peaceful bookshelf reorganizing. She set the book she was holding onto the shelf and looked him directly in the eyes, smiling a natural smile. "Do you have anything by Henry James?"

She nodded her head at once, still smiling her pretty and youthful smile. *I know for a fact that we have something by James, because I just saw it.* "Yes, we sure do." Emmie scanned the shelf with her eyes, finding the book right away. She took it down and handed it over to the gentleman. "I'm afraid that it's the only one we have."

The man looked at the book in his hands and frowned slightly. "Oh, I've read this one already." He handed it back to Emmie. "Thanks anyway."

He huffed as he walked away, back to his group of friends, she presumed. She sighed inwardly and replaced the book. *We're a hotel, not a library,* she thought. *It's a miracle we even have that book.* Emmie wouldn't have minded working in a library, though. The bookshelves were her favorite thing to tidy up in the Stewart House Hotel. She could usually be found hovering there with the books, if she didn't have something more urgent that needed her attention.

"Emmie," Wendy said, walking towards her from the hotel's small diner area. "You're needed in the diner now. Swap with me." She grinned. Wendy was Emmie's older sister. They were thick as thieves, but that didn't mean that they didn't like playfully chiding each other whenever they got a good chance for it. She knew that Emmie disliked working in the restaurant, even if it was much smaller than the original Stewart House restaurant next door. Everyone disliked working in the diner, except for Rita, but she'd come from the restaurant so it made sense for her to enjoy it.

"Where's Tessa?" Emmie asked her sister, looking around for the beautiful brunette who wasn't usually difficult to find.

"Upstairs," Wendy answered immediately. "Managing the rooms. You can't get out of swapping with me."

Emmie sighed. "All right, fine. But I get to borrow your brush first tonight. You always give it to me all full of your hair."

Wendy laughed. "It's not like it hurts you to remove a bit of my hair."

"No, but it disgusts me."

The two sisters stuck their tongues out at each other, having fun in a rare moment where they didn't have to be so prim and proper. The guests had all gone to lunch – some of whom were in the diner, to be sure. Emmie hoped she wouldn't run into the gentleman who wanted that book again. She had a feeling he might still be in the mood for complaining about it.

"It's a deal," Wendy said finally. "Now go before Rita gets mad at me for your delay."

Emmie smirked a little. As she walked to the diner, she made sure to straighten and tighten her white apron strings so she wouldn't look disheveled for the short amount of time her job required her to interact with the public. The diner was only moderately filled, thanks to lunch not bringing in as many hungry souls as the breakfast train tended to do. Rita was already there, serving some of the tables, and she looked up with a smile when she saw Emmie arriving. She sidled over to her as soon as she could break away from her tables.

"Lucky for you, it's not so bad today," Rita informed her. "Just please see to those tables there." She gestured to the tables near the back of the room. Emmie looked over at them and sure enough the Henry James fan was sitting at one of them, surrounded by his group of friends.

Emmie nodded and took a deep breath before walking right over to him. She wasn't the type of girl who generally shied away from confrontation, even if she knew it might be less than pleasant for her. "Good afternoon," she said in a friendly voice, looking from the familiar gentleman to his friends. "My name is Emmie. How may I serve you today?"

The gentleman regarded her a moment and, to her surprise, he didn't seem to recognize her from earlier. "We'd all like to try the meat pies that we've heard so many good things about," he said with a slight smile that Emmie could see peeking out from beneath his thick, gray beard. He looked around at the others at the table and they all eagerly nodded their heads.

Well, this should be exceedingly easy, Emmie thought, her smile growing a little as she regarded at them all. "Excellent choice," she chimed in, not even needing to write that down. "I'll be sure to bring over some glasses of water for you all as well."

"Thank you," one of the other gentlemen said.

Emmie went to the kitchen, delighted that the afternoon was going better for her than she had imagined. Perhaps she'd been a bit groggy when she was working with the books and assumed annoyance when there was none. Or perhaps the gentleman was just better at letting things go than she could be.

She returned to the table a few moments later, carrying a large, silver tray full of glasses of water. Carefully, she passed the glasses out to the gentlemen sitting around the table. "What brings you all to Wallace?" she politely asked them.

"Work," the Henry James gentleman said with a smile. "We're set to start mining next door in McAllaster, but of course we just had to stop in and see what the Stewart House was really like."

Emmie smiled at the men. "Well, we're grateful to have you here with us. McAllaster is quite a ways away."

The gentleman nodded. "It will be quite a journey, when all is said and done. What about you? What brought a pretty young thing like you to Kansas of all places?"

Emmie giggled softly. She wasn't oblivious; she knew that some of the main things that Mr. and Mrs. Stewart were looking for in their lady workers were youth and loveliness. They hoped to lure young men to stay in town by hiring eligible, unmarried women to work in the Stewart House. Well, eventually everyone there except Emmie was going to be married, the way things were going... "Work," she replied. "This wonderful hotel."

This answer seemed to please her customers. They smiled and nodded, murmuring cheerful things to each other. Emmie excused herself after that in order to retrieve the requested meat pies for them.

When Clara came to relieve her to assist with the busier dinner shift, Emmie thought that her help couldn't have come soon enough. She joyfully went to the front desk and collapsed in the chair there, sitting down for the first time in hours. *Ages, it feels like.* She knew that she wasn't supposed to sit there for more than a few minutes, but it was blessedly a slower part of the day for the hotel, so she could relax a little until something called her to attention. Usually, once people were done with their dinner, some of the diners would come over to ask about lodgings. Many of the train travelers didn't stay in town, but Rita and her husband Mr. Stewart had opened this hotel for the express purpose of allowing some people to stick around if they so wanted.

Normally, Clara stayed glued to the welcome desk because it was her favorite of all of the positions, and the one she was the best at – according to just about everyone – but Rita strove to have each of the girls work a little of each position throughout the day.

"Variety will help keep you going," she insisted. "If you remain in one position all day, you won't be allowing yourself to grow and learn new things."

Emmie thought she made a good point. As much as she adored working with the books and helping out in the quieter lounge area of the hotel, she thought she might become bored if that was all she ever did. *I think I've gotten better at talking to people by working in the diner,* she thought. One had to struggle a little in order to improve and Emmie had certainly struggled in her life.

Now that she was able to sit and collect herself for a bit, her thoughts wandered to her journey with Wendy to Wallace. They'd traveled together from Albany, New York as a kind of escape from their parents and their old lifestyle. Often, Emmie wondered if they'd made the right choice in leaving. Their mother worked very hard to support them, without much help from their father who'd all but abandoned them for a posher life in Manhattan. But ever since Emmie and Wendy had started working for Mrs. Stewart, they were able to send along money for their mother, to help her pay her expenses and live a more comfortable life. *It's the least we can do,* Emmie thought. *Sometimes I wish we could just bring her here to live and work in Wallace. It's so much sweeter, and it's never as cold.*

Wendy was even more ambitious than Emmie was. For months now, she'd been attempting to marry herself off to whichever gentleman would have her. She was writing letters to several different men, all thanks to that mail order bride service that was in the newspaper. Emmie disliked the idea of marrying a stranger. She wasn't much for the idea of marriage in general. And she worried every day that her sweet, slightly gullible sister would end up marrying some horrible oaf that she might as well have met back home.

I came out here to work hard and to make a professional name for myself, Emmie thought. *Marriage is all well and good for Mrs. Stewart of course, or Tessa... or even Wendy, if it will truly make her happy. But I shan't be joining them in that endeavor.*

Emmie Sheffield was many things – smart, beautiful, ambitious... and more than a little stubborn. With her shoulder-length blonde hair and bright, China-blue eyes, she was also quite a looker. Wendy, who was equally as pretty in Emmie's eyes, never resisted a chance to tell Emmie how pretty she was. She hoped that it wouldn't actually break Wendy's or her mother's heart if she decided that marriage really and truly was not for her. *I suppose I'm just married to this hotel,* she thought, without an air of sadness or shame. *I think that most people would count themselves quite fortunate to be working in a place that they love so much.*

She once told Tessa that she hoped that she could someday be Rita's assistant and possibly even take over the innkeeper role if Rita ever tired of it or chose to move on. Aside from owning and running her own library – which had always felt like a childish dream, even as she thought of it as a child – Emmie believed that being an innkeeper in an adorable little ranch town like Wallace, Kansas would be such a dream come true.

Rita clearly knew what she was doing when she started this place, Emmie thought, sitting up in her chair and carefully leafing through the pages of the ledger. *I wish that I could follow in her footsteps, without a husband or children to distract me or get in my way.*

Her family and friends may have pegged her as cynical but Emmie knew that she was simply being honest and true to herself.

2

"You really ought to try harder to keep your rejoicing to a minimum when you get to leave the diner," Wendy told Emmie with a wry smile as they sat in their room that night, readying themselves for bed. As promised, Wendy let Emmie borrow her brush before it was full of bits of Wendy's strawberry blonde locks. The sisters both had thick hair and thick hair came with consequences.

"I don't think anyone notices," Emmie said defensively, running the brush through her hair. "It's not as if I dance around the room after we're done working."

Wendy smirked. "You practically do. One of these days, Rita's going to notice and relegate you to hall duties at all times, which she's all but done to Tessa."

"That was Tessa's choice, though," Emmie pointed out. "She hates the diner. It makes her nervous. But I don't mind it; it's just not my favorite."

"Well, don't let Rita know that either," Wendy said. "You know she's loyal to her husband's restaurant. I think it's really noble of her." With that, she pulled out her vanity's shallow desk drawer and produced a small stack of letters. "Speaking of 'husband.'"

Emmie rolled her eyes. "You and your newspaper boyfriends," she scoffed. "I thought you didn't care for the one you recently met?"

"Oh, he was fine. I just wasn't as enraptured with him in person as I was on paper. We still trade letters. I think it might just be easier for me to get to know someone...from a distance."

"You're not so shy in real life though," Emmie said. She carefully removed the few light blonde hairs that had managed to get ensnared in the brush's bristles and then she handed the brush over to her sister. "You should just be yourself. After all, it's not as if you must impress someone who's supposed to know you in your day-to-day life. You're not meant to wear a costume and put on a performance for your husband. At least not *always*."

Wendy looked from one of the letters to her, smiling. "I thought you weren't interested in romance, but here you are dispensing advice about it." She shook her head a little. "I think you're warming up to the idea, even if your mind isn't quite ready for it yet."

Emmie rolled her eyes. "Caring about you and your future isn't the same as wanting it for myself. I just don't want to see my sister brokenhearted or otherwise unhappy."

Wendy gave her a doubtful look and then she went back to reading over her latest letters. The main thing that Emmie was concerned about in regards to her sister getting married was that she didn't entirely know what she was going to do without her. The pair had always been so close, practically stitched together from the same cloth... She didn't know what working in the hotel would be like without her best friend. That didn't mean she was anxious to leave, though. Not at all.

Further emphasizing her disinterest in the eligible bachelors in the newspaper, Emmie got into her bed and curled up under her blankets, burrowing enough so her sister wouldn't be able to see that she was, in fact, still awake. She'd been faking sleep ever since they were children. It was a fun game to her, even though Wendy always went along with it without question, never trying to rouse her once she was burrowed. Emmie closed her eyes, wishing that she could fall asleep so easily. She listened to the sounds of Wendy's pen on paper, knowing her handwriting well enough to be able to imagine it as she carefully scrawled it out of her. From her heart to the page. Emmie knew that Wendy was putting her all into finding a good match for herself. As much as she teased and thought it was silly, she really did hope for the best for her dear sister.

After a time, Emmie fell asleep to the soothing sound of Wendy's writing.

When she awoke the following morning, it was the sound of Wendy moving about that stirred her. She sat up in bed, throwing the blankets from her chest, and looked over to find Wendy shuffling her papers and placing them into an envelope.

"My goodness," Emmie said with a smile. "Have you written him a novel?"

Wendy jumped a bit, surprised to see her awake. Then she laughed softly. "This is what comes of getting to know someone. The letters get longer the more you have to say..."

Emmie got out of her bed and quickly changed into her black dress and white apron. She carefully combed her hair so it appeared less frizzy from her sleep, and then she styled it up in a bun. Wendy was already dressed and ready to go, clearly planning to head off to the post office first. "I suppose I should warn the others that you might be detained?"

Wendy blushed a little as she smiled. "I shouldn't be detained much. I'm just dropping off a letter."

Emmie smiled and nodded her head. "Oh, sure, sure." She knew full well – and likely so did Wendy – that it was entirely possible for her to be stalled while walking along the street. It'd happened before, so it could happen again.

Emmie knew that Wendy hadn't been enthusiastic when it happened last time, so it was fair game as far as teasing her with it went.

As soon as she got into work, her mind focused on the job at hand rather than the romantic longings of her sister. The hotel was quiet and peaceful that morning, as Emmie noticed that it usually was. The days grew more hectic as they progressed until the final calm after dinner. *It's a bit like a wave upon the shore,* Emmie mused. *Rising and eventually crashing. Although that makes it seem far more dramatic.* She was pleased that, for the most part, her job didn't entail that much drama. She'd heard horror stories from Rita about what working in the restaurant could be like at times, and sometimes she wondered if they'd always remain so lucky when it came to their clientele. Surely the rude old men who visited the restaurant would eventually come and visit the hotel, too. Emmie felt strange because she almost wished for it. *I can handle a few surly gentlemen. It would keep me on my toes.*

She found Tessa in the upstairs hallway, dusting the shelves and the paintings on the walls there. "Take a walk around the sitting room," Emmie told her with a smile. "Rita wants me to start up here today."

"Is Mr. Pinchy Hands still here?" Tessa asked her, a scared look in her hazel eyes as she handed over the blue feather duster and old, dust-covered rag.

Emmie laughed. "I'm not exactly sure who you mean, but

a bunch of people have vacated their rooms this morning." She gestured to the doors along the hall, their keys in the locks as an indication that there was no one within them. "So, I think you're safe."

Tessa smiled a little, not seeming entirely convinced, and then she went down the stairs to take care of the sitting room and the lounge below. Tessa was recently married, so it struck Emmie as rather odd that the other girl should worry so much. *If I was married, I should think that my husband could defend my honor if it came to it. She has nothing to fear now that she's a Missus. Not that I need a man to protect me. But girls like Tessa clearly do.*

Emmie made her way into the vacant rooms, removing the blankets from the beds and adding them to a laundry bin. She used the duster and rag on all of the surfaces and the paintings in each room, making sure that all dust and fingerprints were taken care of. The goal was to make each room appear like new so that the guests felt like they were the first ones staying there. After she'd cleaned, she also went around and straightened up the books and newspapers on the desks. Every room was given the daily newspaper so that guests could be informed of the latest information of the day, especially if they were new to town and didn't know about the various things to do there.

Then Emmie did something that she usually didn't do. She picked up one of the newspapers and looked through the pages, seeking out the advertisements against her better judgment. *I know that Wendy frequently picks up the paper while she's out visiting the post office,* she thought. *I wonder if it's worth it for me to read sometimes.* But looking only gave her a dizzying sort of feeling. It didn't seem right to her, reading about men who were basically selling themselves to the highest bidder. *Step right up and meet Mr. Harvey Daniels!* she imagined the advertisements calling like a carnival barker. *He's thirty-nine years old and a lonely farmer looking for love. Could that be you? Write to him now and see if the stars align in your favor!*

Emmie put the paper back down on the desk, scoffing and shaking her head. She didn't need to read the newspaper to know that the gentlemen were desperate. It made her feel bad for them, but she didn't think that she could help them in the way that they wanted or deserved.

When she turned back to the doorway to leave the room, she saw Tessa standing there, wearing a playful smile.

"Uh," Emmie said, feeling her cheeks go hot with embarrassment without knowing why. "What are you doing back here?"

Tessa giggled a little. "I need the rag," she said. "I have to clean the bookshelf down there. It's filthy. Someone seems to have gone around with jam on their fingers."

Probably a child, Emmie thought, pushing the newspaper from her mind at once. "I could go help you," she offered.

"No, that's all right," Tessa said, shaking her head and still smiling at her. "I'm sorry if I startled you."

Emmie handed her the rag, thinking that it would help that sort of mess more than the duster would. The rooms never got as dirty as the lounge area, likely because they were further away from the diner. "So, the breakfast shift must be about over now," she said thoughtfully. "Shall I go down to help with lunch?"

Tessa nodded. "Wendy should be up to switch with you soon," she said. "Unless Rita comes instead."

Emmie hoped that Wendy hadn't been late to work. She hadn't heard anything about it until now, but something about Tessa's tone indicated that Wendy hadn't been to work on time. "Thank you, Tessa," she said. "Good luck with the jam."

Tessa laughed as she went. Emmie got back to work, organizing each room so everything was spotless and ready to greet the day's new visitors. Sure enough, once they had some breakfast in their bellies, people began appearing in the hall to claim their rooms.

"Good morning," Emmie said to each of them as they passed her. "Welcome to Stewart House. My name is Emmie. Please do let me know if you should need anything."

The weary travelers smiled back at her as they each made their way into the rooms she'd just diligently cleaned for them. It gave Emmie a lot of pride to know that she was helping so many people every day. *I know who I can and can't help,* she thought. *The people here need us more than the men in the newspaper advertisements. I wish that Wendy could see that.*

She knew that there was no convincing some people, but she also knew that she wasn't going to change to suit their views either.

3

When Wendy came to trade places with Emmie, she had a strange look. She was smiling like always, but she seemed as though she'd just witnessed something incredible – a mixture of awe and disbelief was on her face. *Something amazing must be going on in the diner today,* Emmie thought, though she was skeptical of that. Nothing that exciting ever happened in the diner and that was the way she liked it. Based on stories imparted by Rita, the restaurant was a better location for spectacles.

"Did something interesting happen during breakfast?" she curiously asked her sister.

Wendy continued to smile. *It must not have been bad, in*

any case. That's good... "Well, yes, it was during breakfast time," she said rather cryptically.

Convinced that she had to be imagining things, Emmie simply smiled back at Wendy. "Better you than me," she said jokingly. "I prefer my diner shifts devoid of anything considered interesting." With that, she began to walk down the steps. Wendy didn't call after her, but she could feel her sister's eyes following her down anyway. Emmie thought that Wendy was acting strange and she didn't like it.

The lunch shift in the diner wasn't bad at all for her, however, and she was soon able to forget about any oddness that her coworkers were causing. Rita was there to work alongside her, although there weren't many customers to tend to as it was.

Halfway through the shift, Rita came over to her. "I'm relieving you," she said in a chipper voice. "You can go back to the lounge and work with Tessa there. As a matter of fact, tell her that she may go home early. Wendy, Clara and I can handle dinner tonight."

Emmie eyed her wordlessly, nodding her head. She wasn't one to argue with the boss. She was glad to be able to work in the sitting room again, but she did worry a little that things might become more hectic as dinnertime approached. *Today has certainly been unusual,* she thought. *Perhaps Wendy's brush was bewitched.* She smiled a bit at the very thought.

"What's got you smiling?" Tessa asked, returning the grin.

Emmie shook her head slightly. "Rita says that you're free to go home," she answered. "I'm sure Mr. Grayson will be happy to have you back."

A light blush painted Tessa's cheeks. "Very well. I'll see you tomorrow, Em. Thank you."

She left the hotel, leaving Emmie standing there in the lounge, wondering why she'd been thanked. "It wasn't my doing," she said under her breath. Turning to the bookshelves, Emmie sighed happily. At least she could get back to her favorite part of the job.

When at last the day was over, Wendy and Emmie met up again and walked together to their room in the dormitory. Though her sister was a bit weary from working the dinner shift with Clara and Rita, she still had that grin on her face as soon as she was with Emmie. *I don't know what's going on, but I'm also not sure that I want to know,* Emmie thought. *It probably has something to do with that man she's been writing to anyway.*

Once they were in their room, Wendy closed the door – something she didn't often do. They usually tried to be friendly and inviting towards the other girls, especially because the others hadn't been there as long as they had. But now that Tessa had her own home and life outside of the hotel, Clara was the only other hotel maid who lived in the dormitory. *Maybe that's why she's closed the door? Not much need to be open for people who don't need it...* Emmie hadn't really been much of a fan of it anyway. If people needed their help, they could always knock.

"So," Wendy said, sitting down in the chair beside her vanity now that the door was closed. She placed her hands upon her knees as if she was about to tell Emmie the most scandalous and riveting tale. "Tessa told me that she found you reading through the advertisements in the newspaper."

Emmie opened her mouth to protest, but it was true. She had been discovered doing just that. *But it isn't what they think!* She rued the moment that she'd ever thought peeking might be a fun idea. "I might've glanced," she admitted. "But I was only setting things up in the room. It's not like I was sitting down and reading the newspaper. I was working."

Wendy continued to smirk at her. "I just knew that there'd come a day when you were interested in the mail order service."

"I'm not!" Emmie protested. "I was merely looking briefly to try and see what all of the fuss was about. And, finding no good cause for fuss, I laid it aside again. Tessa just happened to come in before I'd fully put it down."

Emmie felt silly for even glancing at the ads. Of course, nothing was private while she was at work. Honestly, nothing was private when she was in her room either. She never could find a moment alone. *Maybe I should speak with Rita about this. If I roomed with Clara or someone else – maybe even a restaurant girl – I'd have a better time of things than here, with my sister constantly in my face.*

She hated to think it, though. Even if she and Wendy had their differences, they were very close. They'd been through so much together. She didn't wish to separate, especially since Wendy was likely to run off and get married one of these days as it was... She was just feeling bitter and tired of people nosing into her life. *We don't all dream of marriage,* she thought. And even as she thought it, she imagined the gentlemen writing their advertisements and longing for brides. Could she fit into the picture of what they wanted? She doubted it. And even if she could, would it ever possibly bring her happiness?

Wendy, thankfully, appeared to notice the discomfort she had brought to her sister, so she let the conversation go. She turned her attention to preparing for bed, and to reading one of the other letters she'd received from prospective grooms. "What do you wish for yourself once you've left this place?" she asked casually, not looking at her. "You can't expect to stay at Stewart House forever."

"As a matter of fact, that is my wish," Emmie said, still feeling sore with her even as the subject was changed. "I know that a lot of girls use this job as their first foray into working in the West, but I'd love to stay here and perhaps even become Rita's assistant."

Wendy laughed a little, shaking her head. "I hardly think there'll be a call for an assistant here," she said. "There's only a staff of four as it is. And I don't foresee things becoming busier than the restaurant or any such thing."

The hotel was built as an expansion of Mr. and Mrs. Stewart's home, so it wasn't as if it would someday become bigger. "There's a chance that they'll purchase more land and build more hotels, though," Emmie pointed out. She preferred to be enterprising and optimistic about the Stewarts' business instead of limiting things to how it was *now*. "Things can change. They always do."

"Yes," Wendy argued. "But by that same token, Rita might decide that she doesn't wish to run this hotel anymore and keep the building as a lovely, expansive house. I know Mr. Stewart won't ever change tracks, but that doesn't mean Rita won't want to move on. Think about it... Someday, they may want a family."

Emmie frowned. She'd never thought about that as a possibility; Rita always seemed so interested in her hotel business. Sitting at her own vanity, Emmie let down her hair and brushed it until it was smooth and shiny. She changed into her nightgown and got into her bed wordlessly, facing away from her sister. *I know that she probably thinks I'm being selfish and stubborn,* she thought, eyes closed but unable to fall asleep. *But I just know myself and what I want... I base my opinions of Rita on how she presents herself, too. I suppose I could always ask.*

She slept fitfully that night, her dreams alternating between meeting gentlemen in town and Rita deciding to close her hotel in favor of a sudden slew of children. When she awoke the following morning, she was more than grateful for Wendy's incessant scribbling as she wrote to one of her various beaus. As with the day before, Wendy was fully dressed for work and ready to head off to the post office first thing.

Emmie smiled a little at her as she sat up in bed. She hoped that her sister wasn't angry with her. "I don't think I could ever be as voracious about anything as you are about this whole letter-writing business."

Wendy turned to look at Emmie and smiled. She wasn't mad at her. "I suppose you're voracious about working at the hotel," she offered pleasantly, without any sardonicism in her voice. "I'm sorry I was so quick to scoff at what you want to do with your life. I just don't want you to be disappointed if this place doesn't stay the way it's been for you... I want you to be happy."

And you know just how I can be happy. "I'm sorry, too," Emmie said, getting out of her bed and going over so to hug her sister. "I should take your romances more seriously because they're serious for you. I hope that you find a gentleman who truly loves and appreciates you. Because I want only the best husband for you."

Wendy smiled as she hugged her back. "I'm glad we're not still angry with each other. I shouldn't do well at work if I knew you were upset at me. We're a good team, you and I. Even if life takes us in different directions, I'd like to think that we'd still have each other's backs."

Emmie nodded. "On that, we certainly can agree. And I'll be sure to give some thought to what you said. Perhaps you are right that pinning all of my aspirations on this place isn't the best idea. After all, it's rather out of my hands what Rita decides to do down the line... I can't imagine her giving up this place, but I also don't know what she wishes for. I only know what I see of her."

She got dressed as Wendy finished up her letter and packed it away into its envelope. "I shouldn't be late," Wendy said when she was done, standing up from her chair. "But you may inform Rita that I'm stopping off at the post, so she doesn't wonder where I've gone."

"I shall," Emmie replied. "And hopefully she'll give you double diner duty again because of it," she added teasingly.

Wendy stuck her tongue at her.

It was difficult for Emmie to imagine Wendy ever being mature enough to start a family of her own. She was still childlike in her eyes, and that meant that this topic of marriage was a difficult one for her to adjust to for that reason as well. *She's too young to be getting married and having babies. It wasn't but yesterday that she and I were thirteen and fourteen, helping Mama at our home after Papa went away to the city. I can't believe how much has changed, and how much she's grown.*

Emmie supposed that her dislike of matrimony had more to do with not wanting to grow up and lead separate lives from her sister than it did with an actual aversion to romance. She found men handsome and appealing as much as any young lady... But she still didn't think that she was the right type of woman to get married. Not yet anyway. After all, twenty was so very young.

4

The weeks passed in a similar fashion for Emmie and her sister. Wendy's letter writing and trips to the post office seemed to be an almost daily occurrence to the point where Emmie didn't bother to roll her eyes about it anymore. It was just another part of their days. It took her awhile to pluck up the courage to talk to Rita about the future of the restaurant and what she had in mind for herself. It wasn't the sort of thing that was easy to ask an employer, but Rita was also a friend in Emmie's mind. *She may even be happy that I'm asking. Interest in her life outside of work is a sign that I care about her, isn't it?*

One afternoon, she was working in the diner with Rita and it was only the two of them. The customers hadn't come in from the lunchtime train yet, and it was likely that they would go to the restaurant instead before coming over to stay in the inn. It was the perfect chance for Emmie to speak with Rita. "You know, as much as I enjoy working here when it's busy," she said with a smile, "I do enjoy these quieter moments."

Rita smiled back at her and nodded her head. "Yes, it can be a nice respite from some of the crazier times we experience. Though if you think it gets busy here, you should work in the restaurant for a day!"

Emmie laughed a little bit, shaking her head. "No, no, that's okay. I believe you. Is that part of why you were more than happy to start working over here in the hotel instead?"

"Well, my husband was going to expand his business anyway. It was always just a matter of time. And after we got married, we thought it might be best if I was helping him run things instead of continuing to work as a manager there."

"I don't think just any wife would've been okay with her home being taken over by visiting guests all the time. Strangers, no less." Emmie looked at her with an impressed smile.

Rita gave her an odd look then, as though it'd suddenly dawned on her that Emmie was interrogating her a bit about the business side of things. "Right..." she said a bit more hesitantly. "We do our best to keep our private lives sequestered from the rest of the hotel. Of course, that will be more difficult when we decide to start a family, but we could just get a new home if that is the case."

Aha! So, Wendy's wrong. She wouldn't give up this job, she'd just move out of the inn to have more space. "That makes sense," she said, feeling inwardly relieved but careful to not show it. "I think you would be sad if you had to give up this job entirely."

"Definitely," Rita said, appearing to relax a bit as well. "What's got you so interested? You're not trying to steal my job, are you?"

Emmie could tell that she was kidding, but still she wanted to reassure her. "No, of course not! I've just been thinking about my own place in this town and what I might want to do with my life here. I can't see myself as a hotel maid forever."

Rita nodded. "And you shouldn't. No one wants to do the same thing for the rest of their life, even if they enjoy it." She smiled encouragingly. "Maybe you'll have your own hotel in town someday."

That's so kind of her to say, Emmie thought pensively. She'd never given much thought to actually trying to start her own hotel; she mostly wanted to help run this one. But perhaps she really should think about the grand scheme of things instead of tethering herself to one venue. There was so much potential to be found in that little dusty town. Hence the constant train passengers who stopped in. They were all looking for their own piece of the American Dream. Why shouldn't she?

The customers began pouring into the diner after that

little chat. Thankfully for Emmie, it was actually more of a trickle than a pour. *I'm so glad I talked with Rita about all of this,* she thought. *Wendy probably won't believe me. But then again, she doesn't care about what I do in regards to work, as long as I get married.* She did her best to not roll her eyes at the thought.

As soon as it was time for the dinner shift, Wendy was there to switch places with her. She raised her eyebrows questioningly at Emmie as she came into the diner. Emmie simply nodded her head back at her, not really feeling comfortable discussing the matter anymore, especially not with Rita and the customers right there to listen in. It was nobody else's business what Emmie might be planning to do with her life. Besides, she wasn't even sure herself.

She was glad to back with her beloved bookshelves in the lounge. There usually weren't that many people hanging around in there when it was time for supper, which meant that Emmie could have some time alone with her thoughts. *I can see why Clara is so fond of her front desk position. She's always alone with her thoughts when she's there, too. It isn't as though that's a very demanding shift.* But Emmie preferred to have her books to reorganize and flip through. She knew that she could stand there with her nose in a book and Rita would only complain if she was doing so while guests were around and needed her assistance with something. Emmie was introverted, but she wasn't rude.

Maybe there really is something to be said about starting my own library in town... she thought as she tidied up the books. *Wallace doesn't need another hotel, but it could certainly use a library.* Wendy would likely laugh at the very idea, though. Her friends wouldn't quite take that seriously. The town had necessities like places to purchase and eat food, a bank, a mail office, tradesmen like butchers and farmers... A library wasn't needed. That's what they'd say. There wasn't a crowd for it. *But surely, I'm not the only person here who likes to sit back and read a good book every now and then.*

Emmie decided to put the idea aside for now, because after all she wasn't planning on leaving the hotel any time soon, despite what Wendy thought was necessary. She focused on her work in the lounge, mainly cleaning things and being a silent observer of the guests who chose to recline in there. Many of the hotel's guests liked having the maids in their view, if only so they could feel like they were being helped even if there was nothing that they currently needed help with. It gave them a feeling of security to know that Emmie was there, and as silly as it might have been to an outsider, that made her happy.

At the end of the day, she met with Wendy outside of the diner entrance. "You're so lucky that you got to work the lunch shift," Wendy said to her as they walked together back to the dormitory. "Dinner wasn't very busy, but it's generally busier than the calm lunchtime crowd."

Emmie smiled and shrugged. "I think Rita gives you the dinner shifts more often because she knows that you're good at working in there and can handle it, whereas Tessa and I are relegated to the slower times."

This seemed to pluck up Wendy's spirits. Her shoulders noticeably straightened back and she walked with a bit more pep in her step. "I like to think that I do a good job there, even as I'm trying to move on. Speaking of, how did it go with Rita? Did you discuss matters with her?"

Emmie nodded and filled her sister in on the details of their little chat, including Rita's suggestion that Emmie could open her own hotel if she so chose to stay on that path. "I'm not sure that I wish to do that, though. For one thing, I'd become competition for Stewart House and I don't think I have either the tenacity or the desire to do that. I love this place so why would I wish to compete against it?"

Wendy was thoughtful. "You might wish to learn from the Stewarts and improve upon what they started," she offered. "But I can also see you taking up the mantle here and doing the same. It's up to you what you do with your life... Although I do wish you wouldn't always see yourself as going through it all alone."

"I wouldn't necessarily have to go it alone," Emmie replied. "You could keep on working here with me after you get married. Rita allows that."

Wendy laughed softly as they opened the door to their room and went inside. "You know that's not what I want to do. I want to be a housewife and help my husband full-time.

I've enjoyed working but I also will enjoy being a happy little wife."

Emmie sighed a little. "Then I have no choice but to go it alone."

It was then that she noticed something strange on her vanity. She went over to it and slowly sank into the chair, gingerly bringing the surprise into her hands. It was a news-paper, open onto the advertisements page. Atop it appeared to be a letter, with her name written on the envelope in unfa-miliar handwriting.

Emmie's mouth fell open. She noticed that one of the advertisements had been circled. *Young and reasonably attrac-tive lawyer seeks a wife to be his companion in Wallace, Kansas. Must be young, friendly, and dedicated. Interested parties please contact David Cline.* She read the address that was listed at the end. It was right on the main street of town! "Who put this here?" she asked, looking up from the ad and right at Wendy.

Her sister smiled playfully as she sat at her own vanity, letting her hair down. "It wasn't me. I've been far too busy today. You know that."

"It must've been Tessa, then," Emmie said. She narrowed her eyes and then picked up the letter that sat on the news-paper, placed right next to the advertisement so that Emmie wouldn't miss either thing. "And this is probably what I think it is..." She carefully tore open the letter and read it to herself.

My dear Miss Sheffield,

THE LETTER that you wrote to me gave me such joy and amusement. You seem to be a highly intelligent and witty girl. I'm quite pleased that you took the time to reply to my advertisement and wish to know more about me. As you ascertained, the term 'young' is quite subjective but I do assure you that it wasn't meant to be misleading. I'm thirty years of age. I worked as a lawyer's apprentice back when I lived in Virginia, but now that I've found myself working out West, I'm the only lawyer in town. As Wallace is a small town, with a tight-knit group of townsfolk, I enjoy my job quite a lot, though it does mean that I've got my hands full much of the time, dealing with land disputes and things of that nature which are probably boring to a lady like you.

I find it interesting that you're a book lover. It probably won't surprise you to learn that I'm a lover of books myself and would love to be able to discuss them with you. Even if we haven't read the same thing, it will be fun just to be able to sit down and discuss all things literary for a while. How interesting that the hotel has a small library. Now that I know that, I shall have to pay it a visit. Perhaps I will find you there, too.

You say that you haven't really been looking to marry, but I believe it must be divine providence that you should've found my advertisement even in your slight perusal of the ad pages. This is surely a sign, Miss Sheffield. Please permit me to say so. I would greatly like to meet you somewhere in which you will feel most at ease. Perhaps at your beloved library or in one of the 'courting parlors' I've heard so much about from advertisements about your place of work. Please write to me and let me know what you think, and if I might dare to dream that we shall one day meet!

RESPECTFULLY,

David Cline

5

Emmie sat back in her chair at her vanity, blinking down at the words that were written on the piece of paper in her hands. Words that had been written to and for *her*, in response to a letter that she hadn't written, about an advertisement that she'd never seen before a few moments ago. She felt numb; she wasn't angry, she was just too shocked to quite know what to do about her predicament now that she knew that one existed for her. Someone had written to this – admittedly sweet – gentleman on her behalf, without telling her or warning her about it. She looked over at Wendy, who was still in the process of readying herself for bed.

"Did you do this?" Emmie asked her feebly, holding up the letter. She knew that her expression must've been so hurt and confused, because Wendy looked at her so pityingly.

"I didn't," Wendy replied with a shake of her head. "But I may have told someone that it was a good idea..."

"*Wendy!*" Emmie moaned, throwing the letter down on the desk, on top of the newspaper once more, and rising from her chair. "Why on earth would you do such a thing? Aren't you involved in my life enough as it is? We wouldn't have moved out here if you hadn't said it was a good idea. We wouldn't be working for Rita at this hotel. And now you wish to choose who and when I marry, too!"

Her sister stared at her, raising her hands defensively. "I never chose for you," she said. "I merely told Tessa that perhaps you were looking through the newspaper because you were curious after all. And I guess I may have told her to peruse the ads for you. But I swear, I never directly told her to just write away for a husband for you."

Wendy's voice was so pleading that Emmie knew she was telling the truth. It didn't exactly make her feel better, but at least her sister hadn't gone behind her back and done this. *I suppose I don't* have *to write back to this Mr. Cline...* she thought, feeling miserable even for thinking it. Surely it would be rude to just ignore the poor man now that he had put so much faith into their meeting. Emmie groaned, lying on her bed and feeling ill.

"Does no one mind their own business around here?" she asked rhetorically to the Heavens.

Wendy smiled at her as she settled into her own bed. "You certainly sound like you're planning to write back to him and give this whole thing some serious thought."

"Of course, I'll write back to him," Emmie snapped at her, still lying prostrate on her bed. "But don't think I'll enjoy it. I'm not going to be mean to the poor man. He's done nothing wrong. In fact, right now he feels like the only person I can trust with my feelings about such matters."

But I won't write back to him at this moment, she thought. *I need to figure out what to say, first of all. And then there's the whole matter of him wishing to meet me right away. I don't know what to say to that. He's a lover of books, so that's in his favor. And he's a lawyer, which is far more interesting than a farmer... Oh, it just would've been nice to be able to make my own choice!*

She did her best to go to sleep, but it was a fitful sleep for her that night as her thoughts and dreams continued to wander into the land of newspapers and mail order advertisements. She had no idea what this Mr. Cline fellow looked like, so her unconscious mind had a wonderful time conjuring up all sorts of imaginings of him. Often, he was young and handsome, the way she might've expected, but then a few times he was old or ugly and she found herself rousing from her sleep more than a few times, unable to cope with the idea that she might be exchanging letters with some kind of terrible monster of a man.

The following morning, Emmie felt completely groggy from her night of restless sleep. *I wish that I could roll over and forget that any of this happened,* she thought morosely. She didn't know how she was ever supposed to look Tessa in the eyes again, or how she was ever going to show her face around all of her men-crazy coworkers. Every one of them was in love with the idea of being in love, and she wished that they could just be happy with that and leave her out of it. *Now they'll probably all be constantly trying to discuss this with me, and asking me for updates on my letter-writing.* It was how they were with each other, even though Wendy was really the only one of them who was in constant contact with beaus. As far as Emmie knew, Clara also wanted nothing to do with it. So why were they going after *her* all of the time?

She got ready quickly, pausing to look over the newspaper and letter on her desk again. If she was going to write back to him, she wanted to do it soon. *I guess on my lunch break,* she thought. *Assuming I can get a moment's peace in order to do it.*

When Emmie walked into work with her sister at her side, she begrudgingly smiled as Tessa welcomed them with her usual cheery 'good morning.' She had a few things she wanted to say to her, but it wasn't the time or even really the place for that conversation. The last thing Emmie needed to do was to get in trouble for off-topic arguing in front of guests. It was bad enough when the girls argued about hotel matters in front of the guests.

"Good morning, Tessa," Wendy said brightly. The four girls stood by the front desk, waiting for Rita to appear and give them their schedules for the day. "Emmie's a little peeved about the newspaper she found on her table last night."

Apparently, she's not worried about being inappropriate or getting into trouble, Emmie thought with a roll of her eyes. *At least no one else is around yet.* Tessa was looking at her with raised eyebrows now. Even though her sister had it correct that she was peeved, she didn't wish to upset her friend. They could have a disagreement about the handling of things without being mean to each other. *Right?*

"I'm not peeved per se," she said with a shy smile that was tinged with embarrassment. "I'm more... taken-aback, I suppose. I didn't think that anyone would take it upon themselves to write a letter on my behalf. Or choose a potential beau on my behalf, either. I rather thought that it was the kind of thing we'd discuss. But what's done is done."

Tessa blanched a bit. "I didn't mean to upset you. It was my understanding that you were interested in reaching out to someone but perhaps didn't quite know how or didn't have the nerve. I only wanted to help you." She frowned and looked from Emmie to Wendy. "I should've asked either of you about it first."

I don't really feel comfortable with Wendy being the other person you might've asked, Emmie thought. *After all, she's not my keeper.* But she held her tongue about that, merely shrugging her shoulders slightly. "As I said, it's done now so there's no use getting upset about it. The letter I received was quite nice. You did a good job in choosing someone for me, even if it's not how I would've wanted it."

Tessa continued to look remorseful, even as Rita strolled down the stairs of the hotel and came towards them at the welcome desk. "Good morning, girls!" their boss trilled enthusiastically. Clara and Tessa both looked uncomfortable and Rita noticed this right away. "What's going on?"

Wendy wagged her head from side to side, smiling gaily as if it was all so amusing to her. "Nothing," she answered. "Just a bit of boy trouble, but nothing that's going to interfere with work."

Rita arched an eyebrow and smiled a little. "Still having good luck?" she asked.

"Yes," Wendy replied at once, "and now Emmie is, too."

She's lucky I don't stomp on her foot, Emmie thought darkly, feigning a smile of both innocence and affirmation. "I really don't wish to talk about it right now," she said truthfully, hoping against hope that the subject could just be dropped for now.

Fortunately for her, guests began to come through the front doors of the hotel, which meant that all of their idle chatter had to come to an end for the time being. "I'd like Clara to start on the desk here. Wendy, you've got lounge duty; Tessa and Emmie tidy up the rooms and hallway. I can handle breakfast by myself. Then we'll rotate accordingly." Rita was a professional when it came to calling out their shifts for the day. Emmie didn't know how she managed to plan these things out without prior knowledge of how the day was going to be. It was entirely possible that breakfast would be too busy for just one person.

Then again, when has that ever happened?

Emmie wasn't looking forward to sharing upstairs duties with Tessa at the moment. She had a feeling that their conversation was going to continue as they worked alongside each other. Or, maybe worse, Tessa would simply not wish to talk to her again. Nevertheless, it was a shift that they would both perform regardless of how they felt about things outside of their duties. She solemnly climbed the stairs behind Tessa, wishing to start a conversation but not sure how or if it would be accepted.

"My sister misspoke before," she said at last as they stood together in the hall, cleaning the dust off of the various framed paintings which hung there. "I admit that I was startled to find that newspaper and letter on my vanity, but I wasn't mad about it. In a way, I felt oddly comforted. I know that you meant well and that you only wished to help me."

For a moment, Tessa didn't look at her, but then she glanced over and gave a small smile. "I probably should've asked about it first. It's just that I found you there with the newspaper in your hands, and I thought that you were interested in writing to one of the gentlemen. If this was wrong, I promise I won't bring it up again. You needn't write back to Mr. Cline if you'd rather not."

Emmie smirked a bit, leaning down to wipe the hall table

clean. "Oh, I'm planning to write back to him," she said. "He took the time to write to me and he does sound like a sweet man. It'd be rude to ignore him now that he's reached out to get to know me better. Even if you wrote the initial letter." She looked up and grinned. Tessa looked absolutely thrilled by this decision of hers. It was Emmie's turn to be surprising.

6

After working what blessedly turned out to be a normal day for the hotel, Emmie sat at her vanity that night, feeling more prepared than ever to respond to the letter from Mr. Cline. She wished to be honest with him about the fact that she wasn't the one who'd written the first letter, but decided against it at the last moment. *He might be brokenhearted to discover that it was not me who'd found his advertisement and decided to write to him. That kind of thing can be a terrible blow to a man's ego, I believe.*

Tapping her pen against the table for a few moments as she thought things over, she carefully began to draft a letter, using his letter as a reference so she wouldn't forget to answer any of his questions. She didn't want to leave anything out, even if her answers might not be what he was hoping for.

Dear Mr. Cline,

You certainly seem to be an interesting fellow! I must admit that I had a particular aversion to marriage primarily because it would force me to stop working at the hotel, or at least it would become a distraction for me. Though I'm still not sure that I'm keen on so much change in my thus-far pleasant life, I do know that I'm interested in continuing our correspondence and getting to know each other better. I rather fancy the idea of being betrothed to a well-read lawyer. This is much more appealing to me than marrying a farmer or ranch hand, nothing personal against them of course. Men like that are just more for my sister, I suppose.

I feel that I must be honest with you and let you know that I was a bit pushed into this whole thing. My sister Wendy and our friends are of the opinion that I must meet someone and get married. You know how young ladies can be about this sort of thing. But it's also important to me that you know that I don't regret getting in touch with you. In fact, you're all the proof I should need that this whole mail-order business can be a success.

It wouldn't be prudent if I was to meet you in the hotel's library, although I do very much recommend that you pay it a visit sometime. It's a shame that Wallace doesn't have anything *like a library yet, and I've thought about possibly trying to open one someday, though I don't think there'd be much interest outside you and me. Perhaps some of the guests to this place would enjoy it, but how on earth would they then return the books? I think it's a much better idea for us to meet in the courting parlors that are located on the premises. I know that I'd feel safer that way, not that I'm afraid of you but this is an entirely new experience for me and I'd like to feel like my friends and loved ones are close at hand if I should need their support. You understand, I hope.*

I know for a fact that my sister would be overjoyed about me having a date with a beau from the newspaper. I don't like to let her know that she was right all along, but I agree that you and I really must meet. My boss doesn't know about this situation of ours yet, so I pray that you'll give me a chance to let her know first before our meeting. Let's make a plan for you to stop by the hotel and meet me in its lounge this Friday afternoon. (Afternoon is our calmest time, generally.) Go to the bookshelf and select the book by Henry James. I shall know it's you if you sit on the couch there and read that – or pretend to! Knowing your love of books, I can't help but think that you've already read his Portrait of a Lady *at least once before.*

Please write to me right away if this is disagreeable for you. Otherwise, I shall see you soon!

Yours,

Emily Sheffield

READING HER COMPLETED LETTER OVER, she had to wonder if Tessa had signed the first letter thusly or if it was going to be a big surprise to him that her given name was Emily. It didn't make sense to her to use her nickname in a letter such as this one. Perhaps when Mr. Cline got to know her better, the loving pet name would make more sense. The only people who called her Emmie were her family and her friends at work. It felt strange enough hearing Rita use it, though she didn't mind it.

I really wish that it could've been suggested that I write to him instead of someone else doing it for me, she thought woefully, but the gentleman plainly liked her regardless of who'd written it. And he seemed to have the facts right about her. It wasn't as if he'd said something woefully incorrect in his letter. She appreciated that Tessa had put some thought into it and had done her best to paint an accurate picture of her. *Wendy would've likely tried to make me appear more agreeable to her own tastes and sensibilities,* she thought. *So perhaps it's better that a friend wrote the letter instead of my nosy sister.*

Emmie smile to herself and carefully sealed the letter into the envelope. As nervous as it made her to think that soon she would be meeting the man in person, it made far more sense to her than to keep on writing to someone who was right up the road from where she was at that very moment. *I don't just wish to read what he's like. I really rather wish to see what he's like for myself.*

On her way to work, she dropped the letter off at the post

office in town, greeting the friendly postman with a smile and a nod of thanks. She knew that as soon as she got to work, all the other girls were going to want to talk about was her and Mr. Cline. She did her best to prepare herself for that, hoping that she wasn't just flattering herself now. *I don't wish to be like them – a pack of giddy schoolgirls, the lot of them – but at the same time, it is rather gratifying to feel included for once and have it be okay. They've pushed me and now I suppose I'm in the pool with them. I just hope I don't drown.*

Emmie strolled into the hotel to find the others standing around the welcome desk, like always. Wendy beamed at her and rushed to her side, taking her hand and pulling her towards the rest of the group. "You sent your letter, didn't you?? Oh, I'm so proud of you!"

Blushing, Emmie nodded her head a little. "I mailed my letter. We'll see what happens next. I told him to meet me here in the lounge on Friday, if that's okay." She looked at Rita for confirmation. "We'll go to the courting parlor after that, so we're not taking up space here."

Rita shook her head, smiling. "You may use the lounge for your first meeting, if you like. I see no reason that you should go all the way to the dormitory. You could even go into the diner, provided it isn't too busy."

Emmie felt a little stressed thinking about the possibilities, and the audience that would surely be watching their every move if they stayed in the hotel... Though she knew it would be better to feel that her friends were right there in case she should need their support or help. *Goodness, you'd think I was going into the lion's den instead of having a chat with a gentleman. I shouldn't be needing help, surely!*

"That's very kind of you," she said after considering her options. "I shall tell him that we may stay in the hotel then, if it's not too much of a bother. He will be sitting on the couch, reading a specific book."

Wendy laughed softly. "You sure do love your books. I hope Mr. Cline's prepared to be in constant competition with them."

Rita told them all what their positions in the hotel would be for the morning. Wendy and Emmie were assigned to work the breakfast shift in the diner. "What about you?" Emmie asked her sister as they stood in the empty room, awaiting the arrival of the famished visitors. "Are you still having luck with your beau? What's his name again? I have to admit, I tried not to pay it any mind before."

Wendy didn't seem at all surprised. She blushed and grinned as if she'd simply been complimented. "His name is Geoffrey Murray. Oh! His name sounds like music to me when I say it out loud."

Emmie smiled a little, careful to hold her tongue and not roll her eyes. "And what does this musical man do for a living?"

Her sister continued to blush, which made her feel happy and glad that she hadn't been so dismissive about it this time. As fun as it sometimes was to scoff at Wendy's flirtatious behavior, Emmie did want to continue to see her sister happy. If what made Wendy happiest of all was romance and getting married, then so be it. "He's a rancher from just outside of town," Wendy told her.

Of course he is, Emmie thought, amused this time rather than judgmental. *A rancher suits her better than me.* "That sounds delightful," she said supportively, smiling. "While I can't entirely imagine you working in a rancher's home, I also can't say that it'd be out of your realm of interests and experiences. I'm sure he needs a good housewife to make his house more of a *home*."

Wendy beamed. "He said the very same thing to me, more or less!"

Though she was loathe to admit it, Emmie liked being able to participate in this 'girlie talk' with her sister. At last, she felt like she'd found her place in it, although it remained to be seen if Mr. Cline really could be the man for her. She had yet to meet him, and she thought it was foolish to make such a big decision based completely on what was on paper. *I don't even know what he looks like.* "Do you know what this Mr. Murray looks like?"

"Oh, we've met before. Don't you remember?" Wendy asked gaily, not even pausing for Emmie to answer. "He's tall and broad-chested, with sandy hair and the most darling brown eyes. And freckles! He has the cutest freckles on his face and neck, probably from all of the sun he gets. He's quite handsome, if I do say so myself. And kind and darling."

Emmie wanted to meet this kind and darling person for herself, to see if he was good enough for her sweet elder sister. But of course, there would be time for that if they got married. Surely, she would be meeting him soon, if things were going as smoothly for Wendy as they seemed to be for Emmie. *Why, we might very well both be married by the time this year is out,* she thought with a bashful smile as her sister continued to prattle on about her beau and her imagined happy future with him. Now that Emmie had a handsome and charming beau of her own – she assumed he was handsome, for why shouldn't he be? – talking and listening to Wendy made her feel a great deal more hopeful and excited than it ever had before. She wished that it didn't sometimes. It made her feel rather foolish. But in the moments when she felt such joy and elation, she didn't wish to feel any other way.

7

Friday finally came and greeted Emmie in the form of butterflies in her stomach and flightiness in her brain. She rose from bed and dressed quickly, wondering if perhaps she shouldn't leap to conclusions about Mr. Cline coming to see her, because she hadn't had time to check the post office since sending her letter out into the void. *There's a good chance that he's since written to me to let me know that today's not a good day or he's changed his mind about me. He might possibly be writing to all sorts of girls from all over. He never specified that he wished to marry a girl from town. Why, he also never specified that he wished to marry me. That's just been wishful fantasy on my part...*

Emmie didn't wish to put the thought entirely from her mind, however. She readied herself for work and paid extra careful attention to her hair styling. She wanted to look her best for Mr. Cline, even if he should decide not to come visit her on this day or ever.

"You're up early," Wendy said to her with a sleepy smile as she got out of bed, yawning as she went. "Are you ready for your big day?"

Emmie blushed a bit. *I wish she wouldn't make a big deal about it. Especially when I'm making a big enough deal of it on my own.* "I don't know if I'd ever consider myself ready, but I'm preparing myself accordingly." She glanced at her reflection in her mirror one last time, pinching her cheeks in order to give them some extra color, though she needn't have bothered. She was blushing enough on her own without hurting herself.

Wendy proceeded to get ready as well and then the two sisters went off to the hotel to begin the day's work. "Wendy and Tessa will start in the diner," Rita proclaimed, smiling a little at Emmie. "Emmie will start in the lounge. Clara will work upstairs and I will manage the desk here. Then we'll rotate accordingly."

She's essentially letting me work in the lounge while I need to, Emmie thought. *If I could kiss her without being out of line, I would.* She could hold off on that for the time being and focus on her work and what was to come that afternoon. *Oh, I do hope he comes now especially. Imagine if I caused all of this commotion and he didn't even appear when he was supposed to!*

Emmie followed her orders and happily went into the

lounge. Regardless of the outcome of the day, she was glad to be working in her favorite part of the hotel. She wished for the giddy distraction of a date with Mr. Cline, but either way she would be satisfied. That was something that set her apart from the other girls, who were clearly rapt with anticipation about the meeting. She noticed several times that they were peeking into the room to see how things were going, frowning disappointedly when they discovered that she was still just standing there, rearranging books contentedly.

Honestly, it's a wonder sometimes how this place stays in business, she thought with an amused shake of her head after seeing both Wendy and Rita popping their heads in through the doorways at practically the same time. She knew that the morning could be the slowest time of the day, but this was ridiculous.

Eventually, more people began to come into the hotel and meet up in the lounge while she worked. There were mostly groups of friends or family members, though occasionally a lone gentleman would stroll into the room while Emmie was dusting and organizing, and she would perk up a bit in case they should happen to go to the shelf and pick up the Henry James novel. That was meant to be her cue, though she was beginning to wonder if she'd made the task slightly cumbersome. *Suppose he's feeling as nervous as I am? It might be asking too much and sitting on the sofa in here is as much as he can do...* She cast her eyes in the direction of the sofa, but no one was sitting on it at the moment. Most people chose to stand and chat in the lounge before making their way into the dining area. *Oh, I do hope he comes and follows my directions so we don't fail to catch each other's eye.*

She was beginning to wish that she could be more like her sister. Wendy never seemed to be so concerned about the logistics of things. It was very likely that her plans to meet up with her intended were more along the lines of 'come to the courting parlor in the morning.' Something much simpler than Emmie's attempt to be extra stealth. It wasn't as if this was even a secret from her coworkers, and as far as the guests went she didn't care how they felt about her chatting with a young man in the hotel's lounge. They didn't know her and therefore wouldn't judge.

"Are you okay?" Wendy's voice suddenly whispered into her ear. Emmie turned and jumped a bit when she realized that her sister was right there. "It's lunchtime and so I'm switching places with Clara in the hall... I suppose he hasn't come yet?"

Emmie tried not to look sad or cross. She shook her head. "No, not yet. Although I did say lunchtime, not breakfast..."

Wendy appeared sympathetic. "I can tell that the waiting is killing you."

Shrugging a little, Emmie smiled. "Not really. If this doesn't work out, there will always be another opportunity. It's not like I'm as heavily invested in this as you all apparently are." She laughed softly.

Just then, a gentleman walked into the room. He was tall

and fairly thin, with wavy, dark brown hair and bright eyes that were a shocking mixture of green and blue. Emmie noticed him as he came into the room and somehow, she just knew... She knew that Wendy was saying some kind of retort to her, but she tuned her out as if listening to this young man's every footfall was more important. Suddenly, he came over towards her.

"Excuse me," he said in a voice that was both soft and direct. He leaned in front of her a bit, scanning the spines of the books on the shelf there.

Emmie nearly dropped the rag she was holding as she stepped back slightly, allowing him space to look even though he didn't really need to look any further. "Are- Are you looking for Henry James, by any chance? *Portrait of a Lady*?" she stammered out.

The gentleman was a bit startled to hear her voice behind him. He stopped his leaning and turned to face her, holding the mentioned book in his hands. "Are you Miss Sheffield?" he asked haltingly.

Emmie gulped a bit and she nodded. Her plan for meeting him hadn't gone exactly the way she'd hoped for, but in a way, it'd worked out *better*. She smiled at the handsome gentleman. "I am," she confirmed. "Are you Mr. Cline?"

He smiled from her to the book and then held out to her as if it was the special item that he needed in order to speak with her. Looking down at it in his hands, Emmie saw that it was clearly *Portrait of a Lady*. She blushed as she continued to grin at him. *Well,* she thought. *At least he knows how to follow instructions.* She felt bad now for trying to be so specific and crafty about it... It was far easier to just meet there by the bookshelf. "I'm David Cline," he told her, his smile becoming quite shy. "May I have the honor of sitting with you for a while?"

Emmie continued to blush as she looked into his kind, gentle eyes. She carefully took the book from his hand and set it back on the shelf, not bothering herself with where it was placed at the moment. Organization was the furthest thing from her mind. "It's so wonderful to meet you," she replied. "Of course you may sit with me. My employer has told me that we're allowed to sit on her sofa here, and perhaps have a meal in the diner if you would like. You're likely ready for lunch."

Using her skills from working in the hotel, Emmie gestured an arm over to the couch in the center of the room. Mr. Cline walked over to it with her but stood and waited for her to sit first. Blushing bashfully, she gracefully sat upon the edge of the middle cushion. Mr. Cline sat beside her on her left, careful to keep a bit of distance between them so he was giving her space. "I'm so honored to meet you," he said to her. "I know that our correspondence has been brief thus far, but I've been hoping for this moment for quite some time."

"Me too," Emmie said emphatically, her cheeks feeling blissfully sore from smiling at him. "As you know, I never really fancied myself as a married lady before, but now that I've been getting to know you, I've come around to the idea."

Mr. Cline let out a pleasant laugh, nodding his head at her. "I appreciate that. I imagine that it takes something quite big to make such a change. I pray that I shall never disappoint you or make you change your mind again."

For a moment, they just sat there together, smiling and blushing. It was enough to be beside each other, sharing the same air instead of being far apart and strangers. "What has life been like for you in Wallace?" she asked him once she'd plucked up the nerve to continue their conversation. "What brought you here and when?" *I hope that Tessa didn't cover these sorts of questions already, in her letter to him...* She couldn't recall the answers, though.

If the questions had already been asked, Mr. Cline didn't seem bothered by answering them again. "Life has been rewarding here," he said. "I feel as though I'm helping people, and that's the most important thing to me, in the long run. I wish to be someone that people know they can trust and come to with their problems... Even if those problems are mainly land-related." He laughed again. Emmie liked that his laugh was soft and genuine. It didn't boom or sound at all unkind. "As I wrote to you, I worked as apprentices and assistants back in Virginia. I suppose more than wishing for a promotion, I also was hoping for my own little piece of the American West. I'd heard some great stories from men who've come out here and started a new life or a better life, and that idea appealed to me. What about you? Did you have dreams of working as a maid in a hotel? You certainly seem good at it." He smiled a charming smile and Emmie could sense that he was becoming more comfortable talking to her already.

She giggled a little bit. "I don't suppose that I wished to be a maid," she replied. "I mainly wanted to get away from Albany and explore what else was out there for me. I knew that there were factories in New York, and I could have done just fine in them if it's not immodest for me to say so, but my sister Wendy had her sights on the West and I suppose that I wanted to follow along with her. I always have, after all. I greatly love living here and working for the lovely people who come to visit the Stewart House. I'm not sure it's the place for me for the rest of my life, although if it is I shall be more than happy."

Mr. Cline's smile grew as she spoke and her heart quickened. Had she passed his test?

8

After sitting and chatting on the couch there for a while longer, Emmie thought that it was a good idea to go to the diner and have some lunch. *We don't need to be so secluded the whole time,* she thought. *And besides, he must be hungry.* She looked to him with her big smile still on her face. "Would you like to come and have lunch with me?" she offered politely. "I don't usually dine here at the hotel's eatery, but I've been given special permission today and I don't wish to turn it down."

Mr. Cline nodded his head to her. "I think that would be quite nice," he replied. "I haven't eaten much today. To tell you the truth, I've been a bit too nervous to stomach anything."

She gasped a little and stood up from the couch, knowing

that this gesture would lead to him standing as well. "Me too!" she exclaimed in a friendly tone of voice, as if she was delighted to share something else in common with him. "It's a wonder that I was able to focus on work this morning, if we're being honest. I probably re-shelved the same book for three hours before you arrived."

He laughed as they walked together to the hotel's diner near the front left of the building. He let her lead the way because she was more familiar with the place and he also just seemed to like allowing her to control things. Emmie greatly appreciated that. It wouldn't do, in her opinion, if he started bossing her around. *He's been so lovely thus far,* she thought. *I do wish to see more of him in the coming weeks.*

"I was fortunate to only have one meeting with a client today," he told her as they sat down at one of the tables. The diner was practically empty. Rita was there and she was grinning at Emmie, but she did her best to ignore her boss and focus on Mr. Cline. She didn't wish to become distracted or embarrassed because her boss was there. "Is your office normally terribly busy?" Emmie asked him. "Please don't take this the wrong way, but I can't imagine the townsfolk causing you much trouble, generally. We're only ever busy here because the train brings a lot of travelers who wish to stay and explore the area."

Mr. Cline smiled patiently at her. He nodded his head as she spoke. "You're right. I usually don't have much trouble with the folks in town. It makes my job much easier to form friendships and get to know people here. I'm glad I don't have to deal with the strangers who ride into town on the trains. Though I suppose some of them might decide to settle here because they like it so much, and I can't say I blame them, of course."

"Neither could I," Emmie agreed.

Just then, Rita came over and asked them for their orders. Emmie didn't need to think about it, but she knew that Mr. Cline might need a moment to think over his options. "I'd like one of your cheese and ham sandwiches, please," she told Rita. Then she looked to Mr. Cline. "And what do you recommend for Mr. Cline here? He's never been here or to Stewart House before."

Rita smiled at Mr. Cline and raised her eyebrows a little. "Oh, I see," she said. "Well, our most popular item is our steaks. If you've ever been to Mr. Maddox, the town butcher, you should know that he supplies Stewart House with all of our fresh meats. We've had quite a lot of customers coming back for more of our steaks."

Mr. Cline chuckled and nodded. "Sure, that sounds mighty fine to me. One steak it is!"

Rita beamed. Emmie imagined the dollar signs that Mr. Stewart might be seeing once he received word that the town lawyer had come in to dine and had tried one of their steaks – Emmie would of course see to it that Mr. Cline didn't have to pay for it. He was her guest. Still, Mr. Stewart was always excited by new customers from town, especially prominent ones who would spread the word to more people. *We still don't get too many customers from Wallace itself,* she mused as Rita went off to the back room to prepare their meals. *I think this is a great business move. Not that I care either way personally, but I can see why Rita might be excited.* It was starting to make a lot of sense to her, why her employer had been so insistent about her staying within the hotel for their 'courting session' instead of going to one of the parlors.

"I have never seen someone so excited about steak before," Mr. Cline said amusedly, waking Emmie from her reverie.

She laughed softly. "Oh yes, that's practically the only subject around the restaurant. Over here we do more breakfast shifts than they do, but the demand for steak is still high here."

They sat and chatted a bit more while they waited for their food, talking more about their lives in the past, back when they'd both been young and on the east coast, trying to find themselves. "You know, you mentioned the need for a library in town," Mr. Cline said to her. "And I really do think that's a great idea. I know that there might not be as much of an interest as there is in a restaurant or the like, but I do think that you'd find enough people who love books... There are more of us out there than you think."

Emmie laughed a bit. "I don't think you're wrong," she said. "I think I'm more worried that I wouldn't have the nerve to start my own business like that. I've thought about the possibility of working here as the boss someday or opening my own hotel, and I think that I'm better suited to being a lower status within the place."

Mr. Cline looked at her, furrowing his dark brows slightly. She appreciated that he believed in her and took that to heart, but she still believed that she didn't quite have the wherewithal for that sort of venture. She wasn't very much like Rita, who had a strong, tenacious way about her. Emmie was quieter and mainly just enjoyed order and using her imagination... Things which books helped to satisfy.

Soon, Rita reappeared with their food and their conversation died down while they ate. Several happy 'Mmm' sounds came from Mr. Cline as he ate his steak, and Emmie was pleased that she'd been correct in her assessment about what his meal should be. The steaks never disappointed. Her ham and cheese sandwich was nothing exciting, but she'd grown accustomed to eating such things on her lunch breaks and she didn't wish to try something new while on her date, for fear that she wouldn't like it. She didn't wish for him to think she wasn't eating due to shyness, so she picked something she was sure to happily munch on.

At the end of their lunch, Emmie stood up, smiling down at Mr. Cline. "Well, thank you ever so much for meeting with me today. I've enjoyed speaking with you and getting to know you a bit more. I hope we can do this again in the future."

Mr. Cline stood up from his seat at the table and offered her his hand, which she gracefully accepted. Then he bowed down and gently kissed the back of her hand. "Nothing would please me more than to meet with you again. Please write to me and let me know the time and place, and I'll be there."

She smiled and blushed euphorically. She didn't wish to wait and spend any more time apart than necessary. "We could meet in the courting parlor next time," she told him right away. "Perhaps next Friday at lunchtime?" *I think making this a regular occasion would be delightful.*

Mr. Cline beamed at her and nodded a little. "That would be perfect."

With that date officially scheduled into both of their minds, he gently bade her farewell and Emmie was free to go back to work. She left the diner and went upstairs to relieve her sister from the hall duty. *But oh, how am I ever supposed to get back to work now?!*

Wendy grinned at Emmie as soon as she'd reached the top of the stairs. "How was it?" Wendy demanded excitedly. "How was *he*? He was quite the looker, though he did seem rather shy..."

Emmie laughed softly. "Yes, he was shy but he did open up some once we'd been talking on the couch for a while. He's very sweet, and very good looking, certainly. We mostly discussed life here and why we'd chosen to move out west. I more or less told him that you and I are very close and I simply couldn't let you leave without coming with you. He seemed to appreciate my passion for the job, too."

"Well, you're very lucky indeed," Wendy replied. "I don't know how many gentlemen would actually be pleased to hear that you intend to keep working after getting married."

Emmie shrugged a little. "It worked for Tessa. And anyway, he spends his days working as a lawyer so I hardly think he'd begrudge me my own bit of work. It isn't like he has a farm house that needs my help. Though perhaps he'd like a secretary..." She was rambling some at this point, but she was still feeling giddy from the meeting. So many possibilities were buzzing through her brain.

"Are you planning to see him again?" Wendy asked, her grin indicating that she already knew the answer.

Emmie nodded eagerly. "We've already made arrangements! Next Friday in one of the parlors."

Wendy gasped a bit. "Mr. Murray and I are planning to meet in the parlors next Friday!" she cried. She didn't sound disappointed so much as surprised at the coincidence.

Emmie grinned at her. "Oh," she said calmly. "Well, perhaps we could just make a double date of it."

Wendy shook her head, though she remained smiling. "Rita might not like that," she said. "But I suppose special circumstances may prevail this time. How funny that you and I should be courting at the same time. I never thought I'd see the day."

Now that their excitement had calmed down a bit, the sisters got focused on the job at hand. They went around the hall, cleaning the dust and other grime off of the tables and frames in the hall. Then they went through each of the rooms in order to do the same in each of them, as well as turning over the sheets. They worked together as a professional duo, trading off who did what and who took over which room. *I feel much more efficient when working with her,* Emmie thought. *Though that likely surprises no one.*

At the end of the day, Emmie felt exhausted but satisfied as she climbed into her bed for the night. The coming week promised to be a long one and she knew that she was going to have to work hard to keep her focus and stay positive, even though all she really wanted to do was talk with Mr. Cline and think about what her future could be like. *I know that I still have a lot of options laid out before me,* she thought as she lay there with her eyes closed and her head on her pillow but her mind fully awake. *And all of the potential there is both frightening and thrilling. I don't know how I'm ever meant to relax again, knowing that I'm on the precipice of a whole new kind of life!*

9

The week slowly rolled by like a locomotive leaving a station until at last it was Friday once more. Emmie and Wendy took extra care when they were getting ready that morning, knowing that they were going to be spending more quality time with their beaus come lunchtime. "I really hope that Rita doesn't mind this," Emmie said as she brushed out her hair.

Wendy laughed a little. "You worry too much. She knows what's going on and she'll plan accordingly. There's more than enough girls working for her that she can spare the two of us for a little while during lunch. It isn't as though she *needs* someone in the lobby at lunchtime, no offense."

Emmie hoped that her sister was right. The slowest shift of the day really shouldn't be that difficult to manage with two girls as opposed to four. "You're probably right," she agreed. "I'm just still getting used to this whole thing. I've never asked for much in the way of time off or special lunch periods."

Wendy rolled her eyes a bit. "I know. We all know. You're a goodie-two-shoes and I think Rita is relieved that you're beginning to show some interest in other pursuits."

Emmie thought that was a bit harsh but she supposed that Wendy had a point. After all, it felt like only yesterday that she'd had a hard time imagining herself doing anything other than working in the hotel. *I've started to branch out my goals a bit,* she conceded. *I'm thinking about myself more than the hotel, and it feels wonderful. Rita hasn't ever made it seem as though I'm failing to do my part.*

The two sisters worked that morning – Emmie upstairs with Clara and Wendy in the diner – until it was time for them to take their 'lunch break.' They wouldn't actually be eating lunch; Emmie planned to have a small snack some-time later, once the butterflies had subsided again.

"Make sure you both come back here before things start to get busy again," Rita said to them, seemingly a bit harried but not about to ask one of them to reconsider. Emmie knew that Rita had seen a great many of the so-called Stewart Girls get married and go off to start new lives. She was very supportive of them, even when it sort of got in the way of her business.

She's hoping that we won't leave, Emmie knew. *She wishes us well, but I can tell that she'd keep us on her schedule if we were willing to keep working here.* She wondered if it was too much to ask that the library simply be an expansion of their home. *A full library and study,* she envisioned as she walked out to the dormitory with her sister, hoping to run into Mr. Cline just inside the front door there.

When Wendy and Emmie opened the front doors of the dormitory, they found that the front hallway was completely devoid of people. Wendy went into one of the parlors and then poked her head out again. "This one will be ours," she informed Emmie. "If you see Mr. Murray, please do send him in here."

"Well, seeing as I don't know what the man looks like, I don't quite know how I shall accomplish that," Emmie replied. "But if I can assume an unknown man is him, I'll send him your way."

Wendy sighed a bit at her pedantic sister and went into the selected parlor again. Emmie meanwhile went into the parlor across the hall from that one, believing that this was as close as they could be to being near each other in case one of them needed the other for support.

I suppose that one thing we must get used to is having someone new to take up that position, Emmie thought. *We can't rely on each other forever. Husbands can fill that role, and perhaps even be better at it.* She and Wendy would of course always be best friends who supported each other and cheered each other on, but it would be marvelous if their husbands could take over certain aspects of that. People who'd chosen to be close to them rather than people who'd simply been born into it.

Before long, Emmie heard the familiar footfalls of men in boots upon the hardwood floor in the hall. She stood up from the moss green dais where she'd been resting and peered out of the small doorway of the room. There were two men strolling into the hall, not especially together and in fact they looked as though they were regarding each other with more than a little jealousy. Emmie did her best not to burst out laughing, covering her mouth with her hand in an effort to suppress a fit of giggles.

"Good afternoon, gentlemen," she said to them brightly as if she was merely welcoming them to the hotel. As she stood there in the doorway of her parlor, she made eye contact with Mr. Cline and grinned at him. "My sister Wendy is across the hall there," she said, gesturing a finger in the direction where Wendy waited for Mr. Murray.

The dashing, sandy-haired rancher smiled sideways at Emmie and, with a nod, made his way into Wendy's room. Mr. Cline came over to meet Emmie in the doorway of her own parlor, offering his hand to her at once. She placed her little hand into his larger one and he kissed it much like he had the previous Friday when they'd parted ways. Smiling down at her, Mr. Cline joined Emmie in the parlor that she'd selected for herself. A green dais sat against one cream colored wall, opposite a matching green wing chair. A small, white oak table sat between the seats. Emmie went back over and sat upon the dais and Mr. Cline, taking his cue, took a seat in the wing chair.

"You didn't tell me that your sister was also taking visitors," he said to her, still smiling handsomely. "I was quite surprised to find that other gentleman here."

Emmie blushed a little, embarrassed to have confused him. "I'm terribly sorry," she said to him. "As you probably recall, my sister is the one who has been so very interested in the advertisements and in finding a husband for herself. Were it not for that, I wouldn't have found you. But I should have told you this coincidence that she was meeting with him at the same time and place."

Mr. Cline chuckled and shook his head slightly. "It's all right," he said. "My, my; you two really do everything together, don't you?"

Emmie smiled. "Pretty much," she said with a shrug. "And sometimes it's almost as though we've had the same brain when thinking of something like this. Which never used to be the case, but I suppose one can't avoid one's familial blood bond."

He gave her such a sweet, adoring look at that. She hadn't thought much about it before, but her closeness with her sister was going to affect him, too, if they were ever to be married. It was her wish and hope that Mr. Cline and Wendy would be friendly with each other. *I'm going to have two best friends soon enough,* she thought with a wide grin. *That will be wonderful!*

"How was your week?" he asked her then, seeming a little shy again as if coming up with ways to continue the conversation was the most difficult part for him. "The visitors to town treated you kindly, I hope?"

She nodded. "Oh yes, this week has gone well so far. How are things in your lawyer office?"

He laughed softly. "They've been more or less the same. It's steady work, which was what I was aiming for. I still spend much of my time talking about cows."

"That doesn't sound particularly interesting to me," Emmie laughed. "I couldn't tell you the first thing about cows, other than that they're big and they eat grass."

"My dear, that's all you should ever need to know," Mr. Cline said sagely, laughing even more and shaking his head. "Have you given any more thought to whether or not you wish to stay working at this hotel or if you'd rather open your own place?"

Emmie hadn't given it too much more thought, though she did have a new idea that she believed to be the best compromise for her. "I believe that I should stay here and help the Stewarts expand their hotel. If they were to have a full-sized library here instead of just the few books they currently have, that would be perfect for my wishes. I could be more of a librarian that way."

Mr. Cline appeared thoughtful. "I think that should work out quite well for you. And your boss will be happy to keep you around. The Stewarts aren't strict about their maids being unmarried, are they?"

Blushing, Emmie shook her head. "No, not Mrs. Stewart. The hotel has different rules from the restaurant."

For a moment, Mr. Cline was quiet. She could sense that he was plucking up the nerve to say something to her but she didn't know what it was. She had a few ideas, though. *Is he going to ask me the big question?* she wondered, not fully prepared for how she might react if he did so. *I know that's how these things begin... But it's possible that the question goes without asking, since he placed an ad in the newspaper for its very purpose.* Even though she'd never wished for this before she found his letter on her desk, she quite liked the idea of him getting down on one knee and professing to love her. It felt so unimaginable to her, and that was part of what made it exciting.

Suddenly, he looked her in the eyes and offered his hand from the place where he sat. Emmie reached out and took his hand. "Would you do me the supreme honor of becoming my wife?" he asked her, his voice soft and shy as he smiled so sweetly at her.

Emmie beamed at him. "Yes," she said to him. "Yes, of course I will."

Mr. Cline appeared visibly relieved. "We could marry the same time and day as your sister, if you'd like," he said. He'd clearly given this whole matter some thought. More than she'd allowed herself to. "At the chapel in town. And of course all of your friends from the Stewart House can come."

Emmie laughed a little. "That would be perfect," she agreed. He petted the back of her hand with his soft finger-tips. A rancher or farmer might've had rough hands, but his were gentle and dexterous; the hands of a gentleman who wrote and read books for a living instead of driving cattle across tracks of land. "I can't tell you for certain, but I believe my sister might be planning to get married at the end of their courting session as well. Do you want to go peek?"

Mr. Cline laughed and nodded. They stood up from their seats and walked hand-in-hand into the hallway, where they could just make out the sound of quiet talking coming from Wendy's parlor. Suddenly, there came an enthusiastic cry of "Yes!" and Emmie knew that her sister was now engaged, too.

Before long, Wendy came out of her parlor with Mr. Murray in tow. As soon as she saw her sister, she rushed forward and they hugged each other. "We're going to be married!" Wendy shouted.

"We are, too!" Emmie responded. They happily hugged each other while the two gentlemen looked on, grinning. As soon as they noticed each other there, they shook hands, congratulating themselves quietly.

The plan was set in motion for them to have a double

wedding. Mr. Cline, being that he was a lawyer, took it upon himself to schedule everything. "I will go to the chapel first thing tomorrow morning," he told the three of them. "And soon we shall be wed!" He gazed at Emmie as he said those words. She was overjoyed by how equally excited he was.

10

Rita was absolutely thrilled to be able to help two of her girls get married. Wendy and Emmie naturally went to her right away as soon as their grooms-to-be left, telling her their big news with rising voices. "My goodness, you both have been busy," she said to them with a grin. "I'd be more than happy to assist you both with whatever you may need."

"Me too!" Tessa told them, smiling. "I was in your shoes not long ago, as you know."

Emmie was extremely flattered that her friends at the hotel wished to help on her most important day. "I didn't know what to think or say at first, when he took my hand and looked at me with such reverence," she told them. "I thought he must surely be plotting something like this, but I didn't want my giddiness to get the better of me. It was so amazing to come out of the parlor and hear Wendy's acceptance, too."

The two sisters beamed at each other. They were holding hands. Emmie felt as if the bond she shared with Wendy had grown even stronger now. *Just wait until we get married in the same ceremony,* Emmie thought, getting a bit tearful when she really gave it thought. *It really will be so perfect.*

"I hope Mr. Cline and Mr. Murray know what they're getting into," Wendy said jokingly. "After all, we're already so invested in each other's lives. Now we're even going to be getting married at the same time."

"Well, I'll be sure that you're not getting married in the same dress," Rita said, still grinning. "I can make you each a dress that shows off your particular characters."

Emmie didn't doubt that. She knew that their boss had a large array of gowns from her time in New York City, where she'd been a debutante and needed a new dress for practically every party she attended.

It was decided that Wendy would wear a white gown that was styled with a bit of pink on the sleeves and collar. Emmie wore a gown that included a bit of blue that matched her eyes along the skirt, in the form of tiny flowers. Rita carefully had the colorful dresses dyed so they were white but retained a bit of their former colors. Then she set to work measuring each girl and making sure to take the dresses in a bit to fit their smaller frames. Emmie was always impressed by their boss, but Rita was really outdoing herself now.

On the morning of the wedding, Rita and Tessa carefully helped each sister into her gown, then combed and elegantly braided their hair. "You look like adorable twins," Tessa remarked. "I've always thought that, but this definitely makes you appear like that."

Wendy took Emmie's hand. "Are you ready for this, little sister?"

Emmie nodded her head. "I never thought I would be, but here I am."

The four girls took a carriage together to the chapel on a nearby hill. Clara was more than happy to work the front desk of the hotel all day, with several waiter girls filling in for the absent maids. When they got to the chapel, Emmie, Wendy, and the others went into the small bridal waiting room. Emmie held a bouquet of marigolds and Wendy held a bouquet of daisies. The music began to play and the sisters held each other's hand, the bouquets in their other hands, as they walked up the aisle to meet their handsome grooms.

David Cline was wearing a black suit with a gray tie and vest, standing tall and smiling a shy, nervous smile which ignited a fire in Emmie's tummy. She could foresee many lovely nights of reading together and having philosophical discussions. Mr. Geoffrey Murray was standing there as well, looking dapper in his dark blue suit. His eyes never left Wendy as the two girls slowly walked side by side, eliciting many smiles and 'aww's from the crowd that was assembled in the pews there.

As soon as they'd reached the front, their duo of grooms came to stand beside their respective fiancées. The minister stepped forward. "Dearly beloved," he intoned. "We are gathered here today to witness the union of these souls, who've come together to share the bond of holy matrimony." He looked at each of them in turn. "As it is written in Ephesians 4:32, *Be kind to each other, tenderhearted, forgiving one another, just as God through Christ has forgiven you.*"

There was silence for a moment. Emmie turned to look at David, and he was looking back at her, smiling away. She wished that she wasn't holding her bouquet if only so she could hold his hand as well as Wendy's.

The minister went through the rest of the ceremony, taking the time to speak to each of the four of them, receiving "I do" from each of them. Before long, Emmie was standing facing her fiancé, her back against her sister's. David placed a gold ring onto her finger. *It all feels like a dream,* she thought. She beamed at David as it was announced that they were now husband and wife.

"Husbands," the minister said to David and Geoffrey. "You may now kiss your brides."

David moved slightly forward and took Emmie into his arms, kissing her softly on her lips. Meanwhile, Wendy and Geoffrey kissed nearby. A cheer went up from the crowd of witnesses. The two Sheffield sisters were now married!

EPILOGUE

After Wendy and Emmie were married to their charming husbands, they each took their suitcases of clothes and things from the hotel and moved into their new homes. Wendy lived on a ranch a little outside of Wallace and Emmie lived in a small house near the middle of the city, next door to David's law office. Her head reeled a bit as she was carried over the threshold of the house and then gently set down upon the wood floor. She looked around, wide-eyed with excitement and awe. The home had all the normal furnishings – a reddish brown couch in the living room with matching chairs, a large wooden coffee table, and a small kitchen in the back with stove and plenty of pantries. Upstairs, there was one bedroom and a study, filled wall to wall with books!

"I think I like this room most of all," she confessed.

David laughed and kissed her cheek. "I knew you would. You may use it whenever you like."

It was quite an adjustment for Emmie to go from living and spending all of her time with her sister in the dormitory by the Stewart House. Now, she had plenty of time for solitude and cuddling with her new husband. He showed her his law office and she flipped through the pages of the books he had there as well. She wasn't allowed to read about any of his cases, of course, but sometimes he would come home after a case was over and tell her about it, sometimes in vivid detail.

He was right; his work did revolve around a lot of cows and land deals.

After a blissful week of relaxing and spending time with David, getting used to her new home and her new life, Emmie was gleeful to return to work and let everyone there know how she was doing. "It's not that I don't adore our home," she told David one evening as they sat together enjoying a meal of roast beef and potatoes, "but while you're away at work, there's only so much that I can do to keep myself from being bored. I never thought about it before, but books aren't the same as talking to people."

He was amused by that. "I've found the same thing to be true," he told her. "Which is why I just knew I had to find you."

She was relieved when her sister Wendy returned to the hotel as well. She wasn't sure if Wendy would want to come back, because living on a ranch required a lot more work than a quiet lawyer's office did, but Wendy admitted that she missed the guests and the work that went into running the hotel. "Cows aren't good for conversation," she said with a laugh.

Emmie was amused that once again they seemed to be mirroring each other a bit. The Sheffield sisters just loved to help others, and there was no better place for them to do that than in Rita's hotel. They took to their work after the wedding with renewed energy and excitement, working together during their shifts most of the time. Emmie's favorite was still working in the lounge, where she got to organize the books and help people relax before or right after meals, generally.

The best part for Emmie now was that, at the end of the day, she got to go home and see her husband. She adored cooking dinner for him and talking to him about his day. He always asked her about how things were going at the hotel, too. She was so happy to be able to relax at home and be honest with David about how things had gone, without having to worry about judgment or disinterest. "Everything there seems so much easier now that I don't spend every waking moment at the Stewart House," she told him. "It helps to be able to refresh myself outside of the place, instead of constantly being entrenched in it."

David smiled and nodded at her. "Sometimes it's easier to see the big picture when you're not so close to it. Like when you look at a portrait. If you stand too close, all you might be able to see is splotches of paint."

She nodded her head, smiling back at him. "Exactly." Thinking of that tickled Emmie because she fondly remembered the time that a guest had asked her if she had anything by Henry James. That moment turned out to be very important for her in a way that he would never realize. She'd never been the biggest fan of that author, but now when she saw the copy of *Portrait of a Lady* on the shelf, she couldn't help but smile. That book had been the key to everything, even if it had turned out differently for her than she had initially planned.

After several months went by, it was announced that Stewart House was expanding its hotel to make way for some more rooms. They kept the hotel on the same plot of land but added rooms onto it, the way Emmie had hoped, instead of changing the location entirely. Wendy always suspected that they would need to make some changes once the hotel was more established and the demand was higher, but she'd always thought that they might open up a second location instead of simply making their current one larger. It seemed that Rita had really taken to the idea of having a library and study room for the guests who wished to read or get some work done in its seclusion. Rita also needed more space because she was going to have a child, and a child demanded more than just one small room at the far end of the house.

Emmie and Wendy were overjoyed for their friend and

boss. The hotel was surely going to be a great deal cuter once it had a bigger family ruling the roost. It turned out that Emmie and her sister had both been right about Rita and the future of her beloved little hotel. And if there was one thing that the sisters were good at, it was sharing in all of life's joys and surprises.

THE END

ABOUT THE AUTHOR

Amazon Bestselling author Charity Phillips grew up on a farm in Cherokee County, North Carolina and fell in love with caring for horses at an early age. She currently lives just a few miles from that gorgeous farm with her loving husband of twelve years and their three beautiful daughters. When Charity isn't dreaming up her next clean historical western romance story, she's usually tending to her garden or baking delicious treats for her family.

To keep up to date with her latest releases, you may visit www.hopemeadowpublishing.com and sign up for her newsletter.

FREE STORY!

For a FREE sweet historical romance e-book, please sign up
for Hope Meadow Publishing's newsletter at
www.hopemeadowpublishing.com

Made in the USA
San Bernardino, CA
25 June 2020